EUREKA STREET

Robert McLiam Wilson was born in Belfast in 1964.

ALSO BY ROBERT McLIAM WILSON

Ripley Bogle
Manfred's Pain
The Dispossessed

Robert McLiam Wilson

EUREKA STREET

Published by Vintage 1998

11

First published in Great Britain by
Secker & Warburg 1996

Vintage
Random House, 20 Vauxhall Bridge Road,
London SW1V 2SA

Random House Australia (Pty) Limited
20 Alfred Street, Milsons Point, Sydney,
New South Wales 2061, Australia

Random House New Zealand Limited
18 Poland Road, Glenfield,
Auckland 10, New Zealand

Random House (Pty) Limited
Endulini, 5A Jubilee Road, Parktown 2193,
South Africa

The Random House Group Limited Reg. No. 954009
www.randomhouse.co.uk

A CIP catalogue record for this book
is available from the British Library

ISBN 0 7493 9672 5

Papers used by Random House are natural, recyclable products made from wood grown in sustainable forests. The manufacturing processes conform to the environmental regulations of the country of origin.

Printed and bound in Great Britain by
Cox & Wyman Ltd, Reading, Berkshire

One

All stories are love stories.

It was a late Friday night, six months ago, six months since Sarah had left. I was in a bar making talk with a waitress called Mary. She had short hair, a very round ass and the big eyes of a hapless child. I had known her three hours and I was getting the two-year blues already.

Chuckie Lurgan had sloped out of there half an hour previously after gracefully running out of cash and twenty minutes' worth of heavy hints from me.

In a bar full of waitresses, Mary had been one among many but I'd more than noticed her. She had started by not liking me. Maybe a lot of men might have suspected some reluctant attraction – me, I just thought she wanted to kill me and didn't bother to wonder why. She was hard. She bristled and showed me her sharp little spines. I'm sure she understood that this would make me fall in love with her. I'm sure she knew that.

Then she had begun the amiable waitress routine, teasing me as she served us our drinks. In the end she just sat across from me in Chuckie's vacant seat whenever she had a quiet moment. This constituted a relationship. There was something in the way she looked at me, sloe-eyed, speculative, without warmth. Then there was something in the tilt of her head as she refused my cigarettes and lit her own. I think I thought she liked me. I think I thought I should take her home.

And the special way she looked at me could have been nothing compared with the special way I felt myself look at her. I could feel it written all over my face.

It was me all over. The erotic high-style in the back bar of an Oirish pub. But for all my big talk, I was a blusher, a gulper. I couldn't say anything as straight as a stick. So while I hummed and while I hawed, Mary asked me to take her home.

Sitting late in the bar while they closed up was more disconcerting than you might readily suppose. I looked down the neck of my bottle, ignoring the giggles of Mary's colleagues. The big Protestant bouncer took off his tux, rolled up his sleeves and flashed his UVF tattoos. He tried giving me some old chat while he swept the floor but I was afraid of saying something too Catholic. I ignored him as best I could and tried to think of Sarah. I couldn't manage it.

I suppose it was the first full night of spring and the blunt warm wind lifted my mood as Mary and I left the bar. I ignored my wreck of a car and suggested that we walk.

In her smart dress and sheer tights, Mary looked like something in a crime novel. I wasn't accustomed to girls like that. Somehow it made me feel cheap but, as she smiled at me, I couldn't help but concede that she was pretty. She talked energetically about her job. With all my heart I tried to listen but drifted off, letting the wind make shapes with my hair. But I was glad she talked. I was glad of the noise.

'What do you do?' she asked as we passed Hope Street.

I smiled. 'I do a lot of things. I'm a debt counsellor right now,' I lied, after a fashion.

'That's nice.'

That's the thing about when you lie. If they don't believe you, you despise yourself; if they do believe you, you despise them.

There was a police checkpoint stopping cars at the mouth of the Lisburn Road. As we passed, a cop greeted Mary by name. I didn't like that. There was still enough of the working-class Catholic in me not to like that.

'He comes into the bar sometimes,' Mary said afterwards. The excuse in her voice meant she had guessed what I was thinking. I didn't like that either.

She was impressed by my street. It was leafy. It was green. She even liked the name. I lived on a street called Poetry Street. It wasn't always a good sign when people liked the name of my street. She was impressed by my flat. My flat makes me look like I have a lot of money. She looked at all Sarah's swish furniture and pictures, at all Sarah's faultless taste, and liked me more. She ran her fingers along the bookshelves and smiled at me like I was some intellectual.

I made a pot of coffee all by myself and that, too, impressed her.

'Nice place,' she said.

I didn't know if I liked or admired her but I wanted her. I was lonely that night, womanless. It wasn't the sex I craved. It was the joint cornflakes, the hand on my hip in the dark, somebody else's hair on my pillow. I needed the small presences of someone. I needed Sarah's little bits.

'Do you own or rent?' she asked.

I don't know what I did with that face of mine but hers fell at my reaction. There was a sudden extra width in the big eyes and a tremble of the lips. I hated it when people did that kind of stuff to me – coming out with some duff line and then looking like they were six years old when I frowned.

'I'm sorry,' she said. 'That was a stupid thing to say.'

I didn't disagree but that was when I knew I couldn't sleep with her. I don't know – in my small experience of women, I've found it hard to sleep with them at such times. Times when you get the impression that there's more to them than an opportunity. Sleeping with girls was great, sleeping with people was a bit more complicated. Maybe it was a bad thing, maybe a sign of my immaturity, but I knew that there was some kind of tenderness in it as well.

I stood up as tactfully as I could manage. She stood too. There was nothing to say and little to do. I couldn't think of how to tell her of the big mistake that this had been. I moved towards her and she opened her shoulders and lifted her face uncertainly. It looked like she expected me to kiss her. And then I wanted to, very badly indeed.

'I must go,' she said, surprisingly.

Her cab took twenty minutes. We talked a little. I was oddly flattered that she didn't like me; that she had made her mistake and had corrected it so staunchly. I told her about Sarah and she told me about her policeman boyfriend whom she was going to call when she got home. I thought she was talking about the guy she had greeted when we left the bar but he was just a friend. Mary thought he would tell her boyfriend about seeing her with some guy and she wanted to pre-empt that strike.

'I'm sorry,' she said. 'This was a bad idea.'

'Well . . .' I mumbled.

'I don't do this.'

'Me neither.'

'First night of spring.' She smiled.

'Yeah.'

Then she left me to the rest of the coffee and myself. Much as Sarah had done.

There are those nights when you're pushing thirty and life seems over. When you feel like you'll never tie up any ends and no one will ever kiss your lips again.

I wandered the rooms of my empty flat. I liked my flat. But sometimes, when home alone, I felt like I was the last man living and my two bedrooms were a humiliation of riches. Since Sarah left, I hadn't prospered. Life had been slow, life had been long. She'd been gone six months. She didn't want to live in Belfast any more. She was English. She didn't need it any more.

There had been a lot of killings back then and she decided that she'd had enough. She wanted to go back to somewhere where politics meant fiscal arguments, health debates, local taxation, not bombs not maiming not murders and not fear.

So, she had gone back to London. Chuckie had comforted me with the observation that English girls were a waste of time. She didn't write. She didn't call. She didn't even fax. She'd been right to go but I was still waiting for her to come back. I'd waited for other things in my life. Waiting was nothing new to me. But waiting had never seemed like this. It looked as though I was going to have to wait for longer than I'd got. The clock was running in sprints and I wasn't even off the blocks. People had got it all wrong about time. Time wasn't money. Time was speed.

That night, I lay in my bed with my windows open, the helicopters chuckling comfortingly as they hovered over all those Catholics out west. Sarah had always hated that noise. I had always liked it. It had helped me sleep when I was a child. I hoped it would fail now. It was near four and I was working at half past six. I wasn't worried, though. I knew I had enough unhappy thoughts to keep me well awake so I dozed, feebly wishing that either Mary or Sarah could have somehow found it fit to lay her head next to mine.

Next morning Rathcoole, a Protestant estate on the northern quiff of the city, concrete and cold. Not even eight o'clock and we were doing our third call already. Here I was, working Saturday again. We'd started off at half past six with a three-piece suite from a sleepy, anxious young couple. The woman had cried and the man had gulped nervously as he comforted her and watched our burly forms lumbering about his home. Then we'd picked up a fridge, microwave, electric guitar and mountain-bike from a family on the edge of the estate. Their house looked like it was made of cardboard and they were used to interference. We'd busted in there while all but the seven-year-old were in bed. The dad had grumbled briefly but nobody feels like a fight in their pyjamas. They gave us no trouble.

We pulled up at the third house on our list. We were to take a television from a couple of pensioners. Crab stayed in the van and Hally and I walked up the little path and rapped the door in that hard, hard way we had. I went in behind him when the old guy opened up. We didn't say anything as we stepped over the rubble of the dingy hallway into the sitting room.

Curtains closed, the room was glutinous and dark. A television chuckled in a brassy nook ignoring our incursion like a brave comic shunning hecklers. An old lady sat on a sofa dimly illumined by the blue glow of breakfast television. Her reactions were tardy. She turned towards me. The old guy followed us in, swearing inaudibly, his pruny face slack like he wasn't surprised. The old lady made a couple of efforts to raise the tub of her belly off the sofa. The TV suddenly went to advertisements and the old girl was bathed in Caribbean warmth as she tottered to her feet. She began to shout. 'Get out of here, you dirty hallions! Whoohjoos think y'are? My grandson's in the UDA. I'll have youse kneecapped.'

Blah blah blah, the usual.

Silently, I unplugged the set and picked it up. It was my turn to carry and Hally's turn to be hardman. He flexed himself and looked pretty big in that murky little room. I moved to the door. The old man mumbled some exasperated oath at me and the old lady aimed a swipe of her hand at my retreating back.

Hally stopped and turned round to face her. He bent down a long, long way and put his face within kissing distance of hers.

'Fuck up,' he advised.

Outside I loaded the van and we moved on, Crab trundling through the cheap streets in second gear. Hally was rumbling and red with disappointed aggression. It looked like no one would give him the trouble he sought this morning and even he balked at smacking some old biddy. I looked at him and sighed. I didn't like my job.

Television – retail, £245, outstanding, £135, resale maybe £100 to £120. The company would want £100 back on a gogglebox of that price. Twenty pounds' profit split three ways. We were tycoons. I didn't like my job.

Crab and Hally bitched at each other while I looked out at all the bricks and all the sunshine. The day before they'd picked up a video and stereo in Ballybeen. Hally had been driving and he'd told Crab that the woman they were stiffing was so badly broke that she'd put out to keep her stuff. He'd given poor old Crab some big story about her being an unmarried mother in her late twenties, blonde, big tits: usual list of yob desirables. Crab had gone wild with anticipation. Hally and I had sussed the poor slob was a virgin. Needless to say, it was all crap as Crab discovered when some fat matron had answered the door and smacked him about for trying to take her stuff. This grievance still rankled. It wasn't like Crab had a lot of other things to think about.

I was feeling sour. I worked in the repossession industry. How else was I supposed to feel? Repo work had the capacity to take the edge off my morning and it was always the morning for us boys. That's when we did our best work. People were disoriented in the morning, half dressed, malleable, not generally pugilistic. It seemed that trousers were necessary for confident protest. We didn't work after dark – you never knew what size the guy might be or how much he might have drunk; it was also harder to find women alone after dark and people kept mistaking us for the IRA.

Oh, boy, people were always mistaking us for the IRA. I suppose it was easy to mistake one trio of macho fuckers for another. My colleagues were very basic human beings indeed. Crab was big, fat and ugly. Hally was big, fat, ugly and vicious. I tried not to hate people. Hating people was too tiring. But sometimes, just sometimes, it was hard.

I had a personal theory as to why the people we dealt with

were so easy to deal with first thing in the morning. I had a feeling that poverty like theirs felt worse first thing. It might have been easier to dream or fantasize at night when some optimism or booze could make you bullish but in the pallid light of morning it must have all seemed pretty permanent, this poverty, this shame. It must have seemed fairly realistic.

What depressed me most was that so many people gave us so little trouble. Like they expected our invasion. Like they guessed we had a right and they had none. When an unmarried mother who owes twenty quid on a three-hundred-pound fridge lets you walk out with it and no grumbles, something very odd is going on.

Crab was definitely getting excited about our next call. A sunbed. Crab felt that a sunbed guaranteed some big blowsy tart – just what he needed before breakfast. We pulled into the street and stopped at the address. The house looked smarter than its neighbours: there was a fancy door and some intricate porchwork. Somebody doing well enough to buy sunbeds and build fancy porches had obviously lost their job and now we were coming to take it all away.

I stayed in the van because Crab was so desperate to get a look at the woman his imagination had created. He and Hally knocked and waited. I lit a cigarette and settled down. I felt like shit. Some would say that working-class aspiration always ends like this – hard-faced hoodlums taking all the gaudy baubles away. I still felt like a criminal.

I couldn't get Mary out of my head. I had told her I was a debt counsellor. Which was a big fat laugh. I could never get the hang of being seedy and it appalled me to think of what I had become again since Sarah had left. Some repo thug who lies to the waitresses he takes home. The high life.

Hally was still knocking at the door and Crab was looking disappointedly through the windows. Nobody home. Just as I was beginning to hope that he wasn't going to do it, Hally had whipped out his chisel and jemmied the lock. I hated it when he did that. The cops had hassled us too many times already. I didn't want any more grief. But I said nothing as the two disappeared inside.

I put my head back and closed my eyes. I felt ashamed of the night before. I wondered if I would have felt more ashamed if I'd slept with her. It was just that the girl had somehow shown that she was much better than me. When she had asked me to take her home, it had been a stylish, independent thing to do. Maybe it was always like that when girls did it. But I had smudged it and made it somehow sordid. I wished I didn't have that knack.

A hand tapped me on the shoulder and I jerked upright, eyes open. A man was standing by the open van window. He was unshaven and weary-looking.

'That's my house,' he said. 'What's going on?'

His tone was desultory, certainly not aggressive. Even so, I thought about getting out of the van in case he cut up rough.

'Repossession,' I said, more dismissive than I felt.

'What are you taking?' he asked, curiously.

'Sunbed.'

'Ah, right,' he murmured, without interest. He eyed my cigarette. I offered him one. 'Thanks, mate.'

Crab and Hally were still inside. This man didn't look like he intended moving.

'They'll be ages taking that fucking thing apart.' He tittered grimly.

I flicked something between a smile and a nod at him.

'I'm glad to see it go,' he said, lazily confidential. 'The bitch fucked off so her stuff can fuck off after her.'

Me, I never knew what to say to unhappy people. I never knew what to add or subtract.

'Lost your job?' I asked clumsily.

'Aye, fuck.' The man was briefly energized. 'I was at Short's ten years. Laid me off four months ago. They're letting fucking Taigs in now.'

Yeah, yeah, I thought. There was a new Commission now to make sure that Catholics had fair representation in the work-forces of the province. Equable commentators like this guy blamed this Commission for all the economic, social and moral ills of the planet generally. They had liked it the old way, when Catholics were glad of an indoor bathroom and a couple of raw spuds. But what could he have expected? That kind of stuff couldn't have gone on for ever. Not because it was wrong or anything like that, because it was embarrassing. Would he have been comfortable if he'd known I was a Catholic? I wondered. Probably.

'When did she go?' I asked, to change the subject.

His Catholic-hating smile hardened into his wife-hating smile, a much uglier thing. 'Last month. Told me she was fucking her cousin and pissed off the day before Christmas. Didn't miss her. Drunkest I'd ever been. Drunkest anybody's ever been. Didn't miss her. Won't miss her.' He nudged me. 'Gives me a chance to have a go at all the wee tarts running round the estate. That's the life for me.'

A tear tracked down the tired lines in his face while he talked all his tough talk. Here we go again, I thought. He talked more hardman bullshit like he didn't know I knew how soft and small and sad he was. I didn't listen with either ear.

Crab and Hally finally lumbered out of the house carrying both parts of the sunbed. The van door was open so they loaded up without my assistance. The guy ignored them all the while and continued cajoling me with his man-of-the-world stuff. Crab got into the driver's seat, grumbling about not getting a look at the tart with the sunbed. The man's face did not flicker. Hally pushed him out of the way and climbed in.

And it was when Crab started the van and we moved off that it happened. I looked back and the guy waved at me. A tired, amiable, clapped-out gesture. I don't know. I'd taken stuff from old folks, from women, from kids even. It's supposed to be easier to feel sorry for them but I'd never felt sorrier for anyone than I felt for this tired guy, this silent weeper who'd waved at me as I'd driven away with the last remnant of the woman who had left him.

And that was enough to do it. The low-rent street, the crappy houses, the sky pale and drooping, the waving man with the wet face. It all looked like I felt and I decided that I wanted to go home. I was going to take the rest of the day off. A morning's worth of repo work was enough sadness for anybody.

The van was getting full and we decided to drive back and unload. Crab and Hally bickered on as we drove back to the garage from where we worked. Soon they guessed my mood and left me out of their banter. I couldn't get the picture of the guy with no wife and no sunbed out of my head and I couldn't swallow the taste of shame.

Back at the garage, I left my two colleagues and walked into Allen's office. He owned the garage and ran his debt-collection gimmick from there. He was talking money into the telephone. He motioned me to wait. I waited without patience.

'What do you want?' he asked, when he had finished. Allen was an ex-dipso, car salesman, repossessor, loan shark, all-round wide-boy. He was the only sixty-year-old bald guy I had ever seen in a pair of leather trousers. He was not a man with much grace.

'I'm going home. I'm sick.'

'The fuck you are.'

'Stop me.'

He frowned and decided to stop trying to look menacing. He wasn't any good at it. That's what he'd hired Crab, Hally and me for.

'What's wrong with you?'

'I'm sick.'

He looked out of the small window to where he could see Crab and Hally unloading the van. 'Have you gotta problem with this work, Jackson?'

'Nah, I find it massively rewarding. I thank God every day for the fulfilment of it, the sense of achievement. What do you think?'

He didn't smile – he couldn't, he didn't understand all those syllables.

'Why don't you go be a fucking brain-surgeon, then?'

'I'm thinking about it.'

'You get up my nose, you know.' Happily reminded, he started to pick the organ in question. 'Crab and Hally don't have a problem. Admittedly, they're stupid cunts but they don't have a problem because they know that what you don't pay for you can't have. We take stuff from scumbags who shouldn't have bought it in the first place. Don't buy things you can't afford.' He dislodged a wieldy piece of snot and paused thoughtfully. 'If you don't like it go get another job. I'll live with the disappointment of losing you. Fuck me, who cares if we're not nice – we're necessary. That's more important.' He smiled and flicked the snot from his fingers. Just in case I thought he was justifying himself or anything like that, he added, 'Anyway, do you think I could give two fucks?'

'Can I go home now?'

He dismissed me with a wave. 'Yeah, fuck off. And don't do this again.'

At the door he called me back. I turned reluctantly and looked at him without interest.

'You're a real soppy prick, you know.'

'Yeah,' I said, 'I've been told.'

Back home in Poetry Street, I smacked a cup of coffee into me. Fancy coffee; black as Mick beer and strong as radiator paint. The only way to drink it. Cost me three quid a pound but a man had to have good coffee. Since Sarah had ironed out my tastes it had become a first principle. I lived at the posh end of town now so I ground my coffee and drank it from overpriced, underglazed kitchenware. This was Poetry Street. This was bourgeois Belfast, leafier and more prosperous than you might imagine. Sarah had found this place and moved us in to lead our leafy kind of life in our leafy kind of area. When her English friends or family had visited us there they had always been disappointed by the lack of burnt-out cars or foot patrols on our wide, tree-lined avenue. From my downstairs window, Belfast looked like Oxford or Cheltenham. The houses, the streets and the people were plump with disposable income.

From my upstairs window, however, I could see the West; the famous, hushed West. That's where I'd been born: West Belfast, the bold, the true, the extremely rough. I used to send Sarah's visitors up there. There were plenty of those local details up West.

A radio waffled softly from the flat downstairs. It was barely ten o'clock and the student kids downstairs were probably just getting up. I pulled my curtains wide and Saturday sunlight slapped itself around my room like a coat of paint. I squinted out at all the Belfast birds in all the Belfast sky. Across the Lisburn Road, a diminutive cleaning woman chucked some flaccid garbage from the doorway of the fancy Indian chicken-house. A group of cats appeared from nowhere and started filling their faces. I recognized my own prominent amongst them. He was the fat one with no testicles. I thought about calling him in for his breakfast but I decided not to bother. I didn't particularly like my cat. My cat was a bit of a wanker.

I looked to my own breakfast – coffee, dry toast and cigarettes. I ate in good heart, a neat trick on two hours' sleep and a baby hangover. I went to the door and looked again for the mail that never arrived. I picked up the local paper and took a read at that instead. Another taxi-driver shot the night before. Taxi-drivers were fashionable victims just then. It was all the rage. It was all the hatred. At the bottom of the front page there was an ad for a Christmas pantomime. *Snow White and the Seven Dwarfs* WITH REAL DWARFS!!!

Everything was looking local.

Under the circumstances, Belfast was a pretty famous place.

When you considered that it was the underpopulated capital of a minor province, the world seemed to know it excessively well. Nobody needed to be told the reasons for this needless fame. I didn't know much about Beirut until the artillery moved in. Who'd heard of Saigon before it blew its lid? Was Anzio a town, a village or just a stretch of beach? Where was Agincourt exactly?

Belfast shared the status of the battlefield. The place-names of the city and country had taken on the resonance and hard beauty of all history's slaughter venues. The Bogside, Crossmaglen, The Falls, The Shankill and Andersonstown. In the mental maps of those who had never been in Ireland, these places had tiny crossed swords after their names. People thought them deathfields – remote, televised knackers' yards. Belfast was only big because Belfast was bad.

And who would have thought it thirty years before? Little Belfast could be such a beautiful city. Squatting flat in the oxter of Belfast Lough, hazily level with the water, the city was ringed with mountains and nudged by the sea. When you looked up the length of most Belfast streets, there was some kind of mountain or hill staring back at you.

But, yeah, Belfast continued to fail to surprise me. A couple of days before, a bomb had gone off near the police station just across the road from my flat. I'd watched from my window as the Lisburn Road was evacuated. The flower shop, the newsagent's, the hairdresser's. After sealing off the road, they did a controlled explosion. Jesus! Blew in two of my windows and scared the chocolate out of me into the bargain. How controlled were these controlled explosions? It fucked half the street – the other half was pretty fucked already. What new definition of the word 'controlled' was this?

It was, of course, nothing serious. As Belfast bombs go, it went. Little to relate. Nobody died, nobody bled. It was no big deal. That was the big deal. It was dull stuff. Nobody really noticed. What had happened to us here? Since when had detonations in the neighbourhood barely raised a grumble?

It had been a while since I had been that close to an explosion, what with me moving to this middle-class end of town and all. It was strange. You forget what they're like. But when it went off, I remembered what they were like, quicker than I wanted to.

What were bombs like? Well . . . explosive, naturally. And loud. And frightening. They were loud and frightening in your gut like when you were a child and you fell on your head and couldn't understand why it hurt like panic in your belly. They were fairly irreversible too. Bombs were like dropped plates, kicked cats or hasty words. They were error. They were disarrangement and mess. They were also – and this was important – knowledge. When you heard that dry splash, that animal thud of bomb, distant or close, you knew something. You knew that someone somewhere was having a very bad time indeed.

It wasn't the bombs that were scary. It was the bombed. Public death was a special mortality. Bombs mauled and possessed their dead. Blast removed people's shoes like a solicitous relative, it opened men's shirts pruriently; women's skirts rode up their bloody thighs from the force of the lecherous blast. The bombed dead were spilled on the street like cheap fruit. And, finally, unfuckingbeatably, the bombed dead were dead. They were so very, very dead.

(Incidentally, the controlled explosion was carried out on a bin bag full of discarded Kentucky Fried Chicken. There were little pieces of singed white-meat all over the place. My cat was a very happy cat.)

It was Saturday. I couldn't look for another job on a Saturday and I had the purposeless day to get through. I thought of my cheap friends. They would do. It was Chuckie Lurgan's thirtieth birthday. It would be a big event and his present wouldn't need wrapping. The only decision would be which bar to get him lushed up in.

I left my flat and found the Wreck still unstolen. Nobody was ever going to steal the Wreck. It was the only thing I liked about it. I called my wreck the Wreck for obvious reasons. It was a hugely shitty vehicle but it had incredibly clean windows. Rusty bodywork covered in three-year-old filth but the windows gleamed. I cleaned them every day so that I could see my city when I drove.

I headed for Chuckie's house.

We ended up in Mary's bar again. It was very present tense. The usual cast: Chuckie Lurgan, Donal Deasely, Septic Ted, Slat Sloane and me. The boys, the crowd. Oh, boy, I needed new friends.

Mary was there, working her tables, making no tips. My chest tightened when I saw her and I found out what I'd only guessed. That I'd made myself want her. The way I do. The way we all do. I'd caused myself to need her. When she took our order she said hello to me in a voice commendably level, admirably sure. Mary was just a working-class Belfast girl waiting table but she had a bit of style.

Chuckie's cousin came in after a while. He had the girl with him. They were getting married, apparently. Chuckie's cousin seemed unhappy. From the way he followed her gaze, from the way he looked where she looked, I guessed he thought that she was too pretty. He was right. I wouldn't have married her. Chuckie told me that the cousin was so jealous he dusted her breasts for fingerprints.

And, as usual, the talk got big – the talk was always big in Belfast bars. The old mix, constitutional democracy, freedom through violence and the eternal rights of man. We used to talk about naked women but after a few years we stopped believing each other's lies. Chuckie hijacked the high moral ground which was a bit rich for someone as stupid as Chuckie. I mean, history and politics were books on a shelf to Chuckie and Chuckie was no reader.

Some guy from Delhi Street started guffing on about revolution. I got involved. I got angry. I was only there to see if Mary would go home with me again and, as always, I got involved.

It felt like another of our wasted nights. Six hours of flapping our gums about things we didn't understand at a cumulative cost of about twenty quid per head. Donal and Slat were talking crap about morality and genetics while Chuckie chimed in with his usual dumb-fat-guy routine. The talk seemed easy, like it had fallen off the back of a lorry. But the talk was truly difficult. It was hard, hard work.

Chuckie's cousin and Chuckie's cousin's girl had a row. One of those two-way tiffs conducted in the Irish manner (pretty shrill). I couldn't be sure but I came away with the distinct impression that the whole thing blew up because the girl refused to shave her bikini-line. They went home in separate taxis. I must say, it seemed a lot of fuss about a haircut.

And, as the night passed by, Mary served us our drinks and I failed to talk to her. Sometimes she looked at me, sometimes she didn't. I knew because I looked at her every time she breathed. It looked like we'd drink out our time and I'd miss my chance if chance I had.

And soon enough there was that grim business of barmen shouting time while my drunken pals tried to jostle me into leaving. I kept meeting Mary's eye and leaving messages there. I panicked like a general whose army is retreating. Chuckie was so drunk that he seemed to have lost the ability to speak English but even he seemed to have worked out what I was about.

'You taking her home?' he leered.

I blushed at him for want of anything better. Slat was mouthing about moving on to Lavery's but Chuckie silenced him with the broad flat of his hand and leaned to me confidentially. 'Iss awright. Iss ma birthday. I'll take care it.'

And then he did. To my horror, he stood and called Mary over. She answered his summons, her face sceptical but tolerant.

'Whass name, love?' asked Chuckie, with bland patronage.

'Mary.'

'Well, Mary . . .' Chuckie paused to wave a mild goodbye to some exiting group of yob mates. 'Well, Mary, my friend here, who's a good friend, a good man, my friend here wants to take you home.'

Mary smiled no smiles and promised no promises. She took Chuckie's beer glass from his hand and turned to me. 'Wait for me,' she said. 'We'd better talk.'

For the second night in succession I sat near the door while the punters stumbled out and the staff cleaned up. It was somehow less embarrassing the second time. This time, the bouncer, a different, bigger, Saturday-night kind of guy, wore Republican tattoos. I didn't talk to him. I was scared of not seeming Catholic enough.

And I watched Mary as I waited. In blue polka-dot dress like the other waitresses, she bent to wipe the tables. She was the kind of girl I wouldn't even have pissed on when I was sixteen (I learnt that phrase from girls who had used it to decline my own tender offers). But now she had all it took. I loved that about girls. The odd things that could make you want to make them your own. Who was responsible? Where could I complain?

When she had finished, she put on her coat and stood beside me. She didn't smile and I knew that what was coming was meant to be bad. But there was something in her face that made me hope it would not be so.

We left and walked out into the overstocked streets of after-hours Belfast. Everywhere, the pavements were blistered with drunks and bums. We weren't the only boys and girls standing on those pavements but I think we were probably the soberest. They were all doing their shouting, laughing, crying, getting arrested thing. We felt like the small still centre of some unpleasant weather.

She turned to face me, lowered her eyes to the pavement and then back up towards mine. A big move. There was no fun in that face of hers any more. It was all serious from here on in.

'Look, I just don't know what's going on.'

Was it just me or was that everybody's favourite line? It's not a complicated line. But when some grave big-eyed girl tells you that, doesn't it make you want to run around and punch the air like a footballer?

The street was full of drunks and noise, her face was blank with some pain or fear and her line was blunt enough for two. I had to say something decent.

'Let's walk,' I said.

That night she was so beautiful it was stupid. I wanted to ask her who had made her so beautiful and why? What was it for exactly?

We walked a very round walk to my flat. We dodged the chuck-out crowds in Shaftesbury Square, with all their shouts and pukes and fights. Ours was a more lyrical path. We took in the special streets with the nice trees and the big lamps. We walked by the river where everything could feel briefly eighteenth century.

The night was too good, too big and dark to believe. The weather broke and a light rain fell like retribution. She looked like a love song that night and my heart leapt in dumb, frantic syncopations.

We were talking the usual talk of people who want to make love but who haven't quite brought it up – ospreys, horticulture, synchronized swimming, all that stuff.

I shook like litter (leaves don't shake, I've always thought, whereas your average litter habitually trembles like demons). I shook, hands, lips and heart, which proved, somehow joyously, that I was alive after all, that some bits still worked.

I stopped her dead in the middle of Governor's Bridge and we faced each other. She looked tired from her six smoky hours in the bar but nevertheless! Her face was framed by the dark sky, the wide, wide river and the lights of the streets that straggled down the hill. What with the crisp cold and all that street-lamp glitter in her eyes, it looked so great that I could only think she had rehearsed it. Nipped up the previous evening with a set of mirrors and measuring tapes and worked out the best possible angle in which to make my heart stop.

'Would it be terrible,' I said, 'if I asked you to kiss me?'

And, well, that's the way it goes, isn't it? I was standing there arguing the toss with this girl about whether we would walk and talk or stand and kiss or just part in the middle on that most medium Belfast bridge and suddenly something happened in me, something so big it near blew us both away. It was like God had come and spoken to me, like the best bit in your favourite song and I knew that she had everything I'd ever wanted, ever needed and I could hold this big-eyed girl and still miss Sarah and it was all all right in some way.

And, hey, I'm pretty handsome too and I think that helped, I think that argued my case.

And she kissed me and I remembered that I'd forgotten what that was like.

I realized, when she took her clothes off, that I hadn't even tried to estimate what her breasts might be like, which was pretty sensitive going for a guy such as me. And her breasts were eventually strange soft things, pale and unobtrusive. She thought I was disappointed, making the woman's mistake of not understanding how little her breasts mattered in the scheme of love.

And I knew when my skin touched her skin that I probably wasn't going to kill myself for a while, that life was fundamentally a pretty sound commodity when it could include a girl like Mary. And when she touched me she touched the matter in me. She touched me through.

'Jake,' she said. 'Jake.'

Why not? That was my name.

She left before dawn. She wanted to get home in case her rozzer beau called when he came off his night shift. Our second taxi-waiting conversation in two days. She was trying to make me understand that this was all, a new one-night habit that girls had developed; these days it was the guys who spent weeks waiting by the phone.

I don't know why I couldn't take that seriously, why I couldn't make that matter. After all that love we'd made, we'd opened a dialogue that she couldn't end by stepping into a taxi in the middle of the night.

She told me that she liked me. That in different circumstances, in another time, on another planet, something might have come of it. But she said that we had to be sensible. She loved this cop of hers and she couldn't wreck her life because of the way my eyes crinkled when I smiled.

I smiled.

When the cab came, I walked her out. She got into the back seat and rolled down the window. The driver stayed where he was and pretended, commendably, that he had no ears.

'This isn't it,' I said confidently, as I bent over her.

'Yes, it is.' She'd reapplied her lipstick, she was redraped in tights and heels and no longer naked; some of her erstwhile firmness had returned.

'Can't be.' I smiled for all I was worth.

'Don't wait around for anything.'

'You can't stop me.'

'I can ask you.'

She told the driver her address and he put the car in gear. But then, just as she'd finished all her tough work, her face cleared of its purpose and she lurched towards me and clumsily kissed my face through the open window. Her eyes bulged with the promise of tears, she bumped her head as she sat back, hair and lipstick messed, and she was gone.

I stood on the street watching her go and thought how difficult it was not to fall in love with people when they did things like that.

I smoked some cigarettes and drank some coffee and spent my night looking out of each of my windows.

I'd had an unhappy childhood. My folks had fucked me about in complicated and uncomplicated ways. A poor boy's childhood is thought to be a bad thing. It's supposed to fuck you up. It's supposed to teach you not to care. It's supposed to make you sad. I don't think having that childhood of mine ever really made me sad. I just think it made me fall in love with girls all the time.

Before I went to bed I called my cat in. He took his usual ten minutes of hunting crouches, slow stalks and cavalry gallops to come. Before I closed the door behind him I noticed a new graffito on the wall beside the police station.

The local kids would write things there for the purposes of bravado or initiation. But it was no big deal – the cops were too bored to hassle them. Every month or so some civic-minded old guy who lived nearby would come and paint it over. And then the kids would start all over again. It had become a ritual and it was how I told what time of the month it was. It was an epic and somehow touching battle, very Belfast. The kids wrote the usual stuff of both sides: IRA, INLA, UVF, UFF, UDA, IPLO, FTP (Fuck the Pope), FTQ (Fuck the Queen), and once (hilariously) FTNP (Fuck the Next Pope). But tonight's graffito was a new one on me. It was early in the month. The old guy had painted recently so the wall was nearly clean, and someone had chosen to write in white three-foot-high letters:

OTG

I was too tired to wonder what it meant.

Two

Chuckie Lurgan walked across the Ormeau Bridge with unsteady step and the dust of a hangover pill in his pocket. He winced at the Lagan, which gurgled and bubbled loud, bright water. Under his feet, the bridge felt unsteady as though it, too, were drunk. Frightened, Chuckie picked up his pace to cross the intoxicated bridge.

A car horn blared cruelly and Chuckie almost fainted. The sun broke through some sluggish clouds and Chuckie felt aggrieved by its shine. The day's incidentals seemed malevolent. But, despite the sardonic morning, Chuckie felt that much was beginning for him. Though in the pockets of his grimy trousers he had only three pounds and something near sixty pence, Chuckie was large with potential. Chuckie was thirty now. Chuckie had plans.

He turned into Agincourt Avenue, a street he had never liked. It was without trees and the rustic in him objected to so much undiluted brick and pavement. As Chuckie walked, his thoughts grew confident and steady. After another useless night, he had decided to get things organized. He was tired of the incoherence of his life. Two days before, he had turned thirty. Things must change, he sensed. On this momentous Monday, he was walking the long walk from Four Winds because he had concluded that he was too old to ride on the bus any more. Such transport was undignified for a man a weekend more than thirty.

He was walking from Four Winds because he had woken that morning to find himself crashed and damaged in Slat Sloane's two-up, two-down in Democracy Street. It has been the usual boneheaded weekend. Forty-six pints and two meals. Chuckie's pastimes were a form of reverse evolution. He spent time and money making himself less capable, less evolved. And it seemed to take a whole load of money and time to end up a protozoic reptile on Slat's kitchen floor.

'I'll kick your nappies round the block, wee ba!'

Two warring boys swore at each other as they rolled fistfully on the pavement of Damascus Street. As Chuckie passed through the Holy Land, he rehearsed his plans. He needed money. He needed much money. But Chuckie was not foolish enough to consider looking for a job. Employment was the goal of fools. Chuckie had decided that he would set up in business for himself. He felt that only self-employment would entirely satisfy his independent instincts. Chuckie knew that he had some way to go, but phrases like start-up capital, overheads and profit margins peppered his thoughts and felt quite as good as money in the bank.

He passed the dingy launderette on the corner of Collingwood. He smiled prosperously at a slovenly girl who sat at the window awaiting her wash. She frowned and turned away. Chuckie fancied this some form of reluctant coquetry. He was pleased and ran his hand complacently through his thin hair. As he glanced down the length of Jerusalem Street, Chuckie was realistic enough to understand that his project was as yet hugely initial. But the thought of an eventual office, an eventual secretary (hugely bosomed) and an eventual desk cheered him enormously. The three pounds and near sixty pence seemed to grow heavier in his pocket. Despite a sudden urge to vomit or sneeze, Chuckie felt a grander man.

'How's about ye, Chuckie!'

Chuckie stopped dead and stared at the speaker. He searched the rubble of his sludgy thoughts for the man's name and was surprised by his success.

'Hiya, Wilson.'

Stoney Wilson smiled too greedily at the compliment of his surname. Chuckie concluded that this would take some time. Wilson's bony hand poked him comically in the sternum.

'You're looking bad, Chuckie.'

'I'm dead but I haven't the wit to stiffen.'

Again, Wilson smiled his eager smile and his equine teeth and gums glistened in the sunlight. 'Been a while since you saw this time in the morning, I'll bet.'

Soon-to-be-prosperous Chuckie took exception to this. 'I take exception to that.'

'Easy on, Chuckie. I was only messing.'

Chuckie frowned an unmollified frown and looked at the pavement. He tried to dislodge a splat of old chewing gum with his blunt toe. Wilson searched for a way to continue the dialogue.

'I heard your Ned's getting married to that girl with the great knockers. What's her name?'

'Agnes.'

'Yeah, Alice. I wouldn't mind walking round the block with her on my own account. When's the happy day?'

'I don't know.'

Wilson's weak mouth was mobile with feeble merriment.

'You'll be the last of the single Lurgans. A great responsibility.'

Chuckie frowned again. He remembered a night spent in Wilson's wigwam on Constitution Street when Wilson did his country-boy-in-Belfast act. Three hours of the halcyon days in Portrush-sur-Mer. Wilson had dropped out of the technical college after a couple of months but he still presumed upon his brief brush with tertiary education. Chuckie wanted to escape before the geek started up about Dostoevsky or somesuch.

'Listen, Wilson. Gotta run. I've an interview for a big job this morning. I don't want to be late. You know how it is.'

Wilson's eyes narrowed with incredulity. His mouth flapped open, ready for some comic reply, but his wit deserted him. He muttered some thick valediction and patted Chuckie's arm manfully.

'See you about,' said Chuckie, walking on quickly.

He crossed the road towards Palestine Street. A large car swooped just past his burly form, swerving and blasting its horn. He turned mildly as the receding driver leant out and shouted at him. Chuckie raised his arm in a gesture of squat profanity and apologized as best he knew. 'Go fuck yourself, shit for brains!' he suggested.

Placidly, Chuckie trundled up Palestine Street. Soon, he mused, when he had a car of his own, he would make a point of sounding his horn at pedestrians whenever possible. He promised himself that if he didn't own a car by the end of the year then he would steal one. He wanted a car very badly. He wanted that chattel under him. He wanted a steering wheel in his skilful hands, a sunroof over his head. He wanted to visit car washes and garages. He wanted to go to car parks with something to park. Chuckie longed to be a solid automotive citizen.

By the time he crossed Botanic on his way to the public bar of the York Hotel, Chuckie had decided on the manufacture, colour and engine size of the shiny car that all his plans would bring him.

The distinguishing features of the Lurgan clan were that they had historically loved fame and that the Lurgan women too often were not married to the fathers of their children. The Lurgan lineage was matriarchal. And the Lurgan family were starfuckers one and all.

In 1869, Mortimer Lurgan, a shabby copying clerk at the Ulster Bank in Donegall Place, spent eighteen cold hours on a pavement outside the Chandlers' building in College Street. A reading was to be given by the famous English novelist Charles Dickens. It was his first visit to Belfast and probably his last. Mortimer Lurgan wanted to be in the front row for such an event.

His desire was fulfilled and, that night, Mortimer could be seen sitting in the very centre of the very front row of seats, greasy with delight, even though he could hear nothing since his night on the street had rendered him temporarily deaf.

After the reading, one of the organizers introduced Mortimer to the exhausted novelist. When Dickens was told that Mortimer had slept on the street in his eagerness to attend, his old, lined face flickered with brief interest. 'Well, Mr Logan,' he said, 'it is pleasant to meet such a true aficionado.' Smiling kindly, Dickens was bundled into a curtained carriage.

For the next six weeks, Mortimer Lurgan walked on air as he replayed the details of this brief but touching interview. The spot on his right hand where Dickens had touched him felt livid and ticklish with transmitted greatness. Mortimer resolved two things: that he would one day get round to reading one of the great writer's novels and that he would find out what 'aficionado' meant.

During the summer of 1929, John Lurgan and his family holidayed in a small cottage near Bundoran. The family of their local doctor in Belfast, the Flynns, had found a cottage close by. Dr Flynn was famous in Belfast for his work in the poor areas like Sailortown and the Short Strand. He was accompanied by his wife, two sons and one daughter. One of the Flynn sons fell horribly in love with Jenny, John Lurgan's pretty eighteen-year-old daughter. But Jenny soon found herself bored with the youth. Early in the holiday, the entire county had buzzed with the – inaccurate – news that the great actor Charlie Chaplin had rented a large house on the coast for part of the summer. Jenny had been beguiled by the possibility of meeting him and plotted many entrances to the famous actor's home, including:

faked injury or heart attack, nude bathing in the lake and impersonation of minor Swedish royalty.

Young Flynn, though a good-looking boy, could scarcely hope to dent Jenny's lust for the movie star. Her family were keen on the lad. He was amiable and soundly bourgeois but Jenny wouldn't, couldn't listen to their plans of dull advancement. Her hopes were bent on that touch of celebrity, so close she could almost reach out and bathe in its glow. While Jenny wasted her summer, trying to scrape an acquaintance with Chaplin, young Flynn made desperate, disappointed plans. None came to fruition and he spent the summer failing to fill his arms with Jenny's fragrant young form. That autumn he left Ireland, a rejected and unhappy youth. He went to America, changed his name to Errol and, within a brace of years, he became a movie star. Subsequently and lastingly, Jenny was sour.

In 1958, Jenny's daughter – Chuckie's mother – Peggy, ceased washing her left hand for eighteen months to preserve the ghostly trace left on her flesh when she had touched Eddie Cochrane's jacket sleeve as he left at the stage door of the Ulster Hall following his concert. Though the hand became first black then brown and finally blue with dirt, and a small piece of chewing gum stuck to the inside of her left index finger actually crystallized with age, Peggy would not wash the imagined mark that Cochrane had left. Her hand was finally washed (two hours of scrubbing in which the skin came off like paper) on the day she heard that Eddie had died.

Chuckie's father, though only belatedly his mother's husband, had been immune to this fame-lust. He was not a Lurgan. Chuckie had taken his mother's name when he was born. His father had been a businessman who had spent his best years down Sandy Row selling love pills to middle-aged matrons. He refused to marry Chuckie's mother for two long years, in which time he planted the seed of Chuckie. He had married her on Chuckie's first birthday. Then, tired of the Lurgan opprobrium, and finally exasperated by the mother's collection of sixties pop-star portraits, he had debunked, leaving behind a lingering impression that, if suicide failed, he was bound for Idaho.

Chuckie knew this to be lies or storytelling. He had seen his father a couple of years previously, lie-down drunk in a docker's bar that never closed. He had briefly considered approaching him and having some mannish hug thing there with him on that line of cheap bar-stools. He didn't, though. His father's face was flushed with the sunless tan of the full-time dipso. The man lived in the country in which all Irish alcoholics lived. Chuckie didn't want to see what that would look like.

Chuckie himself demonstrated his family's weakness on a number of occasions. When Ronald Reagan visited Ireland, playing the big Mick card in a tiny two-house town in Kerry, Chuckie had slept fruitlessly in a nearby field for the chance of pressing the palm of the American President, a man he despised.

But more importantly, more massively, Chuckie had flipped when the Pope came to Ireland.

Now, Chuckie was a Methodist. And in God's own country, the substantial, upstanding Protestant was meant to reserve a particular hatred, a particular fear for the evil Kommandant of all the Romish hordes. All his life Chuckie had been capable of shouting, 'Fuck the Pope,' with the hardest and most Protestant of his friends. But when he heard that the man in question, the new Polish Pope, was coming to Ireland, he was in a quandary. Sure, the guy was a Taig, a Fenian, the logical extension of all that was Catholic in the world. But no one could deny that he was famous.

Helpless in the glare of the Pontiff's undoubted acclaim, Chuckie secretly arranged to go on one of the special buses down to the big outdoor mass at Knock. He signed his name as Seamus McGuffin, hoping that would lend a Romish air to his broad Ulster features and his wide-apart, deeply Protestant eyes.

Thousands of people were there. The sun beat down and the Catholics broiled in that heat. Chuckie felt like he was the last

Methodist left.

The Mass itself was a dull and mystifying affair. Chuckie sweated at his ignorance of the responses that the rest of the crowd made as though it were second nature. He had been under the impression that the Catholic Mass was still celebrated in Latin and had planned to mumble meaninglessly when required to make those Taig noises. He was horrified to find that they now said Mass in English and that his lunatic mumblings were no effective disguise. He panicked for a while before it dawned upon him that the people around him thought that he was merely some physical or mental unfortunate who'd been brought to this event instead of on a more reliably miraculous pilgrimage to Lourdes.

The Pope was a windswept dot on a raised altar in the distance. Chuckie was disappointed. But a rumour had circulated that the Holy Pole intended to have one of his favoured walkabouts on the periphery of the enormous throng. Just before the end of the service, Chuckie pushed himself right through to the front, just on the off-chance.

Chuckie's gamble paid off gloriously. The Pope did, indeed, amble briefly along the crush barriers nearest the altar. He touched hands and gave blessings. The people around Chuckie went wild with delight and, as the Pontiff passed by where he was standing, Chuckie threw out his hands amongst the forest of stretching limbs and brushed the Pope's own fingers.

When the Holy Man had gone, the people around Chuckie crowed and bubbled with excitement. He had never seen faces so edified, so glazed with glee. Their lives had been touched with some piety, some great sacredness they craved. But Chuckie's pleasure was more substantial. His hand buzzed with surplus blood, it felt suffused, electrified by the touch of fame, the touch of serious global celebrity.

A shabby photographer, who'd been snapping crazily, touted his wares to the crowd, telling them that he'd got shots which featured themselves and the Pope simultaneously. Chuckie despised the gullibility of the others but ordered a couple on his own behalf anyway.

Two weeks later, a package arrived with his photographs. One was meaningless, a blur of arms and a white cassock out of focus; the other, however, was perfect. The blur of arms was fainter, less chaotic, and out of the mêlée of people, two figures were clear. The Polish Pope faced the lee of the crowd, one arm outstretched. In the midst of that crowd, Chuckie stood five feet distant from the Pontiff, his right arm stretched towards the Pope, his fingers six inches from the Pope's own.

It was a big moment for Chuckie in a number of complicated ways. He felt he had entered the annals of his ancestors' fameseeking activities with some style. But also, swollen with the joy and pride of this famous encounter, Chuckie was forced to take the clement, ecumenical step of having the photograph framed and mounted on the sitting-room wall of his most Protestant domicile.

And from this a moderation was born in Chuckie. He was still only seventeen, and when some of his coarser faithmates heard of what he had placed on his wall, they judged him still young enough to take the meat of their schoolboy beatings. And amidst the biffings and bleatings and bleedings, Chuckie, who only defended the Man because he was famous, began to see an absurdity in this hatred, in this fear. Could it matter that the Pope was a Taig if the Pope was in the papers?

And in the next few years, this new moderation led to a change in the people Chuckie knew. He met Slat Sloane, Jake Jackson and a series of other Roman Catholics. He spent time with them, ate in their houses, met their parents and, crucially, saw the pictures on their walls. It irritated him to find, as he developed this extensive Catholic acquaintance, that everybody's parents had been in Knock when the Pope came to Ireland and that everybody had the same kind of photograph on the walls from that day – the Pope on the periphery and some family member close to him amongst the scrum of devout others.

For the first couple of years Chuckie had failed to bring any of his Catholic friends back to his home, partly because he was unsure of the reaction of his Methodist mother – they had never discussed ecumenicalism, so he couldn't be sure where she stood – and partly because he was wary of bringing friendly Catholics to a street so firmly set in the red, white and blue epicentre of the Protestant Loyalist belt of the city.

However, he also had to admit, it was because he didn't want them to see his Pope photograph. With their experience of Pope photographs, he knew they would fail to be impressed. Chuckie decided that something would have to be done. He had an idea. He took the frame from the wall, the photograph from the frame and brought the picture to Dex, an alcoholic one-time commercial artist who lived on Cairo Street. Dex had been dubbed Dex on account of his remarkable facility for painting two-handed. The guy was a spray-paint genius who never boasted that he had once painted for a national Coca-Cola advertisement. Chuckie promised him two bottles of Bell's for good work and absolute discretion. Then he told him what he wanted.

Two days later Chuckie retrieved his photograph, reframed it and put it back on the wall. His Cairo Street friend had carefully painted over all the human figures apart from Chuckie and the Pope. What was left was the Pope and Chuckie, arms stretched towards each other, in some murky brown dreamscape.

After only an hour, Chuckie had taken down the photograph and returned to Cairo Street. He slapped the second of his bottles out of the painter's hand and set him back to work. The picture was now patently unrealistic. It needed a landscape.

Another two days passed. Chuckie had already promised Slat and Jake that they could soon come and visit down at *chez* Lurgan. He was so anxious, he nearly lost some weight.

The second time he picked up his photograph, he was

happier. Dex had painted some highly realistic trees and hedges, some good green grass, an unlikely sky and even a garden bench – it looked like Chuckie and the Pope were hanging out in some pleasant garden or hotel grounds. Chuckie put it on his wall, called Jake and told him to come round later that afternoon.

But the hour he waited was fatal and when Jake found his Catholic way to Chuckie's Protestant door, Chuckie lay on the floor for twenty minutes ignoring his friend's increasingly irritated knocking. The exterior scene of him and the Pope wasn't special enough. It looked too much like a chance meeting, a casual and unwelcome acquaintance. He went back to Cairo Street.

Dex's liver was suffering as Chuckie gave him his fifth and sixth bottle of whisky in a week. Give me an interior, he said. Give me walls and a roof and stuff. Dex looked at him in trepidation. Then I'll be happy, said Chuckie, without conviction.

And he nearly was. Having apologized to the furious Jake, Chuckie was delighted to see the latest of Dex's handiwork. The old saucehound still had it in him. Now the Pope and Chuckie stood in some modest but spacious room, possibly domestic, possibly of some seminary. There were walls, ceiling, chairs, bookshelves, even a bay window, which shed an excessively transfiguring shaft of light close to the Pontiff. Chuckie stuck it on his wall and promised himself that this would be it.

Chuckie invited every Catholic he had ever met to come round to his house on the following Saturday. His mother would be out – his glory complete.

Chuckie woke early that Saturday. He drank sweet tea as he stared at his photograph and flinched as the shame began to rise. Despite the delicacy of Dex's spray technique, the picture had visibly thickened. Chuckie's heart sank as he could only concede that something was still wrong. The posture of the two figures was now too dramatic. In the exterior version the fact that they were standing, arms outstretched towards each other, had not seemed too incongruous. But now, in that calm interior setting, the attitudes were quite absurd. The outstretched arms above the bookcases would get a belly laugh.

It was still a few minutes short of nine o'clock. Chuckie dressed and headed round for Cairo Street.

He found Dex lying on his own front doorstep, his clothes a stained geography of the night before. It was past ten o'clock before he regained the power of speech. Chuckie explained the remaining problem with the photograph and told Dex to sort it out somehow and make it less ridiculous. Chuckie told him he had one hour. He went home without hope.

When Slat, Jake and the others arrived, Chuckie stalled as best he could. He directed them into the narrow kitchen where they smoked, drank tea and lied about drugs and girls for an hour. Septic Ted, who was hung over, kept asking that they should go into the sitting room so that he could lie down and fart some. Chuckie, who had often boasted of the superiority of his Pope snap, was finally giving up hope when there was a knock at the front door.

Dex stood on the step, his face hideously pale and sweaty. He held the framed photograph in his hands like a desperate peace offering.

'Put it on the fucking wall and get out of here,' hissed Chuckie.

Humbly, the cowed Dex sidled into the living room. Chuckie returned to the kitchen, marked conversational time for ninety-five seconds and then heard the retreating Dex close the front door. Young Lurgan suggested that everyone adjourned to the sitting room.

His friends filed out and filed into the front room. Chuckie entered that room at the tail of the procession and already he could hear murmured exclamations of surprise and edification:

God, who'd have thought it?

They're all at it.

All dipsos.

Fucking typical.

From across the room, Chuckie tried to press a modest smile on his features. He could make out the photograph between the heads of his friends and could see no difference. He could see the two figures in the pictured room, arms out to each other. He shuffled towards the picture promising cruel revenge, though conceding that he hadn't given Dex enough time. Until, two feet from the famous photograph, he saw that Dex had really fixed it, that he had rendered the absurd postures unremarkable, and Chuckie finally understood the genius of the man.

For there they stood, Pope and Chuckie, arms still outstretched towards one another, a whisky bottle in the Pope's hand, a glass in Chuckie's.

Six weeks later, Dex was dead. The kids shouted that he was now an ex-Dex and much amused themselves. The local matrons stood in armfolding pairs on doorsteps. That's where the drink always took you in the end, they would say, loud enough for any passing husbands to hear.

Chuckie, however, hid his photograph and silently disagreed.

In the lizard lounge of the Botanic Inn, Chuckie Lurgan told a joke. No one laughed too hard and Chuckie was conscious of failure. He began to think about going home. He was tired from his unaccustomed early waking and a day's fiscal planning in six different bars. He had drunk too much cheap beer, bought by too many people he didn't really know. As he looked around the thickly peopled gloom of the bar, he was groggily conscious of dissipating his entrepreneurial energies.

Resolute, he drained the last third of his last pint in massive rolling gulps and set the defeated glass on the bar. He bid an unnoticed farewell to a man from Pacific Avenue and struck a path through the crops of people. He urinated odorously in the toilets and then left the bar, never – he felt sure – to return.

Outside, it was briefly wet and the rain fell like fingers on his face. Chuckie looked for a bus stop.

*

Eureka Street, 10 p.m. The darkness was soft and coloured. In No. 7, Mr and Mrs Playfair mumbled in their tidy bed, a brand new Easi-sleep reduced to £99 in a bomb-damage clearance sale in a broken store at Sprucefield. Across the street in No. 12, Johnny Murray, by the half-light of a shaded lamp, offered the beauty of his erect penis to a wardrobe mirror. In No. 22, Edward Carson watched television and drank deep from a can of beer; he was pleased that his children (Billy, Barry and Rosie) were finally asleep and that his irritable wife was, at last, having her protracted bath; in his general pleasure, Edward laughed at something on the television that he didn't find funny. In No. 27, the rococo legend BELLEVUE painted on a wooden plaque by the door, Mr and Mrs Stevens were absent, holidaying in Bundoran; Julia, their daughter (gladly left behind), was showing both her breasts to Robert Cole, who previously had glimpsed only the upper portion of the left one during a memorable party in Chemical Street. In No. 34, a silent man smoked his sixty-fifth cigarette of the day and thought of his policeman son, dead ten years.

In No. 42, Chuckie Lurgan sat in a second-hand armchair of cheap construction. It was getting near eleven and his time felt wrong. Like himself, his time felt sluggish and inert. He was waiting for nothing yet felt himself goaded by a sensation of attendance. He rose from his armchair and went to the window. He looked out onto the street. His gaze swept over Nos. 7, 12, 22, 27 and 34 without comment. He was aware of some vague inflation, some massiveness in Eureka Street. It did not worry him. He imputed it to the inevident God and regained his seat.

He heard the muffled impacts of an argument between the Murtaghs next door. He winced at the sludgy sound of their proletarian controversy. Chuckie was ashamed of the way his fellow citizens spoke. The accents of his city appalled him. His own accent was as thick as any, but to Chuckie, other Belfast people sounded as though they had lighted matches or burning cigarettes in their mouths. He longed for elocutionary elegance.

But this irritation was momentary, for Chuckie was big with love. Shocks of lissom bliss puckered his flesh and he shuddered down the length of his cerebrospinal axis. He had seen her, all of ten hours previously, in the quartered sunlight from the four-paned window of the upstairs room in the Botanic Inn, the perfect girl in the perfect bar. He had fallen, he deemed, in love.

She was having lunch with friends as Chuckie was beginning the serious part of his day's drinking. Glancing over at her while trying to persuade Pete the Priest to buy him a drink, Chuckie had felt profoundly heterosexual. A quick look at the mirrored wall beyond the optics told him (mistakenly) that he was looking well. It wasn't that she was beautiful. She was pretty, certainly. It was more that she somehow reminded Chuckie of himself. He ambled over to her table.

He had given her some old chat. To his amazement she had been polite, even friendly. Chuckie was accustomed to the brutal end of brush-offs and her amiability encouraged him more than it should have. She was an American so her friendliness might just have been constitutional with her. But, try as he might, he couldn't prevent himself from flopping into the chair that her hard-faced girlfriend had vacated to head for the pisshouse.

He hadn't told her too many lies and hadn't looked exclusively at her breasts. That was good going. Relative honesty and looking at her face while she spoke was good behaviour by Chuckie's standards. Briefly, he had felt like a plump David Niven.

She was called Max and had been living in Belfast for a year. She told him that she worked in a nursery or kindergarten. Her friend, who had a funny name, told him later that Max owned the nursery in which she worked. Chuckie's bowels had melted sharply at the thought that she might be rich as well.

Too soon, Pete the Priest was busting his balls to move on to Lavery's, preparatory to the mid-afternoon crawl and then the usual Monday night saucehunt. But he had done big work with this girl. He had made some decisions. He had made some moves. She had magically given him her phone number.

He had left under protest with a new feeling creeping under his flesh. A big feeling for the friendly American girl that felt consonant with his imminent tycoon status. He and Pete drank the rest of the day, as usual, losing each other in a tight clinch in the Rotterdam between the beer and the spirits. He had somehow got back across town to the Bot in the vain hope she might still be there, and in the more serious hope that her drinking habits would be much too moderate for that to be possible. She had not been there and Chuckie had just looked at her phone number on its paper scrap and scrounged a few beers off people who couldn't say no. As the night had wound down, he couldn't help feeling that it was all starting for him.

And, now that he was home, that excitement had not left him. Even the dissipation of his half-cut booze-buzz did not daunt him. The thought of her lent some curious reality, some warm flesh to his dreams of wealth. Somehow, she made it possible. Maybe it was because he knew she was high-grade, top-notch. Maybe it was because she made his dreams necessary.

He wasn't sure but all he could do was think of her. When she had smiled, her lips had stretched like they would split. Maybe it was the shape of her skull or the tone of her skin. All he knew was that he liked it, and later that evening, in all the other bars, it was with him when she wasn't.

Chuckie rose from his chair and decided to go to bed. He was ashamed to retire at such an unmanly hour – he had not gone to bed before midnight since he was twelve years old. He knew that he would be insomniac with passion but he did not care. The open-eyed idleness of his armchair was insupportable to him. He would see better and calmer in the dark.

He switched off the lights and climbed the narrow staircase.

In the bathroom, he urinated copiously once more but did not bother to brush his teeth. He calculated that he drank a pint and a half of good Ulster tapwater every day and concluded that this represented enough fluoride for any man. His teeth were clean enough. Chuckie gilded no lilies.

He switched off the bathroom light and crossed the tiny hall to his bedroom door. Before entering his own room, he glanced through the open door of his mother's. His eyes adjusted quickly to its small gloom and he could see the massive form of his chubby mother, wrapped and warped like a slug in her bedding. She slept fast. Her mouth hung open and he detected a tiny glint of drool on her cheek. He wondered what she dreamt.

(Mrs Lurgan dreamt of the cold night of Tuesday 2 November 1964 when, at the age of twenty, in a polka-dot dress shorter than it should have been, she had ridden one hundred and seventy yards, scrabbling and weeping on the roof of the heavy black car in which the Beatles were being driven away from the ABC cinema and on up Fisherwick Avenue until, solicitous for her, the car had stopped and she fell off onto the tarmac, which had been considerably harder than it looked.)

Chuckie undressed and crept into bed. He waited and shivered as the mattress warmed. He thought of his perfect, perfect girl and his penis unfurled itself slowly. He was surprised by his desire and wrapped his arms firmly around his chest. He decided not to touch himself for her. He felt strongly that he should at least call the girl before he took the liberty of masturbating about her. He started to paint dim pictures of her calling him at the office or sitting in the passenger seat of his phantom car, complete with steering wheel and sun-roof, as they idled lovingly through the car-wash.

Soon, disappointingly soon, he fell asleep.

Three

Within the week, Chuckie had made his meet. After some persuading, John Long had agreed to talk to him. Chuckie thought at one point of using his suspicions that Long had knocked off his mother when Chuckie was a kid but in the end he didn't have to.

John Long was a local boy made good, originating from Eureka Street. He had gone away to England for three years and had come back, still a teenager, with an unexplained two thousand pounds in the bank. He had bought a couple of shops on the row and then a couple more. He had moved away, and the Eureka Street residents only heard of his other expansions by hearsay or on those occasions when he returned to the street of his birth to flirt with the old women and patronize the old men. John Long, sadly named since he was unusually tiny, was now a prosperous if unpleasant-looking man in his fifties, who drove big cars and lived in Holywood, in a big house so spankingly new that it looked as though it had just been unwrapped.

They met on Thursday in one of Long's warehouses near prosperous Bangor. The trip was two buses and a three-mile walk in the rain for Chuckie, who arrived just as Long's Mercedes rolled noiselessly into the car park. Long got out of his car, a parody of the cigar-chomping, camel-coated, yob-made-good. He eyed Chuckie's bedraggled form with some disfavour. Chuckie silently promised himself that he would nurse this grievance, this entrance.

In his untidy box of an office, which was somehow more daunting, more impressive than a swish one, Long was blandly expansive. 'Haven't seen your mother in years. She used to be a lovely-looking girl. How's she keeping these days?'

Chuckie remembered Long's visits, the sleek-haired man with the expensive smell and the bags full of unIrish fruits: grapes, melons and peaches. He hadn't liked him then but had loved that expensive smell, the thick car parked outside and the rumour of magazine glamour that the man always brought with him. He remembered the complicated whispers that had bothered and frightened him. He remembered how he had hated it when the man had offered him the fancy fruit and told him to go and play.

'She's fine. She asked to be remembered to you.'

'Aye, I'm always thinking of Peggy these days. We're all getting old. Tragedy for the women especially.' Long raised his hand over his sparse hair. He had always been vain though never handsome. His complacency was misplaced. He had aged terribly. His face had collapsed and his wrinkles were like ancient scars that ran in little rills all over his face, following the local contours of nose, eyebrow or ear like fault lines.

'Ma looks pretty good, you know.'

'I'm sure she does. I'm sure she does.'

Chuckie sensed that early antagonism wasn't apt. He hoped that Long was going to help make him rich. He tried to smile amiably. His teeth were too apparent in the attempt.

Long decided that that was enough badinage. 'So you wanted to talk to me, son?'

'Aye.'

Long sat back, placed his feet on his messy desk and lit another cigar without offering one to Chuckie. The man was not too fussed about making it easier for him. There was a bad pause, which Chuckie committed to his growing grudge book, and then he made his pitch.

He told Long about his plans of setting himself up in business, about his plans for getting sponsorship, government grants, all kinds of funny money. While keeping the specifics unspecific, he waxed about his dreams of networks of companies, each servicing the others, of monopolies, empires. He talked blithely about sums of money he could barely count. He grew hot and indiscreet, and as the talk got bigger, his voice got smaller. Eventually, it just dried away and he fell silent.

Long chewed on his cigar with an air of spurious concentration and sighed with unfaked satisfaction. Chuckie knew that the local mogul was enjoying this. It was nice to be able to patronize the past, to prove to yourself that you'd really left the place you came from. Long swept his feet from the desk and leant forward, theatrically dynamic. His eyes narrowed with pleasure. 'I won't lend you any money.'

Chuckie tried to say that he hadn't asked but Long waved his objections away. He spat in the wastepaper basket. 'No money but I'll offer you some advice. How does that grab you?'

'Not very nicely.'

Long ignored him. He extinguished his cigar and looked through the glass partition at the goods that lay neat in his warehouse. It looked as though he liked the view. He turned his eyes on Chuckie, almost emotional. 'You're just a wee ballocks from Eureka Street, son. But I started out the same way. I worked hard and now I've got everything you want. And do you know what? It was easy. I never had much to do with women, bar tarts.'

Chuckie was careful not to flinch. He knew that Long was too dim to realize exactly what he'd said, though Chuckie silently damned his mother for making the mistake of this man.

Long stood, concluding the interview and lending effect to his pause. 'Do you wanna know what the recipe for success is?'

'What?'

'No women. I started off thinking that the recipe for success was work now, fuck later, and then I thought it was fuck now, work later, but then I worked out that it was, of course . . .

He left the pause there like a weary schoolteacher, waiting for young Lurgan to rhyme it off by rote.

'What?' said Chuckie.

'Work now, work later. Don't bother fucking at all.'

He smiled the smile of a seer.

The rain had eased to the grey slant typical of Irish funerals. Chuckie, neither sugar nor salt, knew he would not melt but he felt keenly the humiliation of the walk back to the bus station, especially when John Long's Mercedes passed him. The two short greeting blasts of the horn had a satiric lilt that wounded him.

In the hour it took to get to the bus station he had stoked his anger and grief so that the eventual retribution to be visited upon unlong John had become a visceral component of his dreams of wealth. He had had two options, two plans for raising the initial sums so necessary to the commencement of his capitalist career.

The first plan had been to ask Long for the money.

The second plan had been to think of another plan.

He broke his second last fiver in paying his bus fare back to the city. He hoped his dole would arrive the next day. But as the bus moved out of the station and Chuckie looked around at his damp fellow passengers, who had started to steam slightly from the heat of the vehicle, his mood lifted inexplicably. Despite the multiple humiliations and grievances of his present life, he knew that he could spend a warm forty minutes with his head against the window thinking of the American girl.

He planned to call her tonight and his thoughts were nerveless as he wondered what he would say. He wiped some steam from the window and settled his arms on the shelf of his belly.

Already he drew comfort from the thinking of her. Again, his plans seemed more plausible. Having her in his life would definitely be an expensive business. He would definitely have her in his life. *Ergo*, somehow, he would definitely have the money.

He loved her name. Max. He was very glad that she was American. He wasn't entirely sure that he would or should love her. Love was a little ambitious. Exchange of bodily fluids would do to be going on with.

Chuckie always wanted sex, but on his own terms; terms more lyrical and tremendous than might be imagined. He sought forms of mystic union he considered impossible with the women of Belfast. They were not natural docks for his living liquids. He was *very* glad that she was American.

Chuckie thought often of his old girlfriends. Recollections without haze, like erotic memoranda. He thought of the year he was seven and he fell in love with a piano teacher, who played Mozart and the blues. He thought of the bad old good old days when he was sixteen and his mother didn't allow girls in the house; when he lost count of the number of nights he spent in phone boxes after the pubs were shut, ringing round everybody he knew trying to find someone who would lend him a bed or even a quiet corner for a shag, quick or slow.

He liked to think of the scores of Belfast girls who bore his invisible graffito on their inner thighs:

Chuckie was here
Briefly but memorably.

Many of Chuckie's thirty wasted years had been devoted to the search for erotic congress. He had spent much time wandering the city, searching Belfast for sex, tramping leprous streets in pursuit of some quality lewdness. He had found it first in the Central Library, with its lemony reference room, with a girl repeating her O levels at the College of Business Studies. They had sat by the twenty-volume collected speeches of Winston Churchill and somehow it became the scene of Chuckie's twenty-eighth orgasm, the first by the hand of another.

And thus had started an erotic career much more successful than he had a right to expect. Chuckie was not handsome. His sandy hair had started to recede before his twenty-first birthday, his belly rolled like a full balloon and he had the breasts of a thirteen-year-old girl. Nonetheless, women slept with him with something close to monotonous regularity. He had always been proud of his penis – plump and pink as a baby's forearm – and he attributed some of his success to this, his best feature.

But no girl, no woman had made a dent in the marsh of his selfhood. And Chuckie lamented this. Chuckie wanted to be lost in someone. Chuckie wanted a girl who would make life burn in his heart like a heavy meal. Chuckie wanted to discover the secret of true love.

'Got a light.'

An old woman stood over his seat, her damp coat trailing off her shoulders. She brandished her breasts at him.

'Mmmm?' asked Chuckie.

'A light. Got one?'

Chuckie, who rarely smoked, always carried a lighter. It was meant to grease the wheels of conversation with foxy, dark-haired girls in bars. He fumbled in his pockets and passed the cheap, disposable thing to the old woman. She lit her cigarette and made to hand it back to him.

'No, you keep it,' said Chuckie. 'I've given up.'

The old woman paused with her hand held out in an exaggerated posture of surprise. 'Ach, God love you, son. That's very decent of you.'

She lurched back to her seat. Chuckie could see her sitting four rows forward in the no-smoking section, telling her companion – an equally corpulent, equally decrepit lady – of his largesse. The exclamations of surprise were audible through most of the bus and Chuckie had to suffer a complicated series of nods and smiles from the old women, who had both turned round to favour him with their acknowledgements of his *beau geste*. Some of the other passengers also turned and there were some quiet smiles at his expense. Chuckie blushed and worried.

He tried to stare through the wet windows. The fields and houses drooped in the aquatic exterior. He was glad to be abus in such weather. As he looked around the vehicle, he could not repress a sensation of cosiness, as though this Ulsterbus with its condensation, its body heat and smells was some kind of biosphere that sustained them all. He would almost miss it when he was rich.

When Chuckie got home, his mother was in the kitchen making smells he didn't like. He heard her call out some greeting. Without answering, he went upstairs to his bedroom. There he exchanged his wet apparel for dry. Then he sat on his bed and combed his thin wet hair.

Chuckie slept in the larger bedroom that faced onto the street. His mother had made it so years before, so long ago that he had forgotten his gratitude and her sacrifice for a decade or more. His window was open and, after a few minutes, he could hear his mother's voice from the open street. She was standing on the doorstep swapping talk with the other matrons of Eureka Street. It felt like all the evenings he had ever known. Sitting in his eight-foot bedroom, listening to his mother talk, her head six foot from his feet. The houses were tiny. The street small. The microscale of the place in which he lived gave it a grandeur he could not ignore.

In Eureka Street the people rattled against each other like matches in a box but there was a sociability, a warmth in that. Especially on evenings like this, when the sun was late to dip. When finally it did dip, there was an achromatic half-hour, when the air was free from colour and the women concluded their gossip, the husbands came home and the children were coaxed indoors from their darkening play.

He put down his comb and looked out of the window. Mrs

Causton had come across the road from the open doorway of No. 24. Her husband was still working and her kids weren't young so she had twenty minutes to talk away until her old man came home. His mother had known Caroline Causton for forty years or more. They had been at school together. As Chuckie looked down on them talk, with bent heads and folded arms, he couldn't help feeling something close to sorrow for his mother.

Chuckie's mother was a big woman, built historical, like a ship or a city. He found it hard to picture her as a girl. But something in the quality of the light or his mood, some insipidness in the air, suddenly helped him to strip the aggregate of flesh and years from both women and he glimpsed, briefly, a remnant of what they had been. As always, he wondered what she had dreamt. He resolved that he would stop being ashamed of his mother.

Chuckie had been ashamed of his mother ever since he could remember. Shame was, perhaps, the wrong word. His mother provoked a constant low-level anxiety in him. Inexplicably, he had feared the something he could not name that she might do. Since he had been fourteen years old, Chuckie had lived in quiet dread of his mother making her mark.

Sometimes, he would comfort himself with thoughts of her incontrovertible mediocrity. She was just an archetypal working-class Protestant Belfast mother. Not an inch of her headscarf nor a fibre of the slippers in which she shopped departed from what would have been expected. She had *doppelgängers* all along Eureka Street and in all the other baleful streets around Sandy Row. It was absurd. He spent too many hours, too many years, awaiting the calamitous unforeseen. Nothing could be feared from a woman of such spectacular mundanity.

Nevertheless, she worried him.

For ten years, Chuckie had dealt with his unease most undutifully. After his father had left home and Chuckie was faced with the prospect of living with his mother, he decided simply to avoid her as best he could. And he did. There had been a decade's worth of agile avoidance. He couldn't remember when they had last had a conversation of more than a minute's duration. It was a miracle in a house as tiny as the one they shared. The sitting room, kitchen and bathroom were the flashpoints in this long campaign. She was always leaving little notes around the house. He would read these missives. *Slat called at six. He'll meet you in the Crown. Your cousin's coming home at the weekend.* He told her almost all the things he needed to tell her by telephone. Sometimes he would leave the house just so that he could find a phone box and call her from there. Sometimes it felt like Rommel and Montgomery in the desert. Sometimes it felt much worse than that.

Caroline Causton looked up and saw him at his bedroom window. He did not flinch.

'What are you up to, Chuckie?' quizzed Caroline.

'Nice evening.' Chuckie smiled. His mother, too, was looking at him now. She couldn't remember when she had last seen her son's face split with a smile of such warmth.

'Are you all right, son?'

'I was just listening to you talk,' explained Chuckie gently. The two women exchanged looks.

'It reminded me of when I was a kid,' he went on. His voice was quiet. But it was an easy matter to talk thus on that dwarf street with their faces only a few feet from his own.

'When I was a kid and you sent me to bed I would sit under the window and listen to you two talk just as you're talking now. When the Troubles started you did it every night. You'd stand and whisper about bombs and soldiers and what the Catholics would do. I could hear. I haven't been as happy since. I liked the Troubles. They were like television.'

As Chuckie's mother listened to those words, her face fell and fell again and, as Chuckie finished, she was speechless. She clutched her hand to her heart and staggered.

'Shall I call him an ambulance?' asked Caroline.

Chuckie laughed a healthy laugh and disappeared from the window.

Caroline faced his mother. 'Peggy, what's got into your boy?'

But Peggy was thinking about what her son had said. She remembered that frightened time well but his memory seemed more vivid, more powerful than her own. She remembered soldiers on the television and on the streets. She remembered parts of her city she'd never seen being made suddenly famous. She remembered the men's big talk of resistance and of civil war, of finally wiping the Catholics off the cloth of the country. Chuckie remembered pressing his head against the wall underneath his bedroom window and the whispers of his mother and her friend. For the first time, she glimpsed how beautiful it might have seemed to him.

Caroline was unmoved. 'Is he on drugs?'

Chuckie's mother smiled her friend away and went indoors. She found her son in the kitchen. She had to catch her breath when she saw that he was happily cooking the meal that she had begun.

'Nearly ready,' said Chuckie.

An hour later, telling his mother he wanted to do some work on a job application (she was still unused to the heady sensation of such a ball-by-ball commentary), Chuckie went upstairs to his bedroom.

There he opened the little desk he'd used, or mostly not used, when he was a schoolboy. He took out a sheet of paper, an old pencil and his school calculator, a massive thing, unused for a dozen years. He switched it on and was amazed to find it still worked. The omen was propitious.

Before he wrote anything he looked around the tiny room. He felt a lump in his throat at the thought that he had slept almost every night of his long life in this tiny room. The walls bore the marks of old posters ripped and replaced as his passions had formed and formed again; footballers, rock stars, footballers again, and then beautiful big-hipped girls in their underwear. These were the signs of his growth as surely as if someone had marked his height on the wall as he grew.

He looked at the picture of Pope and self above the little desk. It was one of the few photographs of himself that Chuckie possessed. He was young in that photograph. He was not so fat but neither was he an oil painting. Actually, thought Chuckie smiling, in that photograph that's exactly what he was.

He took the photograph/painting from the wall and slipped it into a desk drawer. That was then and this was now. He composed himself, drew breath, looked round one more moist-eyed time and started to write.

It had been more difficult than he might have imagined. He judged that he should not count the past week and should only tot up the totals until his thirtieth birthday since that was the day that he had made all his big decisions. Most of it was, by its nature, imprecise and he had spent much time hazarding estimates. However, he was confident about most of them.

He wrote his list. This is what his list said:

On my thirtieth birthday	
I had been alive for:	360 months
	1560 weeks
	10,950 days
	262,800 hours
	15,768,000 minutes
	94,608,000 seconds
I had	
urinated approx:	74,460 times
ejaculated approx:	10,500 times
been asleep for approx:	98,550 hours (11 years, 3 months)
smoked approx:	11,750 cigarettes

consumed approx:	32,000 meals
drunk approx:	17,520 litres of liquid (approx: 8,000 of which contained alcohol)
walked approx:	20,440 miles
sustained an erection for approx:	186,150 mins, 3,102.5 hrs, 129.27 days
grown approx:	5.40 metres of hair
had sex approx:	175 times
earned approx:	no fucking money

He tacked the paper to the wall where his Pope photograph had been and sat back. It pleased him to think that he had been asleep for so long. That was exactly how it had felt as he considered the waste of his past life. He felt that he had always been sleeping. But it was not a depressing statistic. If you took a sanguine view, it meant that he was still young: it meant that he was really only eighteen years old.

He smiled to think how much and how long he'd pissed. His bladder was famously weak and it had been, perhaps, pressed into more work than it deserved. Some fastidiousness had prevented him from calculating his defecation rate. That was something he hadn't wanted to know.

The aggregate of his copulations depressed him. Though the total duration of his life's waking erections was fairly impressive, he hadn't had anywhere near enough sex. It was only 12.5 times per year since he was sixteen. There'd been enough girls – they just hadn't hung around for long. Max would change all that. He didn't know anything about her – he couldn't even claim her surname – but he had a feeling that she would improve his averages.

He was going to telephone her now, he decided. It would wait no longer. Despite the new rapprochement with his mother, he didn't want her listening in. He decided he would sneak out to the phone box on Sandy Row. Leaving the sheet tacked where it was – at which his mother would marvel while he was out – he went downstairs.

The night was conditional, as dark as undark chocolate. Chuckie loved the gentle commencement of his city's mild summers and, though the rain began again, his mood lifted further.

The phone box was empty, which somewhat daunted him. He had counted on a wait while he marshalled his thoughts for this big call. But he stomped in there with the full vigour of intention. Doing it was the only way of getting it done.

He picked up the phone. He pressed its cold plastic against his cheek, sharing the streptococci of a double hundred Sandy Row Protestant neighbours. He dialled her number.

Chuckie was confident. Chuckie was more than confident, he was adamant. The telephone was his instrument, his device. He preferred the telephone to the non-electronic conversation. On the telephone he was incorporeal, he was all voice. Chuckie knew that he wasn't thin. He was fat but he was ambulatory. On the telephone, the plenty of his flesh hindered him not. On the phone, he could be as slim and pretty as he needed to be.

'Hello,' the telephone said.

Chuckie exhaled. 'Hi. I'm looking for Max.'

'You found her.'

'Hello. This is Chuckie Lurgan. We met last week. Lunch in the Bot. The Botanic Inn.'

'Yeah, I remember.'

'You said that I could call you if I liked.'

'Yeah.'

'Well,' Chuckie smiled audibly, 'I liked.'

They talked. For twenty-three minutes while a queue formed and grew, they talked. They talked of America, of Ireland, of her mother, of his mother, her flat, her flatmate, his prospects, her passport, the way the leaves were just showing on the trees, of horticulture generally, of the chances of a good summer, of his friends, her friends, alcohol, love, secrets, life, God, and what was showing in the Curzon that weekend.

As the twenty-fourth minute arrived, and there was audible grumbling from the four-strong queue, the proposal was made. Max started a winding précis of her commitments for the weekend while she made up her mind. Chuckie stuck his hand through the broken window of the phone box and gave his neighbours a little wave.

She talked on. Chuckie didn't listen. Idly, he inspected the graffiti scratched or scraped into the metals and plastics of the phone box interior. All the favourites: Red Hand Commandos; Diane Murray sucks for free; No Surrender; Hughie loves Deb; KAI (Kill All Irish); UVF; UDA; UFF. Square on the plate of the box itself, just above the numerals pad, someone had laboriously and elegantly gouged the legend:

OTG

Chuckie double-took and peered question marks. What did that mean?

'. . . but, yeah, what the hell, why not?' Max was saying.

He'd never seen it before, nor anything like it. The letter O didn't feature much in Irish or Ulster graffiti.

'So, OK, I'd be glad to,' she went on.

He frowned with irritation. He hated not knowing. 'OTG,' he murmured to himself, 'OTG.'

'What?' Max asked.

'Mmmmm?' mumbled Chuckie.

'What did you say?' Max's voice was sharp.

'I said, oh, I agree.'

'What?'

'Oh, I agree.'

'To what?'

'To what you said.'

'So it's a date, then?'

'Ah,' Chuckie panicked, 'yes, absolutely.'

'OK, see you there.'

The phone clicked in the American style, without formality.

The door of the phone box opened.

'Listen, fuckface, I've had it,' said Willie Johnson, an impatient Eureka Street neighbour. 'If you don't want that phone stuck up your arse, you'll give me my turn.'

Chuckie stumbled out of the box. He hadn't a clue to what assignation he had agreed. Max had said, 'See you there.' Where?

Chuckie stepped to the end of the now five-strong queue. He waited. After an hour, during which his neighbours delighted in taking much time over their own conversations, he called Max back and checked the details.

'Maybe you should write it down,' she advised.

'Yeah,' said Chuckie. 'Maybe I should.'

After his call, he ran into Stoney Wilson again. Stoney had been walking in the other direction but his life was such that he had nothing better to do than change direction and walk with Chuckie wherever Chuckie might choose.

Stoney was one of those people to whom Chuckie always promised himself that he would be much more unpleasant but to whom, unerringly, he was shamefully amiable. Chuckie was always helpless when faced with people about whom he had made private resolutions.

Nevertheless, he didn't want to walk back home because he knew that Stoney would follow him to the door and expect to be asked in. Chuckie didn't feel that he had the energy to refuse him. So, though it was now dark and though the rain had begun its fun again, they walked aimlessly up and down the length of their little local streets, passing the dirty shops on Sandy Row with their windowfuls of spiders and flies, and passing quartets of ambling policemen, all submachine-guns and flak-jackets.

Stoney was full of some story he'd just heard on the radio about some UVF robbers who'd ripped off some jewellery store in Portadown. The punchline was that they'd called a taxi as their getaway car. Typical Prods, said Stoney. The joke was meant to be the ineptitude of Protestant paramilitaries, that despite the blood-drinking myths of Protestant tumult, they weren't as good as the Catholics. But it seemed to Chuckie that they operated on simpler lines than the other lot. Political complexity wasn't their thing. They wanted to terrorize Catholics. They terrorized Catholics by killing Catholics. It had always seemed to Chuckie that they were pretty good at that.

'Were you using the phone box?' Stoney asked, with circus-style slyness.

'Aye.'

'Didn't you used to have a phone?'

'Still do.'

'So why—?' Stoney broke off theatrically. They passed the Rangers Supporters' Club where the coats and gloves of famous Loyalist killers were encased in glass and hung on the walls.

'Fancy a pint?' asked Stoney.

'Not in there, I don't.'

Double-chinned double-Protestant Chuckie could barely have pronounced the word integrity but there was no place in his big gut for the hatred and fear they peddled there. He glanced unfavourably at his companion and promised himself again that one day he would insult this man so dreadfully they'd never have to talk again. But, for now, he merely turned on his heel and started retracing his steps towards his own street.

Stoney followed, not unaware of the sudden impediment in their good fellowship. To mend it, he assumed a comic tone. 'So why were you using the phone box, Chuckie?'

Chuckie stopped dead and turned to face him full.

'What's with the questions? While you're at it, why don't you ask me whether space is curved finitely or infinitely?' Stoney opened his mouth. 'I'm fucked if I know whether it is or not,' Chuckie added quickly.

Stoney was delighted with Chuckie's brusqueness. 'Were you

calling some girl?' His eyes glinted greedily.

Chuckie walked on. With Stoney, it was impossible to be irritated for long. 'Yes,' he said.

'Where's she from?'

'I don't know exactly.'

'Is she a Taig?'

'Fuck's sake, Stoney, she's American.'

Stoney clapped his hands with delight. 'American. Very good. I always wanted a Yank girl. They've got very clean teeth.'

Chuckie laughed.

'Have you shagged her yet?' asked Stoney.

Chuckie paused to decide whether or not to be angry. He decided not to be angry. 'Yes,' he lied.

'How was it?'

'Demonic.'

'You're a lucky fucker, Lurgan. There's your cousin's got himself a wee honey too and you're both fat bastards.'

'Where's the light of your life tonight?' Chuckie asked him. It was a good subject change. In his experience, married guys always talked gleefully about everybody else's love life. Chuckie thought he'd depress him by asking him about his own. Stoney had a dreary wife and a dreary two-year-old kid who shared her mother's button nose and amazed expression.

'She's round at her ma's. Didn't fancy the trip.'

'Yeah, yeah, and you're left to wander Sandy Row on the pull. Hard times, Stoney, hard, hard times.'

Chuckie gestured at the wet streets, empty of people other than themselves. He laughed harshly and walked on. Stoney's little legs had to skip to keep up. They passed the bookie's on the corner, the bookie's that swelled and burst every lunchtime and where Chuckie would see men like his father in a thousand different guises. The place was doing powerful trade because, nowadays, even Catholics were venturing within its doors. They were becoming too frightened to bet in their own betting shops. There'd been a couple of simple massacres in

Catholic betting shops over the past couple of years. Chuckie was sure that these new customers comforted themselves with the thought that money was money and that no one cared whether it was Protestant or Catholic money. Chuckie was also sure they were fooling themselves.

'What'd you say?' he asked Stoney, who'd been breathlessly mumbling something to him.

Stoney swallowed and puffed. 'I hear you're going into business.'

'Do you?'

'Aye. What kind of business exactly?'

Chuckie frowned. They were near Eureka Street now. Then he could be happily free of this fellow. 'I'd rather keep the details to myself for now.'

'Oh, until you hold your press conference, no doubt.' Stoney laughed carefully. He didn't like to overtease. He went on more gently, 'Good business is getting paid a hundred grand a year for watching television all day. That's good business.'

They reached the corner of Eureka Street. Chuckie turned down towards his house. Stoney stopped and said goodbye to his back. Chuckie waved once without turning. Stoney shrugged and moved on. He didn't care. Chuckie was just a fat shite with no da.

Chuckie walked blithely down Eureka Street. His mood was unaccountably tremendous; he was impervious to Stoney's mumblings about good business. No badinage would deflect him. He was going to be rich. If only he could find a way of getting some start-up capital. If only he could persuade somebody to give him something for nothing.

Something for nothing. In a sense, Stoney Wilson had been right. Good business was getting paid as much as possible for as little as possible. That was capitalism in essence. Something for nothing. He needed the impossible. John Long was right. He was a fantasist. Something for nothing. Where could he find a dick who would give him that?

In that rainy moment as he stepped over the cracked paving stone between No. 36 and No. 38, it struck him like some soundless klaxon. That last mental phrase burgeoned in his mind like some thermonuclear aftershock. He stopped stock still on Eureka Street and looked for stars he could not see. The clouds were low and the mist of rain was thick. Even where the land rose towards the West, nothing beyond the lit precincts of the city was visible – even the mountains had disappeared. Rain always made Belfast seem smaller, more itself. Rain always made Belfast look to Chuckie as though it was the last place left in the world.

But now the rain washed and cooled the fever of his ecstatic face. He was transfigured, amazed. Afterwards it would always seem to him that he had been touched by something godly, something almost famous. Afterwards, it seemed that the whole strange evening had been the simple etheric precedent for this moment: the eavesdropping on his mother, their first conversation for ten years, his life-list. It was the indication that, before the day was through, his world would change for ever.

For five minutes Chuckie stood thinkfully in the rain two doors down from his own. And in the shabby, damp, poorly lit theatre that was Eureka Street, the tangle of his thoughts untangled, smoothed themselves out like paper and Chuckie read there an idea so tremendous, so grand, that he felt like a bigger man already.

Four

The way my head banged, when I opened the curtains that Monday morning, I knew it had just been the weekend.

I remembered as I peed and made coffee, practically simultaneously. I'd spent the weekend in the Crown. I'd all but slept there. Slat, Chuckie, Donald Deasely and Septic Ted. I had been chugged naturally. Drunk was hardly the word. A few pints of Bass and I'd been telling eight-foot Protestants why I was a lapsed Catholic. Well, I don't really drink. So, when I really drink . . . it's grief.

Chuckie had been weird. He hadn't been there the whole time, which was weird enough in itself. Chuckie had never met a beer he didn't drink and his missing any of our carousing was unheard of. The sensation of being drunk without him was most uncustomary. He'd met some girl, he told us, some beautiful American. We laughed, naturally, but we were worried. There was a new light in Chuckie's face, a new angle to the way he carried that blunt head of his. I always hated it when my friends surprised me. That wasn't what they were for.

I thought about having a shower but pulled on my working clothes instead. I had forty minutes to get out of the house and coffee was more important than hygiene. I checked for mail (no mail) and let my cat in.

Another wasted weekend. Nothing said worth saying; nothing done worth doing. I wanted to do other things. I wanted to see Mary and find out how reluctant she could be. I should have made my weekend a fruitful thing including her. But no. I pissed it away down the Crown.

Even as I drank my coffee, I tried telling myself stories about it. I tried to remember and believe what fun it had all been. But it had been no fun. We had all hated it. Slat had practically wept with despair on the Sunday afternoon and even Septic Ted, not known for his delicacy or depth, had said that there had to be something else.

So why had we done it? None of us had drunk that much for years. We hadn't been so childish, so objectionable, so male for years. Why? I don't know about the others but it was simple for me.

It was because I knew Mary wouldn't call. It's because I didn't want to be there when the phone didn't ring.

My cat was screaming at me. He was getting noisier – maybe it was the way I'd had his balls cut off. He was trying out a series of new miaows and yowls on me. There were diphthongs, voice-throwing, operatic quavers. It was seven o'clock. Too early for this shit. I piled his dish high to shut him up but he could miaow while he ate these days. I switched on the radio to drown the noise.

'A part-time UDR soldier was killed last night in an explosion in the Beechmount area of West Belfast. Two other soldiers were injured. The incident happened just after ten o'clock. A coffee-jar bomb was thrown at the soldiers' Land-Rover. A security force spokesman said that . . .'

I switched off the radio. In Belfast the news was an accompaniment like music but I didn't want to hear this stuff. Coffee-jar bomb. Yeah, that was another big craze. I got the idea that people were impressed by this new thing, this wheeze, this caper. Me, I wasn't impressed. It was easy to do that ugly stuff.

Suddenly I longed to leave Belfast. Because of an inadvertently heard news story, the city felt like a necropolis. When the bad things happened, I always wanted to leave and let Belfast rot. That was what living in this place was all about. I got this feeling twice a week every week of the year. Like everyone here, I lived in Belfast from day to day. It was never firm. I always stayed but I never really wanted to.

Depressed, I grabbed my coat and left my flat. In Mullin's I bought several cigarettes and a pint of pasteurized. I lit a fag and drank the milk while I drove down the Lisburn Road and on to Bradbury Place, still grubby and paper-strewn after its usual festive night. It was early and the people were soft and pretty, most still rumpled and creased from their recent sleep. Men in suits walked with habitual confidence, unaware that their hair stuck up endearingly; trim women didn't notice that the labels on their dresses were showing and their lipstick was slightly crooked. Belfast was only half awake and its citizens were mild and lovable as children.

As I drove there under the pale sky, I weltered in sentiment. And it was briefly good to be doing what I was doing. Driving to my hard day's toil. In my big boots, my artisan's shirt and my rough trousers I felt dignified, I felt worthy, I felt like the nineteen thirties.

Then I remembered what I did for a living.

I was a repo man. I was a hard guy. I was a tough. I'd been doing it for nearly six months. I'd been doing it since Sarah had left. I'd just gone back to the way I'd mostly been. Before Sarah, I'd sometimes earned my living by fighting people, hitting people or just by looking like I might do any of those things. Bouncer, bodyguard, general frightener, all-purpose yob, I had had the full range. It wasn't that I was big. It wasn't that I was bad. It was just that I was so good at fighting.

In the years after I went to college, I used these skills and butched my way round London, punching heads for cash-in-fist. I went to America for a short stint, quickly discovering that they were all much too good at fighting, and then back to my imperfectly macho hometown. I seldom had to do any real harm. When sporadically called to punch a head or two, I punched a head or two. It seemed easy then. I was like an actress doing a nude scene. I told myself I didn't really mind.

Then one night, doing the door at a dockers' bar, I'd had to mash some old guy who'd been goosing the barmaids. He'd turned bolshie when I'd chucked him out and had kept coming at me. No matter how many times I hit him, no matter how hard, he was so roofed that none of it hurt. In the end I'd laid him out cold. As he lay there on the filthy pavement, his face red and ragged, his gut exposed, I'd felt like chucking my stomach.

And soon afterwards, Sarah had come and ironed me smooth, pressed the tough stuff right out of me. It was only then that I worked out why it was always so easy to hit people. It was because I had no imagination.

The human route to sympathy or empathy is a clumsy one but it's all we've got. To understand the consequences of our actions we must exercise our imaginations. We decide that it's a bad idea to hit someone over the head with a bottle because we put ourselves in their position and comprehend that if we were hit over the head with a bottle, then, my goodness, wouldn't that hurt! We swap shoes.

If you do this – if you *can* do this – then violence or harm becomes decreasingly possible for you. You hold a gun to someone's head, hammer cocked. If you can see what this would do to that head, then it is literally impossible to pull the trigger.

I had happily hurt people because I had no imagination.

Because of Sarah I didn't fight for two years. Then Sarah left. A fortnight later, a guy from Ottawa Street told me what a cunt I was outside the toilets in the Morning Star. I decked him. I picked his teeth out of my knuckles.

People talk about the red mist of the angry, of the sociopath.

Only people who've never fought say that. There's no mist. Things are distinctly uncloudy. Rather, there is a great philosophical clarity, an absolute reliability about the decision to throw the arm. Everything seems fine and sensible and punching someone's head away seems like the dignified, democratic thing to do. And the other secret about being good at fighting is to know that you're no good at fighting. That's for the movies. No one can ward off blows and dodge swipes like they do in the movies. Being good at fighting is simply knowing which bits hurt, which bits break and just having a swing at those. That's all.

I'd tried giving up. When Sarah had been with me, it had been hard to think I'd ever done it. But when Sarah had left I'd started again. It had been a natural progression, an inevitable decline. I'd known Marty Allen all those years before. We'd been involved in a variety of bellicose enterprises and he was glad to bring me in on his repo thing. He'd yuppied up since the last time I'd seen him. He even called his new trade Credit Adjustment but I knew I was back to punching heads and baring teeth.

Crab, Hally and I worked North Belfast. It was mostly poor up there so we had a lot of ground to cover. We were thrillingly ecumenical and we raided Protestant estates with all the *élan* and grace with which we raided Catholic ones. I could never see the difference. There were grim estates and their multiple greys. There were pale, flabby people and their crucial lack. There was the damp, moneyless smell. Both types of places were simply deep cores of poverty. They could paint their walls any colour they wanted, they could fly a hundred flags and they still wouldn't pay the rent and we would still come and take their stuff away from them.

It was Povertyland. It was the land where the bad things happened. Solvent abuse – six-year-olds snorting Evostik down an alley in Taughmonagh, keeling over and drowning in a two-foot puddle. Going out with a sniff and a gurgle. It was the land of Love on the Breadline. Kids here used clingfilm for condoms; they bought their £15.99 engagement rings (½ carat) from the Argos catalogue. They shacked up together for warmth, for forgetting. It was the land where they wrote things on the walls.

I was never surprised that they bought all this stuff they couldn't afford. That's what I'd have done. That's what I *had* done. The only times I'd ever truly shopped were when I had no money. Buying things is the only activity that makes you feel better about not being able to buy things.

And it was such sad stuff. Mail-order stuff, catalogue stuff, penny-a-word, poundstretchers' stuff. Sometimes, after a few runs, the back of the van would look like a 10p stall at a church fête. It amazed me that anyone could want this garbage back. But someone did. So back we took it.

Old, young and medium, the people all looked like I felt. Which was truly, impressively bad. They lived in countries of poverty, in climates of poverty. They ate it, slept it, breathed it in and out.

But they'd bought on, unsurprisingly. They were still allowed to purchase, to consume. They'd shored themselves up with comfort goods. They'd committed the crime of wanting what they could not have and they all came quietly. I had not hit anyone since I'd started working in repo again. I hadn't needed to. I would never need to. They were already beaten, these people. There was nothing more I could do to them.

The really surprising thing was that we never got any grief from either of the forces of national liberation. Both sets, aboriginal and colonist, had been paid off by Marty Allen. They left us alone mostly. The cops, too, just about tolerated us. But it was tricky. IRA, INLA, IPLO, UVF, UFF and the Royal Ulster Constabulary. A whole horde of dumb fucks with automatic weapons and the three of us wandering in and out taking people's televisions away. Luckily, Crab and Hally were too stupid to give it much thought, but me, I had a lot of executive stress.

*

After the first couple of hours of that morning, I should have realized it was all going wrong. We were working the little streets off the Shore Road. Albino Protestant land. Some furniture in Peace Street, a microwave and multigym from Parliament Street and a stereo, video and camcorder in Iris Drive. We'd made ten people unhappy and frightened. The Iris Drive address was a couple with six children. The kids had cried – that wasn't untypical, we were used to that – but one of them, a girl of about six, had become hysterical. She screamed and wailed. I was amazed that she could be so terrified. Was she incredibly fond of luxury electrical goods or were we just frightening men? Whatever, we really scared the piss out of her and I felt bad. I felt worse that we got no abuse. Neither father nor mother, brothers nor sisters said any bad words to us as we tramped in and out of there.

But just as I went to close the door behind me, the mother had stared at me. Just once, and not for long, but I had never seen such contempt, such fear. I wondered what I looked like that she could look at me like that. It didn't take me long.

Afterwards we drove back up to Rathcoole. We were a little irritated as we'd been there only last week, but Allen had said it was a big deal, a special pick-up and that we had to do it today. Hally looked through his list (with his literacy skills no mean or brief feat).

'It's a bed,' he said.

'What?' Crab was driving, his mood suitably foul.

'A bed.'

'We're going back up there for a fucking bed.'

'Aye. I think it's some kind of big fuck-off bed. We're taking it off somebody called Johnson. Marty says it's worth a lot of money.'

Crab grunted some Neanderthal grunt and turned into the estate. On one of the walls, he spotted some graffiti. 'Have you seen that, Hally?'

'What?'

Crab pulled to a halt. He pointed at the smeared, scribbled pebbledash wall. 'That.'

Hally leaned across him and looked out. 'What, "Tina sucks my cock"?'

'No, no. The big letters.'

'OTG,' said Hally.

'Aye.'

'What about it?' Hally asked, mystified.

'Have you seen that before?'

'Nah.'

'What about you, Jakie?'

I ignored him. I wasn't in the mood.

'What does it mean?' said Hally.

'How the fuck do I know?' snapped Crab. 'I've seen it around a couple of times. Some of the lads are getting fucked off about it. They wanna know who the fuck these OTG cunts are.'

Hally pondered. 'What, you think they're like a movement, an organization?'

'Yeah, probably.'

'And nobody knows who they are.'

'No.'

'Have they done anything yet?'

'Like what?'

'I mean have they claimed responsibility for anything yet?'

'Nah, don't think so.'

'So, how do you know it's an organization, then?'

'What else would it be?'

'Could mean anything.'

'Like what?'

'I don't know – anything. Old Thick Git, Open The Gate, Omelettes Taste Good. I don't know. Fuck.'

'Then don't fucking blather about things you don't know, you thick fuck.' Crab pouted. Oops, I thought, and blinked.

I missed the blow. I just heard the wet slap and the sound of

Crab's head bouncing back off his headrest. When I opened my eyes Crab's nose was bleeding and Hally was looking aggrieved.

'Don't call me stupid,' said Hally, mildly.

It took us twenty minutes to find the house. A bad twenty minutes. Things were tense enough without navigational difficulties. That was the thing about yob friendships. They were so very blunt. Mild controversies were conducted bone on bone. None of these people ever agreed to disagree. They were both psychopaths but Hally would be able to kill Crab every time. This consciousness weighed on Crab's mind. His neck grew red with hatred and suppressed rage. By the time we lumbered out of the van, the air between us was thick and hot with violence and anger.

But we got on with it. We did our usual thing. We knocked on the usual kind of door. The usual kind of fifty-year-old fat guy answered. We had our usual conversation with him. He made the customary mild objections and made the characteristic attempt to close the door. Hally put his typical boot in the way and pushed his way through in the traditional manner. The man had the expected change of heart and decided, as always, to co-operate.

It was routine. It was standard.

Inside, the blinds of the front room were still closed. The man, Mr Johnson, stood in shorts and vest. Crab stood close to him, invading his airspace. On the wall, a plain devotional hung, an unCatholic tract. God is Love, it said. Yeah, I thought, we'll see.

Crab asked the man where the bed was. Hally asked him where the fuck he thought it would be. Crab's face convulsed with fury. An itch started at the base of my skull.

'Listen, fellas,' said the man, his voice pressed flat with false bonhomie, 'my wife's really sick. She's had a stroke. The bed's for her. It's a special bed, like a medical one. It cost me fifteen hundred quid. I've only a few payments to make. Can't we make some kind of deal? She's really sick.'

'It's not our job, mate. We have to take it away.'

'All right, listen. She's up there now, my wife. It's hard to move her. If you lads come back in an hour I'll have her moved and then you can take it.'

Crab bridled. He leaned into the man's face. 'Fuck away off. Do you think we have all day to waste on your fucking problems?' He turned on his heel and ran up the staircase. He looked really crazy. We all piled after him.

When we got there we found him standing in a bare but neat little bedroom. He was staring at the tiny woman lying wrapped on the massive metal bed. Mrs Johnson was awake (probably) and her eyes stared out at us through the rictus of her distorted features. The itch in my skull heated and spread.

There was a pause then. A silence. A moment of shame, of something. A moment that showed us all what we'd come to: the sad couple, Crab, Hally and me. We all had a little time to see where we were and what we were doing.

And, who knows, anything might have happened. The three of us might have thought better of it. We might have left those people alone. We might have gone back to Allen with some bullshit or even cut a deal with the ugly fat guy who looked at his wife with such tender eyes.

But Hally had hit Crab and Crab was still angry and he badly needed some trouble. Silently, suddenly galvanized, he strode over to the bed and grasped the mattress with both hands. With one shudder of his huge shoulders he yanked the mattress high and the sick woman rolled off the bed and hit the floor and the wall with a weak thud. I nearly puked with shame.

But then things happened quick. The husband went nuts and jumped for Crab. I knew Hally would kill him so I weighed in there and tried to drag him away. The guy's face was distorted with rage and pain for his wife and he was swiping wildly. It was bedlam. He was screaming, the wife was bellowing in some horrible paralysed way and I was shouting at the guy to calm down. I was really scared. Not by the fight but by all the shame, all the horror. He caught me one on the right temple and I was surprised and impressed by the unexpected quality of that blow. I jerked my head away and became calm.

Doctors and nurses always say that when some horrible accident happens and the mangled victims start coming in, they can always cope with the horror and madness. They say that their professionalism takes over and they can get on with it. That's what happened to me. My professionalism took over. I grabbed a fistful of the guy's gut and squeezed as hard as I had ever squeezed anything. All the fight went out of him.

It was a great ploy, this belly-pinching routine. I'd learnt it in America when some big bouncer had done it to me. The pain was unbelievable and all you could do was whimper and wait for it to be over. It was as much about humiliation as pain. I always thought I was its only European practitioner. I was proud of it. It was a real winning move.

Crab and Hally were manhandling the bed onto the stairs. The thing was huge and even apes like them were struggling. I couldn't figure out whether I should give them a hand or keep my mitt on the husband's guts. He was crying by now. Looking over at his wife, I decided that he was all finished and I let go of him. I joined the others.

It took us twenty minutes. Hally got so fucked off that he kicked the wooden banisters away. That made our job easier but it was still a drag. I was very glad, though. I was happy that it was hard. It gave me something to think about.

After we'd shunted it into the van, Crab turned back towards the house. He looked ill. He looked like he had a bad heart. Like it worked but it was wicked. There were still some bits of the contraption up in that bedroom and he told us he was going to get them.

'No. I'll get them,' I shouted, and raced past him.

Back in the bedroom it was all very unpleasant. I hadn't wanted to go back but it was better me than Crab. The old guy was sitting huddled in the corner, his broken wife lying across his lap, his arms tight, tight around her shoulders. He was murmuring to her, apologizing, soothing.

I picked up the bed rails and turned to the man. He looked at me but just continued to rock the woman in his arms, murmuring. Her eyes stared out at me as well, her face twisted and unbearable. Ludicrously, I felt a pricking at the back of my eyes. 'Look,' I said, 'I'm sorry.'

They didn't reply. She couldn't and he wouldn't. Perhaps that was what made Crab come into the room from where he'd been standing, walk across the kneeling man and slap him backhanded across the face. Perhaps it had been some spurious gesture of comradeship with me, offence taken on my behalf. I don't know. It's also hard to say for how many seconds I fought the impulse. For I did fight it. I didn't want to do what I then did, I passionately didn't want to do it. But I skipped over and gave it to him across the back of the head with the metal rails and laid him out beside them.

It was mayhem after that. Hally came in and there was the usual back and forward. He and I shouted it out, hands carefully pressed to our hips. We didn't want any more fighting. Hally terrified me but I knew he'd never been sure of me. He could never figure out how tasty I was. Crab was conscious but he didn't look good. His hair was matted with blood and it looked like he would throw up at any moment. In all the bickering, the Johnsons, whose house we were in, remained absolutely impassive.

In the end Hally took Crab down to the van and said that he would drive him to Casualty at the Mater. When they'd gone I just left the room and closed the door behind me. I didn't think I'd try to apologize again. But, before I'd escaped, the crippled woman started grunting her strange noises at me. The same meaningless phrase over and over again. It was speech but it took me a few moments to understand what she was saying.

'You,' she was saying. 'You.'

She was right. It was definitely me.

I walked back to Allen's. It took me an hour and a half. It wasn't a sure thing that Allen would fire me for what I'd done to Crab but I knew it was over anyway. I'd seen enough. I could wait table. I could carry bricks. I could give blowjobs down the docks. I just couldn't do this stuff any more.

Back at the garage, I tripped into Allen's office. Once again, he was on the telephone when I walked in. It sounded like some telephone sex line this time. I pressed the cradle down and cut him off. He didn't smile.

'What the fuck did you do that for, you wanker?'

'I quit.'

'Yeah? Well, good fucking riddance.'

'I've got two hundred coming.'

'Heard you whacked Crab.'

'He called a press conference?'

'A big mistake. He'll fucking kill you for that. Then he'll eat you.'

'My two hundred?'

'Your one hundred, you mean.'

He took out his wallet and counted out a hundred in twenties. It was more than I'd expected and that was fair enough. He'd sold me my dodgy stolen wreck of a car for two hundred. He didn't owe me much. He smiled some unpleasant smile he must have seen in the movies.

'Is it Crab or have you just lost your balls for it?' he enquired.

I had no explanation for him and I couldn't think of any tough-guy quip so I left. Downstairs, Hally was unloading the van, swapping tit jokes with a group of Allen's pre-pubescent mechanics. He didn't seem inconsolable about Crab's predicament and he was unconcerned about my presence. I headed for my car.

Hally followed and stood between me and the door.

'How's Crab?' I asked him.

He laughed. 'How the fuck should I know? I took him to the hospital but I didn't fucking wait. I'm not his fucking ma.'

I moved to put my key in the car door. He didn't get out of my way. I stood up straight.

'You quit?' He was squaring up for something. I knew he didn't like me but I knew he wouldn't hit me. That would be so upsetting that it just couldn't happen.

'Yeah, I quit.'

He nodded some internal assent like it was something he had predicted for years. 'Do you mind if I ask you something?'

'What?'

'Are you a Catholic?'

I laughed a big sad laugh. 'What do you think?' I asked.

'Well,' he said ruminatively, 'I always figured you were a poof but I couldn't work out whether you were a Fenian as well.'

'Get a life,' I said, as I got into my car. 'Nah, get two.'

Hally was too pleased with his insult to bother hitting me and he let me drive away unmolested. As I pulled onto the main road, it occurred to me that I'd never buy enough petrol to get far enough away.

So now I was unemployed. It had been a good move. I suppose I should have felt cleaner after that primary integrity but those gestures cleanse only in films. If I felt cleaner at all, it was a micro-feeling. It was a small, small thing. I didn't want to take anything away from anybody again. I knew how they felt. England had repossessed Sarah from me and I was still sitting there fat and sad with that loss.

When I remembered the Sarah stuff, it was like reading a book someone else recommended. You wanted it to have been so much better than it was.

She was a broadsheet journalist from London. I'd just got a shitload of compensation for a beating I'd had a couple of years before from soldiers outside a bar down Cornmarket. I'd only been in hospital for a while but the soldier angle had helped and the Northern Ireland Office was glad to give me forty grand to shut me up. I bought the place on Poetry Street. It was an old Church building, half wrecked and split into three. I got it for almost nothing so I bought it outright. Sarah moved in and made the old place breathe. We lived it out amongst the trees and it was good. For two years of side-by-side, we were happy.

Two years. We practically rebuilt the flat. Sarah made it beautiful. I put stubby pencils behind my ear and nails in my mouth and felt like a real man. I tried to like her friends. She tried to resist the impulse to have mine arrested. It was a pantomime of happiness, a parody of bliss. I loved her like I didn't know was possible. I loved her more than I thought was legal. The sight of her handwriting made my eyes fill with reasonless tears. When I heard sirens I convinced myself that they were ambulances going to the site where her shattered body lay. Sometimes at night, when she slept and I couldn't, I lay with my arms around her, just loving her. I felt that if I had a zipper running down the front of me from throat to belly I would unzip myself and cram her inside and zip her up in there. I could never hold her close enough.

Sometimes I worried about her work. She hated her job. Her paper would only run Ulster stories if the details were particularly appalling, if the killings were entirely barbaric. London editors were not interested in everyday Ulster. Sarah had to go to grimmer places and speak to grimmer people every time.

So, sooner than it should have, it started to go wrong. The reports she had to write, the things she had to see couldn't have helped Sarah fall in love with my city. She started talking about going back to London. I started ignoring her. Then she did three days' reporting on an Armagh pub massacre in which six people died. She quit her Ulster job and bought a plane ticket.

The night before she left was long. She pleaded with me to go with her. I refused. Her pain was inordinate. It was not a situation without remedy. London was an hour away. I could always change my mind. She could change hers. It was bad that she was going but it appeared to me that there'd always be the possibility of rewrites.

But within a fortnight, she'd told me the thing that I couldn't bring myself to believe, to understand. She'd had an abortion in her first week back in London. I hadn't known she was pregnant.

And then it was six months of nothing. Six months of something less than misery. She had crushed my heart flat. I didn't know how much I would have wanted to be a father but I didn't know how much I didn't either. It was always a surprise how much that hurt. How could she make the mistake of not loving me as I loved her?

Since she'd left, my love had been measured by the object it lacked. Since then, I'd been sitting alone late at night, smoking, wondering what it was like to be her.

After my big resignation, I got back to Poetry Street to find Chuckie Lurgan sitting in a chubby heap on my doorstep waiting for me to come home. My cat was sleeping on his knee. For some reason, my cat seemed to like Chuckie. I needed a new cat.

I let them in and fed them both.

He had called work and Allen had told him I'd been sacked.

'Jesus, you're not popular there any more,' Chuckie said.

While we were eating, he grew more and more excitable. He talked rapid nonsense and blushed often. He had a grubby tabloid in his hand. I made coffee while I waited for him to get to the point.

I asked him about his big-deal American girl. He was uncharacteristically reticent. Slat had told me that she was pretty nice and that, for some reason, she seemed keen on old Chuck, but Lurgan was giving me no change from all my blunt enquiry. He told me he was seeing her that night but then he changed the subject.

'Have you seen this OTG thing?' he asked me vaguely, as I headed for the kitchen.

'Yeah. Do you know what it means?'

'Nah, it's a new one on me,' he called from the other room.

'Is it an organization or a slogan?'

'Fucked if I know.'

'I've asked around,' I said. 'Nobody has a clue.'

'What do you think?' asked Chuckie.

'Jesus, I don't know. Odyssey To Glengormley. Orangemen Try Genocide. Oxford's Too Green.'

I could hear Chuckie's chubby chuckle. 'Ominously Taut Gonads,' he suggested enthusiastically. 'Optimum Testicle Growth. Osculate This, Girls!'

I let him have his laugh out while I got on with making the coffee.

'I saw Bun Doran limping up the road on the way over,' he called out to me.

'Uh-huh,' I grunted noncommittally, while I fiddled with the coffee beans. I wondered when exactly Chuckie was going to tell me what was on his mind.

'Yeah, apparently he's also bought a big house with the money he got from his settlement.'

There was the muffled crump of a distant explosion.

'Sounded like Andytown,' surmised Chuckie from the living room.

'Nah,' I shouted back. 'City centre.'

'Sounded big.'

'Didn't sound small,' I concurred.

I came back into the room with the coffee pot. Chuckie was toying with the newspaper on his lap.

'How much did he get?' I asked.

'Who?'

'Doran.'

'Oh, yeah. He got a hundred and twenty grand, the bastard.'

'He's got legs like an Action Man now. It's hardly excessive.'

Barry 'Bun' Doran was a guy we knew. A weirdo from Bosnia Street with whom Chuckie had been to school. Doran only worked as an office clerk but he had a big bee in his bonnet about personal freedom. He didn't like authority. A couple of years before he had decided that, most of all, he hated traffic lights. He felt that they interfered with his personal autonomy, his right to walk where and when he wanted. He started a campaign of ignoring the commands of traffic lights. He was run over by a bus on the Dublin Road. His legs were so badly broken that even when fixed up they were stiff as boards.

Chuckie was unrepentant. 'A hundred and twenty grand, though. You two had the right idea. I'd break my own legs for that.'

I poured myself some coffee. Chuckie didn't really drink coffee so I opened a can of sucrose, comminuted oranges, sodium benzoate, sodium metabisulphite drink for him. His fat face split in a smile and his eyes disappeared in his cheeks.

'Did you see the papers on Sunday?' he asked, with a poor assumption of nonchalance.

'There are lots of Sunday papers, Chuckie.'

'The local ones.'

I lit the hundredth cigarette I'd smoked since I gave up giving up. 'No, I didn't see the local ones.'

Chuckie pulled a facial expression I'd never seen him do before. Chuckie pulled a facial expression I'd never seen anyone do before. His mouth turned down, his lips turned out and his nose turned up. It was amazingly unattractive.

'Take a look at this.' He opened the paper he was holding and pushed it over to me uncertainly. I picked it up. It was the small-ads page of the only mucky paper that Northern Ireland produced, a paper with sexsational stories about mythical locals and pictures of Derry girls with large pale naked breasts.

I started reading through the ads page:

IRELAND'S NEW X-RATED CHATLINE

Now available to 18–21-year-olds
never before allowed to telephone these numbers.

OMAGH COUPLE DOES IT	*0898 300 ---*
LISBURN SWAPPERS	*0898 300 ---*
BELFAST LADY TEACHER	*0898 300 ---*
BALLYMENA VIBRO MISTRESS	*0898 300 ---*
FERMANAGH FETISH	*0898 300 ---*
BELFAST WETNESS	*0898 300 ---*
LIMAVADY LOVE PUMP	*0898 300 ---*
DERRIAGHY WIFE	*0898 300 ---*

I looked at Chuckie.

'Underneath,' he said, in a small voice. I read on.

GIANT DILDO OFFER!!!

BIGGEST DILDO EVER!

BUY NOW! THE MASSIF (16")
NOW AVAILABLE AT A SENSATIONAL £9.99.
THIS LOVE TOOL WILL THRILL EVERY WOMAN.
SEND CHEQUES OR POSTAL ORDERS NOW!
OFFER ONLY WHILE LIMITED STOCKS LAST.

SATISFACTION GUARANTEED.
***FULL REFUND** IF OTHERWISE!*

There was an address underneath. A box number. I looked quizzically at my plump chum. This wasn't all that funny. This wasn't all that surprising. It was hardly worth a trip across town to tell me about. But there was something in Chuckie's little eyes that made me tremble.

'Hey, Chuckie, this has nothing to do with you, has it?'

He looked at me plaintively. He spread his fat hands wide in a placating gesture.

'Chuckie!'

'I told you I needed start-up capital. I couldn't get any fucking grants if I didn't already have some capital. Apart from doing a Doran and getting myself run over, there was nothing else for it.'

'But Jesus, Chuckie, selling sex aids? You can't do that. This is Northern Ireland.'

He looked offended. 'I don't intend to sell any sex aids.'

'What?'

He reached into his little canvas bag. He pulled out a long paper package and unwrapped a massive fake rubber penis. Veined, knobbly and bizarrely pink, it looked faintly like Chuckie himself. Chuckie set the thing on the table between us. My cat growled in fright. I was speechless.

'That's the only one I've got,' Chuckie said.

'You what?'

'I've only got one dildo. I gave Speckie Reynolds fifteen quid for it down the market.'

'I don't understand.'

'Watch,' whispered Chuckie.

He pulled a little rectangular tin out of his bag. He opened it and pulled out a rubber stamp, which he dipped in the ink sponge. He stamped an envelope that lay on the table. I picked it up and read the legend:

GIANT DILDO REFUND

Chuckie smiled the smile of the just-published poet.

'It's simple,' he said. 'I've had seventeen hundred and forty replies already. That's seventeen hundred and forty cheques for nine ninety-nine. That's seventeen thousand, three hundred and eighty-two pounds. I opened a bank account this morning. I'll have ten chequebooks by next Wednesday.'

'But you can't keep the money.'

'Don't worry. I'm going to write refund cheques for all of them. Nine ninety-nine a pop – the full whack. And before I send them I'll take my little stamp here and I'll stamp GIANT DILDO REFUND on the cheques.'

He paused. He bent down to stroke my cat, whose fur was still rising in fright at the thing on the table.

'Can you honestly imagine anyone toddling down to their bank to lodge a cheque that has GIANT DILDO REFUND stamped all over it?' He smiled beatifically.

'Isn't capitalism wonderful?'

That night, I went to see Mary. I still didn't know where she lived so I landed up at the bar where she worked. As I went in, the Protestant bouncer showed me, with a turn of his puffy shoulders, that he was sick of the sight of me. My eye had already turned dark where the man with the bed had hit me earlier. I must have looked insalubrious. I guessed the bouncer might show some form if I pissed him off too much so I gave him a special smile.

Mary's face went sick when she saw me. I saw a mumbled word between her and a colleague and the colleague approached me and asked me what I wanted to drink. I lied and she brought me some beer.

I sat there for two hours, beer upon beer. I hated bars but it was a difficult city in which to lead a life without them. In the end, some shame in me made me just walk up to her and ask her to talk to me.

'Give me a minute,' she said wearily.

She whispered some more with her friend and then grabbed her coat and stood by my table. Her face was grim. She didn't look like she meant to go anywhere nice with me.

'Not here,' she said.

She took me to a swish hamburger joint nearby. We sat and drank cheap coffee.

'What happened to your eye?'

'I was moving some furniture.'

'What?'

'I hit my head against something.'

'I don't believe you.'

'You don't have to.'

There was a pause. Not a comfortable one. She looked at me. Her eyes shone and I knew there was bad news and bad news. She gave me the bad news first.

'I want you to leave me alone,' she said.

It wasn't easy to take this talk from her but I guessed that she had made a lot of things not happen. She wasn't treasuring any memories and I was making myself one big drag. But there was that love we'd made which she could not delete. It was less than a week and my mouth still tasted of her mouth. I felt like I could breathe her breath.

'Mary, I can't leave you alone. I don't want to leave you alone. That makes it complicated.'

Her face went slack and her mouth trembled in a way that made it so very difficult not to just kiss her right there.

'What do you want from me?'

And what did I want from her? I wanted her hand on my face, her head bent for me, her lips on mine. I wanted her to say soft words that would make my heart lurch and my face burn.

I gave her that. Exactly. Word for word. That wasn't bad going and I imagined there'd be some big reward for all that unblank prose.

'You don't understand.' Her voice was gentler, more permissive after all my fancy talk.

'What don't I understand?'

'It's impossible.'

I had a series of great speeches in stock all about possibility and impossibility. And it was hard not to feel optimistic sitting there amongst the bright plastic and the teenage bon vivants with all the primary colours making shapes in Mary's eyes.

'Impossibility never stopped anything actually happening.'

'But I love Paul. I don't want to hurt him.'

Paul was the cop boyfriend. I couldn't muster much feeling

for his civilian predicament.

'It's just impossible,' she continued.

I was energized, ardent. 'You're right. It isn't possible. Or likely. Or even democratic. Nobody gave you the right to make me feel like this.'

'And what about Sarah?'

I was briefly surprised by her high-grade memory. 'Sarah? That's old love, that's dead love. That's love that never was. I do her no disservice. I doubt that she remembers me at all.'

The sick look returned to her face. The one she had worn when she saw me first that night. Her mouth pursed under some assumption of sisterhood. 'Two years' time, you'd say the same of me.'

'Would I?'

'Yes.'

'Would you like some long odds on that?'

She smiled, pleased and flattered despite her firm intentions. I'd never had a problem with vanity.

'I'm going to marry him,' she said.

'That's what you think.'

'What would you know about it?'

I was confident. I was sure. That was always a bad sign.

'Do you often sleep with someone when you intend to marry someone else?'

My mouth was still moving with those last couple of words when I knew how badly I'd blown it. Her cheeks flushed and she sat straighter. She pulled her coat tighter around her and pushed her coffee cup away from her. She looked like she was going to go.

And then for the first time I experienced lust-free lust. I wanted someone's flesh pressed to mine in a way that was almost completely without desire. But she walked out. She just stood up, shook her head, mumbled something I couldn't hear and walked away. My head fell upon the table. It made a hollow noise.

I left soon after. Though it was not late, the streets hummed with discontent and wintry malice. There were lots of cops around. I even thought I could see Mary talking to one of them but I couldn't be sure. I hoped that if it was her then it wasn't her boyfriend she was talking to.

It was near chuck-out time for the bars and there'd been a couple of big bomb scares in the city centre. The siren sounds wafted in the wind and down Arthur Street I could see some desultory scurrying and white tape stretching. The cops were always jumpier if there was a series of bomb hoaxes. I think they preferred real bombs to endless hoaxes. It was like Russian roulette and I don't think they liked waiting for the one that would be real. It had been a pretty busy day for the boys with bombs. One at lunchtime in a multi-storey car park. A mortar had been fired at some soldiers and there had been the one Chuckie and I had heard earlier. And then all the hoaxes.

But as I looked at the people on the streets, I couldn't help thinking that it was still no big deal. It used to be different. We all used to be much more scared. After the biggest blasts in the seventies (recently revived for a second successful season), the colour of the streets always seemed drained and muted as if the colours, too, had been blown away.

But now it was all just an inconvenience, all just a traffic jam.

I found the Wreck in a side-street. A couple of cops and soldiers were loitering there. I got in and tried, ineffectually, to start it up. Just as it was beginning to chug into some semblance of life, a soldier sauntered over, his rifle slung across his pelvis in a carefree fashion.

I wound down my window and put on my I-don't-mind-being-questioned-by-the-security-forces-I-know-you-have-to-do-it face. It was a pretty complicated expression.

The young soldier leaned down to my open window. His face was adolescent and his accent was Lancashire prole. 'This your car?' The inevitable start to the litany of enquiry.

'Yes.'

'This your only car?'

'Yes.' My voice was untesty. It might have been a tense day for these guys with all the ordnance going round town. I reached for the glove compartment to get some papers to prove that the Wreck was indeed mine.

The soldier snorted briefly. 'No, no, that's all right, mate. It's just we thought you were driving it for a bet.'

I didn't need to laugh since he laughed so hard he laughed for both of us. I could hear his colleagues pissing themselves across the street. The soldier bent double and squeezed some feeble words of apology between the whinnies of his laughter. The Wreck, showing rare form, started amidst all the mockery and I drove off.

A couple of hours later, I was at home, making chase with my cat. He'd peed in the bath again and the sight of that little yellow pool around my plughole had sent me spare. It was so yellow. Somehow, you didn't expect it to be yellow. Like it was almost human. Unlike the cat itself. I'd chased him down the stairs, under the chairs, over the tables and so on. He was fucking quick, my cat.

I suppose that being pissed at my cat just because I was already blue wasn't fair. Mary, Sarah, my job: none of it was his fault. But he was unlucky enough to come near the end of a story he wasn't really part of. So, I ran after him with murder in my heart.

I'd got home depressed. Mary had left me making no mistake. When I got back there were a couple of messages. I had nearly wept at all this human contact, even though one had been from Marty Allen, telling me what an asshole I was – as if I didn't know already. Chuckie had called too. He sounded jugged again. Apparently, he'd just had a big date with his American girl. She'd agreed to go out with him again. But apparently she wanted a double date with her flatmate. That was where I came in. Chuckie had happily volunteered me to field the friend. Next Thursday, the message said.

I would think about that later. But for now the important thing was to catch my cat and kill him. I'd nearly cornered him between a bookshelf and a sofa when my doorbell rang loudly. I froze. I thought the Pet Protection League were on my case. I looked at the big clock on my wall. It was after midnight. Belfast isn't the best town for those after-midnight social calls and, as I walked to my front door, I had the familiar fifteen-second feeling that there were two men in bomber jackets and balaclavas with Browning automatics standing at my door with some sincere political objectives. I shucked through it, as I always did, and opened up.

A policeman stood there, his hand raised to the bellpush. I sighed with a mixture of guilt and relief. I spent most of my life thinking that I should be arrested so cops made me uneasy. I wondered if I was going to get grief for hitting Crab. A complaint to the cops wasn't his style, but Marty Allen might have done it just for fun.

'Yes?' I asked.

The cop narrowed his eyes and asked me in a shaky voice, which surprised me, whether my name was my name. What now? I thought, as I answered that, yes, my name was indeed my name.

The bang on my chops seemed to happen all by itself. I'd seen no arm, no hand. The blow knocked me back against my open door and he followed up with the other glove across my mouth.

Imagine my surprise!

He'd come in on me now and swung me round onto the staircase and I felt the stairs bang into my spine. After he'd cracked me in the balls and headbutted me a couple of times, I began to understand I was in a fight there. I was upset, naturally, and it was beginning to hurt as well. I was wondering what to do when he started giving me some elbow to the side of the head.

In my experience, sudden fights had always been like this. When somebody really surprised you, it was really surprising. In the movies, tough guys always handled surprise fights with lightning reflexes, immediate escalation. Us real-life tough guys needed time to get used to the idea, we needed written invitations, consultations, legal advice.

I was getting messed up rapidly by the time I'd summoned the verve to consider a response but by that time the cop himself was puffed out. He stepped back to catch a breath. Then I realized that something was missing. Where were his colleagues? How come the others were missing all this fun?

I sat on the stairs and waited for the next instalment. His hat had come off and I got a good look at him. He was probably about my age, but that clean-shaven, short-haired cop look made him seem like a kid. He looked at me, too, and all his steam was blown. I guessed it was over and raised my hand in a vaguely pacific gesture just to make sure.

'Jesus, take it easy there,' I said placidly.

I think the guy was amazed by my moderate tone. He looked like he didn't know what to do next. He bent to pick up his hat and glanced up the hall. He frowned at something. I turned to see my wide-eyed cat peeking round a doorway. I nearly laughed.

The policeman turned to me again. I was calming down. I wasn't too badly hammered. Despite the neat elbow work, the guy wasn't much good at fighting. I'd worked out that this was private business, that there was nothing official about this brand of violence. I was also beginning to guess who he was. As he stood there, unsure what to do, I felt like giving him some help.

'You stay away from Mary. Hear me?' He tried to hiss the words. The threat was pallid under the circumstances.

'I hear you.' I figured this was the best way of getting rid of him. I don't think she'd told him everything he needed to know. His anger was too shambling to be cuckolded anger. He was being too reasonable about this. He'd seen us earlier and

Mary had obviously told him I was hassling her and no more.

'You'd better,' he said. He looked at my cat again. His confusion intensified. Maybe he thought there should be something more. But he decided there wasn't so he turned and walked out.

I closed the door behind him, close to laughter again. I did a systems check at the bathroom mirror. There wasn't much damage beyond blood and puffiness. My nose and mouth felt hot with the unmistakable heat of fightmarks but all the teeth were intact and my jaw did all the things it should do. He was a weed, this cop, this Paul.

But it still hurt. Fighting had certainly become much harder since I'd given up fighting. But it could have been much worse. He could have brought his copper chums with him. The whole squad could have helped him out there. They could have banged me about down the station. Jesus, the way things went in this country he could have had me serving seventeen years for knowing the first three lines of the Hail Mary. It was nice that it was all just fair in love for a change. I found myself admiring his self-control.

My cat padded to the open doorway of the bathroom. Unusually silent, he looked up at me. I looked down at him. Maybe it all looked like justice to him because, if I hadn't known it to be impossible, I'd have sworn that the furry little shit cocked an eyebrow at me.

Five

The Thursday evening of the next week. It had been the first sunshiny day of the year. Clocks forward, sky wide, the mood good, I drove home from work. I'd found a new job already – I was humping bricks on a hotel refit down the town. The day was late and the sun was low and orange with age; the city looked so light that you could have blown it away. The multiple windows of Belfast's dwarf skyscrapers turned red in pairs like there was a fire inside. Between the trees dogs reddened in the sudden blush of sun.

It was the night on which Chuckie had arranged our double date. My heart much misgave me. I showered. I changed out of my work gear and into my blue suit. Double-cuff white shirt, old gold ladies' cufflinks and black oxfords that shone like a wet street. So, I was a fop. All the really working-class guys I knew were fops. Whenever I'd worked in shitty jobs (wasn't that always?), I'd generally made a point of dressing well after my day's work. It was a kind of nineteen-fifties Northern England fiction thing. It made me feel better.

It didn't quite make me look better. My face was pretty unrepaired after the previous week and all its fun. Bruises, shiner and a swelling on my right jaw that gave me something of the air of a damaged hamster. I didn't mind. I wasn't the vain type.

In my nearby supermarket I bought all the mushrooms I could buy and cooked them in a single pot. With my mushrooms and a baguette, I filled my face while the cat ate his usual double tin. I was conscious of the unpleasantness of having to play the beard on Chuckie's double date but even that prospect didn't dent my mood. I'd noticed that the big OTG across the road had been joined by a smaller, less typographic one. The mystery increased. I ignored it. I read some Erasmus and then I took my cat for a walk while the sun went down.

I stopped at the top of my long, long street. My cat circled my legs as I stood there. The trees were budding – there weren't any blossoms exactly but there was an attempt. I was lonely still but I was happy to be around. My mood had improved. I was glad to be me. It had been a while. Sarah had soon tired of me being me and Mary had taken only a very temporary dose. I'd paid heed to those votes of no confidence.

I looked down at my cat. He looked up at me. Startlingly, my cat was a comfort. My cat hadn't left me. I couldn't really say he liked me but he stayed around, he hung on.

Walking home, cat and cigarette, I prosed on to myself for a while about how good I felt and why. But it was simple. In the supermarket where I'd bought my mushrooms, there was a seventeen-year-old girl who was cracked on me. She was dying for me. I'd noticed her a few days before. She had gone all clumsy when she served me, her blush was minute-long and her smile painful. I knew she liked my bachelor thing, my suits, my cufflinks and my vegetables. Despite the bruises, my life obviously looked liveable to her. I felt old enough to be her daddy's daddy but she didn't care.

That was me all over. A schoolgirl with a crush on me and suddenly life felt worth living. That was the big secret about me. I was so shallow.

It was one of those things I liked about myself.

Well, that wasn't entirely true. I had other reasons for feeling good. It had taken me more than a week but I had finally managed it. I'd had to sell my stereo, my television and my video. I'd had about eight hundred set by and I cadged a couple of hundred from Chuckie. A few other sales, a bit more cadging and I had enough money. It took me a day to find a company that sold them. It took me a morning out there, going through their catalogues, trying to recognize the right one. It took me an hour to persuade the fuckers to knock a couple of hundred off the price and another hour to make them deliver it within the week but in the end it all came right.

I'd called the company before I went mushroom-buying. They had delivered it that morning. When I asked how the Johnsons had reacted when they got their new bed, the guy on the phone said that they'd been confused. They couldn't work out who'd sent it. The delivery guys had told them it was a surprise just like I'd asked them.

'I'll call them tomorrow,' I told the guy. 'They're always like that. You know what parents are like.'

I was glad I'd done it. I'd needed to do it. But I hadn't started feeling better yet.

I drove the Wreck to the riverside bar where I'd arranged to meet Chuckie. It was a new place, an old lock house converted to a yuppie paradise. People who looked like they went yachting frequented it. I didn't like it.

Chuckie bought me a drink and we went out into the Biergarten. *Biergarten*, Jesus. We sat on wooden chairs and looked blankly at the river. They were still dredging it. Some riverside corporation was beautifying the riverside. (Belfast had discovered these frivolities as all the other cities in Britain had decided, expensively, that they didn't work.) There were millions going down round there. All it seemed to be producing so far were waterlogged tractors and a bad smell. I gave Chuckie a bit of disaffected lip about all this.

'I like it,' he said.

I brought my beer bottle to my lips and nearly choked on

the lime some twat had stuck in it. Chuckie patted my back mildly. It was progress, he said. Belfast had to swing with the times. He liked all the new stuff. I couldn't see the point of a lime in the neck of a Harp bottle but I kept mum.

It had to be said that Chuckie was cheesed off that my face was still a bit wrecked. He'd hoped that I could occupy Max's flatmate that night and he thought my chances were impaired by my unbeauty. I tried to quiz him again about what the friend was like but he was vague. He hadn't even told me her name. He couldn't remember it, he said, though he blushed when he said it. I knew there was something dodgy going on and I wondered how much anxiety I was going to have to get through.

'Relax,' said Chuckie. 'She's nice.'

'I'm keeping my fucking trousers on, Chuckie. I hope you understand that.'

Chuckie chucked his shoulders. 'Have I asked you to remove them?' He changed the subject – too rapidly. 'How's work?'

'A constant delight,' I said. 'I'm always conscious of how lucky I am. What do you think, Chuckie? I'm a labourer. It's the same as always.'

Chuckie smiled blandly. 'My name is Charles, you know.'

I choked again. Serious this time. Chuckie – Charles – patted me again. Some yuppies looked round and frowned. Blow it out your ass, I thought.

'Could you run that by me one more time, Chuckie?'

Chuckie frowned, unselfconsciously. 'Well, I'm thirty now. I'm getting tired of being called Chuckie. I mean – Chuckie. It's not very dignified, is it?'

I'd known Chuckie for fifteen years and I swear to God that it was only as I looked closely at him then that I noticed he was wearing a suit and tie for the first time since I'd known him. 'Shit, Chuckie. I dig the duds.'

He surveyed himself complacently. He smiled happily. 'Good, huh. Bought it all today. Took a leaf out of your book.'

I rubbed the cuff of the suit. Classic English cut, double-weave wool. 'Not cheap,' I suggested.

He looked at me with rare sincerity. 'Quality never is.'

I gulped some beer and asked him where he was getting that kind of money.

'My boat came in.'

'What?'

His voice became hushed, conspiratorial. 'You remember my dildo?'

I laughed. 'Bet you say that to all the boys, Chuckie, sorry – Charles.'

Chuckie didn't laugh. Then he stopped me laughing. 'I got four thousand three hundred and twenty-six letters. That's four thousand three hundred and twenty-six cheques for nine ninety-nine. So far, one hundred and eighteen people have cashed their refund cheques. That was under twelve hundred pounds. Seventy-five quid on envelopes and eight hundred and twenty on stamps.'

He drank his drink. He fished inside his jacket and handed me a slip of paper. It was a balance slip from a cash machine.

'£41,138.98,' it said.

'Fuck me,' I replied.

We drank up. We drove off. Chuckie, newly mindful of his wardrobe, looked unhappy about sitting in the Wreck. His fat ass shuddered at the grimy touch of my Wreckseats. I ignored him. I switched on the radio. The news told us that a taxi-driver had been shot in Abyssinia Street and that the Tile Shop had been blown up again. I switched it off.

'Tell me more about this girl,' I asked, trying to rid myself of the envy of Chuckie's new wealth.

'Max says she's nice. That's all.'

'What does that mean?'

'Look, everything I know, you know.' He glanced at me. 'Except how to make money and how not to get hit.'

Laugh? I nearly started. 'You're so funny, it'll hurt,' I warned him.

He smiled. 'Behave yourself and she might even shag you.'

I stopped at some traffic lights. All around me unmodel citizens screeched on by. 'You better marry this American, Chuckie. I wouldn't do this for anybody.'

'Relax. She'll be great. You need some love in your life. After all that Sarah bollocks, you haven't distinguished yourself. And that wee waitress wasn't exactly a great move.'

The lights changed and I fingered my face. The bruising wasn't desperately disfiguring and in the rear-view mirror, my shiner looked almost raffish. In my experience, girls didn't mind if I looked beat-up. In my experience, some girls quite liked it.

The restaurant was near the bar where Mary worked and I was briefly tempted to sail in there with that attractively damaged, unkissed kisser of mine. I knew Chuckie wouldn't swing for it, though, so we headed into the swish eaterie he had selected.

The girls were waiting for us there. In the tangle of being shown to our table, of sitting down and smiling, of figuring out which girl was which, I had enough time to be surprised and impressed by Chuckie's girl. Tall but shapely, she had that healthy American hair and those Yank teeth that glittered like jewels. She looked like how you knew you should live.

'Good to meet you,' she said. 'Chuck often speaks of you.'

Chuck? It was getting complicated in Lurgan Land.

'I'm Max and this is . . .' she turned to the dark-haired girl who sat beside her.

'I'm . . .' She made a noise like someone choking.

'Would you like some water?' I said politely.

She looked at me like I'd pissed in her pockets.

'What?'

'I said, would you like some water?'

The girls exchanged looks. Chuckie frowned at me. 'That's her name,' he said.

'What is?' I asked, perplexed.

The girl made the choking noise again.

'That,' said Chuckie.

It took ten minutes and they ended up borrowing a pen from a waiter and writing it down on a napkin but in the end I determined that the girl was called Aoirghe. It was Irish. And the thing about people with those kinds of names was that they didn't enjoy lexical comedy at their expense. It still sounded like a cough to me.

It got worse.

A few minutes of chit-chat passed. The cough girl and I were silent. The American threw anxious looks Chuckie's way. He shrugged chubbily. Max took it on herself to grease the wheels after my bad start. 'Chuck tells me that you went to university in London?'

I dreaded the prospect of making conversational headway with this. 'Ah, yeah, that's right.'

'What did you study?'

Chuckie tried to smother his laugh.

'Political science,' I said.

Aoirghe didn't bother to hide her laugh.

'You liked London?' Max asked quickly, her smile too sweet.

'Yeah, London's OK.'

Aoirghe chipped in. 'Why did you go to London?'

'Mmm?'

'What was wrong with Irish universities?' Her face was humourless, adamant.

I tried the Noël Coward approach. 'Well, Irish universities remind me of God. A lot of people seem to believe in them. I respect their faith but there's no real proof.'

Her face was a smile-free zone.

'As a matter of fact,' I went on quickly, 'I've no idea why I went to London. I think I just wanted to avoid going to Queen's at all costs. There have to be some standards.'

'I went to Queen's,' she said.

I didn't blink, I didn't pause. With my voice all bright and interested I ploughed on. 'What did you do?'

'History.'

'Ah, right.'

She set down the glass she'd picked up. 'What does "Ah, right" mean exactly?' she asked.

Who knows what would have happened if the waitress hadn't arrived to take our orders? Silently, I blessed this profession to which Mary belonged. Silently, I damned Chuckie's fat little eyes for getting me into this. I could have been doing something better, like having an unusual and interesting bowel disease.

We ordered and we talked on. Max and Chuckie took the burden of the conversation so Aoirghe and I could take a breather between rounds. I was amazed at all these new skills of Chuckie/Chuck/Charles. He'd be speaking French and quoting *haikus* next. Slat had once told me that Chuckie was a man of possibilities but I felt sure that Slat would shit himself if he could see any of this.

I calmed down a bit and checked out my date. She was about my age, blue-eyed, big-chinned. There was a definiteness about her that appalled and attracted me in equal measure. As she listened to the others talk, her mouth twitched slightly, unable to remain set in the position that she desired. I wondered if this was a tic or her irritation at my presence. And when she glanced my way, it felt like a fight would start. She was pretty Irish, this girl, and it looked like I was never going to be Irish enough. It was very hard. Last week, I'd been beating people up for a living. I wasn't sure I had the delicacy required for this task.

Unfortunately Chuckie let the cat out of the bag once more by letting it slip that I'd been born up West there. I'd figured this girl for a middle-class republican – the worst type – and I knew she wouldn't be able to resist the lure of all those credentials of mine.

'You're from West Belfast, then?' she asked me, a new glitter in her eyes. I nearly laughed. Nobody in Belfast says West Belfast. That was TV news talk.

'Yeah,' I said.

Max brightened innocently and Chuckie looked at his plate.

'I wouldn't have guessed it,' said Aoirghe.

And I could have gone in there and then, both hands swinging, but I still tried to let it all slide.

'There you go,' I replied amiably.

She continued, blithe, animated. 'In fact, I was sure that you were a Protestant.'

I looked around. I could only see the top of Chuckie's head as he minutely inspected his asparagus. What the fuck was Chuckie doing eating asparagus? Max smiled at me guilelessly. At adjacent tables an eavesdropping couple stared. I'd tried to let it go but, really, who was I to refuse?

'Why would you have thought that? The space between my eyes, the gapless front teeth, the fact that I'm wearing no green?'

I wasn't exactly shouting but my voice was sharp. Some prick had once told me I looked like a Prod because I wore suits and had short hair. I had a low threshold for this stuff. In fact, I didn't have any threshold for this stuff at all.

Max coughed and Chuckie snorted. I even sensed a rumble of encouragement from the other diners. Aoirghe looked unmiffed.

'I don't know. You just don't seem very Catholic. You don't seem very West Belfast.'

I wasn't a big double-dater. I'd no real experience of the forms but even I guessed that what I went on to say wasn't good blind-date technique.

'I'm sorry but I haven't heard anybody talk crap like that for years. Not very Catholic, Jesus! I'm tired of all that bullshit.'

All the lights in her face switched on full beam. I hated, I *really* hated to admit that it was quite arresting.

'Very good,' she taunted. 'Does that amount to a political position?'

It was time to start shouting. I was punctual.

'A political position. Oh, for fuck's sake.'

Max creased her face at her friend, hoping she'd stop. Chuckie's face was touching his plate. Aoirghe's chin, already prominent, set further.

'Oh, I'm sorry, do you have some problem with politics?'

She was shrill. Max put her hand on her friend's arm. Chuckie looked up at me and shook his fat cheeks at me. All the fight in me dried up.

'Yes,' I replied, my voice low. 'I do have a problem with politics. I studied this stuff. Politics are basically antibiotic, i.e., an agent capable of killing or injuring living organisms. I have a big problem with that.'

Aoirghe was practically purple now and, despite Max's restraining arm, she was winding up to some big barrage when Chuckie piped up in a weak voice. 'Hey,' he said, his face bright with lunatic inspiration, 'you know the way they call Britain the UK—'

'Actually, Chuckie,' I said, swallowing my anger, 'Great Britain and the UK are separate entities. We aren't invited to one of those parties.'

Aoirghe snorted volubly. It sounded like she was saying her name again.

Chuckie smacked half a glass down and went on, 'Well, I was thinking the other day that it shouldn't be called the UK at all. It should be called the UQ. It should be the United Queendom. Where's this king they're talking about?' He turned to the rest of us, his chops chubby with his grin. Peacemaker, wit, Lurgan.

There was a big, big pause. There was even a tiny ripple of applause at an adjacent table.

We all ate silently for some minutes, I was fuming and I didn't want to look at the asshole I'd been saddled with so I watched Max and Chuckie instead. It was odd to see Chuckie make out with a girl like her. Again, I was oppressed by the uneasy sensation that Chuckie was going places. It worried me unaccountably. I mean, I wanted him to do well. It was just that I didn't want him to do well enough to show me up. With this swish girl on his arm he was already assuming a patrician air, already giving me grief for not having a girlfriend.

But after a while Max and Chuckie's talk dried up. Aoirghe had caught their eye. I looked where they looked and saw her staring at me with an extraordinary expression. I even looked behind me just to make sure. Chuckie giggled nervously.

'What happened to your face?' she asked.

I poured my wine while I failed to find a quip. Chuckie looked nervous.

'Somebody hit me.'

'Who?'

'I don't know his name.'

'Where?'

'Around the head mostly but—'

'No, I mean where did it happen?'

'Oh, right. On my doorstep.'

'What?'

'At my door.'

'Somebody just rang your bell and beat you up.'

'Yeah, more or less.'

'Why did you answer your door to him?'

'He was a cop.'

That was foolish. That was my big mistake. I should have known better. Her eyes gleamed with sudden fellowship. She was not a big fan of the Royal Ulster Constabulary, what with her being a Republican and thinking it was a good idea to kill them and all.

'That's disgusting.'

'Well, you know, it wasn't that simple.'

She sat back and included our mystified co-diners in her indignation. 'There is an average of one hundred serious assaults by the RUC every year. There is an average of three prosecutions every year. There are no convictions.'

I threw the rest of my wine down my throat. 'So, Max,' I said, 'what part of America are you from?'

'Don't change the subject,' Aoirghe bellowed. 'How can you

let yourself be beaten like that and not grow angry?'

'Well, it wasn't really political.'

'What?' she screamed – at last I was stoking her fire. 'It's always political.'

I gulped the rest of the wine. Soon I'd be home and everything would be fine.

'I deserved it.'

She was furious. I think she caught fire or something. 'Deserved it. Oh, you poor bastard. Is that how you feel about being Irish? This kind of thing will just go on and on until this whole country is united and we are one Ireland.' She half rose out of her chair and looked at me as though she expected an orchestral swell to underline her drama. The other diners were openly staring now and even the waiters looked anxious. Such talk was never profitable in public Belfast, no matter how swish, no matter how bourgeois. People got nervous. People got annoyed.

I spoke up. 'Listen, Earache, or whatever your name is, why don't you give it a rest and let us finish our dinner?'

She snarled defiantly at me. It was amazingly arousing under the circumstances. 'Don't you want your country united?'

'What country?'

'Don't you consider yourself Irish?'

'Sweetheart, I don't consider myself at all. I'm humble that way.'

At last, she started to get really pissed off. 'Don't call me sweetheart, you prick.'

From that high point, the evening deteriorated.

She gave us the full whack, the entire job lot. The international perspective, the moral imperative and the historical basis for why it was OK for the people she liked to kill the people she didn't like. I'd had many such evenings, many such listenerships – being Irish, I could hardly have failed to – but it had never been so hard to take, it had never been so ugly.

She was particularly good on the history, what with her big local degree and all. She gave us the rundown from prehistory through the Dark Ages to the present day. The old stuff: the island of Ireland had been a free stronghold where human culture flourished at its finest. Then the English came!

There were three basic versions of Irish history: the Republican, the Loyalist, the British. They were all murky and all overplayed the role of Oliver Cromwell, an old guy with a bad haircut. I had a fourth version to add, a Simple Version. Eight hundred years, four hundred years, whatever way you wanted it, it was just lots of Irish killing lots of other Irish.

We swallowed the rest of our meal and swallowed her bullshit too. I couldn't be bothered taking her on any more. She had the impervious faith of the bourgeois zealot, which was OK for her. Nobody was going to come shit in her nest. I envied educated people who got off on revolutionaries. Islington was full of them. It must have been fun if you didn't have to do any of the dying.

When the meal wound up, Chuckie looked like a dead man. This had interrupted all that good work he'd been doing with Max. I didn't know what kind of fantasy he'd had about me and Aoirghe but I wasn't going to take her anywhere convenient while he and Max got it on back at her place. I mean, Chuckie was a friend but Aoirghe gave me the pip.

We parted awkwardly. Max kissed me and I'd liked her. Aoirghe and I stood square to each other and muttered some thick valedictions. Chuckie got into the Wreck with me. I drove him to his place in silence.

When I got home, a car full of heavies had stopped outside my house. I parked the Wreck and opened my front door. My flesh crawled and my blood pounded. As I closed it behind me I was almost disappointed that the muzzle of the Browning had not, in fact, been pushed hard against my ear.

Crab or Hally had been leaving messages on my answering machine. Death threats. Disguising their voices, trying to sound threatening. I didn't take any of it very seriously, but I knew if they got drunk or bored enough they wouldn't hesitate to nip round here or to tell some of their friends with balaclavas what a Catholic I was.

Inside, I looked out my window to see what the heavies were up to. Two of them had got out of the car. They were bad guys, all right, badly dressed, well-moustached. I saw them walk to the graffiti wall. For a moment I thought I'd worked it out. I thought that these were the OTG guys. But then they got out their cans and their brushes and they painted over both the OTGs written there. They drove off. I was relieved. I wouldn't like any mysteries to originate with guys like that.

I lay in bed with the windows open. I couldn't sleep. I'd forgotten what a good night's sleep was like. It was years ago and places distant. I'd used it up, like luck or wishes. In the end I lit a cigarette and switched on the tiny radio, which was the only noise, bar cat, I had left after selling my stereo and my television. A news bulletin told me that they'd shot another taxi-driver. Maybe I'd sell my little portable too.

Next day, I worked through my Friday.

It had taken me a weekend to find another job. I'd called some people. Some people had called me back. I was flattered, amazed. I was stirred to find how high my stock still stood. A few of my old associates had soon heard I was out of work again and they were tripping over each other to offer me employment.

My answering machine had buzzed all weekend with their unanswered messages: Slug, Spud, Muckie, Rat, Dix, Onion, Bap and Gack. Why didn't I know anybody called Algernon? Fondly remembering my old form, my old skills, they had all made various offers but I didn't do that sort of thing any more. Even a stint of repo work had been a departure. Davy Murray's was the worst offer but it was the most legal. I took it and I'd ended up doing crew work for Davy just like I'd done in the old days. I was a construction worker again. I was a brickie. I was a tiler. I was a big success.

I'd worked this work on and off since I was sixteen. We were doing renovations on kitchens at the Europa, the biggest hotel in Belfast. The famous one – the one they always used to blow up. (Such past tenses are hazardous in Belfast, the one they still blow up, the one they will blow up.) Yeah, the one with no windows, the one with the wooden curtains. It was once the most bombed hotel in Europe but Sarajevo joints were taking all the records now.

My new job was OK. I worked in construction so I did constructive things all day. I liked the work. It was simple. It was legal. It wasn't the best use of my education but at least it was giving me some muscles.

Chuckie phoned when I got back from work. I apologized for blowing his plans the night before. No problem, he said. Aoirghe was going to Dublin for a while, which meant Chuckie was going to have Max all to himself for as long as was necessary.

'So you didn't go for old Aoirghe, then?' he asked.

'What do you think?'

I heard him laugh.

'Yeah, she's bad medicine, right enough. But relax, she hates me too.'

'Well, Chuckie, I hesitate to mention it, but wouldn't you be a bit Protestant for her tastes?'

'No, it wasn't that.'

'No?'

'No. You know the way she's a big Irish speaker. When I first met her, I asked her what the Irish word for constitutional democracy was.'

'What is it?'

'British conspiracy.' Chuckie guffawed. 'I'm proud of that joke. It's the only one I ever made up by myself. It's not that funny but it's dead satirical.'

'I presume Aoirghe wasn't busting her gut at that one.'

'I thought she was gonna nut me.' Chuckie chuffed on for a while about this and that.

'How's business?' I asked him.

'Amazing. You would not believe it.'

He told me how business was. I would not believe it.

That night I sat in the Wreck and waited for Mary to leave work. The bar shut late and it was much unhappiness to sit there while the windows steamed up and to lie to all the cops who gripped their guns and asked me what I was doing. It was madness. For all I knew, Mary's pugilistic boyfriend might have been on duty and if he'd seen me waiting there he'd have emptied his clip into me just for fun.

After an hour and more I saw her leave. Her coat pulled tight, she jumped into a cab with one of the other bar girls. I could barely see her face and it only lasted about twenty seconds but it looked like a nice life she had there. It looked like she wasn't missing much.

Then, stupidly, I drove out to Rathcoole. I drove out to the house where the Johnsons lived. I parked the car in front of their house and sat there for an hour or two. It looked like I was turning into a watcher, a weirdo. I seemed to know all these people who wouldn't want to talk to me. I smoked and watched as the lights were switched off one by one. When the house was dark and I could be sure they were sleeping, I felt better. It was no atonement but it was all I had in me.

I went home. Someone had painted letters on my front door. *Your ded*. The spelling was Hally's; it even sounded like his accent. I knew there was trouble to come. Since when had my life become so controversial? I decided to think about it in the morning. I went to bed. I felt so bad, I was nice to the cat. Uneasy but willing, he took the opportunity of getting into the bedroom and sleeping on my face all night.

The weekend opened out to me like a menu in a cheap café. There wasn't anything I wanted there. It didn't feel good to be single any more. Saturday morning I went shopping, just so someone would talk to me, just so I'd have something to thank somebody for.

Chuckie had gone to ground for the weekend, undoubtedly on some mysterious financial enterprise. I wasn't sure that I could ever remember him being out of touch before. The new Chuckie was taking some getting used to. Slat and some of the others would be around but I didn't want to do any drinking. What with Chuckie being such a cosmopolite now, I thought I should try something a little more dignified than usual. I didn't know any dignified people so I thought I'd have to spend the day alone. I wondered if the Erasmus would last a full Saturday.

It didn't. In the end, of course, I couldn't take the solitude.

So, six months late, I went to see my foster-folks.

Matt and Mamie had been my foster-folks. They sounded like a nineteen-fifties novelty act. And that, after a fashion, was what they were.

Matt and Mamie had fostered me when I was fifteen. When all the bad stuff happened with my real folks, the cops and the social workers had nabbed me. After a few weeks of courtrooms and hostels, they dragged me over to Matt and Mamie's house.

Years later, they'd told me what a wolf-boy I was when I arrived. I was violent, withdrawn, the usual stuff. The various arms of all the state services had recommended institutional care but some optimist, some humanist, had thought I was recognizably human. That was the someone who had thought of Matt and Mamie.

They didn't need to remind me. I'd never forgotten the first day I went to them. They lived on the Antrim Road then. They weren't rich – more, solidly bourgeois – but their home, their belongings were unimaginable to me. After I had mutinously fielded an evening of solicitous non-enquiry from them, they showed me my bedroom.

It had all been so bad, my childhood, my youth, it had all been so terrible – povertystuff, Irishstuff – and I'd seen it all through like a hardwood cowboy. Nothing had finally hurt me beyond endurance and, for all the damage I'd taken, I was still standing. But that night I cried, I wept to die. I sobbed silently until my head was hot and bursting and my nose ran like twin taps.

And it was only because of the coverlet on my bed. Mamie had laid a green embroidered coverlet on my bed. I had no idea what it was made of but it was heavy and felt like prosperity itself. It was only a piece of material but it was too much for me, that coverlet. I had never seen such green. I couldn't really understand that this woman I didn't know would have put this thing across the bed for my comfort, for my pleasure. I rubbed my hot, snotty face in it and slept in my clothes.

Later, I decided that it was no big deal. I decided that it was only bed-linen. Later still, I changed my mind. Perhaps green coverlets are not profound things but I think it made me understand something of what I might have missed – that there'd been nobody around to love me like they should.

I lived with Mamie and Matt for a couple of years. By the number of grateful men of various ages who called on them, I soon guessed that Matt and Mamie had done the foster thing before. I was right. They had had no children and had made up for it by fostering the kids nobody would touch. That basically meant males over fourteen. They'd had some shockers: delinquents, hardmen, wide-boys and paramilitaries of every description. Only one had turned out bad. He was dead already, shot by his own side in some Republican feud.

We kids had stolen from them, cheated them and assaulted them – one kid had even come home one night with a UVF gun with which he was going to kneecap Matt, but Matt and Mamie had continued loving them all, absolutely and unconditionally. Eventually these wide-boys, these halfmen just had to learn that language.

Matt and Mamie had stopped fostering now. Or rather they'd been stopped. They were too old. They'd been retired from the caring business. But they'd done their bit. Seventeen kids had passed through their hands from 1964 onwards. Mamie always talked proudly of having the biggest family in the city. Some of these guys were in their forties. They were lawyers, doctors, builders; they were husbands and fathers.

Matt and Mamie had fostered generations of the city's scum and persistently and without reward made human beings out of them.

Matt and Mamie were weird.

Matt and Mamie had been leaving messages on my machine for months. I hadn't called back. I'd only ignored them because I'd known what they'd wanted. I hadn't seen them since Sarah had gone.

They were both in their sixties now, living in a big house out on the Shore Road. It was in the general area where I'd been doing my repo work. I'd always been a bit panicky in case I bumped into them, doing that work of which they would so disapprove. Mamie hadn't wanted to move to the Shore Road but Matt had insisted. He had partially maritime fantasies. He'd always wanted to work in the docks. He'd even tried to leave school when he was fifteen. Mamie – predictably they'd been childhood sweethearts – had dissuaded him. He hadn't wanted to listen to her but since he had tried fruitlessly to have sex with her at least once every twenty minutes between the ages of fifteen and eighteen, she had a carrot he couldn't resist. The new house was on the north edge of the bay of the city and Matt liked to walk the coast of Belfast, concrete and crane, the docks thick with the quality of the sea. He liked to dream there.

I rolled up to the house about two. Matt was in the garden, his big back bent over some dwarf hedgerow. I called out to him. He stood up and shielded his eyes with his hand. It was not sunny.

'Good to see you, son.'

I shook his hand. There was some muck there. 'Likewise,' I said.

We went inside. Mamie was in the kitchen, cooking something major. Her meals had always been complicated affairs, taking military amounts of time and tasting pretty military in the end. She kissed my cheek with her big cold lips and told me to sit at the table. She went on cooking.

'You've been a stranger,' she said, wiping her brow.

I smiled but nobody was looking at me. 'Yeah, well, you know how it goes.'

'I'm not sure I do know how it goes.'

Matt coughed uneasily. 'You want a drink, son?'

'I'd drink any coffee that's going.'

Matt busied himself with my request. Mamie turned to face me. 'How's Sarah?'

I looked at my fingernails. It felt pretty blithe but I knew it would fool no one. 'She's fine.'

'Mmm,' replied Mamie.

A lot of Mamie's conversation had always consisted of indeterminate noises, grunts, mumbles and grumbles, all invested with their own peculiar significance. 'Mmm' was not a favourable noise.

But then, having finished with coffee, Matt started his own series of peacemaker noises, coughs, chokes, sneezes. I nearly laughed. This wasn't Foreign Office but nobody could deny its diplomacy.

'I must urinate,' he announced.

He left the room. It looked intentional. It looked like Mamie had something to say to me that Matt didn't want to hear.

'You look thin,' said Mamie.

'I haven't been eating your concrete casseroles for near a year.'

She took a swipe at me with one floury hand. 'You should call us more.'

'Yeah, I'm sorry. I will, I promise.'

She stopped what she was doing and stood facing me with her arms folded. 'She's gone, hasn't she?'

'Who?'

'Sarah.'

Matt and Mamie didn't like me to smoke but I lit a cigarette anyhow.

'Yes. She's gone.'

Matt and Mamie had been big Sarah fans. They had dug her. To Matt and Mamie, Sarah had been a good thing, she'd been the only good thing. Mamie knew my news already so she didn't freak but she gave me one of her old-woman looks. It was one of the things I'd noticed about Sarah going. Everybody thought it had been my decision. They were wrong. I hadn't packed any bags. But that stuff, all that stuff, it just took too long to explain.

'Who's for dinner?' I asked.

Mamie didn't mind the subject change but she blushed for me. 'John and Patrick are coming round – nothing special.'

John and Patrick were the first and second of Matt and Mamie's fosterings. They were both in their late forties. She was always ill-at-ease when she split her affections like this. I'd made her feel bad that I wasn't getting my feet under her table that night. She needn't have worried. I was OK. Mamie's cooking was dreadful. She had to take the day off to make an omelette. John and Patrick were welcome to it.

'I'd have asked you but you were being all invisible . . .'

I put my arms around her old shoulders. I put my lips to her old cheek. 'Yeah, yeah,' I said. 'Tell it to the marines.'

Matt came back. He stood awkwardly, empty-handed, semaphoric. 'Can we help?' he said uncertainly. He looked at Mamie. She shook her head. He smiled in relief. 'I was going to take a turn outside. Do you want to come with me?'

I looked at Mamie. She turned back to her mixing bowls.

'Yeah, sure,' I said. 'Why not?'

Matt and I walked for an hour. We went right down as close to the docks as we could. Matt stood on the lip of the land and sniffed. He looked out at all the Belfast fish in all the Belfast sea. He was happy there, some docker's fantasy coursing through his old blood. There never was a more inappropriate lawyer. Matt should have been a stevedore, he should have been a longshoreman, he should have been a contender.

Matt wiped some imaginary sweat from his brow. He turned to me and smiled his favourite John Wayne smile. Matt's version was inaccurately humane and generous. 'We know about Sarah.'

I sighed patiently. 'Yeah, Mamie told me,' I said.

'I thought so.' He threw a stone into the water. The plop was loud. 'She came to see us before she left.'

My heart went all hot. 'Yeah?'

'She wasn't very happy.'

I picked up a pebble. It was my turn to throw a stone. 'Well, Matt. She was the one pushing all the buttons. She was the one with all the choices.' I threw the stone. I missed and it landed in a bush. The entire sea to aim at and I fucking missed.

Matt put his hand on my shoulder. 'We were worried when you didn't call,' he said.

'I'm sorry. There were lots of things I didn't want to talk about.'

He smiled. 'Was it bad?'

'It wasn't good, Matt.'

'No.'

'What happened to you two? It was so great between you.'

A pair of vulgar gulls wheeled low like jets, screeching.

I had an opportunity then. If I'd told him about the secret abortion, they might have stopped flying her flag so much. Mamie, the disappointed mother, would have been particularly outraged. It had always been so hard for me to resist the lure of cheap sympathy.

'Why did she leave?' Matt asked again.

'Well, Matt, you know me – easy to live without.'

The old man's eyes were harsh as he followed the flight of the gulls but his mouth was pursed in admiration for their faded beauty. 'You're not funny every time, Jake,' he said.

I kicked some gravel. 'Jesus, Matt, every time? I'm not even funny most of the time.'

'You don't want to talk about it?'

'Matt, this is disturbingly perceptive of you.' I laughed. I changed the subject to one he could never resist. 'Hey, Mamie's looking well.'

Matt gurgled with delight. 'Yeah.' His eyes glittered. 'She's still a fine-looking woman.'

Mamie looked her age but Matt could never see it so. He was hilariously uxorious. Forty years on and still he could barely contain his lust for her. Matt could never believe that his wife was sixty. He still saw the twenty-two-year-old he'd married. He reminded me of Pierre Bonnard. Bonnard painted his wife for fifty years, standing in the bath, lying buff on the rug. At seventy he still painted her like she was nineteen. I'd always had a thing about soppy old guys. It was an ambition of mine. One day, I thought, I might just end up some soppy old guy.

'I hope I die before she gets old.' He laughed.

'You're barking, Matt.'

He kicked a stone into the oily water. 'Yeah, but I'm happy that way.'

We walked on. In the distance we could see the jutting hulk of old Grosvenor Wharf with its mile-long warehouses. It was desolate now. The thousands who had worked there worked there no longer. Yet this sight always put Matt in a good mood. He was a lawyer. No one he knew had lost any jobs there. I hoped it would stop him talking about Sarah. I didn't need any reminding.

Back indoors, Mamie had progressed no further with the meal she was preparing. Her face was smudged with the disturbing brown of some nameless gravy and a truly astonishing smell was leaking from the oven.

'What's with the whiff? Smells delish.'

This was Matt's attempt at cajolerie. I wouldn't have risked it.

'Jake?' asked Mamie.

She straightened from the job and looked at me. I hated it when she asked me that. Jake? It always meant that there was trouble coming. There was something squeaky and interrogative in the way Mamie sometimes said my name.

'Yes?'

'Do you know a couple called Johnson?'

I should have remembered. I should have thought. Typically, Mamie did a form of community visiting around that area. Not content with letting a whole lot of unfortunates come and live in her house, she had to go and be nice to a lot of others whom she couldn't actually house. I should've guessed that she'd have run into the Johnsons. The best thing to do, of course, was to confess.

'Never heard of them,' I replied vacantly.

'That's strange.'

'Why?'

Matt coughed placidly. Mamie ignored him. 'They live in Rathcoole. She's sick and he's not working. Ring any bells?'

In my confusion, I even dipped my finger in one of Mamie's sauces and tasted it. I had to be very nervous to do something like that.

'Don't think so.' I choked.

'They tell a strange story.'

'Yeah?'

Mamie looked hard at me. She stopped smiling. 'You haven't been going around buying beds, have you, Jake?'

'I've already got a bed, Mamie.'

Matt coughed and chuffed a bit. He smiled a big nervous smile and spoke to Mamie. 'Jake says he's got to go now, sweetheart.'

Mamie ignored him. 'What are you working at now?' she asked.

I told her I was a brickie again. She asked to see my hands. I gave them to her. She inspected them minutely and then grunted half in satisfaction, half in disappointment. It was humiliating but it deserved to be.

'What happened to your face?' It was worse because she hadn't mentioned it before. She knew that.

'I was moving some furniture.'

She almost smiled.

'Stay out of trouble,' she said.

'That would be nice,' I replied sincerely.

That was the problem with Matt and Mamie. Their world was a loving world, a decent world. They couldn't understand shabbiness or harm. They had no imagination.

That night I met the boys. Sloane, Deasely and the others. What with Chuckie gone, it was hard to drink the way we were used to. After a couple, we all got depressed. Slat suggested that we eat. Slat had always had vaguely civilized pretensions. We went to a café. We dined. We didn't drink much. We talked. It was very strange.

I went home almost happy. On the wall by the police station on Poetry Street, someone had written two or three more OTGs. The new lettering was even more plump and prosperous than before. Enigmatic fuckers.

When I opened the front door, my cat came bounding out. In my new mood of goodwill, I bent to stroke him, to bond, to spend quality time. He just shot out past me and dived into the garden for a piss. Fucking cat. I wished he'd grow some new balls so I could cut them off again.

But he'd made the right decision. It wasn't an interior night. I didn't go in. I just sat on my doorstep and thought my way through my day.

There had been one pleasant interlude. A man from Amnesty International had called me. I told him he must have had the wrong number but he told me that it was me he wanted. Amnesty had set up an international commission on human rights violations in Northern Ireland. He was responsible for police brutality. My name had been mentioned to him in connection with an incident of police violence. He wondered if I would like to talk to him about my ordeal, in strict confidence.

Then I worked it out. I asked him if he knew any girls who had names that sounded like chest complaints. Yup, it was the delightful Aoirghe's work. I sorted him out. I told him it hadn't exactly been official police business. He asked me if I thought official police business could include beating up the citizenry on their doorsteps. I lost it then. I didn't like this guy vibing me for not being radical enough about being creamed by a cop. That I considered *de trop*. So, naturally enough, I told him to go fuck himself sideways.

I called Chuckie's number. I got his mum. Chuckie was nowhere to be found. Peggy found Max's number for me anyway but then I couldn't get her off the phone. Peggy was keen to talk. She was worried. I'd never known her so garrulous, so I listened up. She said that something was wrong, that Chuckie was acting weird. Where have you been? I thought. I calmed her down, I reassured her. Jesus, I think I told her something like Chuckie's a unique individual after all. Only a mother would have listened to toss like that. Chuckie had told me that sometimes his mother made him strangely uneasy. Sometimes I knew what he meant.

I called Max's number. I got the answering machine. I left a message for Aoirghe, telling her that I would eschew her participation in my private life. Not quite in those words. I think I was adamant. It had been her voice on the answering machine message. That had helped.

Out on my doorstep, the night sounded like an old record that crackled and hissed. Cars swished by as regular as a second hand. Helicopters droned high in dull Zs. A woman laughed distantly like some urgent bird. Far across the city (Wicked West), a series of dry impacts that may or may not have been automatic gunfire erupted and subsided.

Six

Chuckie Lurgan had the most imprecise notions of what the Augustan age might have been, but in the moment that his hand first met the warm flesh of Max's breasts, he had felt more than Palladian. And, as she kissed his eyes and pushed him back and down on her own sofa, Chuckie's mind was filled with columns: the ardent one that had filled his trousers for the previous half-hour and the double set of credits that ranged on the internalized screen of his greed.

Her brassière snapped and dropped and she seemed to expand under his hands. At three o'clock that afternoon, after two hours of vague talk and big-teeth smiles, the Ulster Development Board had awarded him a start-up grant of seventy-five thousand pounds. She ran her hands under and between the flaps of his open shirt. His skin began to feel like liquid under her touch (he was so chubby these days his skin would have felt liquid under most people's touch). End of the week he'd have one hundred and ninety thousand pounds in the bank. He hoped his dreams wouldn't suffer from all this reality.

He was distracted by the spectacle of Max shrugging off her skirt without the use of her hands. That was good. Slat had told him he had no chance but the UDB said that his business plan was one of the most imaginative that they had seen. Slat's problem was his unprofitable adherence to logic. Her dynamic pants round her ankles, Max stood in front of him. Chuckie's attention, that wavering, troubled thing, centred and fixed.

'God bless America,' said Chuckie.

She:

- kissed him,
- pulled his clothes from him,
- made noises in his ear,
- rubbed herself against him like he was a bath-towel,
- made him blush,
- made him laugh,
- made him forget he was fat,
- vigorously, rigorously,
- wiped the money right out of his head.

And apart from the passage which ended with her saying, more impatiently than was strictly necessary, 'It's called a clitoris, Chuck,' he couldn't help feeling that it had gone very well indeed. Begun in surprise, continued with enthusiasm, it had ended in success.

And he had been amazed to hear the noises she made. She had actually laughed. No moaning, no whooping, no whimper, just a massive, muscular shudder of her hips under his hand and a great belch of triumphant rowdy laughter, not a belly laugh. Something bigger. Something lower.

And then they lay side by side, she brown and naked, he white and baggy as a badly blown balloon.

'Hey, Chuckie.'

'Yeah?'

'You OK?'

Chuckie closed his open mouth. 'Mmm-hhmm,' he affirmed.

Max sat up. She smiled proudly at the wreck of him. 'Can I fuck or can I fuck?' she asked.

Chuckie moaned helplessly, Max sipped at her now cold tea.

'I'm sorry. I should have taken it easier first time round. I just got carried away.'

Chuckie put his pillow over his face and whimpered tinily.

Max laid her head on the pillow. 'I don't know why they call it French sex. The blowjob is a distinctly American phenomenon.'

Aoirghe had been away for a fortnight. Chuckie had spent that fortnight wondering whether it would happen, when it would happen. He liked her more than he could say but that didn't have to stop him thinking about sex. The surprise of her regard was so great that he imagined it likely that she might not favour him with her flesh.

He had been much with her without skin meeting skin. Opportunity had been limited. He had his mother. She had her flatmate. But even after Aoirghe's disappearance, quietus had seemed remote. Nothing had happened. He found himself growing more circumspect. He hadn't even tried to touch her breasts, never really finding the line, the trajectory, which would end with such an action seeming reasonable, unconsidered, legal.

That evening, it had been different. He took a taxi to her flat, his thoughts filled with money. He had rung her bell absently. She had come to the door, sloppily dressed, and mumbled things he did not hear and then disappeared. He had nodded to the taxi-driver and had loitered there, waiting to take her to the restaurant he'd booked. He was wondering whether the UDB money would queer his chances of an IRB grant when Max had reappeared at the door and dragged him indoors by his lapels.

One minute he had been standing idly on the doorstep, the next he'd had surprising portions of her stuffed between his lips.

Chuckie sat upright suddenly. The sheet fell from his face.

'Fuck,' he said.

'Again?'

He looked at her blankly. 'The taxi-driver.'

Despite his protestations, Max had pulled on a gown and walked out to pay the driver. Chuckie watched from the window, just in case the scumbag tried anything on. There was enough chat for him to get anxious but Max returned before he could pull his trousers on. He asked her how much the driver had charged.

'He was so amazed that you were porking a girl like me that he only charged me ten. I think he felt sorry for me.' She smiled, somehow delightfully.

'Come here,' said Chuckie.

It was then nine o'clock. It took two hours for Chuckie's pub itch to leave him. His ear was filled with the silent ticking of his internal clock. Time for three or four pints. Still time for a couple. Just time for a quick one.

It wasn't that he wasn't happy. They made a couple of extra stabs at love, long blunt enjoyable stabs. They drank coffee and wine. They talked. They listened to music she liked and which he found magical for her liking. It was just that they were staying in. Without the noise of barmen's complaints, shouts for orders, the look of woozy mirrors and the smell of beery piss, Chuckie was rather at a loss. He couldn't entirely manage the concept of an evening out being an evening in.

Third time around, his penis felt as barnacled as an ancient crab and there was a distinct fishing fleet odour in the air. Third time around, he got the point of the staying-in notion. Afterwards, as he gasped and chugged and choked, Max said, with some admiration, 'Jesus, Chuckie, I thought this was supposed to be fun.'

To his disbelief, they ended the conscious portion of the evening watching a late-night black-and-white movie on the television. Everything in him and about him changed. In common with all the other fat working-class Protestants he had ever known, Chuckie had always felt a certain shame in watching television. It was an onanistic vice, the resort of the deracinated.

It was what friendless folk did when they didn't want to talk to their mothers or wives.

Now, as Max chuckled at fifty-year-old American jokes and cooed at the cleft in Cary Grant's chin, television seemed a dignified, elegant thing, a box at the opera, the enclosure at Ascot. It was only in the way of looking. That grim pursuit, that last resort had all kinds of resident beauties. As he began to relax, he started laughing at all the hard-jawed humour, and even privately conceded that Cary Grant was not entirely without appeal.

When he found himself settled by her sleeping form under the single sheet that the heat of her body made unnecessary, he was surprised. The subject of his staying over had not come up. Had he asked? Had she offered? He lay there a full two hours, blissfully sleepless, amazingly unfiscal. Trapped within the walls of his generous flesh, Chuckie had always wanted an out-of-body experience. He wanted to know what it would be like out there in the slim, attractive world. Flat on his back with Max breathing American beside him, Chuckie came closer to the incorporeal than ever before. He felt less than light, more than airy. He hoped that other yuppies did this.

Next day, Chuckie met up with the IRB, the Industrial Resources Board. A government agency set up to encourage investment in Northern Ireland, the IRB had vast sums of British government money at its disposal, much of which Chuckie coveted. He had thought much about how to persuade them to give him some. It was hard to know what the IRB looked for in an enterprise. They were mostly famous for giving enormous sums of British cash to American motor manufacturers who built expensive factories producing cars so ludicrous that they ended up only being sold to film companies, who used them as the comic props for celebrated time-travel comedies. American textiles manufacturers were given hundreds of thousands of pounds to investigate the possibility of opening companies in Northern Ireland. They always returned home, profitably discovering that such moves were impossible. Colombian gentlemen with dark glasses and white powdery trails from nose to lip met the IRB and walked away with a million or more. Chuckie felt sure he had a chance.

At eleven o'clock exactly he strode into the plush IRB offices. He was kept waiting for only about a minute and a half, a thrilling departure from his previous experience of waiting rooms. No fewer than six besuited timeservers descended into the foyer to greet him. He shook hands half a dozen times, giving confident, up-tempo snorts as he was introduced to each in turn. They moved on to a glossy boardroom with pictures of rare IRB successes on the wall. They gave him coffee and biscuits. They chuffed on about how good it was to see an internal initiative getting off the ground, pressed their smiles smooth and waited for him to speak. Chuckie coughed and looked around him. It was nice in here. The six men looked at him. There was silence.

Chuckie hadn't actually thought of anything to say. He had no ideas. He had no real reason to offer them to explain why they should give him thousands of their pounds. He had not thought it entirely necessary to have a plan. Up to that point, he had been right. Now, as he prepared to speak to these six men, his mind was blank.

He walked out four hours later, dizzy and hungry. John Long was wrong. Slat was wrong. John Maynard Keynes was wrong. Malthus had no idea. Chuckie had simply made it up as he went along. He had dished out a whole series of off-the-cuff pipe-dreams and improbabilities, inventing non-existent projects and ideas never intended or likely to exist. After three hours of bullshit, lies and fantasies, some of which he couldn't even understand himself, they had agreed to grant him eight hundred thousand pounds over the first eight months of his operation. A hundred grand a month.

That night, he booked a table in the most expensive restaurant in Belfast – a restaurant so expensive that only civil servants and IRB men ate there; the food was revolting and came in tiny portions but Chuckie planned to sneak a hamburger and chips before he went. He bought a bottle of champagne that cost more than he had earned in the previous year and went round to Max's.

Of course, the table at the restaurant languished Chuckie-less and the champagne was used mostly to douse Max's astounding breasts in a particularly vivid moment. The evening stretched before them as an endless potential of interior fun. Max tried to have sex with him in most of the square feet on the property. Chuckie wondered if she had had to train for this. If she'd been to sex university and had taken refresher courses. I'm too fat for this, he thought to himself. I'm too ugly, I'm too Irish. But then he remembered the eight hundred grand and went for it as though qualified.

Max called a pizza joint and they delivered some food, which saved Chuckie around two hundred and fifty pounds and gave him the opportunity of doing something he had never done before with pepperoni in his mouth.

They broke for an hour and Chuckie thanked her. He told her she was something special. He told her he was on cloud eight.

'Don't you mean cloud nine, Chuck?'

They talked.

Chucked had often wondered what conversation was for. When he had been young, he had, in common with most children, no patience for what adults did with their lives. They just seemed to talk. They didn't run around or play or have any real fun. There was a lack of dynamism, an existential lack of point. This irritation had stayed with Chuckie, and sometimes he had found himself unaccountably depressed by what adult life amounted to. What was the point of all this talking? Why did he have to do it? Why did he have to listen to it?

The irony was that Chuckie had always been so fat and lazy that he had never run about, or played or had fun anyway.

But that night, Max taught him what talk was for. She showed him why he should be interested. She told him her story. He hadn't even asked.

She told him this:

Max had loved her father like she loved herself. He was a negotiator. He persuaded people in foreign countries not to kill each other. She could see why they listened to him. He was very good at talking. His face was nearly as soft and brown as his eyes. His reassuring, deep voice always made her sleepy and happy. It always made her feel that it was a good world that such a man could live in it.

When Max was thirteen, her mother left her father. Everybody but her mother was surprised. Her mother hated New York, anyway, and any fast-track advancement her husband made was nothing to her. His younger brother, however, was a comfort. After a year, they wanted more than splendidly illicit sex swapped in cars, bathrooms or the beds of either brother.

Max's father looked after Max for a week while his brother and his former wife flew to Miami for a week to get things organized. He told his daughter that her mother was going to marry his brother. Max was scared of all the new rules now that her uncle would be her father. She wondered why her father didn't cry.

He cried when he saw her off at the airport. In the departure lounge, he looked the way he looked when she saw him on television, tall and slim in a neat blue suit amidst the scrum of people.

Miami was not as bad as she might have supposed. She went to a new school and it was OK. She made some friends and they were OK and pleasantly impressed by her New York credentials. Her mother seemed happy and John, her father/uncle, was indulgent. Most of the time, Max didn't even mind the way they pawed each other in front of her.

By her fifteenth birthday, she was the only virgin she knew. At school, her friends were all getting laid with an abandon and a courage that she could barely understand. When they asked her about herself, she invented cousins, even brothers with whom she did what they did. But they did not believe her and fixed dates for her, sometimes with boys who had already passed through their hands. She didn't like the boys, she didn't like the way they tried to make their muscles bulge, the tightness of their jeans and the swollen look that all their faces shared. One of them had cornered her on the back seat of his car, had scratched at her nipples with his fingernails and had thrust her hand into his open trousers. She had grasped his penis while he kissed her and mauled her breasts. It was so hard and felt much too big. It struck her that it did not feel fully human. It excited her like a crime but she had stopped him and he had never seen her again.

Max didn't trust the idea of sex. It was not something that she could square with her idea of manhood. Of who her father was. His gentleness, his charity were her ideal of how a life should be lived and that ideal was sexless. The only role that sex had played in the life of her father was to induce his wife to run away with his brother. Sex was an acid that corroded. It was something that stopped people being good.

For two or three years, it worked well. She saw her father every two or three months. She always saw him in New York. He was busier than ever and was becoming quite famous for his placid skills. He was a common sight on television news.

On her sixteenth birthday, her father took her out to dinner in a Manhattan restaurant where everybody smiled and some blushed to see him. She was proud of him. She was proud of the way he dealt with the people who stopped at their table to talk to him, the men confidential and trusting, the women openly admiring.

Her father told her that she was beautiful.

The band played 'Your Kiss Is on My List of the Best Things in Life'.

Six months later, there was a talk of the possibility of a Nobel

Peace Prize. He had just negotiated a settlement in a tribal dispute in a Central African Socialist Republic that had cost ten thousand lives a year. He was invested with almost saintly status, and television pictures were beamed all round the world of her tall and handsome father surrounded by happy villagers. Then he was sent to Northern Ireland.

He was shot dead twenty minutes after he stepped off the plane. He didn't even make it out of the airport. The police and the Army were amazed. The airport was one of the most heavily guarded spots in Northern Ireland. They reported that the Protestant and Catholic paramilitaries had joined forces to execute such a daring attack.

The IRA and the UVF both claimed responsibility. An American newscaster told the camera that her father had been executed because he was too good at his job. The Irish didn't want him persuading them away from their war. The Irish liked their war.

Max cried through the ten lost days until they flew her father's body back and burned it at an unprivate private funeral. Her mother sobbed without tears for the cameras and her uncle/stepfather made husky eulogies of his dead brother for reporters. Some of those ghouls shouted her name and took her picture when she looked at them.

That night Max ran away.

She ran to Jacksonville, she ran to Pensacola, she ran to Fayetteville and Tulsa, she ran to Amarillo and Lubbock, she ran South again to El Paso, she ran to San Antonio.

She stopped running in Phoenix. In a bus-station coffeeshop, she looked at her watch and saw that two years had passed. She took a pile of dimes and called her mother.

Max had changed. She talked now. She talked in the tough rhythms of cheap crime novels. She talked funny talk about giving head, spit or swallow. Men liked the way she talked. They were impressed by the shell of her independence.

She was a virgin no longer. She'd lost that in a rented room in Sarasota when she fucked a boy she didn't love. It had been a relief but she'd left him that night, unable to sleep beside his animal heat and noise. In the rest of those two lost years, it seemed to her that she had disinterestedly fucked half of the men in America. They'd mostly been grateful but it had touched nothing in her. It had been less than exercise. It had been nothing. Anyway, she only really liked alcoholic men. And they liked her. In sympathy with their own poisonings, she started to find comfort in amphetamines and barbiturates. Stoked on benzedrine in the sweaty arms of some bum in a hotel room, she could sometimes feel free of pain. In two years she thought of her father no times.

Then a very bad thing happened. She didn't tell Chuckie what it was. All he needed to know was that a bad thing happened.

Her mother flew to Phoenix and took her home. She spent a month in Miami. She tried to be calm and she tried to be good. But her mother's smile made her face itch. So, without pleasure, she fucked her uncle/stepfather in her old bedroom and then she ran away again.

She rode Greyhounds for near a month. She had everywhere to go and nowhere to stop. There was nothing for her in New York now that her father was dead. She could not go back to Miami. And all the places she'd stopped in the two years after she left home were only motels and dirty rooms to her. So she just rode buses along and across, up and down America.

On a two-day stop in Reno, she asked an old man where she stood on the map she'd bought. He'd looked at it long and then smiled at her sadly. 'Oh, you're not even on this map, honey.'

In a truckers' bar in North Carolina, she tried to pick up the girl who worked behind the bar. Brown-haired, brown-eyed, the girl had served her beers for two hours, her hips twitching without artifice as she walked. Max cornered her in the restroom and pushed her against a wall. The girl had peeled her off like a dirty shirt.

She came to a stop the night she slept in an alley near the bus station in LA. The air was full of big-city noise and she trembled as she slept. There were cries and gunshots. It seemed to her that the whole of this big city was angry. Suddenly tired, she slept till dawn and then boarded a bus to Kansas.

She hadn't seen her grandparents since her father had died. Her father's father had sold all his land but they still lived in their old house sixty miles from Wichita. Her grandfather's straight back had bent from his years in the dirt he owned and he did not mourn its loss.

Her grandparents, Don and Bea, had fought for twenty years. Two decades ago there had been an argument so divisive that they had split their sitting room into two. One side was feminine, brushed and clean. It had furniture, curtains, there was well-swept order and peace. Her uncle's side was greasy and hardly furnished at all, apart from a buggy old armchair beside the fire. The border between the two regions was only visible because of the unwavering margin between the shine of her floorboards and the dull glisten of the accumulated dirt on his. The strange thing was that they never went anywhere without being together. Always separate inside their home, they walked, sat or stood firmly side by side when they confronted the outside world. Speculation was rife about whether their bedroom was divided in a similar way to their living room. It seemed impossible that a couple who could bear each other so little would sleep together.

She stayed there a year. In that year, she talked of her father with her grandparents. In that year her mother visited once to tell her she was getting divorced and remarried to a doctor from San Diego. Max decided to go to college.

Just before she was to leave, Don died. Bea was deranged with grief. When the family came to see Don's body lying in its coffin, she stopped the procession half-way through. She clambered onto the coffin and hunkered over the body like a child, sobbing. The rest of the family were astonished to see these protestations from the woman who'd split the room to get away from her husband. They buried him next day. Bea allowed only one mourner – herself.

Afterwards, she did not change the layout of that divided room. She cleaned her own half and maintained his own portion in its usual disarray. She conceived a particular fondness for Max and it was thus that Max finally saw the bedroom and knew the truth about whether it, too, had been divided so starkly. She sneaked in one day while Bea was sleeping in her armchair.

She was surprised by what she saw. She told no one about the ordinary room with the deep curtains and the one plump double bed.

She went to UCLA a month later.

It felt like two years of summertime. She sat reading on lawns. She smelt the fragrance her friends brought with them. She talked politics. She talked school.

She fell in love with her philosophy professor. He was a handsome, untidy young man who smoked secret cigarettes in his office. Half the girls and a quarter of the boys on the humanities campus wanted to fuck him. Some had tried and so far all had failed. His smile was as crumpled as his suit and there was something generously ill-fitting about him in general.

One day she saw him in the coffee bar with a couple of young children. Max's heart sank a little to see him married. She joined their table. The young professor was gracious and friendly as always. He introduced her to his children. Married or not, he was made more beautiful by the children crawling over him. She understood why his suits were always crumpled.

Max made cutesy with the kids. She found out their ages. She asked them about their favourite toys and television shows. In a calculated moment, she praised the beauty of the little girl and asked her if her mother had made the ribbons in her hair.

The young professor's smile tightened. The little boy stopped his play and the little girl frowned.

'We don't have a mom.'

The young professor swallowed and spoke to her in a low, level voice, the kind of voice to which children did not listen. 'I'm a widower. Their mother died in a car crash a year ago.'

They talked there for an hour. At one point he excused himself to go to the bathroom. The little girl took the opportunity to tell Max that her mother was gone and her daddy looked after them and how sometimes their daddy's face was sad when he looked at them and how sometimes he cried when he was putting them to bed at night.

The young professor returned and took the child on his knee once more. He whispered something lumpy to her and kissed her soft cheek. He looked at Max, at the mist of her eyes and his smile was gracious. 'Ah, has Alice been telling you sentimental stories about me?' he asked, gently amused. 'She thinks it will make people fall in love with me.'

The little girl was right. There was a month of moves at him. He was unfailingly polite, unfailingly busy with something else. Some other girls told her she was wasting her time. The young professor didn't sleep with his students. If they had failed, Max had no chance.

But there was a night after a late lecture when it rained. She had walked from the theatre with him and they had shared her small umbrella, which kept neither of them dry. They talked under there, the umbrella keeping them close. She had wished it was smaller yet.

The young professor had given her a ride home that night. When he pulled up, she knew by the rigidness of his neck as they parted that he had considered the possibility of feeling something for her. It was easy from there.

Within a month they were spending most nights with each other. She was astonished by the heat of his desire and the wildness of his remorse. She had never met a man who didn't want to. It made her want to very much. And, afterwards, as the young professor lay, naked and grieving for his dead wife, her eyes were full of his flesh.

When he lectured, she marvelled at how her fellow students listened. She flushed with pride to hear him talk. The low red of the evening sun through the windows would make his hair shine like memory and she would want to take him publicly where he stood.

And when he touched her, his touch was courteous, his kiss gentle. He seemed to have a remnant of the manhood her father had possessed, a tender, fightless thing.

Everything in her changed. For both of them she began to believe in a time soon to come. A time when they could forget the damaged process of their lives and be married.

The young professor's children loved her and she was warm with them. But she noticed a stiffness in his face when she touched them. She could tell when he was thinking of his dead wife and she would ask him about her. She asked him about her clothes, about her habits, her tastes so that she could avoid doing anything that reminded him of her. Sometimes, she would find photographs of the dead woman and would feel unpardonable jealousy.

And when they argued, she cried bitterly and hated his wife and said cruel things. It was easy to love the dead, the silent, forgivable dead. He was angry when she talked of his wife.

Her grandmother died. She blew her brains out with Don's old rat-rifle. The young professor was gentle with her while she arranged to fly back to Kansas. There, her mother cried in her arms and was sorry for all the things she could not remember. They buried her grandmother beside her husband. Bea had left Max most of the money she'd had. It was over a million dollars. Max's mother cried again. She was already rich but Max's legacy wounded her.

She spent two weeks in Kansas, clearing up the crazy old house. When she returned to the West Coast she went to the young professor. It was a weekend. He was with his children. They greeted her like a stranger. They had retrieved the world they'd had before her arrival, the world centred on the unspoken, unseen presence of the dead wife and mother. Later, when he put the children to bed, he lingered with them for an hour and more.

That night she fucked him like a whore, like he was a whore. She mauled and moulded his flesh in her hands. Then, when he started to cry, she got up and packed a bag. Before she left she took a picture of his dead wife from the drawer in which she knew it lay. She stood at the foot of his bed, while he sobbed, and threw the photograph onto the empty space she'd left on the pillow.

As she had always done, Max ran away. She flew to San Diego and fought with her mother within an hour. She flew straight back to LA. She packed some bags and boarded a plane for New York. It used to be she would run away by bus. Now, with her grandfather's money, her flights were properly airborne.

In La Guardia, she telephoned her mother, she telephoned the young professor. Neither gave her a reason to come back. She wept briefly.

And then she left America.

She flew club class New York to London. JFK to Heathrow. It had been two airborne and airport days. LA to San Diego. San Diego to LA. LA to New York. New York to London. The plastic airports had seemed more substantial than the cities themselves on the flightsome night.

She was going to Paris. Her father had spent a year there before his marriage. He had always talked about how beautiful it was, how happy he had been.

At Heathrow, she grabbed her bags and wheeled her trolley to a stand-up coffee bar. Numbly, she drank her feeble drink. London looked like New York – at least, the airport did. The men were shorter and their teeth were bad but everything else was much of a muchness. She hoped Paris would be better.

She wheeled her trolley to the Air France desk. A viciously pretty British woman dressed in multiple nylons asked if she could help.

'Yeah, gimme a ticket to Paris.'

The woman's smile twitched briefly. 'What kind of ticket, madam?'

'A plane ticket, honey. Like I'd ask you for a bus ticket.'

Her smile flattened completely and disappeared. 'My name is Helen, I don't answer to Honey.'

'Fuck it,' said Max. She walked away.

She spent six motiveless hours sitting on her bags, numbly avoiding an alternative destination. Paris was a city she had sought without much reason. It hadn't worked out. She would have to go somewhere else. It didn't really matter where. She looked up at a departure screen and saw the word that made up her mind:

BELFAST

She stepped off the plane at Aldergrove. Sticky drizzle immediately coated her hot face. This had been the first time that she had been in the exterior of any place for the previous two transitional days.

She stepped through the airport nervously. She knew it would be OK if she managed to walk past the spot where her father had been murdered. She remembered the place well from the television reports. It had looked to her like all the places she would never know. Her heart was hot and rapid but she walked on bravely. She passed it without trauma. She was almost disappointed.

She took a squat bus to Belfast. There she disembarked and waited. Trolleyless, laden with bags, she couldn't think of what to do. Her travelling had lost its energy. She felt heavy and motionless. She simply sat on the pile of her bags once more.

She lit a cigarette and pulled her collar tighter round her neck. She was breathless with the strangeness of this new town, with all its sticky cold and its planetary fame. It was like walking into a cowboy film. There was an open rank of blue and white buses with mysterious names all rolled above their windshields: Enniskillen, Dungannon, Omagh, L'derry. There was an unreality in this, an unlikelihood that pleased her.

That night she sat on a broken chair and stared out of the uncurtained window of the room she had rented. The window looked out to a road on which people congregated on the warm evening. A shop was still open and groups of women chatted outside its bright window. Across the road she saw two small queues for a cinema. The queues made her unaccountably happy. She watched as they grew and then shrank to nothing and it was quite, quite dark. She did not feel alone.

It pleased her that her life could be so random. The passage from Los Angeles to this obscure Belfast street had been entirely without volition. Unfortunate glances, involuntary decisions, chance conversations. It seemed a suitable way to move herself around the planet.

That night she slept deep and true . . .

When she had finished all her talking, all her story, Max looked down at Chuckie. He lay beached on the bed, the meagre sheet drawn around him. There was a look on his face she had not seen before; a warmth for him flickered in her belly. She hadn't talked so hard in years. She wondered what it was about this dumb, fat guy that had produced all this narrative in her. She smiled. He had done an admirable amount of listening. There were depths to chubby Chuck. Looking down at his lap, she saw the rim of his erection against the sheet. She was surprised but not upset. She laughed. 'Hey, Chuck. Have I been turning you on?'

He looked up at her and paused. His face was pale with the strain of new emotions, unplumbed depths. His eyes were moist with love.

'How much is a million dollars in sterling?' he asked.

Seven

Later that week, Chuckie Lurgan walked a street for the first time in his life, new in the thought that he loved her. This was absolutely it. When he wasn't with her, he thought of her; when he wasn't with her he wanted to see her, hear her; all for reasons he could never satisfactorily explain. He needed her like you might need a drink or a cigarette. When he saw her, they didn't have to do anything special for it to be special. They didn't have to make love, they didn't have to go out. An hour of sitting side by side with her in silence was somehow magically different from the same experience without her. At one point, she told him that she had met Clint Eastwood. Chuckie, starfucker, fameseeker, forgot to get excited. He just looked at her mouth while it moved. Chuckie was worried.

Aoirghe had come back from Dublin and Chuckie had not cared. The last six days had been a series of evenings spent in their flat with Max climbing all over his bibulous form. The night before, even the neighbours had complained, so noisy had been their glee. In all the smutty roll of Chuckie's copulatory history, amongst the countless couplings and ruts, this had counted high.

But adipose Chuckie knew that it was all wrong. Fat Lurgan

knew that he didn't deserve her. Ugly Chuck was conscious of an imbalance. He wondered what arcane satisfaction the beautiful and intelligent Max drew from his company. Chuckie had the sense and grace to know that he was a chump. It worried him that he was getting this unchumply girl.

And all this chump-free money.

For Chuckie now found himself rich. He looked at the statements of his four bank accounts and found a total of £272,645 there. It seemed like an awful lot of pounds.

It lent him ballast as he walked from Eureka Street to Bedford Street. He had returned home that morning as though from a holiday. His mother wasn't there and he had picked up his stuff and headed out. It was an unshiny, pleasant day. He looked at the sky with a proprietorial air. The sky was albino. The sky looked like eggs to him. Two hundred and seventy-two thousand, six hundred and forty-five pounds. He walked down Great Victoria Street, mumbling the lyrics of a cheap love song. He felt what he could only call tremendous, enlarged, a bigger man.

Basking under the double shine of topmost admiration, Chuckie Lurgan walked through the glass doors of Patterson's, the Mercedes People. His dream was coming true. He was about to buy his big, expensive car. He was about to buy a car too big to park.

'Can I help you, sir?'

The pristine young woman's tone was just uncertain enough and the 'sir' faltering enough to be insulting. Chuckie's suit was good but he knew that his face still did not convince. He looked at her tight skirt and her trim heels. He looked at her pretty, prissy face and grinned. 'Yeah, I wanna buy a car.' He stared at her. He fingered his cuffs. He smiled in her face. 'Fuck it, maybe I'll buy two.'

Forty minutes later, Chuckie sat thoughtfully in the corner of the glossy showroom. He looked around him vacantly. Even the sunshine in there looked like it earned good money. The leather in his chair squeaked prosperously as he shifted but, under Chuckie's big ass, it sounded furtive.

The salesmen were doing some paperwork on his behalf. As he glanced around the big shiny cars – so strange, so beautiful indoors – he could scarcely remember which one he had selected. The tanned toothy men had taken some time to treat his intentions seriously. Like the girl at reception, they had figured him for a dreamer, a fantasist coming in to look at stuff he couldn't afford. When he had made his choice and announced his desire to write a cheque on the spot, one of them had openly snorted in disbelief. When he had given them his yob address, they had frowned and bristled, almost ready to eject this overdressed proletarian timewaster.

But when he had given them one of his account numbers and they had called his bank, everything had changed. The men's smiles became extraordinarily elastic. One of them told the receptionist to get Chuckie some coffee, that was, if Mr Lurgan wouldn't prefer a glass of wine. When the insolent girl had returned with his coffee, she gave Chuckie a look of such melting sexual intention that he suspected he might have wangled a blowjob without too much trouble.

When his newly acquired mobile phone had rung and he had blushingly fished it out of his wallet pocket, they had been even more impressed. It had only been Max calling him to tell him some of the things she would do to his genitals that night. At his end, Chuckie had persisted in trying to make it sound like a business call. Max, delighted by this subterfuge, had become more obscene. 'Yeah,' said Chuckie hilariously, 'give me a report on that. Send me some figures.' It was an entirely wasted effort since both salesmen and receptionist had clearly heard a woman's voice bellow, 'I'm gonna fuck you till you scream,' before Chuckie got off the line.

He should have been delighted as he waited there while they clucked, their faces filled with his reflected cash-heavy grandeur, but he was merely depressed. Their initial reactions had caused him too much shame. They had dented him. The subsequent obsequiousness held no charm. Without the actual proof of all those pounds, he didn't look, feel or smell like a wealthy man. He was all wrong. These people knew money. They knew he was all wrong.

For no easily detectable reason, his life had become spectacular, thrilling. He was rich. He was successful. He was in love with a beautiful girl. He was Chuckie Lurgan.

He panicked.

Without doing any work, without producing anything, he had amassed all that money and had the promise of nearly as much again every month for the next five months. It was dreadful. It was frightening.

Chuckie knew that something bad was going to happen. He would be found out. The world would come to its senses and take back all those pounds it had given him. Justice required it. Likelihood dictated it.

Meanwhile, the besuited salesmen had clustered round him again. They were eager to amuse and please.

'Well, Mr Lurgan. She's ready for you now.'

'Who?'

The men laughed indulgently. At the reception desk, the sharp girl laughed too, although she could have heard nothing of what was said.

'Your X series.'

Chuckie looked vacantly at the man's broad, straining face.

'Your car, Mr Lurgan, the one you've just bought.'

'Yeah, right enough.'

The men looked genuinely impressed by Chuckie's patently unfeigned abstraction. A man who could absent-mindedly pay cash for a Mercedes was the kind of man they dreamt of, about whom they masturbated. The receptionist's eyes flashed at him.

They led him out the back way to a side-street where his new car was parked. It was blue, shiny and very big.

'It's taxed for eight months and we took the liberty of calling our insurance company. They've covered it in the meantime and they'll be sending you their literature over the next few days.' The man smiled, his voice was heavy with significance, with drama. 'She's all yours. You can take her away.'

After an emotional farewell, Chuckie opened the door and sat in his glittering new purchase. The salesmen still lingered on the pavement, obviously intending some valedictory waves as he drove off. Chuckie sat mutely looking at the sleek dashboard. Chuckie did not know how to drive.

He pushed a button. The passenger window slid into the door with a marvellous electric hiss.

'Listen,' he called out to the salesmen, 'you go on in. I just want to be alone here for a while.'

The men both nodded their complete understanding – Chuckie could have sworn that they had lumps in their throats – and went inside. He paused. Then he started the engine.

By some quirk of town planning (typical of Belfast's most unpaternal City Fathers), the monotonous ghetto in which Chuckie lived was only about eleven hundred yards away from the car saleroom. Belfast low-income areas often pressed ass to ass with its more prosperous slivers. Admittedly complicated and lengthened by a series of complex one-way streets, it was still impressive that it took Chuckie twenty-five minutes to drive the eleven hundred yards back to Eureka Street.

By the time he had pulled up near his house, he felt confident that he could master most of the difficulties that driving presented. Unable to park the monstrous machine, he abandoned it in the middle of the road, vaguely close to No. 42. He got out. He stood on the pavement. He looked at his car.

It was Austrian or Bavarian or something. He liked that. He had to admit that it looked pretty Nazi, wallowing hugely there in the middle of the dwarf terraces, a car that cost more than most of those houses put together. Parked on Eureka Street, it looked extraordinary, freakish. It looked like the miracle of money.

Some of the kids who lived on the street had come out of

their houses at the advent of the monster motor. They obviously expected John Long or some such plutocrat. When they saw Chuckie emerge, their jaws dropped and their eyes bulged. Some of the mothers came out too. They drew their children back with expressions of fear and bewilderment on their faces.

Blissfully, Chuckie beckoned one of the Eureka Street ten-year-olds. The boy approached uncertainly. Chuckie smiled patronizingly. He held up a five-pound note.

'Here, son. Keep an eye on the wagon, would you?' He gave the boy the money and walked to his own front door, a faint ripple of stunned applause breaking over his shoulders. He hoped it was not excessively childish of him to enjoy this moment. He had lived a long time on Eureka Street, chiefly remarkable for his girth and his Catholic acquaintance. He had earned the right to make this splash. He had earned the right to enjoy.

Inside, he found his mother staring through her front-room windows at the massive car that bisected her street. The small boy was now sitting squarely on its expensive bonnet.

He had not seen her for a week. He had been sleeping over at Max's flat and that morning, when he had returned home, she had been out. It was only when he saw the ghost of himself reflected in her grey eyes that he understood how far he'd come, how much had happened.

His mother lifted her hand towards him in a weak and untypically Irish action. Her face was full of fear and pain. 'What's happened, Chuckie?' she breathed. 'What's going on?'

Chuckie felt congested, he felt a traffic jam in his heart. His fearful week, terrifying month welled up in him. His face heated and crumpled. He felt tears prick at the backs of his eyes.

'Oh, Ma,' he said anxiously. 'I'm fucked if I know.'

Peggy Lurgan understood Chuckie Lurgan as no one could. As no one really wanted to. Flesh of her flesh, she knew the extent of his limitless proletarian shame and fear. She knew how this small city in which they lived could expand or contract at will, leaving them feeling claustrophobic or agoraphobic as paranoid circumstance demanded. As she had aged, her own life had constricted chokingly to its present confines. She lived in a tiny house on a little street with a fat son who didn't talk to her. She only slept with chemicals. Ten years of nitrazepam had warmed her life and made it more than the sum of its parts. But she knew her life was a small, small thing. She had been terrified when Chuckie had started to change. She had been relying on an unaltering, unalterable future. Futile, tedious but gladly unsurprising. Her son's mutations threatened her precarious equilibrium and she needed to know what was worth that risk.

But even after Chuckie had told her about all the money he had made, she was still unsure of how he had done it, not realizing that so was he. But she fully sympathized with his naked panic and terror, the feeling that, soon, the police would come to arrest him. She hoped that it would be only the police.

The weeks since Chuckie's big idea had passed bewilderingly for her. She was confused by her son's sudden suits, the mysterious international phone calls and the glistening fax machine in her scullery.

Chuckie tried to explain things to her. He tried to explain the ease of raising money. He saw the blankness of her look. He kissed her sweetly on the cheek. Which was going too far for Peggy. Which, for her, was much too much to take.

'Cut that out, Chuckie,' she snapped. 'Just cut that out.'

He asked her what was wrong.

'You've changed, son. Something terrible has happened to you.' Her eyes filled with tears. 'When did you get to be so nice?'

Half past eight the next night, Chuckie sat in the Wigwam on Lower Crescent. The boys were there: Jake, Slat, Donal and Septic Ted. He had called them all an hour ago. Telling Max that he had to see the boys after so long, he had slipped brokenly out of her flat. Eight o'clock and she'd boffed him twice already. The day before, Chuckie had noticed that, for the first time in his adult life, he had lost some weight. Four pounds gone. With Max around, he suspected he'd be on vitamin boosts and meal supplements before too long. He was managing the idea of himself rich and horny but the notion of a skinny Chuckie might be too much for anyone to bear.

The Wigwam was a theme café near the university. Bad food and good coffee. Small groups of attractive, intelligent young women seemed to dine there regularly. Naturally, Septic Ted had discovered the place a month before and had been, more or less, camped out there since.

'What do you fancy, Chuckie?' he asked, with a proprietorial air.

Small, dark-haired women with big hips, thought Chuckie. But a waitress glided up and prevented the comment. Septic Ted bristled up and ran his fingers through his hair, which was too short to be significantly altered by the process. Jake gave the waitress his order, Deasely told her what he wanted and Septic confessed his desires. She turned to Chuckie.

'What would you like?'

'What's nice?'

'The chicken's good.'

Chuckie smiled dismissively. 'I'm sorry,' he said. 'I don't eat anything beginning with the letter C.'

The waitress blanked this completely but the boys were delighted.

'Nothing at all?' queried Donal.

'Nah,' replied Chuckie. 'Courgettes, cabbage, cauliflower, carrots, celery, cucumber, celeriac, Cos, cheese, coffee, cereals, chicken, candy, crackerbreads of any type. I wouldn't touch any of those bastards.'

'What about . . . ?' Septic Ted pronounced a coarse synonym for female pudenda.

The waitress didn't bother to blush.

'You're a charmer, Septic,' said Jake.

'What's the fish?' asked Chuckie.

'You wouldn't like it,' said the waitress.

'Cod?'

'Yup.'

'OK, gimme a salad but can I have extra chemicals in that? If it doesn't come wrapped in plastic, I don't eat it.'

The waitress sidled off, uncharmed.

Jake gave Septic some lip about sleazing the waitress.

'Relax,' retorted Septic. 'From what Chuckie tells me, you've a bit of a weakness for the serving classes yourself.'

'Blow it out your ass.'

'Witty.'

Chuckie smiled fraternally upon his friends, bickering and unbickering. He felt better with them. Somehow, the panic and strangeness of his new success was rendered harmless by their presence.

He was closest to Jake but fond of the other three to varying degrees. Slat Sloane was the only socialist that Chuckie knew. He was a lawyer who worked for city community groups and charities. He was better educated than anyone Chuckie had ever met and probably earned less money than the waitress here. He was big on dignity and contribution. Chuckie suspected that Slat just wanted to be Swedish. He'd been in Sweden a couple of times and it seemed to have made a lasting impression. Jake had told him that Slat had not bought his own toilet roll in the ten years since he'd left home. Slat did his own ironing, cooking and cleaning but he was just too fastidious to buy toilet roll. Apparently he didn't want the check-out girls in supermarkets to suspect that he defecated. His mother bought it for him. Slat never had any girlfriends.

Donal Deasely worked for the Government. He dished out all the money that flooded in from the European Community, the International Fund for Ireland and all the other pass-the-hat agencies the Irish loved so. Deasely earned quite a lot of money and spent most of it on fashionable clothes, haircuts and obscure books about science and medicine. He was always reading about something new – cancer, genetics, thermodynamics, prime numbers or swanky astronomy. That's why he'd bought all the clothes and haircuts. He said he really wanted to be a *himbo*. Donal never had any girlfriends either.

Septic Ted had plenty of girlfriends. Septic Ted had too many girlfriends. Septic Ted sold insurance so his erotic success was that bit easier to bear.

'Guess who I saw today,' Donal challenged.

'Marilyn Monroe,' suggested Chuckie.

'Fyodor Dostoevsky,' said Slat.

'Spiderman?' hinted Septic.

'Nah, Ripley Bogle.'

'Who?' asked Chuckie.

'A guy we were all at school with,' explained Slat. 'He was some kind of tramp or something but he went away to England. Cambridge, I think. Haven't heard of him for years. Smart guy.'

'A tosspot,' said Septic.

Then Chuckie remembered their stories of this man – the boy who slept rough in the grounds of Belfast Castle through the last of his unElysian schooldays. Apparently Jake had met him once in London where he had been homeless also. Bogle had told him that he had spent a night sleeping in the *Blue Peter* garden. Jake had considered this a class act.

'Where'd you see him?' asked Jake.

Donal became unsure. 'I think it was him. I saw some bum down near the City Hall. He was reciting Mallarmé in French for fifty p a go.'

'That's him,' said Slat.

'He's a bum again?' asked Chuckie.

'He was made to be a bum,' said Septic. 'A bum from a bum family. Somebody told me his ma used to work the docks for brown money.'

'Brown money?'

'Coppers – loose change.'

'Fuck, Septic,' bellowed Chuckie. 'Brown money – you make this stuff up.'

'Nah, traditional Irish rhyming slang – doesn't rhyme.'

There was some faint guffawing; the five men made their stab at bonhomie. Chuckie was fond of his friends. He was the only Protestant there and still, after ten years and more, that felt like a proud claim, a distinguished thing. When he was seventeen Chuckie had been beaten up for these people.

They'd been friends on and off for twelve or thirteen years. They had mostly gone away and come back. Slat had gone to England to read law at Manchester. He had come back and started fighting fights for the deracinated proles of his hometown. Deasely, bizarrely Francophile, bizarrely polyglot, had lived in Bayeux for a couple of years, then Bremen, then Barcelona. He too had come home. Septic had worked a couple of North Sea rigs and lived in Scotland for a few years. He had come back. Jake had truly disappeared. He had gone to America and no one thought they would ever see him again but he had left America for university in London and had come back eventually. Chuckie? Eureka Street to Eureka Street, Chuckie had never left. They'd gone away, they'd come back. It used to be that Northern Ireland's diaspora was permanent, poor denuded Ireland. But everyone had started coming back. *Everyone* was returning.

Girls, too, had come and gone in their lives but there they still were, still together, still doing the old stuff. They had history. Mostly a history of wasting their time in each other's houses when their parents were away, bogus sophisticates, drinking instant coffee and discussing platonic love.

The waitress brought their drinks. No one commented on Chuckie's ostentatiously alcohol-free mineral water.

'*Salut.*'

'*Prost.*'

'*Slainte.*'

'Beat it down ya.'

They sucked their drinks with ceremony.

'Heads down!' hissed Deasely. 'There's Tick.'

All five started examining their fingernails, coughing into their chests, tying their laces.

'Where is he?' asked Slat.

'Up at the front by the till.'

They looked round furtively. An old tramp had come into the café. In the distance, he could be seen hassling the waitress for money. They were all, except Chuckie, vaguely fond of Tick. They had named him so when he had told them proudly that he was the only Northern Irish indigent ever to have been fitted with a pacemaker. Several medical research bodies had (in print) declared that Tick could not actually exist, that the success of such a procedure was not compatible with Tick's high-octane lifestyle. But Chuckie dreaded him. Tick reminded Chuckie of his father. Tick had always reminded him of his father. In the seven or eight years since Chuckie had first encountered Tick, he must have dished out about six or seven hundred pounds to the old *clochard*. On Chuckie's then limited resources, this had been a strain. But whenever he saw the guy, he couldn't help but think of his father. He couldn't help but dip his hand.

Septic tittered. 'Haven't seen him in a while. He looks pretty shit.'

'He's never dazzled exactly,' said Jake.

'Uh-oh, here he comes.' Deasely blatantly ducked under the table.

'What's the bets it's the Kennedy one?' hazarded Septic.

'A fiver says it's not,' rumbled Deasely, from under the table.

'You're on,' said Septic.

They were referring to Tick's spiel. Chuckie used to think it was charming that Tick had a spiel. None of the other pissed old farts around town bothered much with such finesse. But Tick had dozens of spiels. Propping up the downstairs bar in Lavery's, he used to tell the gullible that he was an out-of-luck songwriter who had written most of Elvis's hits. He charged 10p for a joke. He did 'Guess Your Star Sign'. He sang a crackly chested version of the 'Fields of Athenry' until people gave him pounds to go away. He had even earned good money for a couple of years down the markets by eating fleas for bets.

'Gentlemen!' he barked thickly. He looked penetratingly at Jake. Septic mouthed the words as Tick spoke. 'Where were you when Kennedy died?'

'I was being conceived in a cheap rut in a damp alley off the Donegall Road,' replied Jake.

'Son!' cried Tick, as he never failed to do.

'Father!' wept Jake, as he always did.

It was an ancient exchange, oft-repeated, much-loved. The second time it had happened, Jake had even embraced Tick extravagantly. Tick's almost visible stink had prevented a repetition of that particular move.

'My five pounds, please,' said Septic.

As he looked at the old tramp, Chuckie saw that Septic was right. Tick looked dreadful. Dirt and sweat marked out the craquelure of his ancient face and the whites of his eyes were completely unwhite. He looked like a Rembrandt. He looked hundreds of years old.

'Hey, Tick,' asked Septic, 'what are you drinking these days? Furniture polish? Windolene? Toilet cleaner?'

'Cut it out, Septic,' warned Deasely.

Tick stared hard at all their faces. Touchingly, he recognized them. 'Ah well, fuck the health advice, lads. Just gimme some money. I'm gasping.'

A man approached from behind him and laid a hand on his shoulder. Tick swivelled round to face him.

'Right now, leave my customers alone and be off with you.'

'Eat my bollocks,' suggested Tick.

The manager grabbed him two-handed and started shoving him. There was a chorus of protest from Chuckie and his friends. Jake stood up silently and laid a firm hand on one of the manager's arms. The man stopped and looked uncertain.

'He's our guest,' said Chuckie.

'He's that man's father,' said Septic, pointing out the silent, grim-faced Jake.

Tick smiled beatifically at the man. He gestured at Jake. 'Can't you see the family resemblance?'

'Don't push it, Tick,' warned Jake.

The manager gave up. All the firmness fled and he looked uneasily around for an exit.

'We'll take care of it, thank you very much,' said Jake.

The man walked away, just slowly enough to be dignified.

Tick licked his lips and spoke. 'Did I ever tell you boys that I wrote "Jailhouse Rock"?'

They all laughed.

'Fuck's sake, Tick,' said Septic. 'Remember who you're talking to.'

'How much money do we have to give you to make you go away and leave these people alone?' asked Jake.

Tick, entirely unoffended, adopted his business expression. He frowned, calculated, did a brief headcount of their table and smiled. 'Five of you at a pound each is not, I think, unfair.'

'That's extortionate,' complained Deasely.

'But you know how unpleasant I can be,' Tick explained simply.

'There's a point,' said Slat.

Chuckie stood up. 'I'll sort him out,' he explained hurriedly. He shepherded Tick out of the café. Once on the pavement, Tick, suspecting he was about to be deprived of a multiple contribution, complained so loudly that he could still be heard clearly inside the café. The other boys saw Chuckie give the old tramp something that reduced him to silence. They could have sworn that they saw Tick briefly lose consciousness. When Chuckie came back one of the others asked him how much he'd given Tick. Chuckie lied.

They drank their drinks. They talked about Chuckie's girl.

They talked about Chuckie's money. They talked about Chuckie. His friends cajoled him affectionately. Chuckie knew that he should have loved it, that this praise from his friends might have been something that he valued, but his recent sense of unease had returned. Tick had made him feel uncomfortable.

Septic's head was swivelling monotonously, like a bodyguard beside a president. Chuckie looked around the café and saw the various tables of women that Septic was 'scoping'. Septic Ted was obsessed with sex. He was marvellously adept at getting it. He had made his discovery when only seventeen or eighteen. Septic just pratted about whenever there were any girls around. He knocked things over, he stumbled, he wore unfashionable clothes and blushed when he said stupid things. He got a bad haircut. Most of all, with thrilling success, he told girls he was crap in bed, useless, embarrassing.

It always worked. His friends suffered a tortuous form of collective amazement to see the lines of girls lie on the pavement before him, begging, moist, absolutely, completely seduced.

Stirred by Septic Ted's massive turnover, Chuckie had tried this line a few times himself. Unfortunately, when Chuckie told girls that he was crap in bed, they believed him. But for a decade the line had continued to work for Septic Ted. Chuckie had to hand it to Septic. Everybody else did.

The only hitch Septic ever faced was when girls asked him why his male friends called him Septic. He always told the truth. Only some of them liked it.

(Septic, more properly Edward Gubbins, had been so named when he was fifteen years old. An inveterate and publicity-seeking masturbator, Septic had delighted in giving his school-friends updates every day on the progress of his campaign of self-abuse. He told them of new record diurnal aggregates, new fantasies, new techniques. Towards the end, he started experimenting by including a variety of moistures in his onanistic efforts. He robbed his mother's make-up bags and bathroom cabinets of a mélange of ointments and unguents. Next day, he would pass lordly verdicts on the qualities of Nivea, Pond's, and Vaseline. But one fateful night Septic had absent-mindedly swiped a tube of Immac hair-removal cream from one of his mother's drawers. Blithely, he spread the astringent substance over his eager penis.

It had taken ten or twelve seconds to really make itself felt. Septic always refused to talk about those following moments, but over the next few days, he was happy to appal his school-friends with brief flashes of his mutilated organ. Several boys fainted at the sight. Looking so like a mutant raspberry, a nuked strawberry, it had only been a matter of days before Edward Gubbins had become Septic Ted.)

'I'm in love,' groaned Septic.

The others looked where he had been looking. A few feet away there was a table of three women. Mid to late twenties. All attractive.

'Which one?' asked Slat foolishly.

'Fuck. All of them.'

'One of them is Janine Stewart. Isn't that Janine?' Deasely was excited.

Slat looked closer. 'God, yes. It is.' He paled. 'I used to go out with her.'

'Yeah, I remember,' said Septic. 'Father's girl. Gorgeous but legs like something off a cheap chicken.'

'That's the one.'

'When was the last time you saw her?' asked Jake.

'Jesus.' Slat smiled uneasily. The others knew that he was a little strange about sex. A little too discreet. Slat would have claimed that this was just his rigorously correct political attitude to women but the others suspected something more. 'I haven't seen her for five or six years. Someone told me that she's gay now.'

Septic sputtered in his glass. 'Christ! Janine Stewart a dyke. That's criminal.'

Slat looked at her. 'She's still lovely,' he murmured.

Amongst this little group of men there was something

unconvincing in the casual way they talked about women. Chuckie had watched it become less brutal over the years but there was still a cavalier dash to it that was hard to believe. Chuckie, now Max-happy, suspected that each went home and thought differently and thought tenderly, each suspected that the others did the same but when together there was always that air of raillery, of musketeerish bombast.

Jake stood up and excused himself, heading for the toilets. Septic followed him with his eyes. He was still a little bruised by his ticking off in front of the waitress.

'What's wrong with him?' he asked.

'Maybe it's Sarah,' suggested Slat kindly.

'Ancient history,' said Chuckie.

'What about the waitress you told me about?' asked Septic.

'Nah, she dumped him.'

'Poor old Jake,' laughed Septic, 'he's always been more dumped upon than dumping.'

Deasely had been silent. He spoke now with some authority. 'I know what's wrong with him.' Furtively, he fished in his inside pocket. He pulled out a copy of the *Belfast News Letter* free sheet, a soundly Protestant newspaper that had been printing soundly Protestant news for two hundred and fifty years. He passed it to Chuckie. 'Read that.'

Chuckie read the headline:

SECRETARY OF STATE MAKES STATEMENT ON OTG

Yesterday the Secretary of State for Northern Ireland, Ronald Moncur, voiced his concerns about the possible emergence of a new terrorist force in Northern Ireland.

'We have no definite information about who this new group might be or what the letters OTG even stand for. The police and the security forces are treating the matter with utmost seriousness. It could all be a harmless prank but we will monitor the situation. Anyone with information about this matter should telephone the confidential telephone number and assist the police with their enquiries.'

'What's this got to do with Jake?' asked Chuckie, mystified.

'What do you mean?' asked Deasely. He looked at the paper. 'No, no,' he said impatiently. 'Underneath. Read that.'

Chuckie read:

> Republican agitators have accused the RUC of conducting a campaign of police brutality against a South Belfast man. The accusations concern Jake Jackson, a 29-year-old debt counsellor and Roman Catholic. Allegedly, Mr Jackson was seriously assaulted earlier this month by a number of uniformed but off-duty police officers who broke into his home in the early hours of the morning. Sources claimed that Mr Jackson's injuries were serious and that he is currently too frightened to talk to the press.
>
> Security spokesman for the Just Us party said:
>
> 'This is a typical breach of human rights by the parliamentary forces of the British Crown. The Catholic community has historically been subjected to just these kinds of abuses. Just Us has been accused of being the political wing of the IRA. With this incident we can see again that the Royal Ulster Constabulary is merely a semi-legal group of Loyalist vigilantes. This young man is obviously too disturbed to come forward. Just Us extends its protection to Mr Jackson.'
>
> The RUC said last night that they were aware of no such incident and had received no complaints from any member of the public. Despite this,

> Amnesty International have said that they will be setting up an investigation. Mr Jackson was last night unavailable for comment.

'Shit,' said Chuckie. He passed the paper round to the intrigued others.

Jake came back from the bathroom. 'I hate that,' he announced.

'What?' said Chuckie nervously.

'Ungrammatical toilet signs. Male and Female Toilets, it says in there.'

The others were still reading the newspaper.

'So?' Chuckie persisted.

'Male and Female Toilets? Should we expect that one type is taller and hairier than the other?'

The waitress came and slapped some cutlery down on their table. Jake glanced at her with helpless admiration. Chuckie tried to think of something to say.

But Septic Ted read too quickly. 'Hey,' he said, 'can I have your autograph?'

Chuckie blushed.

'What are you talking about?' Jake snapped.

Septic Ted passed the paper over to Jake. Jake glanced at the story and his jaw tightened. The waitress looked on with new interest and even craned her head to try to read the paper.

'Thank you,' said Chuckie, 'that'll be fine.'

She moved off sulkily.

'You're famous, man,' said Septic.

'It's not funny,' said Jake.

'Is this because of . . . ?' Chuckie dried up.

Jake looked at him unkindly. 'Aoirghe?'

'Yes.'

'What do you think?'

There was an uncomfortable pause. Septic smiled. 'Look at the waitresses,' he said.

They all looked round towards the till. They could see that their waitress was telling the other girls about Jake. She had a copy of the *News Letter* and they were all reading the offending story. Jake groaned.

'Don't knock it,' said Septic. 'You might score some freedom-fighting pussy.'

'Give it a rest, Septic,' chided Chuckie.

'Who's Aoirghe?' asked Slat.

Chuckie gulped. 'She's Max's flatmate. Jake and she met through me.' He glanced at Jake's black-hat features. 'They didn't really hit it off.'

'So what has she got to do with this story?' asked Deasely.

Chuckie smiled eyelessly. 'It's a long story,' he said. He started telling them about it.

Two minutes in, the waitress arrived at their table with the food they had ordered. She delivered their meals in two trips. Second time around, she inclined her head and gave them a muttered and insincere, 'Enjoy your meal.' Then something strange happened. She bent close to Jake and looked intently, piercingly into his face. Chuckie leant closer to hear what she would say. To his amazement he heard her say his name. 'Chuckie Lurgan,' she said. 'Chuckie Lurgan.' Then, satisfied, replete, she walked away.

'Did that girl just say my name?' he asked Jake.

They all laughed.

'No, she said . . .' Jake said something that sounded like Chuckie Ar La.

'What?'

'It's Irish for 'our day will come'. It's a nationalist rallying cry.'

'Chuckie Ar La?'

'Yeah, *Tiocfaidh ar La*. It's the slogan of the Just Us party.'

Chuckie's friends looked at each other.

'We never told you, Chuckie, but that's the funny thing about your name, what with you being a Protestant and all.'

'Your name sounds like a supremacist republican slogan.'

'Yeah, it's like a Jewish guy being called *Deutschland über Alles*.'

'It's a laugh.'

They stopped.

He looked at them unhappily. 'Let's eat,' he said.

The rest of the meal had passed mostly without incident. Jake had been mutinous and the supernumerary political attentions of the grumpy waitress did not assist his mood. Tick had astoundingly come back to the café with a bunch of flowers for Chuckie. There had been a big fuss on the door as the manager had tried to refuse him entry and then Chuckie had to do some very imaginative talking when the boys asked him why Tick had brought him flowers. He told them several things, which did not include the fact that he had given Tick eight hundred pounds earlier.

The next day Chuckie had a big lunch meeting. He'd slipped off to London a couple of weeks before to try to find out if he could hide his ill-gotten money in Cayman Island funny banks or discreet Swiss drug-dealer accounts. He had met a fancy financial adviser who had recommended Luke Findlater to him. Findlater was some kind of posh money man who helped companies expand, contract, upsize and downsize. Chuckie, Protestant Belfast, had imagined that he was just some guy who sacked working-class people but his adviser told him that he had other skills.

Amazingly, said the adviser, Findlater lived in Northern Ireland. He still worked all over the financial world but he chose to live in the wilds of Ulster. Chuckie considered being offended by the man's surprise at this decision. He told Chuckie he would get Findlater on his case when Chuckie returned to Belfast. Chuckie paid the man twelve hundred pounds for telling him that someone else would do the work.

As he prepared to meet this man, Chuckie was nervous. Englishmen always made him feel below-stairs. Most of the Englishmen he had met had been working-class Northerners with berets and automatic weapons but, like many people, he still clung to a notion of Englishness based on Kenneth More in old war movies.

It sounded as though Findlater was a representative of this breed. Chuckie's adviser had told him that Findlater was an aristocrat, a baronet's son or something like that. Chuckie put on his suit and unwrapped a new shirt. With an imperfect understanding of the old-school-tie business, he even put on the orange and blue striped tie of Fane Street School for Methodist Boys.

They were to meet in the Europa. When Chuckie arrived building work was going on in the foyer and he thought he saw Jake. He ignored him and hurried on to the restaurant. He was directed to a table at which Findlater already sat. Chuckie walked up and nervously shook his hand.

'Charles Lurgan,' said Chuckie Lurgan.

'Luke Findlater. Glad to meet you.'

They sat. Chuckie was appalled. Findlater was tall and elegant. His suit might have belonged to his grandfather but it looked much better than Chuckie's five-hundred-pound barrow-boy effort. He imagined a satiric bent to the welcoming smile with which Findlater favoured him. Mutinously, hot-faced, he prepared himself to be patronized.

That did not happen. There was something soft in Findlater's patrician armour. Chuckie found the chip on his shoulder easing away and began to tell this man his troubles.

At last he found someone who understood. Findlater seemed unamazed by how Chuckie had amassed his £272,645. He seemed undaunted by the prospect of the rest of the IRB grant coming in. He understood that Chuckie was manufacturing, selling, producing nothing. Chuckie even told him about the prosperity-bringing vibrator. Findlater laughed delightedly.

Chuckie tried to dampen his humour by talking of his concern at being given nearly a million pounds for doing nothing.

'You see a problem in that?' smiled Findlater.

'Yes, don't you?'

Findlater laughed. 'Mr Lurgan, I think that this is a precious skill of which you should be proud.'

'Yeah, but I'm going to get found out. I'm going to get arrested. It's all going to fall apart.'

Findlater asked him how he managed to persuade these people to give him so much money. Chuckie replied that he was fucked if he knew.

'No. That's not what I meant. What did you tell these people you were going to do with the money?'

This was what Chuckie had wanted to avoid. With shame, he recounted the details.

Chuckie had known that his big chance was to play on the ecumenical angle with the grant agencies. In divided Northern Ireland, the Government thought that solution and resolution lay in schemes that would bring the warring tribes together. No idea was too lunatic to be rejected in this expensive cross-community effort. Chuckie had told the UDB that he was starting a business that would bring the Catholic nationalist sports of Gaelic football and hurling to Protestants, and the English Protestant pursuits of rugby and cricket to Catholics. These sports were sharply divided and a significant emblem of the apartheid in Northern Ireland, or so he had persuaded Slat to write on his application form. Since the men who worked in the UDB were all witless ex-executives from a multinational toothpaste company, this struck them as an excellent business proposal and they had given him fifty thousand pounds on the spot.

He told the IRB that he was going to set up a chain of ecumenical Irish restaurants in Paris. When they asked him what his restaurants would cook that would be distinctly Irish, he nearly said that he couldn't give a fuck but he wasn't sure that employees of a Northern Ireland Office department would understand that sloppy concept. He had hastily changed the subject and had told them that an employee of his was working on the biodegradable gas television receiver. He told them a number of lies and when he ran out of cogent mistruths he just ran through the menu of his own absurd and megalomaniac fantasies.

When poor, Chuckie's daydreams had been modest: a car, an easy job, oral sex with a constantly updated series of film stars, weather girls and game-show hostesses. Any of these things would have been a massive extension of any waking or likely aspirations he might have had. But now Chuckie dreamed of buying the Department of Social Services and the Royal Ulster Constabulary. But, in particular, Chuckie dreamt of buying Ireland. He could already visualize the estate agent's description for the Ireland auction: FINE OLD COUNTRY, RECENTLY PARTITIONED. IN NEED OF MINOR POLITICAL REPAIR. PRICED FOR QUICK SALE.

Chuckie's detailing of his methods faded away. He saw Findlater staring at him fixedly. He blushed.

'That kind of thing,' he said. 'More of the same. Can't remember most of what I said now.'

Findlater continued to stare at him in fixed silence. Chuckie felt his blush spread.

'You mean you managed to persuade government agencies to give you hundreds of thousands of pounds with that witless amateur bullshit?'

Chuckie gulped hotly, too ashamed to be angry. 'Yes,' he squeaked, like a schoolboy.

To his horror, the Englishman fell to his knees in the middle of the restaurant. There were tears in his eyes. He raised his hand in supplication. Dishes clattered to the floor. Other diners looked round sharply.

'Mr Lurgan,' gasped the stricken man, 'you are a genius, a master. Let me follow you.'

Chuckie helped him to his feet.

Luke Findlater would accept nothing other than full employment from Chuckie. He wanted to give up all his other interests and devote himself entirely to Chuckie's projects. The honour of having his ludicrous pipe-dreams called projects thrilled

Chuckie but he was anxious. Historically unadmired, Chuckie was deeply unaccustomed to making such a favourable impression on anyone. He felt the unease of the plain man approached by a beautiful woman. Which of his friends had put her up to it? Was she a working girl? Was it a bet?

Within a week, they had offices. Chuckie moved his fax machine out of his mother's scullery. They had a secretary, a girl from Enniskillen chosen by Luke for her competence and her lack of beauty. They were writing proposals, making contacts and generating documents in a manner that satisfied and mystified Chuckie to an equal degree.

That weekend, he and Luke had what the Englishman persisted in describing as brainstorming sessions. This seemed both strenuous and most unproletarian to Chuckie. They spent the entirety of Saturday and most of Sunday morning sitting in their offices staring guiltily at each other across an unstrewn desk. Chuckie was growing mutinous by Sunday lunchtime when Luke was struck with an idea.

He took Chuckie to the Ashley bar and got him hammered. The Ashley was a dreadful, dank, unreconstructed Loyalist bar. Many of the men who drank there had done time for chasing, beating, baiting, or just killing the Catholics of the city. There was a poster for the ANC over the bar. With its freedom-fighting connotations and left-wing associations, this had puzzled Luke until one of the more cosmopolitan drinkers informed him that the poster was there because of an unshakeable belief amongst the regulars that ANC stood for Absolutely No Catholics. This seemed just the place to Luke. He proceeded to inebriate Chuckie as quickly as he could.

He was right. The combination of witlessness and the milieu of primordial Protestant ignorance induced Chuckie to fantasize wildly and to ramble around the grimy bar telling his hairy-knuckled confederates all his plans for making a million. Luke followed him round, notebook in hand, keeping him out of the worst of the brawls and carefully annotating every useless boozy aphorism.

Within the next week, this eccentric planning session had borne fruit. Chuckie, only truly recovered from his hangover by Thursday afternoon, found to his bewilderment that his company was already heavily engaged in several ventures. Capital had been committed, people hired, money moved.

They had broken into the Irishness business. They were engaged to import half-wool Aran sweaters, made by slave-workers in Romania. By sticking a Made in Ireland label on them and shipping them to New York and Boston, they would make a fortune. They had already bought out a small mineral-water supplier in Kansas; they had contracted to ship the water to East Coast restaurants and wine bars. The shipments stopped off in Philadelphia where they were decorated with the legend IRISH WATER and a picture of an Irish brook. They couldn't afford the water company but, by the time they had to pay for their purchase, the profits for the half-wool Arans would have it covered.

Most eccentrically, and Luke had swallowed hard before he had carried out this one, they had gone into the ethnic accessory business. He had hired cohorts of small boys from around Chuckie's street. He had sent them to the foot of the hills to pick up twigs for which they would be paid a pound for every hundred. The kids thought he was a looper but went to it with a will. Fifteen thousand twigs arrived in the first day. He gave a furniture restorer three hundred pounds to dip them all in a varnish vat and by Wednesday had persuaded an American importer of miscellaneous luxury items to take ten thousand genuine Irish leprechaun walking sticks (RRP $9.99) off his hands for four bucks a go. They had forty thousand dollars by Thursday. Sale or return, but who would bother?

Luke had already started investigating the possibility of setting up some small utility companies, one in New Jersey to be called Irish Electric and perhaps a gas company in Massachusetts called Irish Gas. The office was full of papers, monstrous piles and bulging files. He had set up different diversification headings: Agribusiness, Finance, Industry, Service Sector. They were expanding like the yawn of a lunatic octopus. It was all mad, all impossible.

Chuckie had to lie down.

Eight

I lit another cigarette and groaned. I was breaking my fast at Rab's Rotten Café – I swear it was called that – an early bacon and eggs joint near Sandy Row. This was one of the places that had made Chuckie what he was so it may have been a poor idea. It was only eight in the morning. A morning when I'd already had a bad breakfast of poached eggs and smoked the café blue, while the booze of the night before flattened down in my gut and I felt a year's worth of regret.

I'd had the piss scared out of me when I woke that morning. Two plain-clothes cops had made a seven o'clock call at my house. They'd only come to interview me about the newspaper reports that I'd been beaten up by a cop. I made them no coffee and gave them no help. They'd only called so early to annoy me. I stood at my door and told them I didn't know how the newspaper story had happened and that none of it was true. I didn't particularly want to get Mary's boyfriend into trouble but I did it mostly because I knew it would annoy Aoirghe.

'A delegation of bereaved relatives met the Just Us party today to request that the IRA reveal to them the sites of the graves of their murdered relatives, officially termed missing. It is suspected that as many as twenty-five bodies lie buried under various building sites and housing estates in West Belfast. Just Us said that they had no control or responsibility in IRA actions.'

'Hey, Rab, turn that off, will ya?' I called out.

Rab, an obese and hairy man with the most ill-executed tattoos I'd ever seen, called back grumpily, 'Does your dick reach your arse?'

'What?'

'Does your dick reach your arse?' he repeated patiently.

'Why?' I asked nervously.

He glared.

'Because if it does, it'll be easier for you to go and fuck yourself.'

'Thanks. That's nice.'

The fat fuck went back to cooking his horrible meals. I looked around the other breakfasters. A motley crew of four or five, none seemed at all put out by Rab's customer relations. They were used to it. He was no maître d'.

I paid up and went to work.

At lunchtime, we all went out onto the roof of the hotel. So long in dark indoors, we blinked and winced at the light. We'd been cleaning out one of the big kitchens before retiling. My colleagues and I were greasy from our work; our clothes were covered in smears of industrial cleaner and adhesive scraps of dead food.

My workmates sat or lay down, they lit their cigarettes, they opened their newspapers and their lunchboxes. An eggy smell lingered briefly in the open air. Ronnie Clay, of the famously flesh feet, threw me an apple in an uncharacteristically munificent gesture. I bit into it and walked away from the indolent others to the edge of the roof. From seven hundred feet up, I looked out across the city, towards the lough. The water in the bay glittered with tiny crests.

It wasn't a dream come true, this job. I wasn't the manual type. I was educated way beyond my station. I looked at my hands. They were already chapped and grotesquely scarred from their work. I'd never liked tiling. I had to get another job.

But I loved this roof. It was the only good thing about working there. Failure always has some upside. The hotel was one of the tallest buildings in this flat, flat town and I could see all Belfast from up there. I could see the City Hospital like a biscuit box with orange trim. I could see the bruised, carious Falls. I could see the breezeblock rubble and trubble of Rathcoole, fat and ominous in the thinned distance. I could even see the Holy Land. I could see all the police stations, I could see all the Army forts, I could see all the helicopters. But, from up there, the streets smelled sweet and Belfast was made of cardboard in the mild and cooling air.

And, besides, any kind of work was better than kicking arse for Marty Allen. I'd had a call from him, asking me if I'd changed my mind. He told me he might give me my old job back if I had. It was easy to refuse. He asked me what big-deal employment I had now. I told him I was working in a bank. He told me I was humping bricks down the Europa. He knew everything, Allen, I'd forgotten that. I said goodbye. He said that Crab and Hally had been asking for me. I'd told him they couldn't have me and hung up.

Crab and Hally had been up to their old tricks again. I'd had lots of dark wide-boy abuse on my answering machine. I could tell that it was mostly Crab but Hally had left one or two messages. It was simple vituperation and threats but it still sounded like they'd had to write it down on their sleeves to remind them.

A couple of days before, I'd found a Jiffy bag full of shit in my letterbox and the legend 'Taigs will dy!' chalked on my front door. They were extending their range. I was sure it was taxing them heavily.

There was trouble coming, I knew, but I would deal with it some other time. I was just going to do my work and fail to get laid.

'Don't do it. Don't jump! Life can be beautiful.'

I didn't even turn to acknowledge Ronnie's big joke. I'd been coming up there every day for a week and every time I walked to the edge of the roof Ronnie cracked this joke. Ronnie was a Democratic Unionist. If you hadn't known, you'd have guessed.

They were in a comic mood. They'd been laughing at me for an hour already. I'd asked the site boss for the next day off. I'd hoped that I wouldn't have to say why. I had to say why. They laughed like drains.

The night before, I'd made a promise to Slat. Slat was always busting my balls with his high-grade integrity. A lot of South Belfast's concerned classes had hired a train to go down to Dublin as a protest against all the IRA bombs that had been planted on the Belfast to Dublin line. By all accounts, it was meant to be an emblem of the community's protest against terrorist violence but it sounded like a satchelful of shit to me. Anyway, in his cups, old Slat had been all for this Peace Train. I agreed I'd go along. Chuckie and Max were going. I balked a little when I discovered that it was running in a couple of days – that was, tomorrow when I'd probably be hung over still.

I knew now that I should have been smarter than that but I hated to see Slat sitting there with a faceful of Guinness, telling me what I didn't know about democratic responsibility.

This Peace Train thing was a new development. It had been started by Sam McDuffin, a local celebrity (in the loosest sense). He thought that it was time the intelligentsia of Northern Ireland stood firm against the gunmen. Intelligentsia? McDuffin was some old geek from Sandy Row who did a local radio show about the good old days when the soda farls were hot, the doors were always open and nobody minded if you were a Protestant or a Catholic – as long as you were a Protestant. I wished Slat hadn't goaded me into going to this thing. McDuffin was the last thing I needed.

But at least my esteemed workmates all had a big laugh

when they heard I was going to ride the Peace Train. Honestly, such fatalism was most unbecoming. Ronnie said, and I quote, 'There'd be peace quick enough if the Army were allowed to go into every Fenian ghetto, guns blazing.' I'd always imagined that the Army were allowed to do precisely that. Ronnie didn't know that I was a Catholic. I had told him I was a Methodist from Fivemiletown. He believed me.

I looked across at my lounging co-workers and noticed that little Rajinder was sitting, as always, on his own, the Belfast Asian. Rajinder wasn't quite white, and this was a problem for Ronnie Clay and his pals. The week before, Ronnie had told Rajinder that black people all looked the same to him. Rajinder's smile had been a pale, pale thing. I think he'd heard that one before. It was an ugly moment but, in fairness to Ronnie, I had to admit that black people all looked the same to me as well. But then white people all looked the same to me too. To me, we all looked pretty awful.

We finished up about four. At Ronnie's suggestion, we all headed off to the Bolshevik for a couple of pints. I didn't want to go but it would have been impolitic to refuse. I didn't want to look like a university graduate or a human being or something like that.

The Bolshevik was an old city-centre bar of imperfect design and cleanliness. It had been opened in the early twenties by Ireland's only communist. At first called the October '17, the name was changed to the Lenin, on account of customers continually asking what happened on 17 October. From the Lenin, the name was changed to the Trotsky, the Stalin – briefly popular during the latter years of the Second World War – the Khrushchev, the Gagarin, the Revolution, swiftly changed at the start of the Troubles, and finally to its present title. The original owner was long since dead but his descendants held fondly to the tradition of Soviet nomenclature.

Unfortunately, the Bolshevik was commonly dubbed the

Bullshit by the citizens and was mostly frequented by reactionary Protestants of the most decided kind. There were no revolutionaries and Rajinder never joined us. Ronnie was always immensely happy in the Bolshevik. He and the other colonists felt that this was their kind of place, their kind of fate.

There was some old chat with my workmates, some old crap. They chided me again for my imminent journey on the Peace Train. They grew serious. They lamented their lot. They talked the talk of Protestant fear and conspiracy. Catholics were moving in everywhere, including across the table from them if they but knew. The Fair Employment Commission was putting them in the workplace. They were then getting enough money to buy property in good Protestant areas where the houses had no shit on the walls. The RUC weren't allowed to shoot them any more and if any good Protestant took a couple of the dirty bastards out, he was, appallingly, sent to prison just as though he'd committed a crime. Bar the tits and the university education, these guys reminded me of Aoirghe. I didn't mention this.

I was, as you'd expect, bored pissless with this. Belfast hatreds were multiple but unvarying. I'd heard them all before, the details and the emphases never changed. You could sing along if you liked. These fulminations were faded and dog-eared with age.

The tragedy was that Northern Ireland (Scottish) Protestants thought themselves like the British. Northern Ireland (Irish) Catholics thought themselves like Eireans (proper Irish). The comedy was that any once-strong difference had long melted away and they resembled no one now as much as they resembled each other. The world saw this and mostly wondered, but round these parts folk were blind.

Interestingly enough, Protestant/Catholic hardmen would still routinely and joyfully beat the shit out of Catholics/Protestants even if those Catholics/Protestants didn't believe in God and had formally left their faith. It was intriguing to wonder what a bigot of one faith could object to in an atheist who was born into another. That was what I liked about Belfast hatred. It was a lumbering hatred that could survive comfortably on the memories of things that never existed in the first place. There was a certain admirable stamina in that.

I sat in the grimy bar and listened to those boys, happy but mistaken in the belief that I was a Protestant. In my early years, I had often hoped that the future would be different. That from out of the dark mists of Ireland's past and present a new breed would arise. The New Irish. When all the old creeds and permutations in people would be contradicted. We would see the Loyalist Catholic. The liberal Protestant. The honest politician. The intelligent poet. But, as I sat and listened to my workmates, I decided I wasn't going to hold my hand in my arse waiting for any Utopia.

The flow of debate was halted when a skinny, grubby kid approached our table with an armful of newspapers. He softly ululated some mysterious phrase which, though it sounded like *Oyoyillooiiethkckooiy*, we all knew meant, 'Would you like to purchase the latest copy of the *Belfast Telegraph* newspaper?' At least the kid did this quietly as a concession to being indoors. Out on the streets his (sometimes extremely mature) colleagues belted out these Nordic challenges with some gusto.

Nobody wanted a newspaper so Ronnie told the kid he had no sale. The kid stood where he was, wiped his nose with his sleeve and said: 'All right, ten p for a joke, then.'

One of my workmates, Billy, groaned. 'Ah, fuck, it's not you, is it? I didn't recognize you. Had a bath this year or something?'

The kid's murky chops grew murkier. 'Does your dick reach your arse?' he asked.

I stared.

'What?' said Billy.

'Does your dick reach your arse?'

Billy was unamused. 'What do you mean?'

'Well, if it does you can go and fuck yourself easier.'

Billy slapped the kid hard across the face. The child dropped his newspapers. He bent to pick them up, snuffling, trying to cover his face with his hands.

I put my glass down.

'What did you do that for, you dumb prick?' Ronnie inquired mildly of Billy.

'None of your business, wankstain,' he riposted.

The dirty kid looked up briefly, a bright look amidst his tears. Obviously he had not heard that *bon mot* before and was now carefully committing it to memory. You could almost see his lips move as, imperfectly, he spelled out the letters.

Billy lifted his hand as though to take another swipe at the boy.

'Touch him again, and I'll break your fucking skull,' said Ronnie.

Billy was a sparky enough young man and might have gone for it but Ronnie had surprised us all so much. Billy was smart enough to make no ungenerous assumptions about anyone's pugilistic skills. Wisely, he decided that experience was always an unknown quality and let it go.

The kid picked up his papers and moved off, sniffling.

'Aye, Ronnie, you're my fucking hero.'

'SuperClay.'

'You fancy him, do you?'

'Ronnie wants to fuck the wee snotbag, right enough.'

'I'm sure he'll let you for a fiver.'

I drank up and got out. Outside the Bolshevik, the kid was picking up his papers again. Reasonably, the landlord had thrown him out for getting hit in his bar and the papers had spilled. I helped him.

'They're pretty fucked, son. Nobody will buy them now. I'm sorry.'

'Bollocks,' he replied.

'What?'

'Forget it.'

A window rapped behind us. I looked round. Ronnie Clay

and his pals were hooting and jeering at us, obscenely pantomiming a variety of sexual acts. Ronnie was back to normal, I was glad to see. I didn't want to have to start liking him.

'Let's move on,' I said to the kid.

We walked on, no doubt confirming the delighted predictions of my workmates.

'Hey, kid, what's your name?'

He skipped further away from me, his dirty coat flapping. 'You're not going to fruit me up, are you? You're going to try and fuck my bum, you dirty poof. Help!' he started shouting to passers-by. 'Help. I'm being raped. Help!'

'Jesus, kid. Stop it. You're safe.'

'Help, help! Rape!'

To my panic and horror several concerned citizens looked like they were thinking of stopping and rescuing the poor child, sorting me out into the bargain.

'Fuck up, you little shit,' I hissed. 'I wouldn't fuck you with somebody else's dick.'

The kid stopped abruptly. The same calculating and memorizing expression spread over his face. Having stored the phrase, he decided he liked it, and thus he believed me.

'Roche,' he said.

'What?'

'My name. Roche. You asked me my name.'

We walked on through Cornmarket. The passers-by walked on, evidently concluding that he was my younger brother or that he had decided it was OK if I raped him. Either way it wasn't their problem and they moved on.

Needless to say, I wasn't so keen on his company now but I felt I had to keep the conversation going until our way could part. 'Do you often get smacked like that?'

'Aye sometimes.' He stiffened and drew himself to his full half-height. 'Usually, I smack the fuckers right back.'

'You didn't just now.'

'Aye, well, there were six or seven of you. Sometimes I just piss in their beer when they're not looking. I can piss at will. It's handy.'

'What age are you?'

'Fifteen.'

I looked at his tiny, wizened face and his little boy's physique.

'Aye, right,' I said.

'OK, fourteen.'

I laughed.

'Thirteen?'

'If you don't know, kid, who gives a shit?'

'Twelve.'

'Why aren't you at school?'

'It's half past five, you dumb fuck. What school did you go to?'

I began to think that Billy had had the right technique for dealing with this youngster. I glared.

'Ah, don't be so fucking humpy. It was a stupid question,' he chided.

'A great man once said there's no such thing as a stupid question.'

'He didn't have a lot of conversations with you, then.'

'Watch your lip.'

'Why, what's it doing? Tricks?'

I gave up.

'Stop,' he screamed at me.

I froze. He bent down and picked up a coin from almost underneath my foot.

'Fifty p,' he said. 'Magic.'

I walked on. He tripped along beside me.

'Do you ever think about anything other than money?'

'I'm a businessman. I've got to get along.'

'You remind me of a friend of mine.' I laughed.

'What's his name?'

'Chuckie.'

'Is he a fat ugly character with a big fuck-off car?'

'Yeah. You know him?'

'I copped a fiver for looking after his motor a few days ago.'

'Where was this?'

'Up the Falls.'

'Where?' I asked, surprised.

'Falls Road, dimwit.'

Chuckie had a lot of Catholic friends but I couldn't see him being too comfortable in that most unUnionist heartland. But then I was beginning to understand that Chuckie's greed was ecumenical. He would go anywhere to make money.

'What's the big deal?' asked my young companion, 'Is he a Prod? I knew he was a Prod.'

'How?'

'He didn't have any rhythm.'

'I presume you do have rhythm, then.'

'Aye, don't you?'

'Only intermittently.'

'Speak English, you fancy bastard,' said Roche huffily. He seemed sensitive to words in a variety of ways, this prodigy.

'Now who's being humpy?' I chided.

'Aye, well, don't use stupid fucking words you don't even know yourself.'

I let that go and we walked on in silence. I didn't know what delicate emotional corns I had trodden on with this child but I was growing less interested. Near the City Hall I stopped at a right turn. 'Listen, kid, I don't know where you're going but I'm going up this way. I'll see you around.'

I was just moving off when the kid put an indescribably begrimed hand on my sleeve and stopped me. 'Hold on,' he said. 'Have you been to college?'

'Yeah.'

He looked hard at me for a minute. 'C'mere.'

He pulled me up a side-street. Briefly, I began to consider the possibility that he shared Ronnie Clay's suspicions about me and was going to offer me a cut-price blowjob or something.

The world was certainly getting more complicated that way.

We pulled up at the blankish wall of a multi-storey car park. He pointed at it.

'What's that?' he asked.

'A wall.'

'You're not funny,' he snapped.

'So people say.'

'What's that?' He pointed to a small clutch of graffiti four feet up the wall (optimum reading height for the stunted little fucker). It was small and closely written. I moved nearer.

OTG, I read. OTG.

'What does that mean?' asked Roche.

'Listen, kid, I don't know. Nobody seems to know. I've asked around. It's been in the papers.'

'Read out the letters, you tossbag.'

'Read them out yourself, you cheeky little shit.'

He stared hard at me.

Ah, right, that's it, I thought. He can't read. 'OTG,' I said – me and my bleeding heart.

'Again.'

'O–T–G. Can you not . . . ?'

'I can read fine, fuckface.'

I turned on my heel and walked on. He had charm, sure, but it was so obscure. Before I got to the end of the street I heard him call after me. I stopped and turned round.

He stood amidst a clutch of homegoing office girls. 'Hey, does your dick reach your arse?' he shouted thinly in the distance.

Not yet, I thought, not yet.

By the time I'd walked half-way home, the city was weary from all its work. Belfast had quickened and slowed. The traffic was quieter now. It was six o'clock. The homebound workers were now all home and the streets had thinned of people. Though bright, the light had softened. The sky was wispy and vague, a moderate effort. The sky looked distinctly underwritten up there.

I crossed Shaftesbury Square. Though early, the Lavery's overspill was already out on the street. Groups of unusually dirty youths lounged on the pavement with beer glasses in their hands. As I passed the bar, stepping over their outstretched legs, a warm, urinous waft hung in the air outside the doorway. I hated Lavery's. It had to be the dirtiest, most crowded, least likeable bar in Western Europe. Consequently, it was enormously popular. Very Belfast. Einstein got it wrong. The Theory of Relativity didn't apply to Lavery's. Lavery's time was different time. You went into Lavery's one night at the age of eighteen and you stumbled out, pissed, to find you were in your thirties already. People drank their lives away there. Lavery's was for failures. I was working as a tile layer and I couldn't get into Lavery's because I was too successful.

I walked up the Lisburn Road and passed the Anabaptist Church – or double-duckers as we called them – the South Belfast Gospel Hall, the Windsor Tabernacle, the Elim Pentecostal, the Methodist Mission, the Presbyterian Presbytery, and the Unitarian Church of Protestant Mnemonists or something like that. At the door of all the adjacent rectories, broken pastors stood, staring at me with grim expressions. To the old law, they held true. You crap on my grandfather, you crap on me. I found these guys infinitely more frightening than Crab, Hally or Ronnie Clay. I tried not to look like a Catholic. I tightened my Bible belt. I thought they were convinced.

I crossed the junction of Elmwood Avenue and glanced down its treeful length. The Bolshevik fiasco and the business with the crazy kid had depressed me unaccountably. It didn't feel good to be going home on this blue evening. I didn't want to face my empty flat. I didn't want to face my empty evening.

Home, I showered, I ignored my cat, I put on my suit and I headed down to the supermarket. The girl who liked me might be there and I could think of nothing better. I knew I was sad, buying groceries I didn't need just to meet some adolescent girl whom I wouldn't even chat up. I was sad but I was happy that way.

I bought another load of mushrooms. I couldn't think of anything else. The girl who liked me wasn't there. I fell in love anyway. I was served by a spotty seventeen-year-old boy with geeky red hair and amazing, award-winning acne. It was obviously his first week at the job. He couldn't get anything right. He just mumbled inaudibly and blushed collar upwards. He blushed at the till, he blushed at the bananas, the *baguettes* and the *fromage frais*. He blushed infinitely more than my regular girl. I don't think he was blushing because of any passion for me. When he turned his red head I saw the hearing aid nestling behind his ear, unhidden by his hair. This kid just blushed because he thought he was generally a crap idea, a big mistake. It made me want to kiss his lumpy neck. It made me want to die of love.

When I got back, Chuckie had called (Slat had called too, Amnesty had called again and Crab and Hally continued their old guff but I ignored them all). I called Chuckie back. He and the rest of the boys were going to some kind of gathering in one of the new yuppie bars on the Dublin Road. I was too bored and lonely to say no.

I got my cat and forced him to sit on my knee while I watched the old folks in the two houses opposite me. I'd often seen these two playing out their comedy. They didn't seem to talk to each other but they always did the same things at the same times. He was Asian, obviously a widower, a soft-bellied old guy often being visited by various clutches of children and grandchildren. She was true Ulster intemperate stock, a blue-haired old dear often dressed in a miraculous pair of pink semi-nylon stretch slacks (no visitors). That evening they were out gardening in their little patches of green out front. They bent over their shrubs, their heads nearly touching, tugging at a weed bush that bordered both their little gardens. I sometimes suspected they didn't get on but I had to say that, that evening, the races sure seemed united in their mutual hatred of weeds. It was beautiful.

When I got to the bar where I was meeting the boys, I was horrified. There was a sign over the door.

'An Evening of Irish Poetry Tonight 8 p.m.,' it said.

'Oh, fuck,' I replied.

Obviously there were no bouncers that night. What hordes would they be fighting off? I stood on the doorstep and pondered. Could any solitude be worse than this? I was amazed that Chuckie would attend such a gathering. I mean, Slat, Septic and the rest of us were basically yobbish, vulgar and sad but we could claim some form of brush with education, with literature. Chuckie, however, was moronically ill-informed. I suspected Max's hand in this.

Inside, I found that my suspicions were correct and I also found, to my meagre delight, that Aoirghe was with them. I walked up to them. I patted Chuckie's arm, said hello to Max and was greeting the fearsome Aoirghe when I unfortunately coughed.

Her eyes narrowed. 'Are you taking the piss again?'

'Jesus!' I choked. 'I just coughed. Gimme a break.'

Her eyes narrowed more (how could she see anything like that?). 'Yeah, and I got your message. Thanks very much, it was charming.' She hissed the last word.

I blushed and coughed again. 'Whoops, sorry. Sorry about the message. I was pissed about getting nosy calls from Amnesty.'

She turned to Max and started some chat with her. I shrugged my shoulders at Chuckie, smiled amiably at him and grabbed him viciously by the balls.

'Ow.'

'I don't fucking believe it, Chuckie. How come you didn't tell me she was going to be here?' I gave his pebbles another twist. 'Hmm?'

'Fuck, Jake. Let go. It wasn't my fault.'

I released him.

Slat, Septic and Donal arrived. We stood in a bunch waiting for the wimp who couldn't stand the pressure of resisting buying the first round.

'Look,' Chuckie whispered to me, 'she's just staying for the poetry. After that, she's fucking off with one of the poets.'

My relief was tempered with a qualm of jealousy. That moment scared me badly. I shook my head and cleared my mind. I held my hand in front of my face and counted my fingers. I was OK.

'What's wrong with you?' asked Chuckie.

'Never mind that. What the fuck are you doing at a poetry reading?'

Chuckie looked slightly miffed at my surprise. Septic muffled a laugh. 'It was Aoirghe's idea. One of the guys reading is a councillor for Just Us. He wrote a book when he was in the Maze.'

'Oh, great.'

'One of them's famous,' said Chuckie consolingly. 'Shauny . . . Shinny . . . Shamie . . .'

'Sugar Ray Leonard?' suggested Septic.

'No.' Chuckie struggled on manfully, 'Shilly . . . Shally . . .'

'Shague Ghinthoss,' shouted Max.

'Even better,' I complained.

Shague Ghinthoss was an inappropriately famous poet who looked like Santa Claus and wrote about frogs, hedges and long-handled spades. He was a vaguely anti-English Catholic from Tyrone but the English loved him. They had a real appetite for hearing what a bunch of fuckers they were. I liked that about the English.

Max sloped over with a book. Aoirghe trailed along reluctantly behind her. Max smiled. 'It's the launch of this new book. It's supposed to be very good.' She passed it to me.

'According to whom?' I asked grammatically.

Chuckie coughed and old Aoirghe looked ready to tell me.

I dipped into the book to avoid her eye.

'Of course,' she put in acidly, 'I wouldn't expect you to be sympathetic to any writers belonging to the Movement but even you couldn't deny Shague Ghinthoss's reputation.'

'Is that right?'

'There's a beautiful one of his on the first page,' said Max brightly. 'It was good of a writer of his repute to endorse a book like this, don't you think?'

'I bet I can recite it without reading it.'

Chuckie looked impressed at this – sometimes satire passed him by. Aoirghe bristled. I passed the book to Deasely, open at the first page. Donal adopted a pedagogical expression.

I cleared my throat.

'The blah blah under the brown blah of the blah blah hedges.
I blahhed her blah with the heft of my spade
The wet blah blahhed along the lines of the country with
all the blah of the blah blah blackberries.'

I stopped. There was no applause. Deasely looked at me severely. He tutted. 'You left out the fifth blah, Jackson. Go to the back of the class and buy me a beer.'

He chucked the book back to Aoirghe. She looked like she was pissing blood. 'Jesus, Jackson. Your friends are near as bad as you. Do you boys go to asshole support groups at weekends?'

It was a bad, bad evening. Before the reading started we were reluctantly – on both sides – introduced to a number of Aoirghe's friends and associates. To do her justice, they weren't all extremist republicans. There was a man who taught Television-watching Skills at the University of Ulster. There was an old college chum of hers, a man with a Theory of everything. He had a Theory of Poetry. He had a Theory of Parties. A Theory of History. A Theory of Haircuts. He told me all of them. He did not include a Theory of How Not To Be Boring.

Then the reading commenced. We stood still while a series of twats in poetic clothes (a varying costume, always expressing equal measures of nonconformity, sensitivity and sexual menace) drivelled on about the flowers, the birds, the hedges, the berries, the spades, the earth, the sky and the sea. Whatever you said about Shague Ghinthoss's reputation, he definitely had one. All these tossers bore his mark. Unlike Ghinthoss, none of these boys was from the country. They were all pale-faced city boys and most obviously had never seen any of the hedges, berries or spades about which they wrote so passionately.

It was clear, in addition, that these were all nationalist hedges, republican berries, unProtestant flowers and extremely Irish spades. These subtleties were dashed, however, when the penultimate poet did his stuff. This unprepossessing john, we were told, had had his work translated from the original Gaelic into Russian but not into English. He was to read one of his poems in Irish and some guy would translate into English. (I should point out that I had seen this poet at the bar, showing a fine grasp of idiomatic English when he was trying to chat up one of the bar girls – though, admittedly, he seemed to have some difficulty in understanding the phrase, 'Fuck off, you ugly twat.')

This man read, haltingly but confidently, a poem entitled 'Poem to a British Soldier About to Die'. It was hard enough to follow the text in detail, what with the simultaneous translation and the fact that it was crap, but the sentiments were apparent enough. The poem told the young British soldier (about to die) why he was about to die, why it was his fault, how it had been his fault for eight hundred years and would probably be his fault for another eight hundred, why the man who was going to shoot him was a fine Irishman who loved his children and never beat his wife and believed firmly in democracy and freedom for all, regardless of race or creed, and why such beliefs gave him no option but to murder the young British soldier (about to die).

There was silence after he finished. I waited for the boos and catcalls. How foolish. It wasn't until a few seconds into the cheers and whoops that I realized that everybody loved it. Weren't there any Protestants here? I looked over at Chuckie but he was blithe. He hadn't even been listening, a condition he shared with many of his faithmates.

The fat poet milked the applause. Some of the other scribes joined him on the podium. The rapture sounded as though it would never end. These culture vultures were frenzied in their acclaim. After a time the hubbub died down. The chubby humanist waited for total silence, then leaned close to the microphone.

'*Tiocfaidh ar La*,' he bellowed.

Chuckie jumped in his skin. 'What?' he squeaked.

Thankfully, no one heard him in the resumption of the tumult.

It went on. It was as bad as could be. The great man, Ghinthoss, got up and read. He read about hedges, the lanes and the bogs. He covered rural topography in detail. It felt like a geography field trip. In a startling departure, he read a poem about a vicious Protestant murder of a nice Catholic. There were no spades in this poem, and only one hedge, but by this time the crowd were whipped into such a sectarian passion they would have lauded him if he'd picked his nose with any amount of rhythm or even in a particularly Irish manner.

He milked it all. Then he took some questions. I'm not saying they were entirely facile but their content was mostly eugenic. These people gathered close together, snug in their verse, their culture, they had one question. Why can't Protestants do this? they asked themselves. What's wrong with those funny people? Why aren't they spiritual like us?

Ghinthoss was grandly forgiving. He seemed to think it was not all the Protestants' fault. Given a million or so years of Catholic supremacy, Protestant brows might lift, they might start with a few uneasy grunts, invent the wheel and wear bearskins. If we were kind, the poor dumb brutes might be able to manage a few domestic poetic tasks in a century or so.

'Mr Ghinthoss,' I asked in a pause (oh, I didn't want to, I couldn't help myself, I bit my tongue, I put my hands over my mouth but it just would come out), 'Mr Ghinthoss,' I enquired, 'could you tell us, whether, great poet that you are, whether . . . whether your dick reaches your arse yet?'

I was always good at public speaking.

As I was being thrown out I arranged to meet the others. They wanted to go to Lavery's – I was being lifted in the air by two ten-foot revolutionaries at that point so I couldn't debate the venue.

I checked myself out in the bathroom of a hamburger joint nearby. A graze on my forehead, a cut on my lip. Oh, my poor fucking face. It was getting boring, this Jake-beating thing, it was happening every day. I used to be so pretty. I used to be so tough.

I didn't want to go into Lavery's until the others were there so I nipped into Mary's bar just to see if she was there.

She was. Her face fell like I don't know what when I walked in. The place was pretty empty. I knew if I sat at the bar she wouldn't have to wait on me. I could easily have saved her that.

I sat at a table near the wall.

'Can I get you anything?'

'Hello, Mary.'

'What would you like to drink?'

'Mary, no grief. Just say hello.'

'Hello.'

'Double gin. Neat. No ice.'

There was a pause.

'Please,' I added.

The firmness in her face fled. Abruptly she pulled out a chair and sat opposite me. 'Listen,' she said, 'Paul's terrified that he's going to get into trouble for that thing between you. Some detectives have interviewed him. They said they were going to talk to you. They told him he could get a prison sentence, never mind lose his job.'

'They came today.'

'What did you say?'

'I told them nothing had happened. That it was all a mistake.'

'What about the stuff in the papers?'

I told her I didn't know how it had happened. I told her it had nothing to do with me. Then I told her about Aoirghe.

It was lovely for a while there. I'd never had Mary listen so carefully to what I said. I'd never had her so interested. It was because of her concern and love for another man, sure, but I didn't care. It was nice anyway. My aspirations were thrillingly modest.

She laughed about Aoirghe. 'You've got woman trouble, Jake,' she said. 'You always will have. Men like you always do.'

It had been going so well up to that point. I had been deciding that I liked her enough not to care about anything else. That it was OK if she didn't want to sleep with me again, I could allow that. Then she had to go and say such a thing. What kind of man was I like? Where were these men like me? What was wrong with us? Why couldn't we get laid?

She brought me my drink. I dallied there for a quarter-hour. I didn't touch the gin. (I could never drink gin neat. I'd only ordered it that I might seem butch and epic.) As I was leaving I said goodbye and told her that she was beautiful – which wasn't entirely true. She kissed my face. I felt worse.

I went into Lavery's. Slat and Deasely were already there. They'd been thrown out of the poetry reading minutes after me. Slat had asked the poet whether it was entirely nice to kill soldiers and got himself chucked out. Deasely had reacted to Slat's expulsion by bellowing, '*I like Protestants*,' and had soon followed his friend. Feeling some pride, I bought them many drinks. I wondered if anyone at the verse gig could have imagined that they had ejected three Catholics. It seemed unlikely.

By the time the others arrived, I was feeling dreadful. I'd had a couple of drinks. I didn't want to get drunk. Lavery's was horrible. The men, the seeking bachelors and married rogues.

The big laughs, the glittering eyes, sharp after groups of women. The beer-buying, the phonecall-making, the endless pissing. I was tired of the Irish and their bogus dissipation.

There were four main sets of people.

There were the expected groups of Alcoholics-in-Residence, giving their seminars in the corners. All Belfast bars had those – it was no surprise. Lavery's had one enormous difference. Lavery's seemed to be running a training scheme, an apprenticeship. There was a tableful of guys who were beginning their slide. They'd started out in Lavery's; as they passed their wino exams they might fan out to other bars or actual indigence but they'd started here and they couldn't stop. They'd always be Lavery's graduates.

There was a whole set of men in their late thirties, forties or even fifties who had some vague attachment to or yen for the music business. Wrinkled, obese, they were identifiable by their grey ponytails and the remarkable sexual success they achieved with quite attractive women in their early twenties. This success gave these men confidence. It had not dawned on them that this apparent anomaly – all the more glaring because my relatively handsome friends and I couldn't get a sniff – was because the physical laws were in abeyance in the warp of Lavery's time and space. It was because of the special physics prevalent there that they had a chance. On the street, they were just sad old geeks.

The third group was the largest. Students from Queen's. Kids too dumb to go to a proper university, they hammed it up in this bar. Almost all country boys and girls, they did their best to be urban, metropolitan. It was only weeks since they'd been joy-riding tractors and shagging sheep.

And finally, of course, there was a selection of astounding dark-haired girls running their fingers through their hair, walking up and down past the bar, their eyes meeting no man's.

About four hundred and fifty people of various ages on three floors spending around six or seven thousand pounds, they sweated and bellowed through their evening. They tried to make it look like fun but they couldn't manage it. I was one of the few people who could admit that I was there because I had no life.

It was better when Chuckie and his massive entourage arrived. Aoirghe was not amongst them but some of her friends had come. The television-watching man was there and the other man with all the theories but there was an enormously attractive girl with them. Dark-haired, a little full-blown, big-hipped, she looked like a seedy Snow White. She was my callipygian ideal. I wanted her, naturally.

I think Max must have noticed. She introduced us. Her name was Suzy. We chatted for a little while, amiably supervised by Max. After a few minutes, the big group had moved perceptibly away from us. There was a pause between Suzy and me, a consciousness that we were now in a sense almost alone, almost confidential. She looked up at me (she was fucking attractive).

'What kind of music do you like?' she asked (I promise!).

Come on, it had been a difficult month. I was emotional, I was bruised, I was fucking horny. I had some decisions to make.

'Rhythm and blues,' I said. 'Comic opera, early eighties ska, forties crooners, showtunes, big bands, Mozart . . .'

It didn't matter how horny I was, it just refused to pan out with this girl. After we'd got over the music hurdle, we chanced the others. Her face was turned to mine. She was beautiful but she kept giving me the full range of all her enticing routines, fluttering eyelashes, drooping lids, flattering smiles. At one horrible and confiding point she told me that she had a theory of life (it couldn't be a theory *about* life, it had to be a theory *of* life, it had to be an eighteenth-century disquisition, it had to be the fucking *Origin of Species*).

'Would that be your brother over there?' I pointed out the theory man from the reading.

'Yeah. How did you guess?'

'I'm mystic that way.'

'Huh?'

'Nothing. Well, what is it?'

'What?'

'Your Theory of Life.'

'Oh, yeah.'

With an air of infinite mystery and importance, Suzy socked it to me. Her Theory of Life was that whatever she wanted she went out and got it. Jesus, even then I engaged. Free of contempt, I tried to point out some of the flaws in her complex reasoning. What if what she wanted was inimical to the desires and wants of others? Even when I'd rephrased that it didn't make much of a dent in her. That did it. I told her about Rousseau and the Social Contract, the natural right and the social right, the idea that with rights we are sovereign and subject at the same time and that her sovereignty was my subjection and vice versa.

It took her twenty minutes but, in the end, she went away.

I rejoined the bigger group and hung out with my failed male pals while we all watched Chuckie and his beautiful intelligent American. I still hadn't stopped desperately desiring Suzy but I knew if I sat on my hands, bit my tongue and shut my mouth until I left the joint I'd be OK.

Aoirghe came back with her chubby Nazi poet. I'd had a few more drinks by then but I still shouldn't have said what I said.

'Hey, Aoirghe,' I said. 'Don't you prefer your dates to at least look like they might have had some hair once?'

When was I going to learn not to take this girl on? She gave me a whole load of abuse about my remark, she gave me a whole load of abuse about my stunt at the reading, she gave me a whole load of abuse about what a fucker I was. She managed all this in the time it took her date to get her a drink at the bar and return.

'This is Seamus.' She introduced him reluctantly.

'And this was Jake,' I said, as I walked away. It was a crap line but that had never stopped me before.

'Hey, Jackson,' she called after me, 'I hear you're going on the Peace choo-choo tomorrow.'

'Yeah?'

'Maybe I'll see you there. There might be a reception committee waiting for you when you get back.'

I leered at fat Seamus.

'You have fun in the meantime, *buttfuck*.' I really did whisper that last bit under my breath as I turned round. The cow must have been some kind of Batgirl or something. I didn't see her coming. She hit me over the right ear. I went flying into a group of moustachioed hardmen, sending their drinks flying. They needed no further invitation. It had been a dull night for them and I was their only nibble.

They dragged me outside and would have beaten me fuckless if Max hadn't fired out there and done some big FBI routine on them. I think that they were impressed that she was just so American and just so beautiful. They didn't touch me. It was a very post-modern pub fight.

Max brushed me down and tried ineffectually to set me to rights. 'Are you OK?'

'No,' I replied.

'Go home.'

'Hey, Max. What's wrong with me? Why can't I find a girl like you? What's Chuckie got that I haven't? Bigger tits, yeah, but that's not everything.'

She laughed. Manna to the drunk. I liked her so much.

'What's wrong with me?'

'Almost everything,' she answered.

I'd always hated it when people gave that kind of snappy, wisecracking, ultimately meaningless, enigmatic answer.

'I've always hated it when people give that kind of snappy, wise . . .'

I don't think I made it to the end of the sentence.

Nine

Waking is the wrong word for what I did that morning. There was no emergence from darkness, there was no jolt into consciousness. I didn't wake up as such – my disease just got this new open-eyed, standing-up symptom. I drank some water. It felt as though the first few mouthfuls were absorbed straight into the hard dry sponge of my tongue. I made coffee easily enough but then I poured it into the ashtray. I lit the filter end of two consecutive cigarettes. I was so fucked I smoked them anyway.

It was looking grim there until my cat put in his bid for his breakfast. Miaow! That was just what I needed. I chased him for nearly fifteen minutes, finally cornering him in the bathroom. While I was trying to figure out some method of holding him down so that I could pee on him, he escaped out of the window. I peed in the sink instead.

I felt much better for that. I washed, I brushed, I groomed. I had a fat lip and a mark on my brow but I looked better than recently. I made more coffee and switched on the radio. Outside, it looked like summertime. It was July so it had come early to Northern Ireland. It would be over by lunchtime. Not intending to go to work, it had been nice to put on my suit (the dark blue – last night's charcoal was in pretty bad shape) but it still felt like an after-hours Agincourt between my ears. I decided I wasn't going to drink again. It wasn't how bad I felt; it was how bored I'd become.

'A man was shot last night in an apparent punishment shooting. He is critically injured in hospital. The IRA say that he had been repeatedly warned about antisocial behaviour. Police said . . .'

There was me switching off the radio again. Soon, I'd forget what music sounded like. Antisocial behaviour? Fuck, what was that? Did he pick his nose in mixed company? Did he wear bad shoes? The IRA said that they policed their own areas. They sure did. They shot kids in the legs – joy-riders, car thieves, kids who smoked a spliff or two, maybe kids who gave them lip. Hush ma mouth, but that never sounded socialist to me.

I checked my mail. There was nothing too interesting. Until I opened the door, that is. There, on my doorstep, a package lay. I knew immediately that Crab and Hally were doing their stuff again. Nobody else liked me enough to send me parcels.

I picked it up gingerly. I squeezed it. Not squishy. Glad there was no shit, I opened it confidently enough. In it was a photograph of Matt and Mamie's house and some ball-bearings. I went back inside.

I drank some more coffee, I even switched the radio back on. It took me some minutes but I finally worked out why they'd sent the ball-bearings. The dumb shits mustn't have been able to get their hands on any actual bullets so they'd sent the BBs as a kind of air-rifle substitute. I almost laughed outright. I still called old M&M though.

'Hello.'

'Mamie?'

'Yes. Who's that?'

'Jake.'

'What's wrong?'

'Nothing. I just called to see if you were both OK.'

'Jake, I've never known you conscious before nine o'clock, never mind making social phone calls.'

'Yeah, yeah.'

'Are you going to tell me what's wrong?'

'Let me talk to Matt.'

There was some inaudible scuffling and grumbling and Matt came on the line. 'Hello, Jake.'

'You had any surprise callers recently, Matt?'

'No. Will we have?'

'No.' I paused. I'd chosen to speak to Matt not because I was sexist but because I knew Matt was marginally less macho than his wife. If Mamie heard about it she'd be out there with a Kalashnikov. 'Don't say anything to Mamie but if you get any visitors you don't know, you call me.'

'All right.'

'It's nothing, Matt. Just some guys looking for me about some money. They might remember that I used to live there.'

'Right,' he said insincerely.

'I'll speak to you soon.'

Matt was silent. 'Listen, Jake,' he said uncertainly, 'we've got something here for you. You can have it when you call next. If we live that long.'

I laughed. 'You're not going to tell me what it is? You always loved mystery, Matt. Hey, listen, tell Mamie I'm going on the Peace Train today. She'll like that.'

I heard him relay the information and I heard Mamie's unmistakable snort of derision.

'Tell your old lady to give me a break,' I chided him. 'She should be pleased. It's a whole new me.'

'That would be nice,' said Matt.

I hung up. I called Chuckie and told him about my parcel. Let me think about it, he said. He felt that he could help. I didn't hold out much hope. I said I'd meet him at the station for the Peace Train jaunt. He sounded a little vague. Sure, he said, sure. I didn't like the sound of that but he'd hung up and

I couldn't be bothered calling him back.

I decided that I'd deal with Crab and Hally later. I had no real idea of how I'd deal with them but the phrase about dealing with them later made me feel indomitable. That was a comfort.

I looked out. My cat was in the driveway, trying to do his hungry and maltreated look for passers-by. I finished my coffee. I tightened my tie. I put his breakfast out and I went out to do what I could to bring peace to the world.

By two o'clock in the afternoon I was enjoying myself. The sunshine was warm and there was a light breeze that ruffled my hair. The grass was a pleasant seat and it was fun to check out the peace girls as they struggled up and down the bank and congregated in their enviable little groups.

It had started pretty badly. We all met at Central Station. In the crowd – a whole hundred and fifty or so – I couldn't find Slat, Chuckie or Max. I wasn't at all surprised that Chuckie hadn't turned up, but I hadn't expected Slat's desertion.

The gig at the station was typical. It had been the usual worthy Irish pacifist event. A couple of dull speeches by people you would have crossed the road to avoid, a single local TV crew and the desultory crowd.

I was, however, astonished to see Shague Ghinthoss mount the platform and address the audience about the price for peace, which we all had to pay and which we all would afford, Protestants and Catholics alike, if we could only live together in mutual respect and amity. I was going to shout abuse about last night but I thought people might have suspected that I'd been having sex with him or something and, besides, who would have listened? Ghinthoss was a famous face, or rather, several famous faces.

And I must admit I had a sneaking admiration for his style. He might have been a hypocritical Janus-faced tosspot but if there was a camera crew around he'd be there.

I had no sneaking admiration for what followed. A couple of

folk singers got up and did their dreadful stuff. A chick with a harp strummed for a little while and then a group of young painters had an impromptu exhibition of what they called their peace pictures. These heroes were told to move amongst the crowd with their little daubs. I moved up close for that. The TV camera zoomed in on one guy who was holding a painting of what looked only vaguely like a dead fish.

'Oh, yes,' I heard him say into the boom. 'My painting represents the struggle for peace. I had to decide whether the fish should be alive or dead. I think it has great significance that in this painting you can't really tell whether the fish is dead or alive,' you couldn't really tell it was a fucking fish, 'and, of course, the fish also has all sorts of religious and political connotations. It reminds me in a way of Tolstoy.'

I nearly hit him for that. I'd always been fond of Tolstoy and at least old Leo had done some actual work. I'd seen lots of arty bullshit in Northern Ireland. Provincial but famous, it could produce almost nothing else. Subsidized galleries stocked full of the efforts of useless middle-class shitheads too stupid to do anything else, too stupid to pass the exams that their folks paid for. But I'd never seen anything to match the fishboy.

'This fish gives me hope,' he said emotionally. 'I think this fish can give us all some hope.'

The great Ghinthoss embraced the fishboy grandly and people around them applauded.

We got on the train. We set off. It was quite sweet for forty minutes or so. It felt like quite a clean-shaven, cardiganned thing to be doing. Here I was riding a Peace Train from Belfast to Dublin to protest against the IRA planting bombs on the Belfast to Dublin line. There was going to be another meeting at Dublin station.

But we didn't get to Dublin. There was a bomb on the Belfast to Dublin line. Boom boom.

The train was stopped on a bridge over an embankment just after Portadown. People were stunned, not by the irony but by the unexpectedness of it. I thought that odd: bombs were the subject of their efforts. But these were educated bourgeois and they didn't expect that anything *they* did could be affected by these vicious, callous, working-class terrorists. When those guys planted the bomb they must have been tempted to strafe the train as well.

Robbed of their Dublin protest, some of the peace folk just got off the train and waved their placards about on the line. The railway people went nuts but the TV crew loved it. There was some problem with the line on the way back. It looked like being a long delay so most of the rest of us got out too.

I sat on the bank and smoked some cigarettes. Like I said, I was beginning to have fun. And I was glad that we hadn't made it to Dublin. It wasn't that I didn't like Dublin. Sometimes Dublin was OK but sometimes Dublin gave me the shits.

I was only thinking this acrid stuff to avoid thinking about the girl sitting on the grass close by, whom I was definitely considering marrying. Yeah, I was in love. Again. How bored my friends would be when I told them.

I'd noticed her first as we were boarding the train. Mid-twenties, dark-haired, short, grave-featured. I made sure we were in the same carriage and watched her furtively. Like most of the other women there – peaceful, soulful types – she wore no make-up though her mouth was set in a line of pursed, inept lipstick. She was with a small group of enthusiastic girls and good-natured, turtle-necked, clean-shaven boys.

She noticed me notice her. I took no comfort from this because of my suit. I was the only man not wearing some form of woolly jumper. I hoped it lent me a decadent, attractive air, but for all I knew it might have made me look like a secret policeman.

When the train was stopped and we all got out, her group sat close enough to where I was sitting. Without Slat and the others, I'd felt uncomfortably solitary, as though I stuck out. But there on the grass with the event crashing around everyone's ears, I felt that my besuited uniqueness could only have looked pretty desirable.

With the train stopped on the bridge and everybody sitting on the grass or doing community singing or giving desultory TV interviews it was all pretty embarrassing. Even the train looked faintly embarrassed on the bridge, as though fearful of us seeing up its skirt.

Her group seemed comfortable enough. Those girls and boys chatted in some infinitely tolerant, infinitely self-sufficient way. I tried hating the guys she was with but I couldn't. They looked so much nicer than me. I could only applaud her taste.

Still, after twenty minutes or so, I began to hope that she liked me. She looked in my direction with varying frequency but her gaze was grave. And my heart started its business, its racing, charged-up, I'm-still-young routine. I felt all springtime, all happy. I thought about trying out the Reluctant Look.

I had no chat-up lines. Hardly anybody ever slept with me. I couldn't be called a sleaze. But I had one thing that worked. The Reluctant Look. I hadn't used the Reluctant Look for years now. The problem with the Reluctant Look was that it always worked. Always. Anyway, it was banned in several European countries. The UN would get involved. Maybe I'd also thought about growing up to the point where such artifice would seem childish, unworthy, dishonest. But then again, maybe not.

I wound up for the RL. I wrinkled the corners of my eyes, I pouted slightly, I felt a wash of melancholy descend on my features (I was nearly thirty and I was still at this stuff). Just as I was about to unleash the full ballistic terror upon her, a boom microphone was shoved under my nose.

'Do you think it's ironic that the Peace Train has been halted by a bomb on the line?'

'Wha'?'

I looked up to see myself surrounded by the film crew. The cameraman moved in for a close-up while the producer repeated the question.

I stared dumbly at him.

He coughed and tried again. 'What message do you have for the people who planted this bomb today?'

There was another silence. I was staring silently at someone else. I'd just noticed that Shague Ghinthoss was with them, standing there with a proprietorial air. He beamed at me with the *faux*-humility of an everyday evangel. Already, he'd hijacked it so that whatever film they were making had become a biopic. Great.

The producer followed my gaze. It gave him an idea. 'We have Shague Ghinthoss, Ireland's greatest living poet, here. Would you like to ask him a question?'

'Yes.'

He was delighted to get a response from me. 'What is it?'

I addressed Ghinthoss. 'You're a poet?'

'Yes, I have that honour.' He smiled patronizingly.

'I've always wanted to know something.'

'Yes?' smiled Ghinthoss.

'What the fuck do you guys do in the afternoons?'

The producer said, 'Cut,' acidly enough but at least the soundman sniggered. They moved off. Ghinthoss glanced back at me when the others weren't looking. It was a good look. He must have practised. I'm winning, his look said. I searched my memory for a look that said I couldn't give two fucks, but I couldn't find one.

Intriguingly, the camera crew had moved on to the group in which my girl sat. They behaved amiably enough. They weren't inviting celebrity but they didn't tell them to go away either. They also seemed able to bear with the excitement of meeting Shague Ghinthoss. I found my regard for them increasing.

After a minute or so, I stopped watching. I lit another cigarette. I found myself missing Chuckie. It would have been fun to see what that fat fucker would have made out of all this. Money, probably.

'What did you say to them?'

I looked up, startled, squinting into the sun. She sat down

beside me, pressing her skirt behind her knees. I hadn't seen her coming.

'Whatever it was, they don't think much of you.'

I was surprised, gratified (a little disappointed?) to find that she had approached me. I was also puzzled. I had planned to spend the rest of the eventual journey back fantasizing impossible approaches to her, opening gambits, accidental acquaintance-formers. I would have executed none. I would have been quite content to let her leave unmolested. It was part of the joy of it. Her very graveness made it so much less likely that I would ever have said anything to her. Maybe that's why I liked those grave girls so much.

'Ah . . . well . . . I, ah, didn't have much to say.'

She smiled. She was very pretty. Too pretty for me, perhaps. I'd always preferred slightly plain girls. It was somehow so much sexier when they took their clothes off.

'Me neither,' she said conspiratorially. What with my train of thought, it took me some time to remember she was talking about the TV crew. I liked her inclusive tone. It put us in the same Venn diagram.

'The people you're with don't seem to mind.'

'No. They're easy-going.'

'They seem nice, your friends.'

'They're all right.'

I was surprised at the coolness in her tone. I was even more surprised when she asked me for a cigarette. She looked too clean to smoke. When she lit up I knew that was because she didn't smoke. She tried manfully to swallow her chokes but it was pretty clear.

'You're a surprising character to be at a thing like this,' she said.

'Don't I look like the peaceful type?'

She pointed at my face. It was only a scratch and a fat lip but I saw what she meant. 'What happened?'

'I was moving some furniture.'

She gave me an old-fashioned look.

'I move a lot of furniture.'

Somehow I was getting trapped in my usual macho-bullshit routine. I wanted to talk about Racine and Flaubert with this girl but it looked as though she liked the macho bullshit instead.

'You read any Rousseau?' I asked her sadly.

We talked for a while. Her name was Rachel. I liked her such a lot. She looked like the kind of girl I'd die for and, besides, my heart was so full and my mind so empty. I was as nervous as a seventeen-year-old but she seemed impressed, she seemed persuaded.

At one point a bearded guy with a couple of kids passed by. He was carrying the baby but a six-year-old girl trailed along at his hip. She was crying monotonously in some well-rehearsed grievance. The man's patience snapped. He stopped, bent over the little girl and slapped her hard on her bare legs. 'I told you to stop that,' he hissed at her. The child cried more.

That didn't seem very peaceable to me. That was the thing about these peace-lovers – I always wondered who they liked to beat the shit out of. The man walked on a little. His daughter sobbed bitterly. She stood a few feet from me. She saw me looking at her and her sobs were slightly interrupted. I beckoned her to me. She came hesitantly.

I got out my handkerchief and wiped her wet face. Her face was red and smeared but she was a pretty little thing. 'If you cry much more, you'll melt,' I said. It was a bad line but she was tactful enough to pretend to titter. I smoothed her hair down. 'What's your name, sweetheart?'

'Doris.'

I didn't blink.

'Now you look nice again, Doris.'

She smiled at me. I looked over at her pugilistic owner. 'Your daddy's waiting for you.'

She ran on to join him. I was no magician but I always found that children were pretty calm if you denied yourself the pleasure of knocking them about.

I lit a cigarette, trying not to look at Rachel. I knew what I'd done. I'd been doing it for years. Things that I hoped would make girls want to sleep with me. Years before I might have criticized myself for such ostentatious gallantry, such a cynical display of *tendresse*. These days I comforted myself with the thought that I would have done the same if Rachel had not been there. And at least I hadn't decked the father. All the while my heart had pounded audibly and I had been racked by a profound desire to walk up and punch his head in. I hadn't done that. For me, that was a significant step. I was a reformed character.

When I finally worked up the courage to look at Rachel I saw that light in her eyes, the unmistakable glitter that meant that she thought me sleepable-with.

'That was a nice thing to do,' she breathed.

'She didn't deserve to be slapped.'

'You like children?'

She was going the full way here, she was practically gasping. I think she thought I was some well-dressed desperado with a sensitive side that she could unlock. I think she watched too much television.

'Yeah, I like kids.'

'Why don't you have any?' She smiled at me. 'You'd make a good father,' she said. She flicked her eyes my way.

Now, when a woman says something like that to you, there's no mistaking what she means. It had only been said to me a couple of times but I'd always ended up getting bits of myself wet.

I tried winding it down a bit. I liked her. I didn't want her giving me any cut-price cutesy. She was too nice for that. I was too old for that. I wanted to like her too much. I should have eased off but I couldn't help myself. I was looking for love. Again.

I almost felt sorry for Rachel. She hardly deserved me and all my grief. But I didn't want her to stop talking to me. I didn't want her going away. After Sarah, Mary, Aoirghe and the others, my self-esteem was low, their poor opinion of me had kickstarted my own. Such unanimity was convincing. I was feeling more than susceptible. If Rachel said anything too nice to me, I'd lick her hand and fetch sticks for her.

We were stuck there for ages. Rachel and I talked for half an hour before she returned to her friends. Then they herded us back into the train, which rolled slowly back into Portadown. Ghinthoss and some of the others insisted that everybody get out there and have another demo. The station employees tried to stop it. Portadown was hardly the big smoke, the station was just a single long platform and a breezeblock hut but Ghinthoss was adamant so out we got.

We hung there for another hour. By now Northern Ireland Railway's schedule was fucked. There were only two or three lines in the country and we'd done a better job of blocking one than the IRA themselves. The NIR people begged us to get back on the train. In the end they called the police. When the fuzz arrived, Ghinthoss obviously pondered the possible benefits to his career. Having a full pacific battle with the cops might have had an attractive 1960s, Parisian-riots air but, on the other hand, he didn't want to lose any glitter with the authorities: there were too many prizes, grants and subsidies available to the genteel and careful Irish poet, too many knighthoods and laureateships. With a great air of sacrifice and suppressed menace, he told us all to board the train.

With the chaos on the tracks it took us more than an hour to get back to Belfast. I'd exchanged a few words with Rachel at Portadown but nothing had been ratified – she hadn't *signed* anything. I knew I only had minutes left to solidify this liquid situation. I wanted to see her again, desperately.

As we all disembarked at the station it looked like it wasn't going to happen. In the small-scale mêlée I tried to keep as close to her group as possible but we had no chance to exchange any words. We were nearing the outer doors of the station and it looked like she would slip away for ever when fate – or, at least, fascistic politics – intervened.

About forty or so Just Us demonstrators with placards and another couple of TV crews were strewn across the electronic doors of the station. I recognized one as Mickey Moses, the messianic public relations man; he was surrounded by a group of Just Us women, hard-eyed, Maoist, a typical bevy of republican unlovelies. Many of the men looked tough enough and pretty keen as well. I'd seen lots of Just Us demos, they were childish affairs. But this one smelt somehow different. Deep down, right in my molecules I could feel trouble coming.

Our crowd milled to a stop twenty yards away from the Just Us lot. I looked round for Rachel and saw Shague Ghinthoss instead. He was standing uncertainly, close by the TV crew, his expression more confused than those of most of the crowd. Perhaps only I could fully appreciate his dilemma, after the previous night's republican rabble-rousing and this afternoon's beatnik peace-talk. Several of his many constituencies were pressing their claims. There were now three television crews on the scene. That was an opportunity not to be missed.

I saw him slip furtively into the ladies' toilets. Good decision, I thought. Once the grief cleared, he'd be around to give three separate speeches of heartfelt lamentation to the TV crews. He might scam a Nobel if there were any deaths.

Meanwhile some words were being exchanged at the front. I elbowed my way up there just in time to see the first chair thrown. A few bottles and stones followed. (Where had they found stones? They must have brought them in with them, which was undeniably and commendably far-sighted.) Some peace girls started screaming and crying. Elbowing through some more, I got to Rachel and grabbed her hand. The Just Us front rank of beer-bellied heavies had charged our crowd and peaceful heads were being kicked already. Someone shouted to call the police, others thought running was the best idea. I dragged Rachel towards the elevators at the side exit of the station.

Before we got there one of the fat freedom-fighters weighed up to us. Leather jacket, stiff hair, moustache and tattoos, standard wide-boy warpaint. He liked the look of us. His blood was up. He grabbed my collar, called me a Prod fucker and took his swing. He occupied but a rudimentary position on the evolutionary scale so his big paw was easy to evade. I could have reasoned with him but I just busted his nose and teeth with one of those joyous, unrehearsable elbow punches that only come along once a year or so – oddly the moustache made for an easier target.

A couple of guys who'd been following up stopped momentarily. They were surprised. I don't think that we peaceniks were supposed to show such good moves, and guys like that could never fight for fuck. Maybe with Armalites you don't have to.

Their pause gave Rachel and me time to slip out and down the escalator. We tripped through the car park double-time. Nobody followed us. The sounds of the fight receded in the city hum of Belfast traffic. I'd parked the Wreck on the other side of the station and the only way to get there was to walk across the front concourse. I thought it was better to leave that for a while. The cops had just arrived but I didn't want to be there for the sorting-out. And I'd remembered that there was a little patch of river accessible from the station car park. I'd been there before and I knew it was a good place to hide and not a bad place for a first kiss. It wasn't dark yet, when all the glittery lights on the river would have rendered it a *fait accompli*, but it was twilighty, it was pink enough for me.

We headed down there. It was pretty and my heart was swelling. Rachel's internal organs seemed inflated too. I could feel her tremble beside me and she kept talking about the fracas and the way I'd put my guy down. This grated. I had biffed the man but I was proud of the way I'd sidestepped all the trouble. I'd been feeling like Gandhi. But Rachel was all lit up by my fistwork. This depressed me but I decided, charitably, that nice girls like her didn't see much of that stuff so her reaction was bound to be disproportionate.

We sat on the lip of the river side by side. The sky grew

pinker and Rachel's blood cooled. I found myself extremely happy. I was a chump that way. She might have been gauche but she appeared to like me. I wanted to kiss her. The thought that she might want me to was erotic prize enough.

My mouth dried and I grew nervous but I talked on. She was silent and started glancing at me in that wonderful way that says the first kiss is expected, dreaded and desired.

It could have gone on like that for hours but in the end something in her face – maybe she had her own version of the Reluctant Look – made me simply pull her slowly towards me. I did my sensitive, hilariously virginal, puckering-up thing, she just did that grave, pretty-girl, head-tilting thing. My heart surged. Like almost everybody else, in a life littered with the undead memory of a hundred first kisses, I still hadn't got over them. First kisses still made life worth all the boring bits of living – all the going to the toilet, getting headaches and having your hair cut.

There was a girl I knew from Century Street. She dumped me just after the first time she kissed me. 'What could be better than that?' she said. 'When will we ever improve on that?' I didn't like to admit it but she was right.

Rachel kissed me and it was beautiful by the river. By the cadence of her breathing and the way she brandished her nice-girl breasts at me, I thought it had been something for her, too. It was a fresh enough night but I was airless with joy.

It started to rain. Happily we made our way through the car park back towards my Wreck. As we passed the concourse, we saw the cops clearing up from the last of the incident. People were being put in the back of paddywagons, Just Us and peace-folk alike. I saw Ghinthoss vaguely remonstrating with some of the rozzers for the benefit of the camera crews but most of them were in tight on the people being arrested. The poet had a dissatisfied air. I guessed he was thinking that it might have been pretty good television if he'd been arrested like that. A spell in chokey might have been a great boon. It had worked a treat for Oscar Wilde. Maybe ducking into the chicks' pisser hadn't been such a good idea, after all.

We were moving on when someone called Rachel's name. We turned round to see one of the boys from her group being loaded into the back of one of the police vans. His face was covered with blood but he looked more horrified to see her and me together than by his own injuries. He called her name again and then disappeared into the van.

Rachel was for walking on but I stopped. 'Wasn't that one of your friends?'

'Yeah,' she replied vaguely.

'Aren't you going to do anything?'

'Like what?'

'I don't know. He didn't look very happy. Aren't you worried about him? He's your friend.'

She pouted. 'Well, he's kind of like my boyfriend.'

'What?'

'It's been over for ages. I just haven't told him yet.'

'What?'

'It's hard.'

'How long have you been together?'

She pouted again, she set out a foot in front of her. She twisted her heel from side to side and looked at it truculently. Suddenly, this kind of stunt had ceased to be engaging.

'How long?'

'Two years.'

'Fuck me.'

She tried to smile. 'It's no big deal.'

'It didn't look like he agreed with you.'

'That's not my fault.'

I stared dumbly at her. She was the prettiest girl I'd ever talked to and there was a gentleness in her that made me want to put my head in her lap and weep, but why was she behaving like this? Amidst the noise and bustle of the cops and the complaints of the various protesters, she stood staring silently back at me. Amidst all the bullshit, she looked more attractive than anyone had a right to look. I thought about her bleeding boyfriend. I recognized that face he'd pulled as he'd been taken away. I thought about Sarah. I didn't have whatever it took to be able to do what she wanted. As I looked at her I wished I had but I knew I didn't. When I passed twenty-six years of age I had decided to fight the selfishness of lust. I had decided that because I knew that the finest fuck in history wasn't worth twelve seconds of someone else's unhappiness.

'I can see some of your friends over there,' I said. 'Maybe you should join them.'

Oh, her face could harden quickly. She looked behind her. 'Is that what you want?'

'I think it would be best, don't you?'

She smiled without warmth. 'A quick snog enough for you, then?'

So much for that first-kiss magic.

'You were too old anyway. I'm only twenty-one,' she said.

I tried to smile.

'What age are you anyway?' she asked sharply.

'Fifty-seven.'

'You look it.'

'I hope your boyfriend's OK,' I said, as gently as I could.

She walked away. After a couple of paces, she stopped and turned to face me. 'You know, Jake, you're a real sanctimonious arsehole.' She walked away.

Why was it, every time I met someone these days, they ended up calling me names?

I lit a cigarette and wandered towards my car. In two days I had walked away from two attractive, interesting and interested women. I must have been getting old.

'Jackson.'

I stopped and turned round reluctantly. I'd expected some more grief from Rachel. Imagine my rapture when I found myself confronted by the delightful Aoirghe. Of course, I thought, she was bound to be there. She'd even mentioned it the night before.

'I warn you, Aoirghe, I'm not in the mood,' I advised wearily.

'I thought you were.' She glanced back to where I could see Rachel and her friends. 'What's wrong?' she asked. 'You fail to score again?'

'I'm too tired for this.'

I walked away from her. It was a pointless gesture since she followed me.

'I saw you attack Gerry, you fascist. That was a mistake. These peace girls don't like that macho bullshit.'

I stopped. 'I'm a fascist?! What were you all there for? You're the people with all the ordnance. You were looking for trouble.'

She snorted scornfully. 'Those middle-class shitheads wanted to have their pathetic little protest. We just thought we should have one as well.'

'All they were doing was asking for peace.'

She snorted again.

'Don't you want peace?' I asked.

'Not on their terms,' she replied.

'On what terms, then?'

'On our own terms.'

I laughed. 'That's a constructive position. Your folks must really dote on you.'

'We'll win in the end.'

I opened the Wreck door. 'Change the record, please.'

'Fuck you.'

I smiled happily. 'Tell me, Aoirghe, do dogs bark when you're around them? Is there a reflection when you look in the mirror? Do you have an inexplicable aversion to garlic?'

'You're a big laugh,' she spat angrily.

I got into the Wreck. I would have turned the ignition but if the Wreck did its stuff as usual then it might not have been the valedictory gesture I'd planned.

'How did it go with your slaphead Shakespeare last night?' I asked politely.

'Jealous?'

I had told her I wasn't in the mood but I'm not sure that was an excuse for what I went on to say. 'Aoirghe, I wouldn't fuck you if I had a bag of dicks.'

I started the car. It started first time. The old diesel engine drowned her reply. The Wreck had its moments. I blew a kiss and drove off.

Childish, I admitted, but fun, definitely enjoyable. I switched on my Wreck-radio, caught the words 'two suspect devices', and switched it off again. I drove on, musicless. As I turned up Bedford Street, I decided to sing to myself.

A large BMW came skidding off a side-street at about forty-five miles an hour. The driver struggled to keep all the wheels on the ground but the big car went into a spin. I braked hard and skidded up the pavement, just missing the pillars of a theatre. The BMW spun round towards me and I thought I would die. It hit the kerb hard and lost most of its velocity, shunting into my passenger side almost gently.

I gasped for breath. These things always came from nowhere and always made me want to piss myself. I took a moment to get my breath back and regain control of my wildly shaking limbs. I could see the driver of the BMW struggling angrily with his door. Looked like he wanted to sort me out. That was just what I needed to calm down. I jumped out of the Wreck and sped towards him. I dragged the driver's door open and the driver menaced me with his fists.

'Roche!' I exclaimed, aghast.

'Who the fuck are you?' the child asked. He looked at me closely. 'Oh, it's you, the graduate. Didn't clock you in the suit. Good fucking driving, pal.'

'Whaddyamean, good driving? You nearly killed me.'

'I had the right of way.'

'You're a twelve-year-old criminal driving a stolen car. Don't fucking patronize me.'

He laughed delightedly.

'Are you hurt?' I asked.

'Nah, I always wear a seatbelt.'

'How civic of you.'

'What?' he asked warningly.

'Nothing.'

He looked up and down the street. A few passers-by had stopped to watch us, and the traffic was pulling round us gingerly.

'The filth'll be here in a minute. Gimme a lift,' he requested airily.

I looked back at the Wreck dubiously.

'Don't worry,' he said. 'Old bangers like that can survive anything.'

'Hey, lay off my Wreck – I mean, my car. At least it's paid for.'

He climbed into the passenger seat and proceeded to direct me out of the little tangle on the pavement with his erstwhile joyride, commenting all the while on the deficiencies of my driving and my vehicle.

'So you steal cars?'

'I borrow them.'

'It's illegal.'

'Really? I didn't know that. I better stop doing it now. Thanks.'

'Have you done it before?'

'What do you think?'

'Judging by your driving, it's hard to say. Why did you do it?'

'I fancied a spin,' he answered blithely.

'What if that had been a doctor's car or something? What if some medic got an emergency call and he'd come out to find his motor swiped?'

Roche turned his grubby face towards me triumphantly. 'I'd have given him a lift,' he said gleefully. 'He'd have got there quicker.'

I had to laugh. 'That's for sure. You were doing some knots

coming round that corner.'

'Well, why hang around?'

I looked at him in the seat beside me. He was so stunted that the seatbelt swamped him. Mathematically, I could have been this kid's father. It was a horrible thought. 'I hate to think what you'll be like when your balls have dropped.'

'Worry about your own balls, pal.'

I'd crossed Bradbury Place before I realized that I was heading towards home. That was not a good idea. I definitely didn't want Dick Turpin there to know where I lived.

'Where am I taking you, kid?'

'Just drive.'

'I'm taking you home. Where do you live?'

'You promise you're not going to try and snog me at the garden gate?'

'Ah, fuck, not that again.'

He told me, with relatively good grace, where he lived. I turned right down Sandy Row and headed for Beechmount. I should have known. Upper Falls gamin, he was typical.

'You know where Beechmount is?' he asked me casually.

'Yeah.'

'I knew you were a Taig.'

'Good for you.'

He fingered the cuff of my suit. 'Not at work today? How come?'

'I had to go to a . . . funeral,' I muttered. Roche's mockery might just have sent me over the edge.

We were on the Grosvenor Road now. He told me to pull over. I did. It was simpler that way. I pulled up under a streetlight. He pointed over towards the edge of the housing estate.

'Look,' he said.

I looked. In the growing darkness, the streets were lit up but not illuminating. It was a West Belfast housing estate. I'd seen them before. 'Very nice,' I said. 'I'm sure it's lovely in the moonlight.'

He tutted irritably.

'Look at the wall,' he hissed.

I looked at the wall. There were some graffiti there. *Fuck all Prods. IRA are God* and even a few *OTGs*. I looked closer at the *OTGs*. They were shakily, dyslexically written, the work of a child and not a gifted one. Once or twice it was misspelt, *OGT*, *GTO*, *TGO*.

'You got a couple wrong,' I told him.

'What are you – the spelling police?'

I laughed and drove on.

'What's your obsession with this *OTG* thing?'

'What?'

'Why did you write that?'

'I wanted to.'

'Why?'

Out of the corner of my eye I could see his ratty little face adopt an appearance of mystery and importance.

'I saw a guy writing it a couple of weeks ago.'

I was interested now.

'Just one guy on foot. I saw him writing opposite the Orange lodge on Clifton Street. When he finished I followed him. He went into the New Lodge and wrote it up on a wall near the Just Us advice centre. Looked like he didn't like Protestants or Catholics. The lights are green, dickhead.'

I lurched and stalled, cursing the brat. After a while, the Wreck chugged into life and we drove on.

'Then what?' I asked him.

'I followed him for an hour or two. He just wandered round the town stopping to write on walls every now and then. Opposite churches, political headquarters, even a police station at one point.'

'Didn't he get caught?'

'Nah, he was pretty cute that way. It was dark and he was a nice mover.'

'What did he look like?'

'I don't know. About your age. Walked very quiet. Dark

clothes. Jacket and trousers. Like a suit. I nearly thought he was a priest for a while.'

'Why?'

'Well, his gear was dead black and I could just make out a bit of white at his neck.'

'You'd make a good cop,' I said.

'Fuck you.'

'Thanks.'

I turned right into Beechmount. Beechmount looked like Beechmount always looked – small, unprosperous. Little terraced houses with little terraced people standing on the doorsteps. Some kids ran about the pavement as they always did and some broken glass lay around as was habitual. The walls were painted with a variety of crude scenes depicting how much nicer Catholics were than Protestants and a series of inventive tableaux in which large numbers of British soldiers were maimed and killed.

These were the Belfast mean streets, the internationally famous and dreaded West Side jungle. It was no big deal. The scorbutic children and big mamas were stock stuff. You could see worse in any city. Even as nearby as Dublin and London you could find more dramatic poverty, more profound deracination. You mightn't come across the same quality of Armalites but everything else would look much the same.

There was a species of suffering here that was supposed to be different. A crucial disenfranchisement, a particular oppression. These people, we were told, weren't living in the country they wanted to be living in. I'd been in lots of poor places and I'd never found anyone there who thought that that was the place for them.

I came from a place just like this. It was old hat. Dead news. I wasn't buying any of the bullshit.

'Over there.' Roche pointed to the dirtiest house I've ever seen.

I pulled up. A group of short-haired tracksuited youths

looked over briefly and then turned away. That was the real joy of the Wreck. It would never be worth stealing.

The kid slipped out of his seatbelt and opened the door. He glanced at me as though disappointed by something I had failed to do. I lived with it.

'See you around, kid,' I said.

He smiled. 'What's your name again?'

'Jake,' I said.

'Well, Jake,' I waited for the insult, 'you're all right. See ya.'

He tripped round the car and up the little garden path to the dirty house he lived in. No insult, no graphic profanity. I watched him as the door was answered by a big guy in a dirty T-shirt. He looked over at me suspiciously. He thought about coming across and chatting it out but he didn't have any shoes on. He just scratched his balls, threw his fag butt into the garden and turned into the house with the kid. Young Roche there didn't take after his father in terms of stature but they shared a similar charm.

As I tried to move off I stalled again. I tried starting the engine once or twice but it was useless. The Wreck did this sometimes. If I left it for half a minute, it would wise up and start.

In the silence while I waited I heard the unmistakable noise of shouting from Roche's house. I could have sworn I also heard the sound of blows. I couldn't be sure but I was sure. The big guy had looked like he would. He had looked like he did.

I started the engine and drove away. What could I have done? Sometimes it's just not your problem.

But, all the way back to my house, I felt grim. I should have known that there was someone in the kid's life who was beating the shit out of him regularly. With kids like Roche there was always some big guy in a dirty T-shirt in the background. I didn't know why it bothered me so much. Was it that he reminded me of myself when I was a kid? Hardly. Now that I had arrived on the scene, at least Roche had someone in his life who liked him – or tried to. That was the big difference between us.

Through my clean, clean windscreen the city looked dirty suddenly. After a day of calorific politics and no-show romancing, Roche had been enough to make Belfast seem like a washed-out mouth. I couldn't spit the taste of my day away. I hated the way that could happen. Driving around, liking the streets and the people, was one of the few pleasures I had left. I hated it when my life took that away from me.

It was near ten o'clock when I got home. The cat was pissed off and hungry. I was pleased. He was close to missing me. My expectations were low. I'd settled for pissed off and hungry. I fed the fucker and played my messages.

Chuckie told me he'd sorted out my Crab and Hally problem.

Septic asked me to double-date with him on Friday.

The Amnesty guy was back on my case.

The coppers who'd called yesterday said they were dropping it.

Aoirghe told me to go fuck myself.

I kicked the cat. He looked at me like it wasn't his fault. I couldn't argue. I switched on the radio. It was a foolish move. I should have realized so close to the hour that the news would be on. This time, I didn't switch it off.

'Police said that the incident was not serious. Three arrests were made. A Just Us spokesman alleged that one of their members had been viciously assaulted by a so-called peace campaigner and required hospital treatment. The spokesman said that this showed the insincerity of such so-called peace rallies. The poet Shague Ghinthoss, who was at the incident, refused to comment. Sometimes, he said, things were better left unsaid.'

I laughed and started making some coffee. Good old Shague. I even poured the cat some guilt-milk.

'There has been a report tonight that the mysterious group calling itself the OTG has threatened two young Protestant men from North Belfast. The RUC refused to comment but sources have suggested that the men were threatened because they were involved in debt-collecting activities in the area.'

I switched off the radio and picked up the phone. I called Max's house. Aoirghe answered.

'Is Chuckie there?'

'Is that Jackson?'

'Yeah.'

There was a pause.

'I'll get him.'

Jesus, no abuse. What a polite exchange!

Chuckie came on the line. 'Hey, Jake, I'm sorry we didn't make it to the train thing. You know how it is. Sounds like you and old Aoirghe had a good time there.'

I cut him short. 'Chuckie, what exactly did you do about Crab and Hally?'

Chuckie sounded scared. 'Well . . . Deasely and I talked about it and we thought since they were hassling you, the best thing we could do would be to give them some of their own.'

'Did you ring them up and pretend to be the fucking OTG?'

'Well, yes, we did.'

'Brilliant.'

'It worked. Donal called Crab and told him that we'd kill his family, his friends, people he'd only passed by in the street and then we'd kill him if he didn't lay off you. Donal said he was pissing himself.'

'Fucking wonderful!'

'What's wrong?' Now Chuckie sounded wounded.

'It's just been on the radio. If Crab tells anybody my name was mentioned, people will think I'm in a terrorist organization that doesn't even exist.'

'Oh, yeah,' replied Chuckie lamely.

'And what if those two fuckers are in the UVF or something?'

'Relax! You said yourself they were mostly too stupid to be dangerous.'

'What?' I screamed. 'Do Loyalist paramilitaries have entrance exams now? All they have to do is tell someone and I'm dead under a housing estate or doing a hundred and seventy-five years in Long Kesh.'

'Take it easy.'

'I'm going to kill you, Chuckie.'

'Jake, Jake.'

My doorbell rang. I froze.

'What's wrong?' asked Chuckie.

'There's somebody at my door,' I whispered.

'Well, go and see who it is.'

'What if it's the guys with the hoods and the 9-mms?'

'Go to the window and look out.'

I put the receiver on the table. The window was open and there were a few lights on so it felt safe enough. I craned out into the musky dark air. It failed to cool my face. I could see a man at my door. A cop. My heart sank but it might have sunk further. The RUC were better than the UVF. I hoped.

I went back to the telephone. 'Chuckie. The cops are at the door. I'll call you when I can. You're in big trouble, fatso.'

I hung up and answered the door with an upstanding expression on my face. 'Yes?' I enquired squeakily.

The cop turned to face me and I saw that it was Paul, Mary's fisty boyfriend. I ducked.

He laughed. 'Relax,' he said.

I straightened up. 'Are you going to hit me again?'

'No.'

'Good.'

There was a silence. He seemed uncomfortable. I wondered what he wanted. He looked at his shoes.

'Lovely evening,' I said.

He laughed again. There was a glitter in his eyes that made him look young and pretty. I was resolutely heterosexual but I couldn't help nearly liking him for that.

'Look, I haven't got long,' he said. 'I just wanted to say thanks.'

'What for?'

'For not splitting on me to CID yesterday.'

CID? What was that? Oh, yeah, the cops. I was getting very, very tired of three-letter initials.

'Oh, yeah, right. Forget it,' I said mildly.

'I shouldn't have hit you like that.'

'Maybe not.'

He looked at the scratched graffito on my door. 'Who did this?' he asked, shining his torch at it.

'Just some guys I used to work with. No big deal.'

He looked at me with his tough but friendly expression. 'You get any trouble, you give me a call.'

My hero! Jesus, he'd been doing well up to then but I thought this was taking it a bit far. What was I supposed to do? Swoon into his embrace and run my hands up his manly chest?

'Right,' I said.

He smiled uncertainly again. He hadn't planned his exit line. I looked blankly at him.

'Well, anyway. Sorry about hitting you and thanks again for keeping it quiet. I owe you.'

''Bye now,' I hinted.

I watched him walk away. I shook my head. I suppose I should have been glad that it was an amiable end to a fractious day. Then I remembered Chuckie.

'What happened with the cops?' he said, when I called him.

'Nothing. It was a mistake. Something else entirely.'

'Good. There's no problem.'

'Bollocks, Chuckie. I'm still in trouble. I'm still going to kill you.'

'Jake, you've got to calm down. You take things too hard. You've got to sort your life out. You're a mess.'

'You've got a lot of cheek.'

'I'm your friend, Jake. That's why I say these things.'

I looked at my watch. I was too tired for this. 'Hey, Chuckie.'

'What?'

'Does your dick reach your arse?'

'Hold on, I'll check.'

I heard him setting the receiver down, I could even hear the faint whizz of a zipper being unfastened.

I hung up before Chuckie could tell me any stuff I didn't want to hear.

Ten

That night, on Poetry Street, Jake slept like Chuckie and Max, like Slat, Deasely and Septic, like little Roche and big Ronnie Clay, like all the city's citizens – barring the nocturnals, the insomniacs, the dark-workers and the general nightwalkers. With so many of its people asleep, Belfast lay like an unlit room.

The city rises and falls like music, like breathing. The sleeping streets feel free. The southside shopfronts and the streetlit sidewalks echo empty. Near Hope Street, a stray drinker walks late and wavy. In a small house in Moyard, a thin man lies sleepless and old. On Carmel Street, a dark young woman stalks fearfully in slippers, looking for her cat. There are small events everywhere. On Cedar Avenue, on Arizona Street, Sixth Street and Electric Street, the Royal Ulster Constabulary stand around in damp little groups, keeping an eye on nothing, stopping infrequent cars, checking licences, radioing control. Hello, Control?

Under street-lamps by all the city's walls, writing gleams: IRA, INLA, UVF, UFF, OTG. The city keeps its walls like a diary. In this staccato shorthand, the walls tell of histories and hatreds, shrivelled and bleached with age. *Qui a terre a guerre*, the walls say.

Posters and billboards flap in a hundred little winds. They proclaim concerts, religious meetings, theatres, religious meetings, consumer goods and religious meetings. On Brunswick Street a ragged orange poster flaps. 'The Reverend Ramsden's Travelling Cathedral & Disco, Formal Dress, No Catholics', it says.

On some poles, flags perch. From some windows they hang, upon the tops of certain tower blocks they flutter, these flags. There are a thousand flags, but five mere colours and only two designs. Green, white, gold, red and blue. The two three-coloured emblems of difference.

Throughout the city, bunches of flowers lie. They are grouped on pavements, in doorways or they are wedged between railings. The city is dotted with these false little gardens. The flowers bright and new in their wrapping paper, or weary and wilting with age. Any long walk through the city takes you past one or more of these sites. The citizens have placed these flowers on the spots where other citizens have been murdered. If the flowers are old, you pass and wonder who died there. You always fail to remember.

It is only late at night, if you stand up high, that you can see the city as one thing, as a single phenomenon. While all sleep, the daytime jumble is unified and, geographically at any rate, the city seems a single thing. You can see it ringed by its circles of black basalt, mountains, cliffs and plateaux. You can see the dark sea in the wide bay lapping right up to the foot of the metropolis, wetting its very heart.

You can see that Belfast is, quite literally, a dump. Its core is built on level land that simply wasn't there two hundred years before. Earth was dumped into the sea and Belfast was built there. Slob land, reclamation. The city is a raised beach, an abutment. The townsfolk say it rose from the water like some god but the truth is that it was dumped in the sea but didn't sink.

Belfast is Rome with more hills; it is Atlantis raised from

the sea. And from anywhere you stand, from anywhere you look, the streets glitter like jewels, like small strings of stars.

Some say it is a city of 279,000 people, 130,000 men and 149,000 women, and that these people are squashed into 11,489 hectares. Some say that there are half a million souls there – Greater Belfast is Belfast too. Two cathedrals, some docks, a harbour, many hills and mountains. A sea-level town on the lip of the land.

However many, whatever size, it is magical. This night, the streets smell stale and tired, the air is full of regret and desire. Time seems passing and passed. The city feels how it feels to grow old.

However magical or glittering, you can read the signs. You have seen the flags, the writing on the walls and the pavement flowers. This is a city where people are prepared to kill and die for a few pieces of coloured cloth. These are the standards of two peoples with a four- or eight-hundred-year-old difference, national and religious. It is an illogic, a conundrum that corrupts the blood here. There is no revolution, only deadly convolution.

But deep at night Belfast whispers in cool breaths that hatred is something like God. You can't see what you can't see, but if you fight and follow it blindly enough, it will keep you warm at nights.

As your eye roams the city (as your eyes must, as our eyes, those democratic unideological things, always will, giving witness, testimony), you see that there is indeed a division in the people here. Some call it religion, some call it politics. But the most reliable, the most ubiquitous division is money. Money is the division you can always put your money on.

You see leafy streets and you see leafless streets. You can imagine leafy lives and leafless ones. In the plump suburbs and the concrete districts your eyes see some truths, some real difference. The scars and marks of violence reside in only one type of place. Many of the populace seem to live well. Many prosper while many suffer.

Belfast is a city that has lost its heart. A shipbuilding, rope-making, linen-weaving town. It builds no ships, makes no rope and weaves no linen. Those trades died. A city can't survive without something to do with itself.

But at night, in so many ways, complex and simple, the city is proof of a God. This place often feels like the belly of the universe. It is a place much filmed but little seen. Each street, Hope, Chapel, Chichester and Chief, is busy with the moving marks of the dead thousands who have stepped their lengths. They leave their vivid smell on the pavements, bricks, doorways and in the gardens. In this city, the natives live in a broken world – broken but beautiful.

You should stand some night on Cable Street, letting the little wind pluck your flesh and listen, rigid and ecstatic, while the unfamous past talks to you. If you do that, the city will stick to your fingers like Sellotape.

Whether in the centre itself or the places in which people put their houses, the city's streets, like lights in neighbours' houses, are stories of the done, the desired, the suffered and unforgotten.

The city's surface is thick with its living citizens. Its earth is richly sown with its many dead. The city is a repository of narratives, of stories. Present tense, past tense or future. The city is a novel.

Cities are simple things. They are conglomerations of people. Cities are complex things. They are the geographical and emotional distillations of whole nations. What makes a place a city has little to do with size. It has to do with the speed at which its citizens walk, the cut of their clothes, the sound of their shouts.

But most of all, cities are the meeting places of stories. The men and women there are narratives, endlessly complex and intriguing. The most humdrum of them constitutes a narrative that would defeat Tolstoy at his best and most voluminous.

The merest hour of the merest day of the merest of Belfast's citizens would be impossible to render in all its grandeur and all its beauty. In cities the stories are jumbled and jangled. The narratives meet. They clash, they converge or convert. They are a Babel of prose.

And in the end, after generations and generations of the thousands and hundreds of thousands, the city itself begins to absorb narrative like a sponge, like paper absorbs ink. The past and the present is written there. The citizenry cannot fail to write there. Their testimony is involuntary and complete.

And sometimes, late at night, when most sleep, as now, the city seems to pause and sigh. It seems to exhale that narrative, to give it off like the stored ground-heat of a summer day. On such nights, you cross a city street and for a few golden minutes there are no cars and the very hum of distant traffic fades and you look at the material around you, the pavements and street-lamps and windows, and if you listen gently, you might hear the ghosts of stories whispered.

And there is magic in this, an impalpable magic, quickly gone. It is at these times that you feel you are in the presence of something greater than yourself. And you are. For as you look around the perimeter of your illuminated vision, you can see the buildings and streets in which a dark hundred thousand, a million, ten million stories as vivid and complex as your own reside. It doesn't get more divine than that.

And the sleepy murmurings of half a million people combine to make an influential form of noise, a consensual music. Hear it and weep. There is little more to learn on the earth than that which a deserted city at four in the morning can show and tell. Those nights, those cities are the centre, the fulcrum, the very wheel upon which you turn.

Sleeping cities and sleeping citizens alike wait upon events, they attend upon narrative. They are stopped in station. They soon move on, they soon start again.

And as the darkness begins to curl around its edges, the city shifts and stumbles in its slumber. Soon it will wake. In this city, as in all cities, the morning is an assault. The people wake and dress themselves as though arming themselves for their day. From all the small windows of all the small houses on the small streets of this little city, men and women have looked out on first-light Belfast and readied themselves to do battle with this place.

But for now they are still abed. Like Jake they lie, their stories only temporarily suspended. They are marvellous in their beds. They are epic, these citizens, they are tender, murderable.

In Belfast, in all cities, it is always present tense and all the streets are Poetry Streets.

Eleven

Rosemary Daye popped her third tobacco gum of the day. It had been three weeks and she'd smoked only two cigarettes. Both when she'd had a drink with Sean. She had felt that there was an excuse with a new boyfriend. On that second date, she'd been so nervous that accepting a cigarette had helped to establish the cloud of sophistication with which she was trying to blind him. She knew now that it was an effort she did not need to make. Now she knew how gloriously blinded he'd been already. She'd worn her print dress and he had actually whimpered even before she had slowly peeled it off.

The light sunshine almost warmed her skin at the thought. She crossed Royal Avenue and went into her favourite shop. Fashionable girls lounged. She browsed absent-mindedly. It was too expensive and she wasn't sure she liked it but she tried on a green-linen knee-length skirt. The things he had said about her hips – his sincerity underlined by the visual evidence – still made her skin flush. As she modelled the skirt in a half-length mirror, she noticed that it was already creasing beneath her pelvis. A week ago she might have thought it made her pear-shaped. Now she gladly wrote the hefty cheque before she had even changed back into her own clothes. This skirt, those creases, she knew, would make him weep.

The shop assistant smiled at her as she paid and Rosemary wondered if the girl knew her thoughts. Her happiness seemed intuitive, conspiratorial. She wondered if the girl, who was pretty, had someone who worshipped her like Sean worshipped Rosemary. Pointlessly but generously, she hoped so.

Outside, the sunshine had cooled but was sunshine still. Her mood lifted further and she even, faintly but perceptibly, swung her hips when she walked.

She wondered why she hadn't found him handsome until that night. Now, she wanted to chew his smile right off his face. His broad teeth with the tiny front gap, his strong chin and the skin dark with imminent stubble, they all made her feel clumsy and hot inside.

She smiled at herself in a dark window. Mechan's beauty parlour. Rosemary checked that window often. Rosemary checked many windows often. There were few pedestrian routes through the city that Rosemary could not plot for regular intervals of reflecting surfaces. She had a map of the city whose milestones were places where she might look at herself. Dark windows, matt displays, even parked cars. Rosemary was uncomfortable if she was forced to walk more than two or three hundred yards without the possibility of checking how she looked.

It wasn't vanity. It was concern. Rosemary's hair had ruled her life since she'd been thirteen. Idiosyncratic, untameable, her hair had a unique capacity to make her unhappy. For years she had spent hundreds of pounds on cutting it, treating it and shaping it in a variety of clip-joints. She had watched other women and their hair, she had calculated their difficulties, their budgets. If she drove her car behind a car full of women, she could calculate to a nicety the combined annual trichological expenditure represented there.

In the past couple of years, she had established some control over her hair. With the help of an electronic straightening device and a mysterious post-shampoo unguent that seemed to thicken it, she had won the battle. Too often, her hair still looked like an unfashionable air hostess's coiffure, and bad-hair days were more than bad for her, but it was progress.

Nonetheless she had not lost her self-checking window habit. She was not alone, she noticed. Other women routinely checked their ghostly selves in those demi-mirrors, and many more men seemed to do it than women. Even the ugly fat men inspected their images with monotonous regularity. The more attractive men seemed to do it with uneasy fascination but the ugly fat men looked at themselves with entirely candid, undisguised approval. It was only lately that her looking had become an act of approval. She was beginning to like herself. She was beginning to think that if she'd been a man she might have liked to climb all over a woman like herself. She was twenty-six. It was about time.

As she looked out at the broad expanse of Royal Avenue, it seemed that the street was full of men who would desire her and that their desire would be different from the unwelcome, reducing thing it had always been before. It was as though Sean had released or revealed a world that was full of good desire, generous desire. People wanted their flesh to touch flesh, warm skin on warm skin. What could be the harm in that?

Rosemary crossed the street, smiling at a man who hadn't noticed her. He looked at her then, gratified and puzzled by the width and warmth of her smile.

It was a quarter past one. She had only fifteen minutes before she had to be back at work, back to the slender joys of insurance. For the first time in three years, she felt herself yearn for the office and its milky half-light and its somniferous warmth. An afternoon of desultory phone calls could not be too onerous. She would kick off her shoes and knead the warm carpet under her desk with her bare toes – it was the first day of the year on which she had not worn tights and she was pleased to see that few other women had dared on so unsunny a day. There would be plenty of time to think about Sean and his hard/soft skin and the possible futures they might have.

She cut down Queen's Arcade and walked through its murk. This place, normally so tawdry to her, a poorly covered row a man wide, was transfigured and glamorous. Her spirits, not peaking, lifted further. She hoped she would always feel this.

She felt as though he had kissed her every inch. He was her fifth. *Oh, let me be your fifth,* he had pleaded, when she had told him she had slept with four men. No one before had shown his gentleness or his appreciation. The memory of his stunned silences and his sheer gleeful gratitude made her stumble half-way down the arcade, again making her stomach feel heated and wet inside.

She had refused to spend the night and she hadn't smiled when he said he would call her. It had hurt her to have the mood so dispelled by those words, *I'll call you.* They were the only words he had said that she had heard before. As she drove home, she had gained some perspective, made it no big deal. Men were like that. She should feel anger, not shame. But she could not control her joy when she got home and her grumpy flatmate Orla had tersely announced that someone called Sean had just telephoned for her, unconcerned that it was half past three in the morning. Orla said that he sounded drunk, though Rosemary knew that he had drunk nothing – apart from her. Orla went back to bed in some dudgeon and Rosemary called him back. His voice was wide awake but soft and he did sound intoxicated. He told her, cornily, that his bed felt too big without her and that her hips had made him feel that he could now die happy. Maybe it wasn't much but it felt like enough.

She emerged from the dark of Queen's Arcade. A hazy strip of cloud had passed, the sun blushed warmer and she felt its tiny warmth in her already hot face. She smiled and then smiled again at the thought of her reasonless grinning. She loosened her collar. Though lightly clad, she felt wrapped and snug in her skin. The heat of her flesh was marvellous. She thought she would never be cold again. She felt as though every living, breathing inch of her was goaded into some kind of heat, some slow, productive burn.

The light of Fountain Place brought her to some approximation of her senses. She had wandered and bought skirts for so long that she had neglected to get her lunch. She didn't have much time left. She turned into the small sandwich shop to which she always went. She stopped at the door to let a handsome, raffish young man in a green suit pass by. He, struck by the flush of her face and neck, smiled flirtatiously and held the door open with a vaguely gallant air. She smirked happily and stepped under his arm. She turned to murmur some thanks and stopped existing.

The largest part of one of the glass display cases blasted in her direction. Though fragmented before it reached her, the pieces of shrapnel and glass were still large enough to kill her instantly. Her left arm was torn off by sheeted glass and most of her head and face destroyed by the twisted mass of a metal tray. The rim of the display case, which was in three large sections, sliced through or embedded in her recently praised hips and some heavy glass jars impacted on her chest and stomach, pulverizing her major organs. Indeed, one substantial chunk of glass whipped through her midriff, taking her inner stuff half-way through the large hole in her back.

The young man who had opened the door for her – he was thirty-four but still had unlined skin and thick hair, had always been thought younger than he was but what had irritated him in his early twenties now delighted him, as he saw his old schoolfriends married or bald and he could still comfortably date girls ten years younger than himself – was also killed, though he took nearly twenty seconds to stop existing. Some of the display case had removed one of his legs completely and mutilated his groin and pelvis. Glass from the door had smashed open his face, ripping off his nose, and penetrated his brain. His name was Martin O'Hare. He had been to school. He had read *Great Expectations* and had wanted to be an astronomer. He had been in love with people and people had been in love with him. He had a story, too.

Inside the sandwich shop (how unglamorous, how untremendous – Northern Ireland had never dealt in epic murder sites: alleyways, corner shops, betting shops, sandwich shops, mobile shops, crap pubs, bad dance halls, up against a variety of walls painted and unpainted), Kevin McCafferty stopped existing. Kevin had been serving a salad and bacon *baguette*, with Flora rather than butter, to a middle-aged businessman he didn't like. Kevin was poorly paid but was doing the double to get by. He was tired of being on the dole and he wanted to be famous. He sang in a band whose name changed every gig – or rather, every month. He didn't really like music and he knew he couldn't sing. But it was an excuse to wear his hair long, chase girls and perhaps, one day, to appear on television, which he greatly desired.

(Kevin achieved his ambition six months later when an independent film company broadcast a documentary on Channel 4 about the Troubles and used some of the Fountain Street scene-of-crime photographs that were to be taken within the next five or six hours. Kevin, standing so close to the blast, had been impressively mangled but, though decapitated and missing a leg and a large portion of chest and abdomen, there was, crucially, something recognizably human about his meat. Other victims had been blown entirely to bits and though the colour pictures of those people (or *pieces*, more properly) were certainly shocking, the director decided that they lacked that human dimension, that extraordinary *shockingness* that Kevin's beef-like approximation of the human form possessed. The Broadcasting Complaints Authority later upheld a record number of complaints about the programme from people who didn't want to look at that kind of thing and from Kevin's mother who insisted, correctly and miraculously, that she recognized her son's internal organs, his exposed ribs and spine, his headless, grotesque self. The film director's wife refused to sleep with him for nearly three months and the RUC scene-of-crime photographer committed suicide five months later in an incident that wasn't necessarily related.)

Kevin had a story, too.

Natalie Crawford also had a story. She was eight years old so it wasn't, up to then, a very long story or perhaps even enormously interesting to most adult readers (apart from her indulgent parents, of course) but, in the normal course of events, her story would have grown, used a larger cast, involved more scenes and events. Even so, an eight-year-old's story was quite a lot to end so abruptly. She, her sister Liz – a twelve-year-old who was already in love with a boy from Carryduff who, she insisted, despite his impressive spots, had eyes just like Brad Pitt's – and their mother, Margaret, all stopped existing more or less in unison when a blown-apart drinks fridge showered its hot metal on their soft, unresisting flesh.

The Crawford family had its own collective story. The loss of the three Crawford women certainly robbed that story of much of its dynastic heft. In addition, husband-and-father Robert certainly felt that the rest of his personal narrative wasn't quite the ringing thing it should have been. Wifeless, childless, Robert simply refused to live with it. He refused to deal with it. Afterwards television crews, doing pieces about the grieving relatives, used him gleefully for the first couple of weeks. The dead wife and two little girls made such a good story. In the months that followed, with Robert's stubborn resistance to comfort or happiness, the TV crews avoided him. His passionate grief, his lack of development, his unreasonable and untelegenic refusal to forgive didn't make such a good story.

Robert's great grief was that his wife and children had only been in Fountain Street that day because he and Margaret had had such a furious row about his never doing the dishes. The backlog and arrears of ten years of marital resentments had, as always, been exercised and rehearsed in full force and Margaret had stomped off into town with the two children to cry, sulk and get killed.

Robert never got used to how much this hurt; he never lost his surprise at the stormy extent of his grief. It would wake him in the middle of the night. He didn't have to dream about it: it lay like a crust over his thoughts, conscious and unconscious, a massive hurt for which he had no room but which grew anyway like something obscene rising in his gut. The first time he masturbated after the explosion, three months later, he had cried himself to sleep, dead with shame and guilt. It was as though nothing he could do could match the dignity of how he should remember them. It was as though he had only learned to love them after they had been blown apart. Love choked him as much as grief. Dreadful, uncontrollable tenderness that had nowhere to go. He had nowhere to put all the love they had made him feel when they died. He had never known how dreadful, how damaging love could be.

Robert's story became uncommercial. He lost his job. He lost his friends. He drank – to remember not to forget – and it just rained in his heart for the rest of his life.

So, thus, in short, an intricate, say some, mix of history, politics, circumstance and ordnance resulted in the detonation of a one-hundred-pound bomb in the enclosed space of the front part of a small sandwich shop measuring twenty-two feet by twelve. The confined space and the size of the device created a blast of such magnitude that much of the second floor of the front part of the building collapsed into it and out onto the street. There were fourteen people in the sandwich bar. There were five people in the beauty parlour upstairs when it collapsed and twelve on the street in the immediate vicinity of the flying shrapnel and collapsing beauty parlour. Thirty-one people in all, of whom seventeen stopped existing then or later and of whom eleven were so seriously injured as to lose a limb or an organ.

In a glass-fronted bookshop across the street a security guard and two browsers in the travel section were badly wounded when the bookshop window exploded. The security guard lost one eye completely but merely the sight of the other, while the face and scalp of a middle-aged woman leafing through a picture book about Mauritius were permanently mutilated. The other browser lost much of the delicate tissue of his neck and face.

A street bin thrown across the exit of Queen's Arcade by the force of the blast hit a schoolboy sitting on one of the stone benches there and so damaged his pelvis that he would never walk properly again.

There were many people with cuts and scratches, there were many people frightened. Some of the amateur ambulancemen and women, who had waded in when the smoke and dust had cleared, saw dreadful, emetic sights that would rest like a film over everything they would see subsequently in their lives.

In the ringing, piercing silence of the aftermath of the bomb, there were a few moments of something grotesquely like peace. The dead were dead, many of the dying were unconscious, or incapable of speech, most of the injured and the terrified were in shock or simply very, very surprised. Because it had been very, very surprising. An everyday, entirely forgettable, urban situation (any café, any shop, any pub, any street) explosively converted into a slaughterhouse. The living took a few seconds to understand, to start their screams.

Three minutes later, some policemen had arrived. Some stood or squatted by the injured or dying, some clambered over the rubble to look for survivors, one intelligent policeman just turned and ran away. Within five minutes, the first ambulance had arrived. The two paramedics, thinking themselves veterans, waded in with some aplomb; within seconds they were gagging.

Some of the immediate rescue operations were hampered by the delicacy of the police. One of the traditional features of these explosions was that the bombers would plant a second or even third device timed to detonate some minutes later, planted just where they thought the police might set up their cordon lines. Police and firemen took some time to make sure this was unlikely – one sandwich-shop victim, who might not have died, died.

By the time ten minutes had passed, the death-toll had risen. More paramedics struggled with their horror and more police officers and firemen scrabbled amongst the debris. Several passers-by had simply crumpled to the ground like nauseous children, formless heaps, trembling, silent.

After fifteen minutes, most present had grasped the situation. A cordon had been erected. Onlookers and journalists were restrained. Digging crews had been set up. A triage system was working efficiently, supervised by a youthful doctor who would never know how much she had physically resembled Rosemary Daye. It was notable, nevertheless, how many people still refused to understand what had happened. Several of the shocked onlookers sat staring dumbly at the excrement and tissue and blood, incapable of comprehending how political this was. One naïve fireman, upon retrieving what seemed to be a portion of a severed head, naïvely believed this to have been a sadistic act. A woman with a bloody face who comforted her young son near the bookshop had no real conception of the historical imperatives leading to such an event. One French tourist, who'd been closer to Castle Street than to the bomb itself but still had been badly scared, even wondered to himself why anyone who might want the British to leave the Irish alone would announce this by killing Irish people. But he was French.

There was all round a lamentable lack of overview, of objectivity. Those involved refused to put the event in its proper context. And for some unruly souls, this was a process that continued for some time. Indeed, one churlish triple amputee actually told a newspaper some weeks later that he would never be able to understand or forgive the people who had planted the bomb.

One can excuse much of this by their surprise and some of the immediate physical distress attendant upon such an event, but the more consistent refusal of some to listen to reason or explanation is perhaps harder to fathom. Maybe, at such times, many people simply refuse to read between the lines. Maybe they believe the lies that their eyes tell them.

For the men who planted the bomb knew it wasn't their fault. It was the fault of their enemies, the oppressors who would not do what they wanted them to do. They had reasonably asked to have their own way. They had not succeeded. They had then threatened to do violent things if they did not get their way. When this had not succeeded, they were forced to proceed with extreme reluctance to do those violent things. Obviously it was not their fault.

It was the politics of the playground. If Julie hits Suzy, Suzy doesn't hit Julie back, Suzy hits Sally instead.

The rest of the day at Fountain Street was a stretched, slow thing. The hours passed as though time itself had been damaged in the blast. Time passed at the pace it took a man to walk across the rubble. Time passed like death.

They removed the seriously injured. They removed the medium injured. They removed the slightly injured. They removed the shocked. They didn't remove the frightened. Some of the frightened had to stay. They themselves were some of the frightened. Witnesses were interviewed by the police. The police were interviewed by the press. Politicians gave statements. Medics gave statements. There was a round of hearty condemnation and outrage on all sides. Few paused to think how often they'd repeated those words over the last double decade or so. The accessible bodies were removed and then the dig for the more inaccessible remains began in earnest.

Earnest was the right word. Such an endeavour was a committed journey into gravity, into deep seriousness. Some of the diggers were civilian volunteers. Men and women of good humour started this work and felt like there would never be anything to laugh about again. They found many things. They found a partially damaged hearing aid, which was never attributed to any of the victims. They found the sandwich bar menu board, dented and bloody. There was a rumour that they had found a perfect human brain, completely exposed. They found an undamaged green linen skirt, which mystified them – all the female dead were badly mangled and their clothes mostly in tatters – until one perceptive individual spotted that it still bore a large price tag. They found clothes, wallets, toys, handbags, coats, shoes and boots, people, bits of people and things no one could identify.

A man called Francis, a father of two, found a small blue thing he could not recognize. He was about to throw it in the pile in which the discovered clothing lay when he realized that there was a scrap of blonde hair attached. His heart blew like another bomb and he dropped it in horror. It was a bit of a blue hat with a part of a little girl's skull attached. (It was later identified as a piece of the greater remains of Natalie Crawford.) He shouted to the others and sat back on some debris, breathing hard. A couple of firemen came over. Francis pointed to the small blue thing. One of them picked it up. The other patted him on the back. 'You all right?'

Francis nodded, still puffing like a woman in labour. After a couple of breaths, he went back to work and started climbing again over the hill of rubble. It would have been better if a single man had found the small blue thing, or at least a man with no children. But Francis had those two daughters and an inappropriate gift for empathy. Within a couple of minutes he was holding his hands in front of his mouth and nose and sobbing like a beaten child – Francis was also a sloppy thinker and had no real grasp of history or politics.

Such inadequacies were common at the bomb-site. A fair few were also obvious at the two hospitals, which dealt with casualties and fatalities. The Accident and Emergency Department at the City Hospital quickly came to look like a knacker's yard. Other everyday patients, who had come in with sprained ankles or slipped discs, reeled out in horror. In the mortuary, the bodies were laid out bit by bit, assembled slowly from the seventy or eighty pounds of unidentified tissue brought to them there. A difficult task because so much of it was scorched and shredded. Human flesh was famously ill-equipped for withstanding such conditions. What had flesh ever done to merit such treatment? The sins of the flesh must have been big sins for flesh to be treated so.

Such failings were evident also amongst the policemen and women sent to inform relatives of the identified dead. Appalling reluctance was shown to execute this task.

The only real professionalism was amongst the reporters and cameramen on the scene and at the hospitals. They demonstrated real vigour and real hunger for their job. They thrust cameras and microphones everywhere. One German journalist even pointed his microphone at a corpse on a gurney. The other local journalists laughed at that. They had stopped asking questions of the dead a long time before.

By midnight, many of those involved had returned home. The police, the paramedics and medics, the bereaved and the workers at the bomb-site. The day brought an odd unifying phenomenon to many of them. That night, many thought, while drinking a cup of coffee, brushing their teeth, watching a film or locking a door, *What a strange thing to be doing after what I've seen.* Many felt as though their insides were hairy and itching. It was a most unaccustomed feeling, one they could not explain.

There was another unifying phenomenon. All of those people possessed a new knowledge. For all their lack of understanding, they comprehended something of which they had been ignorant. Some had learnt a new respect for the fragility of flesh, some thought they had learnt something about the possibilities of human cruelty, but there was only one knowledge common to all.

They had all learnt that from revolution runs blood, runs all our human waters.

The Fountain Street dead were Rosemary Daye (hips and hair), Martin O'Hare (aspirant astronomer), Kevin McCafferty (unemployed, couldn't sing), Natalie (not a long story), Liz (liked Brad Pitt) and Margaret Crawford (resented washing dishes), John Mullen (never ate his salad and bacon *baguette*), Angie Best (the owner, a forty-two-year-old divorcée with two children and a twenty-five-year-old lover she was about to dump), William Patterson (never met him), Patrick Somebody-or-other, a woman called Smith and six unnamed others. The list is pointless. The list is easily forgotten.

Named, unnamed. Remembered, forgotten. They all did that trick the dead do. Whether they died immediately, more or less immediately or later, they all did that trick. From living human to corpse – the fastest transition in the world.

To sum them up is pointless and impossible. When she was twenty-two, Angie Best passed her driving test and experienced an ecstasy and sense of freedom so extraordinary that no subsequent experience ever matched its intensity. Her driving-test examiner, a man called Murray, remembered her joy for the rest of his life. He liked to recall her on rainy Wednesdays when he'd had to fail more than one candidate.

They all had stories. But they weren't short stories. They shouldn't have been short stories. They should each have been novels, profound, delightful novels, eight hundred pages or more. And not just the lives of the victims but the lives they touched, the networks of friendship and intimacy and relation that tied them to those they loved and who loved them, those they knew and who knew them. What great complexity. What richness.

What had happened? A simple event. The traffic of history and politics had bottlenecked. An individual or individuals had decided that reaction was necessary. Some stories had been shortened. Some stories had been ended. A confident editorial decision had been taken.

It had been easy.

The pages that follow are light with their loss. The text is less dense, the city is smaller.

Twelve

But Fountain Street is an incidental detail. The site itself is a distraction, the event, in some ways, an irrelevance, the toll a technicality. Such bombings, such murders do not really involve the people involved. The deaths and the maimings are a meaningless by-product. The victims are mostly random, entirely obscure. No one is interested in them. Certainly not the bombers. It is the rest of us who matter.

Such events are a message. They are designed and supposed to tell us something. To show us something, at any rate. The actions are not ends in themselves. They are demonstrations. Look at what we can do, they say. Look at what we can do to you.

We are terrified. We are meant to be terrified. That is why it is called terrorism.

Thus the reaction of the general citizenry is the substance of such events, the product, the commodity in this robust PR. And the reaction of the citizenry was this:

Jake Jackson, Ronnie Clay and Rajinder Singh had all comprehended the fact of the explosion at one and the same time. At 1.15 p.m. they stood or sat on the roof of the Europa Hotel with their workmates, lunchboxes on their laps, sandwiches to hand and mouth. They heard the unmuffled bang of a proximate detonation. There was a mild waft in the air. Several went to the edge of the roof and looked about them.

'Came from over there,' suggested Ronnie, pointing westwards towards the Grosvenor Road.

Rajinder gestured towards the city centre where they could see a large dark ball of dust linger, tremble and disperse in the mild breeze.

'Where's that?' asked Billy.

'Castle Street,' said one.

'Nah, Royal Avenue,' suggested Ronnie.

'Looks big,' said Jake.

A siren began to wail, building pitch and volume.

'Didn't hear any sirens before,' said one man.

'Does that mean there was no warning?' asked Rajinder.

'Who knows?' answered Jake. 'They don't need sirens to evacuate buildings for a bomb scare.'

The men looked at one another silently. Several returned to their original positions and recommenced their luncheon. Ronnie shrugged his shoulders and joined them. After a couple of minutes, only Jake and Rajinder were left at the edge of the roof. For some time they stared towards where they could still see the remnants of the dust cloud linger in the air like a stain.

Rajinder looked at Jake uncertainly. 'I have a bad feeling.'

Jake glanced back at the ebbing dust plume. 'I hope you're the only one.'

In common with 84,637 other people in Northern Ireland, Luke Findlater discovered that a big blast had occurred in the very first radio report of the incident on that day. Every lunchtime he listened to an eccentric agricultural programme on Radio Ulster called *Farming Ulster Update*. He heard, with delight, items about silage management, pig-farming and sheep-dip. The Englishman knew that it was probably some crass patrician taste for obscure kitsch but it genuinely charmed him.

Within only twelve minutes of the explosion in Fountain Street, the presenter of this programme had stopped speaking, fumbled with some paper and announced in an uncertain voice that he had received unconfirmed reports of a serious explosion in Belfast city centre and that several people had been killed.

The man's voice, so associated with the risibly mundane matters of manure and chicken-crops, formed those words strangely. The effect was disturbing. Luke felt cold. He sat back in his chair with a peculiar sensation. He looked around the office. He had not lived long enough in Northern Ireland to find such things usual, customary. The furniture in his room, the very stationery seemed grotesquely commonplace under the circumstances.

Luke had been about to send a fax. Now he proceeded to send that fax. He stood by the machine, feeding the paper through, feeling the unaccountable, unanswerable consciousness of something inappropriate.

Fifteen minutes later, when Septic Ted learnt of the bomb he felt nothing quite so complicated as the feelings that had oppressed Luke. He was a veteran. He had lived in that city all his life. He knew several of the scores.

He had taken the day off work and was lounging on a sofa watching daytime television. He had nearly dozed off when the news flash appeared. He drank another mouthful of beer and burped acidly.

'Wankers,' he said.

Septic was not unfeeling. He was used to it.

Chuckie Lurgan learnt of the Fountain Street explosion thirty minutes after the event. He had gone home to have lunch with his mother. To his irritation, she had been absent and had not come back after an hour. He was driving back to the office from Eureka Street when his telephone had rung – or, rather, parped thinly. Chuckie was yet too doubtful of the intricacies of driving to risk combining that task with a telephone conversation, delightful and flash though that would be. He pulled up on some Bedford Street double yellows and answered the call.

It was Luke Findlater. He told Chuckie how they had earned some money in the two hours since he'd been gone and how they were to earn more in the twenty minutes before he got back to the office. Chuckie, as always, liked to hear this but preferred not to be there. 'I've got to get some things in the city centre,' he said. 'I'll park the car, do my stuff and see you in forty minutes.'

'That might be a problem. There's been a big explosion somewhere central. The centre might be cordoned off.'

'When?'

'Don't know. Not long ago.'

Chuckie hung up. He started the car and turned left at the bottom of Bedford Street, getting onto the wide square circuit of one-way traffic around the City Hall. As Luke had predicted, the police had laid stretches of white tape across the approach to Donegall Square. Chuckie's car became hemmed in as those behind him manoeuvred to change their route. He stared down the broad boulevard of Donegall Place. Groups of ambulances, fire engines and police cars clustered near the Bank of Ireland but he couldn't tell where the bomb had been.

A policeman held up the traffic so he could pass by. The man's face was pale and blank. Chuckie didn't like that look. He had seen it on policemen's faces before. Even at the periphery of such incidents, even hundreds of yards away, they often wore that numb, pallid expression.

Diverted, he turned left past the building he had always known as the College of Knowledge. He was irritated that his shopping plans had been dashed, but there was a small, indolent part of him that hoped no one had died.

*

Crab and Hally heard about the bomb nearly fifteen minutes after Chuckie. At two minutes before two o'clock they were in the van, just about to turn into the New Lodge, a Catholic area – a task which, they hated to admit, was more daunting since they had lost Jake, their conveniently Catholic colleague. They were listening to a song neither liked. Crab had just spotted a young woman in a tight skirt and had shouted something that had sounded to the woman like some meaningless elongated howl but which both Crab and Hally understood to represent the statement 'I'd fuck ye any day of the week, big darlin'.'

They had laughed big fat laughs like the big fat men they were.

When they had stopped laughing they found that the song neither liked had ended and the two o'clock news had begun. An announcement was made about the Fountain Street bomb.

'Do you think it was one of theirs or one of ours?' said Crab to Hally.

'Do you think it got more of theirs or ours?' said Hally to Crab.

'City centre. Hard to say how many Taigs there'd be down there.'

'That place is near Castle Street. They're bound to be Taigs.'

'One of ours, then.'

'Aye.'

'Good one. Never too many dead Taigs. Fuck them.'

'Yeah, fuckers.'

They turned into the New Lodge and looked about those Catholic streets with a new sense of triumph.

And so it continued. The city's discovery of its shame was gradual, piecemeal, intermittent.

Slat Sloane had heard when a workmate told him. He had felt a pain and a shame that he couldn't quantify. He had thought of the dead, and his own tender flesh had puckered and tingled in sympathy with theirs.

Donal Deasely had found out when his office on the other side of town had been evacuated by the police. The city had ground to a halt because of several subsequent bomb-scares which the police had treated seriously, concerned about the possibility of a follow-up device. He had heard the earlier blast but it had sounded distant and no big deal. He had been surprised when one of the policeman told him about Fountain Street. He felt momentary shame about thinking it nothing.

Max, veteran of American violence, had been surprised. It had been her first big bomb. There had been many shootings, but she was American, she was used to that. The explosion confused her. What had it been for, exactly?'

Paul – Mary's policeman boyfriend – learnt all he needed to know when his shift was sent to Fountain Street to secure the scene and protect forensic material. He spent two hours standing sixty yards away from the rubbled hole of the sandwich shop. After the first hour, he had given himself a sore neck from not turning in that direction.

Young Roche heard, hours later, when on his way home from school he met a boy he knew – bewilderingly, he had attended school that day. The boy told him that there'd been a big bomb down the town and that forty people had been killed. Roche had sold the boy three cigarettes for fifty pence before they parted.

Aoirghe, Matt and Mamie, Mary, even drunken old Tick all found out about Fountain Street in their various ways at their various times and to their varying degrees of horror or pity. Suzy, Rachel and several of the other women with whom Jake had failed to sleep also heard, learnt and discovered. By the time darkness fell, the knowledge had spread through Belfast with the imperceptible but unstoppable velocity of the fading light itself.

The knowledge permeated the city like weather, like a very local depression. That night's nightlife was desultory, hushed.

Some had found the news heart-stopping, some had found it dull but there were few who had not found it. Some parents held their children in a tighter embrace that night, some lovers spoke more gently, even some fighters didn't quite fight. The citizens were busy, they couldn't think about it all the time but they thought about it all the same, and there were few who would not have wished it away if they could.

The city and the citizens knew that this act had supposedly been committed on their behalf. A mandate was claimed. As the citizens fought, worked or idled their way through their evening, they almost all knew that no vote had been taken, no proposal put forward. Nearly every citizen thought privately, individually, No one asked me. It was a silent but complete unanimity. It was a silent but complete rejection.

The evening passed and the city grew darkly quiet once more. The southside shop-fronts, all the streetlit sidewalks became deserted. From up high, the city looked the same as it had looked the night before. There was one floodlit patch where you might spot rubble and searchers, but generally Belfast looked like it always looked.

The streets still glittered like jewels, like small strings of stars.

Thirteen

'I think she wet her bed last night,' said Chuckie. 'When I went in this morning, the sheets were soaked.'

The doctor gazed at him without replying. Chuckie was growing irritable. The man had been staring at him in this manner for some minutes. Time was short and he was worried about his mother. 'I don't want her taking any more tranquillizers,' he said.

The doctor stopped his hand as it reached for his pen-pocket. He looked blankly at Chuckie.

Chuckie looked around the confines of the little kitchen in which they stood. He kept his temper. 'Is it some kind of long-lasting shock or something? Is she going to get better?'

The doctor gawped silently.

'Why are you looking at me like that?'

The doctor, not a young man, coloured. He was Chuckie's own doctor. He had known the man for fifteen years and more. He had come to Eureka Street several times. He had always been quick to get away. He had never dawdled so.

'Well?' he enquired.

'God, you've changed,' the doctor wondered hesitantly. His tone was awestruck and Chuckie paused, his anger gone.

'What do you mean by that?' he asked narrowly.

The doctor swallowed nervously. 'Well, I haven't seen you since . . . since . . .'

'Since what?'

'Since you were . . . ah . . . different.'

Chuckie chose the calm route. 'I've made a little money. Big deal. I'm not a freak.'

The doctor nodded doubtfully. Chuckie inspected his reflection in the tiny square mirror above the kitchen sink. Bar the swanky suit, he didn't think he'd changed so very much.

He took his Havana from his mouth; the cigar caught slightly on his big gold ring. He tried to bring the doctor back to the subject. 'My mum?'

'Look, Chuckie – sorry, Charles. Your mother has had a terrible shock. She wouldn't be normal if it didn't have a pretty devastating impact on her. She'll recover when she feels capable of it. If you don't want me to prescribe tranqs then there's nothing I can do. I've seen several people in her position. It always gets better with time. Quicker than you'd expect. People are resilient.'

Chuckie looked discontented.

'I don't think she wet the bed. She probably just sweated a lot. What sleep she'll get will be very disturbed. You know she's stopped taking her sleeping pills.'

Chuckie nodded unhappily.

'Peggy's been taking those things for fifteen years. She'll be feeling like a dried-out heroin addict. That plus her recent shock is a heavy burden. You have to be patient.'

The doctor smiled at him. 'And get some sleep yourself. You look rough.'

Chuckie shook the doctor's hand and showed him out. There was a slight controversy on the doorstep when Chuckie tried to tip the man a hundred pounds, but that was soon smoothed over and the doctor was more discomfited than outraged.

Chuckie went back inside. He moved to the foot of the stairs and called up to his mother's bedroom – actually his own room – that he would make her some tea. He took the subsequent silence as assent.

He busied himself in the kitchen. He was growing accustomed to the domestic tasks that had once defeated him, but he still frowned in puffy concentration. He was thinking hard.

Chuckie had been thinking hard for a week now. He had been thinking hard since the night his mother had been brought home bleeding tears, mute but hysterical.

Peggy Lurgan had been walking past the corner of Fountain Street just as the bomb exploded. The freak of the blast wind had knocked her off her feet and, despite her surprise, she had been almost amused. It was an undignified pratfall, a middle-aged woman like her sent sprawling arse over tip. For a few seconds, she had suspected an unusual gust of wind or a collision with an unseen person. For those first few seconds she was fine.

Unfortunately Peggy had sat there, uninjured but motionless, for nearly fifteen minutes. Unfortunately, in the confusion and mayhem, no one had thought to move her before then. Unfortunately, though protected from the blast by the corner of a stationer's shop, she had been blown into a position with an unrestricted view of the sandwich-bar debris. Unfortunately she had been only thirty yards away. Unfortunately her eyes remained open. Unfortunately she didn't look away.

After those nearly fifteen minutes, Peggy was taken to hospital. She waited there for minutes she could not count. She knew she was cold and that was as much as she could easily comprehend. Someone told her she was suffering from severe shock but she didn't really hear and couldn't really care. She was just cold. She was just frightened.

Caroline Causton had called Chuckie at the office. The police had come to Eureka Street on the off-chance of finding a relative and Caroline had quizzed them. For a blank black moment, Chuckie had thought that Caroline was telling him that his mother had been injured or killed. When he heard about the shock, he was upset but unmistakably relieved.

He picked Caroline up on the way to the hospital – the idea of 'shock' had reduced his urgency. The Accident and Emergency Department at the City Hospital was in uproar. Chuckie and his neighbour fought through the crowd as quickly as possible. A nurse told them that Peggy would be under observation for a few hours and that then they might take her home. She wasn't hurt but her shock was unusually severe and they had to be careful.

Chuckie and Caroline waited for three hours. Chuckie had not thought about what had happened until then. He could avoid thinking about it no longer. The evidence, the result was before him. The hospital was thronged with the injured and their relatives. He didn't see anything too dreadful. He had arrived much too late for that. He did, however, see scores of people weep. He had never seen scores of people weep before. Some wept quietly, some hysterically. Some bawled openly. One woman, whose husband had just died, squealed dreadfully, as though she were dying herself. The screams continued. The other weeping stopped as people turned to look at her. Her knees had given way and she had fallen to the floor where she scrabbled and beat her hands. Chuckie felt a bad taste in his throat. Another woman tried to raise the crazed widow. *Calm down*, she kept saying, *calm down*. Jesus, thought Chuckie. Tall order. Let her scream, help her scream.

Before they took his mother home, a medic gave them careful instructions about looking after her. It was vital that she was kept warm and quiet. Caroline and Chuckie decided that they would watch over her that night, sharing the duty. When they got back to Eureka Street, they steered Peggy into Chuckie's bedroom. The larger room was more appropriate, they felt. It was an easy task: she was malleable as a child. Chuckie went downstairs while Caroline undressed his mother and put her into bed.

Caroline went across the street to get some things and tell her husband. The man was mutinous, apparently, but his wife was adamant. When Caroline told him about this, Chuckie was filled by an abrupt and uncharacteristic desire to go across the road and beat Mr Causton's head in with a brick.

Caroline took the first watch. She told Chuckie to get something to eat and then to try to sleep until she called him. Chuckie guessed that if he slept Caroline would watch over her friend all night. He said nothing.

When she went upstairs, he enjoyed four grim, silent hours downstairs in the tiny house. He tried to eat a sandwich but it tasted like rubber. The smell in his throat from the hospital had lingered. He tried watching television but could not concentrate on the flicker of those coloured lights. He saw some news footage of the Fountain Street scene. His mother had been there. It was an impossible thought. An impossible event.

The little house made the event seem even more improbable. The interior of No. 42 was the only scene in which he could think properly of his mother. It was where she belonged. She was so *of* the place that sometimes the distraction between the woman and her house grew blurred, and sometimes it was hard to tell where one ended and the other began. The tiny house was like the tiny woman. Plain, small-scale, indoors.

Chuckie was appalled to find tears in his eyes. His already overblown self felt bloated with emotion. His nose tingled and twitched and he felt wetness on his cheeks. The idea of his useless, small-time mother enduring all that was unbearable. He closed his eyes and tried not to look at her furniture or her pathetically ornamented mantelpiece.

At three o'clock in the morning, he went upstairs and relieved Caroline. She refused to go home. She said she would sleep on the sofa downstairs.

It was worse to watch. His mother slept soundly enough, twitching occasionally, and, at one heart-breaking point, whimpering like a little girl. Chuckie's heart filled. He touched her face and found her cheek wet with drool. He had never watched her sleep before. He felt like a lover. He felt like a father. Silently, guiltily, he wept at the thought that she might have been hurt, at the thought that she might ever be hurt.

A week had now passed since Fountain Street. To Chuckie, his mother seemed little improved since that first dreadful night. She was speaking, true. But not much. Not so as you'd have noticed.

He put the teapot and cup on a tray and carried it up to her room.

She lay in her bed with her small face quarter-turned into her pillow. He put the tray on the little table beside her head.

'There's your tea,' he said gently. His throat was still thick with this unaccustomed emotion so his voice sounded strange to him. He bent down beside her. She opened her left eye and murmured her thanks.

Chuckie looked at the bottle of sleeping pills by his mother's bed. There were three left. There had been the same number for a week now. He knew she didn't sleep. He wondered why she wouldn't take her nitrazepam. He hadn't asked her yet.

'Caroline says she'll come over lunchtime,' he announced to the wall.

He helped her gently into a sitting position. He poured some tea. He made it badly and it looked greasy and dark. Peggy drank a little. Chuckie looked at the untouched magazines by her bed. He had chosen poorly and had mixed up middle-aged knitting magazines with youthful glossies filled with pictures of naked young women and articles about penis size.

'Would you like me to get you some more magazines? Would you like me to get you some different ones?'

She tried to smile at him but there was a droop in her features that made him think she was going to cry.

'I've just got to ring the office,' he said hastily. 'I'll be back in a minute.'

He looked back towards the bed as he walked away. She sat motionless, the forgotten cup cooling in her hand. As he stood at the door he glanced at the wall beside his head. The much-painted photograph of himself and the pontiff was there. He had taken it from the drawer and hung it over his list in its old place in the hope that it might make her laugh. It had not yet succeeded. He touched it fondly and went downstairs.

Chuckie hadn't spent much time at the office in the past week. Events and schemes were afoot there that he barely understood. Luke had tried to explain as simply as he could, but Chuckie, sudden mother-lover, found no room in which to do any new thinking, any new comprehending.

He called Luke. He told him that he would spend the rest of the morning with his mother. 'How are we doing?' he asked.

'You told me not to tell you, Chuckie.'

That was true. It had all become too frightening for Chuckie. His fattest fantasies were being made copious flesh and he could not face all the facts of his id. He didn't know all the grisly details. What he didn't know couldn't keep him awake at night.

'Well, what about the ecumenical dating agency? You can tell me about that,' he said.

'I hired someone to run it yesterday and the ads go in the papers tomorrow. It's moving along nicely.'

'We're not going to make much money out of it.'

'Why not? We always do'

That was fair enough, thought Chuckie, they always did. He didn't want to ask himself why.

'Is the kid still there?' he asked.

'Yes,' said Luke, in some embarrassment. 'I've told him repeatedly to go away but he just asks me whether my dick reaches my arse.'

'Relax,' said Chuckie. 'Send him round.'

He hung up.

For twenty minutes Chuckie cleaned, tidied, and avoided

going up to his mother's room. Every few minutes, his conscience would lead him inexorably to the foot of the little staircase but his dread and love prevented him from mounting that obstacle.

After twenty minutes the bell rang. He answered the door to find Roche, slightly less dirty than usual, standing on his doorstep, looking entirely unimpressed.

'Come in,' said Chuckie.

'Ta,' said Roche.

He led the boy into the kitchen, not noticing the feral looks of calculation on the child's face. They sat by the table and Chuckie poured yet more tea. He'd bought a score of yuppie coffee-makers of various degrees of complexity and ingenuity but he couldn't help yet preferring a cup of tea brewed with working-class over-insistence.

'Do you have a first name?' he asked the boy.

Roche's indignation was immediate. 'Are you trying to get up me again? You're just like your friend – always trying it on.'

Jake had warned him. Chuckie had listened but it had made no difference. Roche was still around. Chuckie had first encountered him when he had gone up to Catholic Land on the Lower Falls and rounded up some kids there to go twig-gathering for him. There weren't enough Protestant urchins to go round and every bone in Chuckie's body, every atom of his being, was ecumenical. This kid had gathered three or four times as many sticks as the others but Chuckie suspected that he had operated some sinister form of sub-contracting. Whatever, Chuckie had recognized a kindred soul and had paid him extra.

That had been a mistake. Roche had been lurking around their offices ever since. Tentative at first, he had become bolder and for the last week Chuckie had been dealing with irritated phone calls from Luke, complaining about the boy's presence around and outside the building. Chuckie knew the kid should have been going to school or something but he had made him run a few errands. Once or twice he had even invented something for the kid to do. Roche guessed this and despised him heartily for his weakness, but Chuckie couldn't help liking him.

'Well?' he asked.

'Well, what?' squeaked Roche.

'Your name.'

He saw the boy's mouth open in some imminent bellow of homophobic accusation. He cut him short. 'Forget it,' he said. 'I don't want to know.'

There was an uncomfortable pause. Chuckie sipped his tea. Roche stared dumbly at him. The boy was unsurprised not to be told why he had been summoned. Evidently he suspected another manufactured task. There was a faintly supercilious curl to his stained features. 'How's your old ma?' he asked suddenly.

Chuckie spluttered his tea. 'I don't know,' he mumbled uncertainly. 'I think she's improving.'

'That's good.'

Chuckie stared.

'These things take time,' Roche continued, with an air of infinite gravity. 'Especially at her age.'

'Yeah. Right. Absolutely.'

'Don't worry about it. It'll be OK.' He patted Chuckie's shoulder with his tiny filthy hand. 'Mind if I smoke?'

Chuckie shook his head. The boy lit up. He sat back in his chair and exhaled comfortably. He looked about the little kitchen with a placid expression.

Chuckie pulled some money from his pockets. 'I want you to do something for me.'

'No handjobs, remember.'

Chuckie tried to smile. 'Go to McCracken's and buy a big bunch of flowers and then take them here,' he passed the boy a scrap of paper, 'and give them to Max.'

'The Yank chick?'

'Yes,' answered Chuckie, somewhat resentfully.

'What kind of flowers?'

'I don't know. Flowers.'

'You're a poet.'

'What?'

'What kind of flowers? Do you want roses, carnations, lilies? What do you want to say to this girl?'

'Just buy the fucking flowers.' He passed Roche some notes.

The boy looked at the notes in his own hand and then at the rest. A smile hinted around the squeeze of his narrow eyes. 'I tell you what,' he suggested, 'why don't you slip me fifty and I'll make sure you say something special to her?'

'And keep the change, right?'

Roche tried to look affronted. 'There won't be much. I'll get something swanky. I'm a bit soft-hearted that way myself.'

Chuckie gave him the rest of the money. The boy left.

After he had gone, Chuckie stood for some minutes in the narrow hallway. He suspected that he should have been wondering all kinds of things about the boy. What were his dreams? He didn't, though. He couldn't. As always now, his thoughts were full of his mother. Possessing all these new contemplative skills was proving as vexatious as possessing all this money.

Having screwed up his courage, he was about to go upstairs when the bell rang again. He opened the door.

A surly man in overalls looked back at him. 'Lurgan, forty-two Eureka Street?' he asked.

'Yup.'

'There are two vans here now and another couple coming this afternoon . . . Are you sure about this, mate? I've never delivered an order this big.' The man had pushed his way past Chuckie and now stood in the middle of the little sitting room. 'Fuck,' the man said. 'We're never going to get all this stuff into a house this size. Sign here.' He thrust a piece of paper into Chuckie's hand and left.

Chuckie read the delivery note. He remembered. He regretted.

Chuckie had always had an intense and troubling relationship with mail-order catalogues. They had always meant much to him. In the tiny, muted world of Eureka Street, they had been injections of colour, prosperity and glamour. His mother's house was not a house of literature. There was a Bible and there were catalogues. It was obvious which the fat, consuming young Chuckie would have preferred.

As he grew older, he became conscious that they were tacky, sad, but some component in his soul made him find the world of commodities represented there glamorous, quite intoxicating.

They had been a joy to him but they had been a sadness too. Throughout his childhood, these tomes had been an emblem of his mother's poverty. When he had been young, she had tried to curtail his endless perusing of their unattainable bounty. He could not understand that she could not supply him with the toys and goods he could see before him in these glorious books. He never understood her pain at the hunger they caused in him, a hunger she could not satisfy.

And although she herself had always looked lovingly through every last bright page, she had only ever selected the meanest items from the least exciting sections. She always had to pay by instalments, weekly sums so small they made him blush. These books, so addictive, so beautiful, had been a part of their mutual shame.

That week, wounded by his mother's pain and gloom, Chuckie had searched his mind for something he might do for her. His limbs heavy with fruitless love for her, he had stalked up and down and around their little sitting room until his eye fell upon one of those catalogues. He had leapt on it as he had used to fall upon them, passionately, convinced they would solve his problems.

He had spent almost an entire afternoon on the telephone. After some persuasion, the girl he spoke to chose to take him seriously. He told her to ring his bank. She did. Then, his heart filled with joy, he bought a book's worth.

For the first thirty or so pages as he and the girl on the phone leafed through the catalogue together, he merely bought every item. It was quicker that way. The girl persisted in slowing him down by carefully itemizing and pricing each item he chose but in the end he prevailed upon her simply to tick them. After a while, the buying of every thing on every page had proved patently absurd. By the time they got to the watches and jewellery, it would have involved buying his mother one hundred and fourteen watches, sixty-one of them men's. When they reached the sports section, although he knew that his mother would have little use for cricket bats and football boots, Chuckie still bought at least one thing from every single page.

It was an epic event. Towards the end, Chuckie could hear that the woman's colleagues had grouped around the telephone and were counting down the total and whooping in delight and encouragement. They had never seen such buying and when he ordered his last item – an electronic personal organizer, with French and German translating capabilities – it sounded as though they were having a party. Chuckie asked the girl to give him the total cost. There were some minutes of keyboard tapping, then a pause.

'Forty-two thousand five hundred and twenty-eight pounds, fifty-two pence,' she said, awed.

'I'll send a cheque,' said Chuckie, with infinite brightness.

Now, he stood aghast as a series of overalled men began to dump endless brown cardboard boxes in the front room. They all shook their heads and laughed. One of them looked around the meagre space and mentioned that three sofas were coming in one of the later vans. Chuckie had forgotten that he had bought five. He had chosen five in case his mother didn't like the first, and also because several pages of the catalogue were devoted entirely to sofas and he had insisted on maintaining his item-a-page record.

As the unloading continued, Chuckie remembered that he

had bought dozens of garments for her with no real sense of what size she might wear. He had bought countless pairs of men's shoes. He had bought exercise bikes, sunbeds, fishing rods, computer games. He had purchased car seat covers, cat baskets, televisions, electric guitars, dumb-bells and attaché cases.

His heart sank as he remembered the part of the catalogue that had borne the brunt of his buying, the first forty pages. He rummaged desperately amongst the growing piles of boxes and found it. He opened the first forty pages. Women's underwear. He leafed through disconsolately. Black bustiers, frilly baby-doll nighties and high-thigh Lycra G-strings. He thought of his stunted middle-aged mother. He felt like crying.

Forty minutes later, the men had finished and Caroline Causton had come across the street to see Peggy. She was appalled but an irrepressible snort of laughter escaped through the hand she held to her face.

'What were you thinking of, Chuckie? Where's your sense? Peggy'll have a fit.'

Chuckie mumbled some feeble apology.

'Try and clear some of it up and I'll go to your mum,' snapped Caroline briskly.

Chuckie watched her mount the stairs, shaking her head. He always felt superfluous in Caroline Causton's presence and he feared her disapproval greatly. As she disappeared into his mother's bedroom, he felt a momentary and additional qualm of jealousy.

He was preparing to return to the office when the doorbell rang again. It was growing monotonous. He answered it irritably, expecting more deliverymen. He was surprised to find Roche there. The boy stood looking at him, a ragged bunch of flowers in his hand. Chuckie did not invite him in.

'She got them?' he enquired dubiously of the besmirched gamin.

'Nah.'

'Why not?'
'She wasn't there.'
'No?'
'No.'
Chuckie considered. He had never known Max miss a day at the nursery. He would call her at home before he left for the office.
'Where's my change?' he asked the boy.
'What change?'
'You're not going to tell me that you spent fifty quid on those?' Chuckie pointed to the listless bunch of carnations in the boy's hand.
'I had more. But I, ah, lost them.'
'What?'
'Yeah, I was chased by a flock of swans and I dropped them.'
'What?'
'Aye, big fuckers.'
'In Belfast?'
'You calling me a liar, fatso?'
'Go away,' said Chuckie hopelessly.
He closed the door on Roche and called Max's flat. There was no answer. He called Aoirghe at work. 'Lurgan?' She sounded annoyed.
'Why can't you call me Chuckie?'
'What do you want?'
'Where's Max? I tried her at work and at the flat.'
There was a pause. When she spoke again, her voice was softer than he had heard it hitherto. 'Look, Chuckie, Max has gone.'
'Gone? Where?'
'Home.'
'I told you. I called her there.'
'No, I mean home. Back to America.'
'What?'
'She left last night, Chuckie. She told me not to say anything.

She's sent you a letter.'

'What's going on?' asked Chuckie angrily.

Aoirghe told him. She nearly seemed to enjoy it.

He had only seen Max once during that week. She had been understanding and sympathetic about his mum. She didn't mind his absence while Peggy was upset or ill. Indeed, she had been so sympathetic that she had even visited his mother a couple of nights ago. Chuckie had been filled with desire when he saw her in all her warm brown healthy flesh, but she had spent almost the entire visit upstairs with his mother and he had felt himself excluded in a very definite manner. When she left, her face had been strange and her kisses uncharacteristically diffident.

For some, almost mystical, reason he could not quite grasp, he had feared that some great event had taken place upstairs with his damaged mother. When he had seen Peggy later, her face had been as strange and muted as Max's. He wondered what they had talked about.

They had spoken on the telephone subsequently. There had been a detachment in Max's words that the newly sensitive Chuckie had attributed to awkward kindness. She had told him that she was tired of violence following her around. She had left America with many people she knew violently dead and now it looked like Belfast was going to be the same. Chuckie had been disturbed by this notion but, in the end, he had decided there was nothing about which he should be anxious.

It was not as though he had given her no thought. Occupied by his mother as he was, Chuckie had dreamed of Max constantly. In these reveries, there was something besides his usual sensual gratitude. In the grip of his changing feelings about his mother, Chuckie found himself concluding that he felt larger things for this American girl than he could easily accommodate, fat though he was.

He hung up on Aoirghe without saying goodbye.

Nine o'clock that night, Chuckie was in the Wigwam with

the boys. They were talking about the fact that the IRA had just issued violent threats against the unknown OTG movement. The IRA had been slow to call in their claim for the Fountain Street bombing (no one knew that this was caused by the number of vandalized phone boxes in the Moyard area). In the interim, a rumour began and circulated for some hours that the OTG might have been responsible for the outrage. Such rumours were quick to gain the currency of fact in Northern Ireland. The IRA, justly peeved, had now made its feelings clear. Chuckie knew that some of this was his fault, after the threats against Crab and Hally, but he had buried the memory with the ease he would have shown with a sexual mishap, a failed erection. Besides, unlike his friends, he had other things to think about.

'You're quiet,' said Jake, looking at Chuckie.

'Yeah,' he mumbled.

'Your mum's going to be OK,' said Jake gently.

The general conversation ceased and the four young men tried to avoid looking sympathetically at their fat friend. There were a few coughs, and beers were slurped.

'It's not that,' Chuckie said.

'What is it?' asked Slat.

Chuckie told them about Max.

He was surprised to find how good it felt to tell them and how good it felt that they listened. He was surprised at the unanimity of their subsequent advice. Go after her, they all said. Follow her. You'll never find another like that.

It seemed absurd at first but, gradually, they talked him into considering it. Even Septic stopped watching women and joined in the general encouragement. Chuckie felt his eyes grow hot and prickly. He had never felt so liked.

'What about my old lady?' he asked.

'We'll look after her,' said Slat enthusiastically. 'She'll be all right.'

The others murmured uneasy assent. Chuckie considered

their proposal.

Ten hours later, Chuckie sat uneasily in the window seat of the fifteenth row of an aeroplane as it taxied into take-off position. He had rushed everything through. Luke had obtained a passport for him a couple of weeks before, believing multitudes of international money-making flights to be imminent. Jake had helped him out, booking the flight, driving him to the airport in Chuckie's own fat Mercedes, of which he had graciously granted Jake the use while he was away. Hesitantly, Chuckie had asked Jake to look after his mother in combination with Caroline Causton. He had thought long and hard about whom he would ask from amongst his friends. Caroline Causton would be around more or less permanently but he wanted something extra. Septic was not an option, Donal was often foolish. Slat seemed the obvious choice – he was gentle, good with women, the all-round socialist paragon. But there was something about Jake he had always trusted. And Jake said he would be glad to keep an eye on Peggy.

When he had guiltily told his mother what he proposed to do, he had been surprised by her reaction. Her face had shown a brief but unmistakable flicker of interest. Encouraged by this, he told her that he hated to leave her and that he would be back as soon as he could but that he felt he had to go.

'Good for you,' his mother had said distinctly, before closing her eyes and turning her face to the wall.

He spent a sleepless night, tortured by the necessity of following Max and abandoning his mother. He was torn between two sets of love – for that's what he could now call them both. One he knew he could never lose: his mother, he felt now, without asking, would always love him. But Max might not have even begun to consider that possibility. He knew that, in some epic transatlantic way, he had to offer her that option.

As dawn approached, he racked his memory for details and venues from the life story that Max had told him. Phoenix.

Miami. San Diego. New York. Hopelessly, he mapped out his search in his head.

That morning, as he had packed and waited bleary-eyed for Jake, he had looked around No. 42 in a guilty daze. All of the mail-order goods had now arrived. Jake and Caroline had already taken a sofa each but that left three. Aoirghe had promised to take another and Jake had suggested Oxfam for some of the rest of the stuff, but the mess in the house was nightmarish. It made him want to cry. It looked absurd, chaotic. It was typical. It looked just like him. It looked like all his clumsy love.

Seatbelt fastened, laces loosened, stationary on the tarmac, Chuckie remembered that he had never flown before. He was gripped by momentary provincial prole panic. He felt a light, almost fashionable perspiration on his face. Take-off, he was told, would be delayed fifteen minutes. Which, he felt, made it worse. As he thought about the take-off and the seven airborne hours ahead of him, he prayed that he would neither disgrace nor wet himself.

But Chuckie need not have worried. The Chuckieness in him meant that within five minutes he was asleep, and by the time the plane was taking off, he was open-mouthed and drooling, small chuffing noises not quite snores escaping from his nose and mouth. Chuckie drooled and chuffed all the way to America.

Fourteen

All along the street, sirens wailed and horns blared. Constant streams of people with hard faces joined the street from the spilling mouth of Broadway. Chuckie shuffled and dodged against the adamant flow of citizens. Small-town boy, he tried glancing at every face he passed. Those faces were keen as the wind, they were tight with tension and time.

The pavements reverberated under their sharp heels like drums or thunder. Chuckie, Belfast-born and Belfast-bred, had always delighted in lording it over yokels from the dark interior of Northern Ireland. If you were from Lurgan, Enniskillen, Omagh or Dungiven, Chuckie Lurgan would become the ultimate in urban, the complete cosmopolite. But now, as Manhattan walked and drove past him, Chuckie Lurgan was terrified.

He expected every face he saw or could not see to do him some form of big-city harm. He waited for someone to pull a gun or a blade. The constant sirens made him walk twitchily, with the delicacy and strangeness of a soldier patrolling no man's land. He was used to the traditions of Belfast brutality and gunplay but New Yorkers looked like they would all do it to you. They'd do it casually, quickly, and they'd enjoy it. Even the women looked terrifying. The women, especially, looked terrifying.

Chuckie was struggling towards Times Square, or so he hoped. He had an appointment to keep and was fearful lest he be late. He had woken with time to spare but had spent a couple of hours wandering around Manhattan blissfully frightened. He had wanted to walk somewhere famous, somewhere he had seen in the movies. But Chuckie had been in New York for only sixteen hours and he felt that he had as yet to stand somewhere that *wasn't* famous. The city seemed rotted by celebrity. Every sidewalk, every lamp-post, every taxicab he had seen before. At first intoxicated by the realization of all his celebrophile fantasies, Chuckie was growing weary of big New York. He was tired of the tingle in his spine. Feeling epic all the time was proving a burden.

His appointment was with Dave Bannon, a New York Irish detective he had hired the previous afternoon. Unsure of what Max's mother's surname might be in the midst of her third marriage, he had told the man what he knew and how her last-known whereabouts were somewhere in San Diego. As Chuckie had described his task to Bannon, he was conscious of what sounded like the impossibility of the search. Bannon, though, had seemed confident, especially when Chuckie had slipped him three thousand dollars for the week.

They were to meet in Bannon's sordid office just behind Times Square. Bannon had been worried about out-of-town Chuckie wandering blithely around such parts of his city and had advised his client only to travel by cab. Chuckie had been much too bullish and foolish to listen to that. Now he wished he had taken the man's advice. It was early evening and the streets were growing dark. The rain that had begun to fall a few minutes before was getting heavier and Chuckie was worried. He would have hailed a cab but was too diffident to try. He felt that, provincial, timorous, essentially Lurgan, he would fail to carry off that gesture with the requisite confidence. He was also unsure of how far he was from Times Square. Every time he tried to stop a passer-by to ask the direction, they walked on without glancing twice. He would die of shame if he hailed a cab only a street or two from his destination. The cabby would doubtless drive the sappy foreigner a twelve-block diversionary route and thus Chuckie would never know. He had too much dignity for that. He preferred to walk.

So walk he did, almost on tiptoe, like some bloated ostrich, skipping over the tripwires laid by his fears.

'Mr Lurgan, you did everything like I told you?' Bannon asked.

'Ah well . . .'

'Two wallets – in case you get mugged you can give one away. Don't look at anyone, don't talk to anyone, don't walk anywhere.'

'Yeah. Absolutely,' said Chuckie.

'Show me your wallets.'

'Well, I did everything apart from that one.'

'Do everything or do nothing, Mr Lurgan. Precautions must be total. This is a bad town. I'm sure Belfast is a pretty tough place but the way you flash your dough they'll eat you alive around here.'

Chuckie stuttered, 'It's kind of you to—'

'I look after my clients, Mr Lurgan.' Bannon patted his shoulder.

There was a pause. He was a medium kind of man, Bannon. Medium height, medium hair. Chuckie tried to drag him back to the subject at hand. 'What did you find?'

'I found everything, Mr Lurgan.' He smiled complacently. 'I always do.'

'What does that mean exactly?'

'I found the mother. She's in San Diego.'

'Brilliant.'

Chuckie's glee elated the detective, who neglected to inform him that since she had not changed her name at her third marriage, and since her second marriage had been to her first husband's brother, her name had remained the same and all that Bannon had had to do was look through the San Diego telephone directory. He thought such details would spoil the moment. He passed Chuckie a piece of paper with two addresses written there. 'I found the grandmother's house in Kansas too. You said your girlfriend hadn't sold it after the old lady died.'

Chuckie very nearly whooped with delight.

Bannon's triumph was almost palpable. 'Way I figure. You say this girl and the mother don't get on. She tries her first. They fight, she moves on to the old lady's house in Kansas. You should check out the mother first.'

'Good idea.'

'You want me to come with you? Slightly higher rate outside the New York area. I could keep you straight.'

Chuckie stared. He was tempted: he felt like a fat baby amongst all the sharp Americans. But he didn't want Bannon around like a bloodhound when he finally tracked Max down. He had elegant, lyrical plans for that. He wasn't sure where Bannon's flat face and spiv manner would fit.

'That's OK. I think I can manage. I'll give you a call if I have any bother.'

Bannon looked carefully at Chuckie. His face squeezed into a smile that was not entirely free of affection. 'Why don't I make a call and get you on the first flight to San Diego? Then I'll give you a ride to the airport. My car's not far and I like you, Mr Lurgan. You paid me more for a day and a half than I've made in the last month or so. I owe you a ride for that.'

Chuckie smiled happily.

Bannon made the arrangements quickly and efficiently, barking his commands into the telephone with some hauteur (the three thousand dollars had made him feel slightly less medium than usual). He locked up his office and the two men left his building, stepping gingerly onto the glossy alleyway, their unhatted heads stooping in the sudden heavy rain.

Within seconds two brown-skinned young men with extreme haircuts stood before them. There was a brief pause. Fat Chuckie noticed that the two young men shook their limbs like athletes warming up for a race. The rain ran off their skin like sweat. They seemed coltish, more highly sprung that highly strung.

'Your money,' one of them stated simply.

Bannon almost smiled back. He seemed unscared. He turned the key in the lock of the outer door of his office building. 'You packing?' he enquired amiably.

The boy who had spoken first opened his jacket slightly and rested his other hand on the butt of the 9-mm automatic pistol that nestled blackly on his ribs.

'OK,' said Bannon. He passed the boy a small brown leather wallet, which he took with some grace before looking enquiringly at Chuckie. 'He's a patient of mine. He's simple. He's not allowed to carry money.'

'Watch,' answered the boy.

Chuckie looked around to see what he was supposed to be watching. Bannon grabbed his arm and slipped off his wristwatch, passing it levelly to the boy.

'Oh, sorry, I . . .' muttered Chuckie.

'What about you?' the boy enquired of Bannon.

The detective shot out his cuffs on straight arms and showed his bare, watchless wrists.

'OK,' the glistening boy murmured. 'That's about it. See ya.'

The boy and his friend slipped away unobtrusively to wherever they had so noiselessly been. Chuckie had an unreasonable urge to thank them, to shake their hands or kiss them. Bannon walked on. Chuckie stood dazed.

Bannon stopped. 'Let's go, Mr Lurgan.' He grabbed Chuckie's arm again. He smiled almost tenderly. 'That's why New Yorkers are always asking you the time. A wristwatch isn't worth the trouble it takes to get stolen.'

'The thing with the wallets. Don't they come back if they find nothing there?' asked the bewildered Chuckie.

'I always leave a few bucks in them and some plastic. Cancelled or out-of-date credit cards. Those kids are too dumb to bother.'

'They were very polite.'

They turned into a larger, wider alleyway where the rain battered them with greater freedom. Bannon wiped his face as he walked. 'Yeah, well, everybody round here is trying to minimize stress. You piss those boys off or don't help them out, they get real fucked off. You take it easy and so do they. They don't want no executive tension.'

'Fair enough.'

'That's what I always thought.'

'How many disposable wallets do you carry?'

'A couple usually, but I got turned over a couple days ago and that was my last.'

'Let's hope we . . .'

Chuckie's voice trailed off as he saw Bannon's face tighten. He looked in the direction of the man's gaze and saw three young white men walking towards them from the parking lot in which Bannon's car was parked. One of the youths carried a baseball bat.

'Shit,' said Bannon softly.

'Haven't you got a gun? You're a detective.'

'Nah. In this city somebody's gonna take it and blow your eyes out with it.'

The boys stopped a few feet away from them. Chuckie felt a little squirt of urine damp his thigh. He thought about running. He thought about how fat he was.

'Give us your fucking money,' said one of the boys, who had obviously seen the same motion pictures as Chuckie. Chuckie looked sideways at Bannon. There was no help there. I'm going to die, thought Chuckie. Murdered by white guys in New York. I'm too Irish for this to happen, he thought. I'm too Protestant.

The three youths were surprised to have their request ignored, but they were experienced enough to attribute this hesitancy to surprise and fear. They underlined the point. The boy with the baseball bat smashed his weapon against the wire-mesh fence. The noise was tremendous, heart-stopping.

'The fucking money.'

This lot didn't have too much trouble with stress, it seemed to Chuckie. Desperately, he glanced back at Bannon.

'Hey, guys,' Bannon said sadly, 'don't fuck this guy off.' He pointed to Chuckie. 'He's from Northern Ireland. He's in the IRA.'

There was a momentary pause and Chuckie could see a tiny calculation in the hoodlums' eyes. They looked at each other.

'Say something,' the baseball-bat boy said to Chuckie.

'What would you like me to say?' asked Chuckie, with inappropriate grace and distinction.

'He don't sound Irish to me.'

'He's a Brit or Scotch or something.'

'He sounds like a fat fuck from North Carolina.'

The boys moved closer, ready for battle.

Gripped by lunatic panic, Chuckie suddenly launched into his – only intermittently successful – impression of the demagogic tones of the Reverend Dr Ian Paisley. 'No shurrender. Not an inch. No Pope here. Home Rule ish Rome Rule. Ulshter will fight.'

The boys stopped dead, frozen in their tracks. They glanced hurriedly at one another.

'I seen this guy on TV. He's a crazy fucker,' said one.

A decision was quickly reached. The baseball bat was lowered. They backed off slightly.

'Listen. No sweat,' said the boy with the bat. 'You guys take it easy.' He smiled uncertainly at Chuckie. 'Hey, power to the people, man. Down with the King and everything.'

They turned and ran off.

Bannon turned to Chuckie. 'Nice routine, Mr Lurgan. Very

nice work.'

Chuckie lay down in the rain.

At the airport in San Diego, Chuckie called his mother. There were several banks of payphones and each rank was occupied by men in suits, clutching perfectly serviceable mobile phones, reluctantly having to repeat *I love you* over the crackle of the lines to California, Boston and Philadelphia. *I love you . . . I LOVE YOU*. It didn't always sound sincere and several of the men were accompanied by lithe young women in costumes of ascending degrees of provocativeness. Chuckie smiled sadly.

'Hiya, Caroline,' he said, when he finally found an unoccupied slot. 'How's it going?'

'All right, son.'

'How's Mum?'

Caroline's voice grew fainter. 'All right.'

'Is she eating?'

'Aye.'

'Is she sleeping?'

'Aye.'

'Is she taking her pills?'

'Jesus, Chuckie, do you want to know if she's pissing and shitting as well? Gimme a break.'

'Sorry.'

'Aye, right.'

'What's wrong?'

'What do you mean?'

'Why are you so grumpy?'

'It's hardly even nine o'clock in the morning, Chuckie. What do you want? Heavy fucking breathing?'

'Has Jake been round?' asked Chuckie.

'He's here now.'

'Brilliant.'

'I'm away across the street to make my man's breakfast and then get some sleep. I'll get yer man for you.'

Chuckie shoved a great many more dollars into the coinbox. He glanced around at all the other besuited men at the telephones; they looked harassed but glamorous. He wondered if he looked like one of them.

'Chuckie?'

Chuckie was surprised at the warmth that flooded his heart at the sound of his friend's voice. He had not felt lonely until now. Tears sprang to his eyes and his nose itched.

'Hiya, Jake.' His voice was muffled in an attempt to conceal his emotion. He had intended a rather swanky, transatlantic, living-out-of-a-suitcase conversation with his friend, but he knew now that it would take all he had just to avoid bawling. 'How's Mum?'

'She's a lot better, Chuckie. She's talking more.'

Chuckie paused and gulped hotly. 'Do you think she'd want to talk to me?'

'She's asleep right now, Chuckie. She sleeps so little, it'd be a shame to wake her.'

'Absolutely.'

'What time is it there?' asked Jake.

'It's after midnight.'

'Where are you?'

'San Diego.'

Jake laughed. 'Cool,' he said.

'What's funny?' asked Chuckie sharply.

'It's just hard to think of you there.'

'What's that supposed to mean?'

'Come on, I just got used to you being around in Belfast. It's not the same without you, Chuckie. Take it easy, I'm being nice.'

Chuckie remembered that his friend was looking after his mother. 'Yeah, look, sorry, Jake. Thanks for looking after Peggy. I'll see you right.'

'Stuff your money, Lurgan.'

There was a pause. Both men, so far apart, regretted that their conversation had veered this way.

'Have you found her?' asked Jake.

'I'm getting there,' a mollified Chuckie replied.

'How d'you like America?'

'It's great. I got mugged twice.'

'That's nice.'

'Hey, Jake.'

'What?'

Chuckie paused. 'I think I love her.'

'I guessed, Chuckie.'

'Right.'

The silence was hilariously manly.

'Hey, Chuckie.'

'What?'

'Roche has been asking for you.'

'Who?'

'You know, the kid, the joke-seller.'

'Well, he can't have me.'

Chuckie hung up. He got a hotel room at the airport. He asked the girl at reception about the street where Max's mother lived. The girl told him it was an easy cab ride. He asked for an alarm call and tried to go to bed. He failed. The flabby clock of his body was lagging and sprinting on its own accord. He lay open-eyed for a couple of hours and then he called a cab to take him into town.

It was nearly three o'clock but San Diego wasn't sleeping. The downtown streets were close to lively. Chuckie went into a bar with two hundred dollars and made some brief friends. He drank numbly, talking nonsense and hearing more. He felt like a small blip on some big screen. He felt empty, deracinated. He missed the Wigwam and Lavery's. He missed Jake, Slat, Septic and Deasely. He missed his mother. He missed Eureka Street. It was as though he missed himself. Those were much of what constituted him.

After an hour he left the bar and walked out into damp San

Diego. The sidewalks glittered, wet and marvellous. Though it was late, citizens still walked those streets. The underlit shop-fronts were lined with pairs of underdressed women whom Chuckie supposed were prostitutes. These girls wore cheap pendants, which flashed in the street-light. San Diego was a naval base and some of the girls wore T-shirts that bore legends such as 'Marine Girls', 'Fuck me, the Navy!'

There was plenty of fight too. Every block or so, Chuckie would see a brawl erupt in some bar, on some street. Men kicked each other's heads to pulp, smashed bottles in faces, pulled and used knives. Outside one nightclub, he saw two marines beat a lone sailor. They banged his face against walls and trashcans, they kicked each of his teeth right out of his head.

And there were the noises of the incidents he did not see. The muted sound of war from the interiors of houses, apartments and bars. The dull shouts of angry men and the stifled screams of women. Sometimes he thought he heard gunfire.

The streets were littered with rubbish and bottles. The walls were littered with billboards and mugshots. On one wall he saw a local newspaper hoarding, which carried a giant version of each day's front page. CONGRESS PASSES NAVY BILL. MORE SAN DIEGO CLOSURES. And just at head level as he passed by, near the foot of the giant page, a headline about the murder of two San Diego prostitutes. Whore murders were not important. They were gestures, indications of mood.

Chuckie began to scan the streets in serious search of a taxi-cab. It was only San Diego but Chuckie was terrified now. He lamented the foolishness of his small-hours adventure. The streets upon which he walked felt splattered with somebody's blood or somebody's semen. He had a sudden and unwelcome sense of how fragile and inappropriate all his chubby, formless Irish flesh was in the midst of all this. He longed for the comfort of familiar Belfast and the understandably butch and brutal Sandy Row. He longed for the safety of some terrorism, some civil war.

It took him an hour to get a cab and he felt that he had walked half-way back to the airport by then. Back at his hotel, he cancelled his wake-up call and almost made a trembling, homesick pass at the bright new girl at reception. Fifteen minutes later, he slept like a dead man.

He woke so late and breakfasted so long that it was nearly five o'clock before his cab rolled up outside Max's mother's house. It was a big house, roughly the same size as the entire compass of Eureka Street. It daunted him badly.

A servant or some kind of housekeeper answered the door and there were a bad couple of minutes while Chuckie explained that he wanted to talk to Mrs Paxmeir about her daughter. There were some more bad minutes when he was introduced to Matron Paxmeir herself and had to explain his mission once more. He was rendered almost speechless by Mrs Paxmeir's appearance, which did nothing to plead his case.

Mrs Paxmeir was a gross facsimile of her daughter. Emaciated, paper-thin, she wore a smile tightened by sunburn and ill-will. Despite her dragonish exterior, Chuckie found himself oppressed by her TV-anchorwoman glamour. She looked like a woman who had never been to the toilet.

She told Chuckie that she had seen Max two days before. She didn't seem to know why her daughter had visited but she seemed conscious that she had disappointed her in some way. That consciousness did not trouble the woman. As she grew older, she said, she found herself growing less interested in her daughter's various dramas.

'I always knew she'd end up with someone like you,' she informed Chuckie.

'Someone like me?'

'Yeah.'

'What does that mean?'

'Well, you know, somebody small-town.'

'Thank you.'

They both heard the housekeeper at the door. It appeared that Paxmeir's husband had come home. She seemed to intend being rid of Chuckie before she had to make any introductions.

'I don't want to keep you,' said Chuckie. 'If you could tell me if you have any idea where she went, I'll take my leave. Her grandmother's old house maybe?'

'Yeah, maybe,' the woman replied indifferently.

Chuckie tried to glare at her but failed. He felt a new affection for Max, a new pride in her. With this harpy as a mother, Max was a genetic miracle. It was astonishing that she could walk and talk when she came from such a source. What she was, she had made herself.

Mrs Paxmeir noticed his appraising look. 'You think I'm a pretty bad mother, eh?'

Chuckie blushed and stammered. Despite his dislike, he did not want to insult the woman. He intended to marry her daughter, after all. 'Hey, listen,' he stumbled, 'a friend of mine once told me that the maternal instinct was a fiction.'

'A real bright guy.'

'So so.'

She stood up on her spindly legs, preparatory to his departure. 'You got big feelings for Max?'

'I think so.'

She smiled thinly. 'That's not always enough for my little girl. I should know. She's strange that way. You watch your step, Irish boy.' She manoeuvred him through the hallway and opened the front door herself.

'I always do, Mrs Paxmeir. I always have.'

'Call first next time.'

'Absolutely.'

She closed the door behind him. He didn't turn round. Across the street, his cabby waited. Chuckie was glad that somebody cared.

He spent another night at the airport hotel. There was a

flight to Kansas City in the morning but he was stuck in San Diego for that night. He clung to the hotel like a piece of driftwood. He ate room-service sandwiches, drank room-service coffee and watched insane hotel television, failing to interest himself even in the miraculous variety of naked young women on one of the cable channels.

Much later he went down to the lobby just to talk to someone. He asked the girl at reception several spurious questions. Joining in the conceit with professional briskness, she answered his questions efficiently but amiably. Then switching into her general-chat mode, she asked Chuckie, with that same efficient amiability, where he came from. He told her.

'Gee, you're Irish. That must be great for you,' she squeaked, with restrained enthusiasm.

'Where I come from, it's not a very distinguishing feature.'

The girl looked question marks at him.

'Well, we're all Irish there.' He realized what he had said. 'Or, at least, so some say. Some people say that we're British and some Northern Irish, but on the other hand . . .' He looked at her blank, enquiring face, which registered no distress at his meandering. 'Forget it,' he said.

'Sure, no problem.' The girl beamed at him. Chuckie was forced to admit that her smile was neither vacuous nor false. Her grace was simultaneously professional and genuine. He had only been three days in America. It was a combination to which he had not yet grown accustomed. Americans were simply frequently in a very good mood.

'Nice talking to you,' she said, with a concluding smile.

Chuckie smiled back at her. 'Definitely,' he replied.

Back upstairs, his head on his pillow, his elbow on his gut and his genitals in his fist, Chuckie decided that he liked Americans.

When he woke, he felt differently. Jet-lagged, lonely, Chuckie struggled around his hotel room, washing, shaving, dressing. His mood was inexplicably black. In the bathroom he raged impotently at all the mirrors in which he could see his extra, his unnecessary flesh. His body didn't look like it could do much romantic pursuing. He could hear the usual faint accompaniment of American hotel bathrooms. Through each thin wall, through ceiling and floor, he could hear people brushing their teeth. It had been the same in the hotel in New York. This was America. People brushed their teeth all the time and the sound of other people brushing their teeth had always driven him crazy.

Mutinous, ugly, Chuckie checked out and found his flight for Kansas City. As he waited in the departure lounge, he knew why he was unhappy. As he came close to finding her, he discovered that he dreaded it. He was supposed to persuade her to return with him. He could think of nothing to persuade her.

On the plane he tried to sleep but the man sitting next to him stirred and twitched in that way that Chuckie was beginning to recognize as the beginning of an American conversation. Chuckie was most unkeen. He grabbed a magazine and scanned its pages silently.

'Hi, there.'

Chuckie looked round. They were already at twenty thousand feet. The man had had several minutes in which to think of an opening gambit more complex than this.

'Hello.'

'You English?' the man asked.

'Not quite.'

'Not quite. What does that mean?'

Chuckie stared. The man seemed almost annoyed by his prevarication. He was a massively tanned fellow of sixty or so with one of those abundant, entirely white heads of hair that Chuckie longed to pull. His head didn't look real. Though white, his hair was as thick and strong as any young man's. Why didn't Americans go bald, Chuckie wondered.

'I'm from Belfast.'

'Northern Irish.'

'Yeah.'

'Not quite British.' The man smiled.

'You got it,' said Chuckie, in American.

There was a lull in their chat and Chuckie returned gladly to his magazine.

'What you doing over here?' the man asked him, obviously rejuvenated by the little pause.

'This and that.'

The man laughed, showing his expansive, expensive teeth. With hatred in his heart, Chuckie tried to calculate how many times he would have to brush them every day to get them to gleam so.

'You're doing some business over here, right? That's the kind of answer I always give if I'm cutting some kind of deal.'

'Not really.'

'What do you do?' challenged the man.

'This and that.'

The man whooped with triumph. 'I knew it. You're cutting some deal.' He began murmuring to himself, as though remembering his multiplication tables. 'San Diego, Kansas City. What could it be?' He looked up at Chuckie again. 'You in agribusiness?'

'Not yet,' said Chuckie.

His interlocutor barked with laughter. Chuckie was amazed to find himself such an effortless comic success. (When he had landed at New York, the immigration officials, after giving him some grief, had asked him whether he had any previous convictions. Yeah, Chuckie had replied. That God existed and Distillery would win the European Cup. Though mostly mystified, the men had laughed like drains.)

'When I said not yet, I didn't mean that I was intending to go into agribusiness,' he explained. 'I just meant you never know. If you'd asked me if I was gay, I would have said the same. Not yet is the best you can say.'

The man stopped laughing and peered at Chuckie with something disconcertingly like awe. Chuckie's homespun metaphysics had always brought the house down in the Wigwam but round here it looked like it would get him published. The man pulled a grave friendly face and thrust his hand towards Chuckie. 'John Evans,' he said.

'Chuckie Lurgan,' replied Chuckie Lurgan.

The men shook hands.

There was the tiny hint of another gap in the dialogue and Chuckie tried to return to his magazine. He was nowhere near quick enough.

'I do a bit of this and that myself,' said Evans. 'In fact, I do a lot of this and that.' He took Chuckie's magazine from his lap and flicked through until he reached the page he wanted. He set it back on Chuckie's knees. 'That's me.' He pointed at the glossy pages.

Chuckie looked and saw a double-page article about John Evans, the San Diego tycoon. He was the man in the photographs, sure enough. The article called him a billionaire. If Chuckie had not been trying to think about Max, he would have been impressed. 'It says here you've got a private jet,' he said, making conversation.

'That's right.'

'Is it broken at the minute?'

'What?'

'What are you doing on this plane?'

'Oh, right.' The man smiled delightedly, as though he'd been asked a question he relished answering, which was indeed the case. 'Nah, the jet's fun sometimes but I like to fly regular airlines when I can. It's the only chance I get to meet ordinary folks and annoy them about how rich I am.'

He belted out his big laugh and Chuckie sniggered politely. This American Croesus was beginning to get on his nerves.

'Tell me more about what you call this and that,' said Evans.

Chuckie told him.

After an hour, Evans was frankly drooling. Chuckie's narrative was not producing the effect he had intended. He had hoped that his brief summation of the paucity of his enterprises would make this super-rich American shut up and leave him alone. His attempt failed disastrously. Evans, experienced businessman, brilliant dealer, had never heard anyone downplay the scope of their business concerns. Chuckie's attitude perplexed him – drove him crazy. He was desperate to know what stroke Chuckie was trying to pull. He made a few hints about the capital he could inject into fresh ventures. Chuckie didn't even listen. He just complained that Belfast City Council had objected to his idea of setting up a ready-to-wear balaclava franchise in Northern Ireland. It was madness. Northern Ireland's peculiar circumstances created a huge market for such a product, he whinged.

Evans grew frantic. He was used to men trying to wheedle his cash out of him. This eccentric, secretive Irishman was refusing to be interested. He must be on to something huge, Evans concluded. There was something in Kansas he wanted to keep to himself.

'. . . and then I bought this big fuck-off car that I couldn't even drive. It was too big to park so I had to abandon it in the middle of the road all the time and then, of course, the Army panics and sends in its bomb-disposal team and they threaten to blow it up because they think it's a car-bomb and . . .'

The fact that he could not imagine any big Kansas deal of which he would not know made Evans more convinced of the truth of his theory. Anything he didn't know about had to be very good indeed.

'Do you do much business over here?' he asked Chuckie, interrupting that steady flow of plaint.

Chuckie looked confused. 'A bit.'

'Oh, yeah?'

'Sold some stuff here. No big deal. Very small-scale. Everything we sell is complete bullshit.'

Evans tried to smile ironically but it was too European for him. 'Bullshit?'

'Total.'

Evans smiled in a more American manner this time. 'Bullshit sells. We like it. Look at our presidents.'

He laughed his huge laugh again. Chuckie didn't bother to join in this time. The time for *politesse* had passed. He started to read his magazine, quickly flipping over the pages about Evans.

Evans's good humour was checked by Chuckie's rudeness but his irritation was soon replaced by an expression of recognition, of approval, even. He seemed to think that Chuckie's handling of the situation was admirable. The fat Mick had big balls, for sure, but Evans had never met a man who could outgonad him. He persisted. 'OK, Mr Lurgan. Let's talk straight. I'm interested. Let's do some fucking business.'

For the next half-hour he badgered Chuckie for more information. Chuckie was growing wild with despair. They would land soon and he didn't want to turn up at Max's door without some preparation. Unfortunately, his demonstrably unfeigned lack of interest made Evans wild with plutocratic desire. Eventually, maddened, Chuckie gave him his office number in Belfast and told him he could speak to Luke. He warned him one last time that it would not be worth his while.

The plane had now landed and Chuckie was standing by one of the exits before the airbrakes had been released. The air hostesses were unable to persuade him to return to his seat. He heard Evans puffing and blowing to follow him. He closed his eyes and thought of Ireland.

'I should have guessed she'd end up with someone like you,' the old lady at Max's grandmother's house remarked.

'That's what her mother said.'

'Yeah?'

'I'm glad I meet everybody's expectations like that.'

The old woman's face was expressionless. 'Her mother's a tramp. She married two of Bea's sons. Bea hated her both times. Sometimes I think she did it just to annoy the old girl.'

'I met her. It wouldn't be a surprise.'

This produced something close to a smile. Her eyes clouded again quickly. This woman's husband rented Max's land. Max had come round a couple of days before and asked her to fix up the house. She was going to stay a while.

'You're not pretty,' the old lady said implacably.

'I have a good personality,' said Chuckie.

There was a definite smile on her papery face this time. 'Max never went much for looks.' Her words were insulting but her tone was distinctly less harsh. Chuckie decided to be happy with that.

It had taken him three hours to get to Max's grandmother's place. He had booked a hotel room in a small town ten miles away and cabbed it out there. He had stood on the gravel of her driveway for some minutes, his fortitude in poor repair. The old lady had come to find out who he was. At first, the bewildered Chuckie thought that she was Max's grandmother but she was just a neighbour. She was the clichéd Midwest matriarch and he was almost surprised to find her without a shotgun on her hip. After a couple of minutes of conversation with her, it became clear that this old lady didn't need one.

She told him that Max was not there. That she had gone to LA for a couple of days. The old woman expected her back the next day. She did not invite him in, but neither did she tell him to go away. Max must have told her about him. Chuckie felt that this was a start.

It had taken some minutes to arrive at this insulting but less harsh situation. Chuckie was confident. He decided to try some drama. That might compensate for his lack of beauty.

'I think I love her,' he said.

The old lady was silent. She brushed a fly from her face. 'You'd better,' she said firmly, significantly.

'Why?'

The woman peered closely at him. Her expression changed in some way that Chuckie did not understand. He saw real warmth in her eyes. Her stiff backbone gave a little and her shoulders sagged into a less indomitable posture. The fly landed unmolested on her hair. 'Jesus, son. You don't know. You really don't know.'

'What? Know what?'

She looked gently right in his eyes. 'You better come in.' She moved back in her threshold and held open the door for him.

Chuckie didn't move. 'What don't I know?'

'Come in, son.'

'Tell me.'

She swatted the fly from her hair.

'She's pregnant,' she said.

They sat for a couple of hours on her wide porch. Chuckie reclined with his dizzy head against the hand-rail. Numbly he stared at the wood. It comforted him strangely. Lacquered, firm, it looked like wealth to him. A plump emblem of prosperity.

He returned to his hotel in a stupor. The cab driver asked him for a hundred and fifty dollars. Chuckie gave him three hundred. It was only six in the evening. He went up to his room and sat on his anonymous bed for four hours staring out of his hazy, unopenable windows.

He watched the winds blowing across the freeway, making the trucks wobble. Somehow he had thought she had left because of the Fountain Street bomb. He watched the cars drive by the little town, which was less a town than an accidental cluster of buildings hanging onto the Interstate.

The people driving past were people he would never meet and who would never meet him. In this America there were scores of millions so. The thought made him lonely no longer. America's massive indifference to him elated Chuckie now. The presentiment that America was unreal had been bothering him since he'd arrived. He'd seen it plenty on television but he had had no real proof that it existed. It could have been a cinematic fiction, a cartographic conceit, a giant *trompe-l'oeil*.

But sitting on his hotel bed, watching the freeway, Chuckie

began to believe that America was a concrete verity. Ignore him as it might, a part of him was there. Somewhere in the blank abundance of America, his child grew. Chuckie had contributed. Son of the son of the son of planters, Chuckie Lurgan had planted something on his own behalf.

He knew that she had gone to LA but he didn't care. For a while, he had been jealous of the young professor. It had been their only argument. Max had lamented the male obsession with the past, her past. Men always wanted to know everything, she said: size, weight, textures, time and place. Some of them had gone so far back into the past that they met palaeontologists. They had discovered the fossils of old love.

But Chuckie was jealous no longer. Chuckie didn't care about the young professor now. The child made it all right in some complete way he barely understood. He had always found expectant fathers risible. But now that it had happened to him, Chuckie knew that everything had changed.

He knew that he would see her the next day. He felt sure that he would make it fine now. The child made it easy. Whether she came back to Belfast or he stayed in America, they would not separate.

Chuckie watched the Interstate until the day grew dark.

Fifteen

Their cries rang out.

'Open your legs and see if we know ya.'

'Get your chubbies out, darlin''.

'I'd fuck ye any day o' the week.'

'Yo, yo, yo.'

Young Billy, unable to contribute a fresh piece of dialogue, simply howled like a hound. The girl walked past, trim, tidy, her jaw set firm, her eyes scanning the other side of the street. Ronnie Clay shouted some more suggestions to her mute well-dressed back. 'Ah, c'mon, sweetheart, ya know ya want to.'

There was a brief pause after the woman had passed out of earshot – in my experience there always was a pause just then.

Ronnie shrugged his shoulders. 'Nice tits but she wasn't up to much.'

I watched fat, bald, ugly Ronnie bend to grasp the handles of his wheelbarrow. Perhaps uncomely Clay just never looked in the mirror. That still did not put him in a position from which he could confidently notice a dearth of pulchritude in others.

We had been doing this for the last three hours. We were dumping the debris of a cleared-out ground-floor kitchen into some skips by the side of the hotel. Every time a woman passed by, she received the tribute of a hundred such taunts. Only Rajinder and I declined the opportunity. This was scrupulous sexual politics, Belfast-style.

I suppose I could have tried to stop them, to dilute their expressions of admiration. It would have been pointless. I'd spent large parts of my life around men like that. They didn't listen to polite objections.

Anyway, Ronnie was running the show and he would have been impossible to stop. He was like a new man. He buzzed and fizzed with surplus energy. Even I had to concede that it was fairly impressive for a man in his fifties. He worked at double pace and barked at these unfortunate women with something like real hunger. During the lunch break, someone had asked him what he was on and Ronnie had explained to us all.

He had been suffering from chronic insomnia for some years. He attributed it to the Anglo-Irish Agreement and the creeping suspicion that his country would soon be in the hands of the filthy Roman Catholic Church. Never having had a day's illness in his life – something always claimed by fascists, for some reason – he had visited his doctor with some reluctance. The doctor had refused to prescribe sleeping pills. He had told Ronnie that there was a new Californian technique, which sounded absurd but worked like a charm. He advised Ronnie to think nice, soothing thoughts in bed to calm him and lull him into sleep. Nothing about sex or work or money. Pleasant green-trees kind of stuff.

Ronnie took the doctor at his word and tried the technique. For weeks it had not worked. No sylvan musings seemed to help Ronnie sleep. Then he decided to personalize the process.

Ronnie began to lie in bed and day-dream idle dreams of pest control, of genocide. He dreamt of ways of ridding the planet of all its dark-skinned humans. He dreamt of starting an underground militia to kill blacks – I didn't want to know what had happened to all the Catholics. Receiving massive financial aid from South Africa and the southern US states, Ronnie and a group of like-minded colleagues and neo-Nazis armed themselves. Thousands of twenty-man cells walked into black towns and villages with their guns (AK-47s, Uzis, Brownings, mortars and flame-throwers) blazing.

Always having been intrigued by sickle-cell anaemia, he dreamt of inventing a bacterium that wiped out black people. He dreamt of inventing a special global neutron bomb that killed only non-whites. He imagined some controversy about the danger to those whites with deep suntans but Ronnie didn't care. The seeking of a suntan was, for Ronnie, sufficient colour treachery to merit death. He dreamt of becoming an international arms dealer, who sold defective weapons to black nations which fatally exploded when used. He bred a hybrid dog, a vicious superdog, which ate only black people. He dreamt pain-filled dreams of black quietus. He dreamt of telling Teacher on them.

Every night since then, he had fallen perfectly asleep, so relaxed, so happy.

That's what I liked about Ronnie Clay. Absolutely nothing.

We worked on for another few minutes until one of the boys spotted a woman approaching our spot. I paused. There was something in her gait I recognized. I couldn't put my finger on it but I felt a sudden foreboding.

Ronnie and Billy started their business:

'C'mon, big girl.'

'Show us your hairy pie.'

'Do ya wanna climb my pole?'

''Mon over here and I'll put some colour in your cheeks.'

Rajinder looked at me and rolled his eyes. I smiled back. I had finally recognized her and I confidently awaited events.

As the woman passed my workmates, her chin was set grimly. They did not abate their compliments and Ronnie grew enormously excited. The tide of his obscenity did not ebb. 'Ach, come on, honey. Just a quick blowjob. I'm dying for ye. C'mon over here and empty my bollocks for me.'

The woman stopped abruptly and looked Ronnie full in the face. Some of the others cheered. They waited for her feeble objection. They became quiet as she walked up to Ronnie. This had never happened before. One or two briefly thought that Ronnie was going to receive some of the sexual services he had requested.

It was not to be. The woman simply grabbed Ronnie's testicles and started to squeeze. Ronnie crumpled, his knees bent but he did not fall. The woman squeezed harder. Ronnie's face went white. The woman looked in my direction.

'Hello, Aoirghe,' I said.

'Friends of yours, Jackson?' she asked, giving Ronnie another tweak.

I looked around my dumb, terrified workmates. 'Not exactly,' I replied.

Some moments passed. I bit my lips. Ronnie had stopped breathing.

'When are you bringing that sofa round?' Aoirghe asked me.

'Any time you like.'

She thought for a moment. Beads of sweat had begun to sprout on her forehead, I could see the muscles in her gonad-squeezing arm, flexed and taut. I bit my lips some more.

'Bring it round tonight. Before eight.' She smiled at Ronnie. 'Empty enough for you?' she asked him pleasantly. She loosened her grip and walked away.

Ronnie dropped to the ground and measured his length there. By the time he had regained consciousness, several attractive women had passed by. No one said anything to them.

After work we all went home. No one suggested stopping off at the Bolshevik. Ronnie was still incapable of consecutive speech.

I walked home happy. Belfast was looking good. Proper summer had come – it was August so it was about time. And it was hot. It boiled. People walked around dazed at the unBelfast balm. Men took off their shirts and decided that it looked nice to go all red and swollen. Girls wore startlingly little clothing and demonstrated many of their beauties, emphasizing the unfairness of the Northern Irish gender pact. The red, swollen men got them, and they got the red, swollen men.

I had to confess, as I walked there, that I watched these women as much as Ronnie and the others. The only difference was that I tried to pretend I wasn't looking and I kept my big male mouth shut.

Looking out my Wreck windows that week, I'd never seen the city so empty, so muted. The streets went unwalked, bars were people-free, and multi-screen cinemas played to four or five people a night. Everybody was scared. Everybody had thought that Fountain Street would produce reaction. Fountain Street *had* produced reaction. Three days later, there had already been four separate murders. Within a week, there had been two more bomb blasts and a betting-shop drive-by. Twenty-seven people had died in eight days. The citizens stayed in their houses, waiting for the extra bomb-and-gun stuff they felt was sure to follow.

So, up and down I drove, the city scarily free of traffic. It made me feel like I owned it even more. There was no one around but me, the police and the Army. They stopped me at roadblocks every six hundred yards. At least it was a social life.

The OTG thing was getting serious. The cops had started laying wall-watching traps to see if they could catch people writing OTG. They succeeded in nailing a few but they had been copyists with no idea what the legend meant. I'd begun to notice, immediately after the Fountain Street bomb, that the OTGs were beginning to be written with a more desperate, hurried air. I didn't ponder much – it seemed an appropriate response.

It was like the seventies: a time when rubble scars marked the city like a good set of fingerprints. But as I drove street to street, I felt sorry for Belfast. It had a guilty, sheepish air, as though it knew it had blundered again, made its name sound dark in the world's mouth again. It was uniquely endearing to me and it chose to look its prettiest in recompense. In the unusual evening heat, I wound down my window and drove slow. The evening was light, fragrant, the air was clear. Look at all my good points, the city seemed to say.

There were many. For all my big talk, this was still a city I loved. Me and the Wreck, we sometimes toured this metropolis in a little haze of directionless benevolence. Sometimes we just drove around late at night, the old car and I, and just watched happily, listening to Heaven 17 songs, looking at all the people and wondering if they knew how multiple and beautiful they were. It never mattered what happened.

I paused as I passed Sandy Row. I stood at the foot of the Lisburn Road. I hadn't checked up on Chuckie's mum that morning. It was the first morning I'd missed. My duty was clear.

Chuckie was still in America. I'd been looking after his mother. I'd stopped looking after his car – I soon perceived that I couldn't handle it. I went back to the Wreck. I knew it was a crap car but I felt it was more me, somehow. Hey, for that matter, I felt it was more Chuckie too.

But I was still monitoring his mother. After the first few days, Peggy appeared to be getting a little better but she still wasn't talking much. At first I'd felt only sorry for her. That Fountain Street thing had been very bad medicine and I could think of no one I'd less like to witness such an event than Chuckie's chubby mother. Poor old five-foot Peggy was half a woman as it was. She was almost the definition of the damageable human. Everything about her had always seemed frail or conditional. His mother's softness had always troubled Chuckie but I had always felt for her.

And though she was better, she still lay for hours on end, staring at Chuckie's bedroom wall. It broke my heart. Some old girl called Causton from across the street was helping look after her.

They talked some. This woman had a proprietorial air about her care for Chuckie's mother. They had been friends since they were schoolgirls so that was fair. But she didn't like me and resented Chuckie's having asked me to hang around. It was some womanly thing, some crucial lack of the feminine in me. I resented that. My dick wasn't my fault. It didn't necessarily make me a bad person.

Notwithstanding her objections, I called in on Eureka Street twice a day or so. I even spent some entire evenings there – with my many social obligations that was such a sacrifice.

For four or five days this had continued amiably enough. Then, a week after Chuckie's departure, it began to unravel. One evening Caroline went home to spend some time with her grumpy husband. I helped her across the road with several remaining boxes of Chuckie's mad catalogue purchases. When I got back I found that Peggy had come downstairs and was clearing up. I was surprised but pleased. I said nothing and began to help. Much of the gear had been distributed around Sandy Row and definite patches of carpet were visible between the boxes and bags.

Caroline had told me that one night she'd found Peggy sitting downstairs amongst all Chuckie's purchases, picking over them and whimpering. She seemed more amused than anything now. We worked for half an hour or so, Peggy even chatting intermittently like some plump, uneasy bird.

When we'd finished I sat heavily on the sofa intended for Aoirghe and puffed. To my surprise, Peggy suggested that she make us some tea. I had always particularly loathed Peggy's tea – green-grey, only partially liquid – but I thought her offer was a good sign so I courageously accepted. She pottered off into the kitchen.

While she was gone I started to examine some of the boxes I'd piled near the sofa on which I sat. They contained women's underwear, reams of it. It was fairly glossy stuff, too. I knew Chuckie's catalogue had been a medium to low-rent affair but those silky things looked the business to me. As I dug further into the boxes I found Lycra high-thigh bikinis, G-strings, lurid thongs. I ran them through my fingers in amazement, horror.

'Sugar?'

I made it a few inches off the sofa without the use of arms or legs. In my shock, I had rendered myself airborne solely by buttock. I glared wildly at Chuckie's mother, who stood by the kitchen door.

She smiled. 'I know! Look at those things. What was Chuckie thinking of?' Then (I swear) she giggled like a milkmaid, looked me full in the eyes, tossed her hair and said, 'What use would those things be to an old woman like me?'

She tripped back into the kitchen.

I felt my skin crawl with shame. I felt sure that she had spotted it. I didn't know how long she'd been standing there, watching me, before she asked if I wanted sugar. I knew she had read the not entirely comic thought in my face.

For, unwillingly but unavoidably, I had just at that moment been wondering what Peggy might have looked like in some of those athletic skimpies.

When she returned with the tea-tray the air in No. 42 was all electrons; it was thick with threat and charge. As she set the tray on the little coffee table, I could have sworn that Peggy had assumed a seductive twitch to her hips. Her ass positively waggled. It was six inches from my sweating face. I couldn't help but look.

As we drank our tea, I realized that this was the first time Peggy and I had been alone. Caroline Causton was in her own house. The sudden thought did not assist my ease of manner.

'Once we get rid of the bigger things, the house will be back to normal,' said Peggy. Her tone wasn't exactly coquettish but there was a bright nervousness in it that appalled me. 'Caroline called Oxfam today and they said they'd be glad to take some.'

I nodded vaguely. I hated to admit it but Chuckie's mother

did look different. It was as though she was undergoing some transmutation, emerging from some matronly chrysalis. She had shed a few pounds since the thing at Fountain Street – she'd never been anywhere near as fat as Chuckie, and I'd always been fond of the generous figure, but the loss suited her. I really hated to admit it but Chuckie's mother had become vaguely shapely.

'Margaret Balfour at No. 22 said she might be interested in the last sofa. I've never really liked her much but I don't see the harm.'

It was weird. I began to have a dreadful suspicion that I was considering the possibility of fancying Chuckie's mother. I wasn't sure what age Peggy was. Fifty, fifty-one. It had never struck me before but she was a pretty handsome woman. She had a good figure for her age. And there was, I hated to confess, that business with the underwear. As she wittered on about catalogue consumer goods, the image of her new intimate apparel rented space in my mind and invited unwelcome images over for long parties. Grotesquely, I thought Peggy was beginning to notice my discomfort and guess its source. I mean, Jesus, I wasn't getting laid. I was very horny, but this – this was too much.

'Do you sleep with enormous numbers of girls, Jake?'

I spat a half-mouthful of bad tea all over the sofa destined for Aoirghe. I coughed. I choked. I sputtered.

Peggy tittered mildly. 'Well?'

I was still having trouble breathing but I blurted out a response before she could say anything else I might regret. 'Jesus, Peggy. No.'

She smiled beatifically. 'Why not?'

Some more coughing. Some more choking. A bit of sputtering too. 'Fuck. Sorry. Ah, Jesus, I don't know.'

'I'm surprised you don't get around more. You're not a bad-looking fella.'

If I'd had any tea left to spit I would have spat.

After a few minutes I managed to steer the chat into neutral space, but the rest of the evening was a nightmare. There was an obscene mutual consciousness between Peggy and me. I was no saint. I'd had that heart-shaking, dry-mouthed, deeply sexual silence with women once or twice but never with a friend's mum.

When Caroline Causton finally returned, after a dreadful two hours, I almost wept with gratitude.

So, I chose not to call in on Eureka Street just then. I was still in my work clothes, I reasoned feebly. I had to pick up the sofa for Aoirghe. That was time enough. I knew it was because I was too frightened, but I walked up the Lisburn Road anyway, concluding that I needed to have some sex. I needed to have some sex really soon.

I got home. I washed my untouched dishes and then my untouched self. I had a few hours to kill and, normally, I would have put on a suit, strolled into my supermarket and looked around to see if my teenage admirer was working. But I had stopped that. I didn't go to that supermarket any more.

How was I, then, to make six o'clock become seven o'clock if I couldn't aimlessly shop? There were other shops on my road but there are only so many cigarettes you can buy. There were plenty of cafés but I didn't have the nerve for solo snacking and, besides, I didn't want to go falling in love with any more waitresses.

I took the cat for a walk.

Poetry Street was radiant. The old lady across the road smiled at me and her Asian neighbour cast an amiable wave my way. My cat hid under the nearest car. He had no social skills. (Before he'd left for America, Chuckie in a fever of fiscal enquiry had calculated that if my cat lived to its proper natural term, then in food, vet bills and moderate fortnightly catty treats he would cost me more than eight thousand pounds before he died. Chuckie said my cat represented an unacceptably low unit profit and advised me to hit him over the head with a brick. I was tempted.) A few paces on, the cat and I saw an attractive young woman coming towards us on our side of the street. This time the cat checked her out and I hid under a car.

Yeah, it was getting bad. I was getting close to thirty and I didn't have a girlfriend. Even Chuckie had a steady squeeze but I felt like that was all over for me now. It didn't help that it was summer and I fell in love every hundred and fifty yards. It didn't help that I felt like the kind of man that I wouldn't have gone out with.

Leaving the cat where he was (there was always a slim hope he might get lost), I headed back home. I jumped into my car and Wrecked it over to Eureka Street. I made Caroline help me stuff the sofa into it while Peggy was still upstairs – struggling into a Dayglo thong? I told Caroline I'd be round later or the next day or something, and drove off.

Having passed through that ordeal, I turned my thoughts to the one I was about to face. What had happened to Ronnie Clay that day was merely the real-time manifestation of what Aoirghe had been doing to me ever since I'd met her. No one had ever squeezed my stones like she did.

I was stopped at two roadblocks on the way to Aoirghe's. One of the soldiers wanted to rip up the sofa sticking out the back of my car. He thought it was a good place to hide a big wad of Semtex. His colleagues dissuaded him. They pointed out the absurdity of the notion of a sofa-bomb and also mentioned what a feeble fucker I looked. I drove on unmolested.

Just as I pulled up outside Aoirghe's, the radio told me that two more soldiers had been shot. The timing was inappropriate. I would have carried the sofa alone if it had been possible. It wasn't. I pushed her doorbell.

She opened the door and glared at me with her habitual lack of grace.

'Hello,' she said, without enthusiasm.

I smiled. 'I'll need a hand to get this yoke in for you,' I suggested.

There was a new reluctance in her face. 'I've someone here who'll help you.'

She called inside. My heart sank. What was she doing having some man in her flat? Somewhere deep in my consciousness, I must have been idly speculating about rapidly showing Aoirghe the true humanist, non-violent political path and then having her roger me to a standstill, all well before midnight.

My surprise was superseded by astonishment and then vexation when Septic Ted popped his head round the door and smiled uncertainly at me. 'Hiya, Jake.'

'Fancy seeing you here, Septic.'

'Amazing, isn't it?'

'No.'

Aoirghe affected to ignore our sloppy chat but I could see that even she was anxious. I was furious. What was sleazy Septic doing there?

'Let's get the sofa in,' I said, grimly enough.

It took longer than it should have. I kept giving the thing sharp nudges, trying to drive it into Septic's groin. After a while, he started to return the favour. This silent battle impeded our progress. By the time we finally deposited it in Aoirghe's sitting room, we were sweating and blowing like whales.

'Boy,' said Aoirghe. 'For young guys, you two are really out of shape. I'll make some coffee.'

Septic looked terrified at the prospect of being left alone with me, even for a minute. 'Ah, not for me. I have to head on. Going to the Wigwam, Jake?'

'Yeah,' I said. 'I'll see you there.'

He blanched and left. I noticed no flesh on flesh as he parted from Aoirghe. That was something.

She turned to me. 'Edward just called round to discuss something with me,' she said nervously.

'Who?'

'Edward, your friend.'

'Oh, Septic, right.'

There was an uncomfortable silence. I prepared to leave.

'Coffee?' she asked.

'Please,' I squeaked.

I followed her into the kitchen. We chatted vaguely. I told her the sofa looked nice in her flat. She said she'd been worried it wouldn't suit the rest of her décor. I said that the occasional incongruity was a mark of style. She said that was OK for small items but that sofas made big statements. I said it didn't matter, the sofa looked well anyway.

The usual stuff that people who don't like each other talk.

It was strange. Both our faces looked hot and our voices were tense. I'd never been in her flat before. We had not often been alone and we certainly had never been polite. I didn't know how long I could sustain my end of the disquisition on interior design. I felt my mouth drying out.

I hadn't thought much about Aoirghe. I had pondered much on her politics and her bad attitude but I had not deeply considered her. What kind of bus had she ridden to school when she was a kid? What was her favourite colour? Did she like lapsed-Catholic ex-tough guys with low self-esteem?

Appraised in this manner, Aoirghe, for a brief moment, didn't seem so bad, after all.

It was a *very* brief moment.

In a sudden access of affection, I asked her playfully what her surname was. I couldn't believe that I didn't already know. I mentioned this to her.

Her face went taut as a drum. 'Are you trying to be funny?' she asked bitterly.

'Ah, no,' I said, doing my innocent face. (It was one of my favourite faces. I don't know what it looked like but it felt superb.)

She muttered something else to me, handed me a cup of coffee and stalked off into her sitting room.

'Sorry?' I said, following her.

'Jenkins,' she spat. 'My surname is Jenkins.'

How I wish I hadn't so precipitately slurped up that first mouthful of coffee. It splattered onto her new sofa close to the spot where I'd spat all that tea in Chuckie's house. I coughed. I choked.

'Jenkins,' I said brightly. 'That's a nice name.'

Old Aoirghe's glare was genocidal again.

'No, really. I mean it.'

You know the way when you're a kid and you get caught doing something really bad and you're in real trouble and the adults confront you and you think to yourself, Oh, fuck, this is serious! And then you piss yourself laughing anyway? Well, I tried not to laugh. I passionately wanted not to laugh – but *Jenkins*. Aoirghe Jenkins. It must have broken her republican heart that she wasn't called something Irish like Ghoarghthgbk or Na Goomhnhnle. I laughed. Like a drain.

'You're such an asshole,' said Aoirghe.

'Fuck, here we go again.'

'What do you mean, here we go again?'

'You're always busting my balls about something.'

Then Aoirghe told me what it was about my balls that they needed so much busting. She told me I was arrogant and sexist. She told me I was naïve and unmotivated. She told me that I wasn't republican because of an innate self-loathing, a deep political self-hatred. I was amazed – and rather touched – that she could have doubted the real intensity of my self-love.

I sipped my coffee. 'At least I'm not a fascist,' I murmured.

'Are you saying I'm a fascist?' she screeched.

'Well, you republicans are always telling me that you're nationalist and socialist at the same time.' I did my wide showman's smile. 'Nationalist and socialist. Now, children, does that remind us of any famous twentieth-century political movements?'

I tried to smile at her. I was doing my best to keep it lighthearted, to accuse her of fascism almost playfully.

'Fuck you,' she said.

'Come on, Aoirghe, it's really childish to fight like this.'

'Childish? That's rich, coming from you. Everything I've ever heard you say has been infantile. Just because I have some political commitment you think you can take the piss.'

'Political commitment is not what you have, sweetheart.' I knew how much she hated being called sweetheart. I cupped my hands over my testicles just in case. 'Fountain Street was not an expression of political commitment.'

'I didn't do it.'

'You fucking support it.'

'No, I don't.'

'Condemn it, then. Say they shouldn't have done it. Say it was wrong.'

She was silent for a moment, her face coloured. 'It was regrettable,' she hazarded.

'Regrettable?' I screamed. 'Tell me it was wrong.'

She pursed her lips together and looked at her hands. I stood up and bent over her, putting my face close to hers. If I could have found it in my heart to say something tender and sensual, this might have been a good move.

'You can't condemn it. You think it was absolutely fine, a regular way to behave. And that, my dear, means you're a fucking Nazi.'

'It was regrettable but the end justifies the means.'

I felt her spit on my face. I wheeled away and straightened up.

'Brilliant. So, it's time for the Maoist-bullshit part of the evening now? The end justifies the means. That's based on an immature attitude about life, never mind politics. There is no end, there is only means. It's fucking pointless.'

I only noticed I was shouting when my throat started to hurt. I stopped. I sat down. I sipped my coffee and looked at my hands.

'A united Ireland is an achievable goal. It will happen. We will win. It's right. That's my opinion and it will never change,' she suggested.

'An opinion that remains unchanged quickly becomes a prejudice,' I said, quite mildly.

Her eyes narrowed. She smiled triumphantly. 'What about all your peaceable stuff?'

'That's different. That's a conviction. Convictions are portable. You take them with you anywhere you go. They always apply.'

'Such as?'

'Violence is wrong. That applies in all situations.'

'You must have forgotten that when you decked Gerry,' she said.

'Who?'

'The Peace Train. The guy at the station with the moustache. You broke his nose. Wasn't that wrong?'

'Oh, yeah. Well, I'm an imperfect follower of my own theories. And, yes, it was wrong.' I lit a cigarette and stood up. 'Anyway, I've given up violence. I bought a violence patch from the chemist. I stick it on my arm and I feel less need to beat people up.'

No, amazingly, she didn't laugh. She continued not laughing for another twenty minutes or so before I finally left. Just before the end of that comedy-free conversation she told me mutinously that Amnesty International were having a Belfast press conference in a fortnight's time and they wanted me to attend and tell the world how I was abused by the police. She had promised them that she would try to persuade me.

At least I got a laugh out of that. I pointed out some of the reasons why that might be a little difficult. I painted her a broad picture. 'Go fuck yourself,' I said. (I was getting pretty slick.)

She threw me out. I liked that about Aoirghe. She was consistent.

I drove around for a while. The streets were less deserted than latterly and my mood lifted again. It was one of those nights when every song on the radio makes your trousers tight. It was a bad night to be without a girlfriend. It was warm. It was almost like any summer Friday night when the girls were out barelegged in short skirts and the boys were wearing linen trousers stained by their sixth pint and innocent Belfast lay bemused and strewn with their drunken litter and everyone laboured under the misconception that I drove a taxi.

I dropped in at the Wigwam. I was an hour late but I wasn't hungry. I found the boys at our usual table. As always they were talking about what really mattered.

'There absolutely has to be life on other planets,' said Deasely. 'To suppose that amongst the multibillions of stars and thus more multibillions of planets, to suppose that ours is the only planet to produce the right conditions for sentience is monumental arrogance. Mathematically, there has to be something in that vast black darkness.'

'What, Ballymena?' quipped Septic.

I sat down and they nodded their greetings at me. Deasely continued. 'The universe has everything we need to think about. Too much twentieth-century science has been micro-science, the science of molecules, atoms, genetics. The real science is the new way of thinking that lying on your back looking at the stars can never fail to produce.'

The nationalist waitress sidled up to me. '*Slan*,' she said.

'Yeah, right,' I replied.

Ever since she'd read about me in the papers, this girl had been giving me the Gaelic thing there. She asked me what I wanted in what she supposed to be a seductive tone. I asked for some coffee. She said something else in Irish that I didn't understand and loped off with a big smile. At least someone wanted to sleep with me, but I still felt like weeping.

'The most beautiful concept in the cognitive universe is the glitch in stellar calculations produced by the imponderable of the speed with which they are moving away from us and the speed with which we are moving away from them. All measurements of distant stellar bodies are unreliable because of distance, speed and time. The mathematics depend on where we stand. From somewhere else, the results would be different. There can be no absolutes. That is so tremendous. It's so political. The act of observation is ultimately vain,' mentioned Donal.

'Maybe that's why Jake can never work out why he can't get a girlfriend,' suggested Septic. Nobody laughed. I lifted my hand. I cocked my invisible gun and blew out his invisible brains.

The freedom-fighting waitress brought me my coffee. I stared at the floor.

'Not eating?' asked Slat.

'Not hungry.'

'What's she saying?' Septic asked, as the waitress moved off muttering her thick dark stuff. 'Does anybody know what she said?'

Without Chuckie there we were all Catholics but, still, none of us had a clue. Septic's finest comic episode had come a few years before when a French girl he wanted to pork had asked him what the Irish word for silence was. Septic had replied, with entire sincerity, that *soilence* was the Irish word for silence. He had been easier to like in those days.

'What have you got against chuckie pussy?' Septic asked me. I ignored him.

'The very difference between the evident manufacture of the basic chemical elements in interstellar space and the non-manufacture in intergalactic space tells us that—'

'Fuck up, Deasely,' snapped Septic.

I hoped that Septic's ill humour – he wasn't even looking at any of the many women dining in the café – showed that his plans to investigate Aoirghe's pants had come to naught thus far. I was sure that this was the case. Septic liked to boast. I asked him what he'd been doing over there and his lips were uncharacteristically zipped.

We talked idly for a while. The waitress brought us some drinks, but we failed to be festive. We missed Chuckie. We'd met a couple of times here since Chuckie had gone and it simply hadn't been the same without him. His was an unlikely loss and I think we were all shamefaced that our fat Protestant friend's absence cost us so dear. But we sat it out for an hour or so, looking at each other unhappily, mumbling incoherently about this, mumbling incoherently about that. Near eleven I announced my intention of going home. Nobody wept. No one protested.

As I was preparing to leave, Tick, in a new suit and shoes, came in looking for Chuckie. When we told the suddenly elegant indigent that his friend was in America, the old man sat on the floor and sobbed like a baby. 'I brought these,' he blubbed. 'He asked me and I brought him these.'

He held some pieces of paper in his quivering hand. I took them. I read. They were *receipts*. Chuckie had actually asked old Tick to *invoice* him. I totted up the total. Eight hundred pounds. I took Tick aside. 'How much money did Chuckie give you?'

'Oh, absolute hundreds,' replied Tick.

'How many absolute hundreds? Eight hundred?'

Tick nodded and started bawling again.

'Jesus, Tick. Why are you crying? I'll make sure he gets them. He won't mind if they're late. He went away.'

'It's not that,' he sobbed.

'What, then?'

Tick wiped a remarkable-looking droop of snot from his nose and mouth with the sharp sleeve of his new suit. 'Chuckie asked me to double every amount. He said it would do no harm. My conscience wouldn't let me. That's fraud. I'm a wino but I'm an honest wino.'

He dissolved in tears. I patted his head gently. I looked at my hand. I wiped it on my trousers. The others were looking over inquisitively at us by now. I helped the broken Tick out of the café. 'I'll talk to Chuckie,' I said. 'I'm sure he'll understand.'

Tick pressed my hand and limped off. I watched him. His sharp suit still looked grotesque on his grubby body. That was the thing about dignity – it was always so surprising, so unwelcome.

I said farewell to the others and left the Wigwam. At the door, the Gaelic-speaking waitress gave me some old Mick chat but I ignored her. I made like Tick and limped off home on my own account.

It was a beautiful night. I left the Wreck parked outside the Wigwam and loped slowly towards Poetry Street. Belfast was tense and scared; there were, doubtless, people being done to death at that very instant but, all in all, it was beautiful. The city sounded like an old record that crackled and hissed. But you could still hear the trouble, distant or close. In the broad night, the sirens whooped and chattered like metallic married couples.

I removed my jacket and opened my shirt. I slowed my pace. I dodged the drunken men and tried not to look at the miraculous girls. I read the walls with a feeling of unaccountable joy. After a few yards, I noticed that there was a smattering of dyslexic OTGs: TGO, ODG, OTD. I stopped and touched the wall in question. I had guessed right. The poor draughtsmanship was characteristic and the paint was still wet.

'Roche!' I bellowed. 'Roche, where are you?'

A few passers-by stopped to stare. I ignored them.

'Roche!'

Several of the passers-by shook their heads and walked off, thinking I was a madman. A small dirty head peered round the entrance of an alley nearby. There were smudges and flecks of paint in the boy's hair. 'Oh, it's you.'

'You're still not getting it right,' I said.

'What?'

I pointed to his imperfect graffiti.

'Hey, Jake.'

'What?'

'Have you got a Postgraduate Certificate in Education?'

'No.'

'You can fuck off, then.' He smiled happily at me.

'Come on,' I said. 'I'll give you a ride home.'

It was nearly midnight, the street was full of drunks. It looked like that twelve-year-old was going to debate the point but I think he recognized I was getting all adult there. We walked back to the Wreck.

Roche had continued to hang around after Chuckie's departure for America. The kid was everywhere. Luke Findlater told me that he was around Chuckie's offices most of the day and I often saw him lurking in Eureka Street when I went calling on Peggy Lurgan. He must have forgotten what school looked like. I taxed him about his education one day and he suggested that I should eat his bollocks. I liked Roche. He had some imagination.

He was also a handy errand boy to have around Eureka Street. Chuckie had left a shitload of cash in a box in the kitchen and I used that to get the kid to stock the house. He had very high wage expectations. I don't know what Chuckie had been paying him but I never saw any change.

As we drove up West, Roche told me that he had seen the OTG man again. He had noticed something else this time. Every time the man wrote on walls he would write some kind of sentence before and after the legend OTG then he would simply paint over everything but those three letters. Every time I'd seen OTG written in the city it had been preceded and followed by bands of paint, the first band slightly shorter than the second. I'd thought it was merely a decorative conceit.

'What does it say before he paints it out?'

I turned off the Westlink and Roche murmured something into his chest.

'What?'

'I don't know,' he muttered. 'It's hard to make it out before he paints over it.'

I stopped at some traffic lights. 'Listen, kid. So you don't read too well. It's no big deal. I was slow at school. All the best people were.'

'You haven't speeded up much,' Roche replied defiantly.

I drove the little prick home in silence. Just as we turned into Beechmount, he asked me to stop the car. 'Let me out here,' he said.

'I can take you up to your door just as easily.'

'Here's fine,' he said, too loudly.

I stopped the car. The kid got out. 'Thanks,' he said insincerely.

I watched him as he walked off. He kept looking back at me. I knew what the score was. I swung the car across the street just as he turned a corner out of sight. I stopped the car. I got out and followed.

As I suspected he might, he walked past the street where he lived. He ducked down a few side-streets and ended up back on the Falls Road. I had an idea where he was going. I went back and fetched the Wreck. I drove to the Grosvenor Park, a dilapidated and tiny concrete and grass esplanade with a few dingy swings and a clapped-out bandstand. I parked and walked slowly up to the bandstand. The bench there was unoccupied. I was surprised. Then I bent down and looked underneath. Roche lay there, his head propped on his schoolbag, a tarpaulin pulled over his shoulders.

I waited for the quip that didn't come. Amazingly, the boy said nothing. He stared at me mutely, with something like shame in his eyes. For once, he looked like he was twelve years old.

'What's wrong?' I asked. 'A bit of bother *chez* Roche?'

'What?'

'Forget it.'

I was squatting on my haunches. It was growing uncomfortable. I lit a cigarette. He stared at me. I offered him one. He lit up greedily. There was silence and the air felt warm and magical on my face. It wasn't such a bad night on which to sleep rough. Still.

'Come on,' I said, standing up, 'you can sleep at my house.'

Roche stuck out his head from underneath the bench and opened his mouth to protest.

'Relax,' I said. 'I'm not going to try to have sex with you.'

The boy shut his mouth, satisfied. He gathered up his meagre stuff and scrambled to his feet. He looked expectantly at me.

'Hey, kid,' I said, 'I think I should tell you something.'

'What?'

'You're much less sexually attractive than you believe.'

That night I dreamt a year's worth of dreams.

Six a.m. Roche ended up pulling me out of bed by my hair. I chased the persistent little shit downstairs but I hadn't a chance of catching him. My cat looked on with interest as I chased the boy round the kitchen.

'The phone,' he bellowed. 'It's your fat friend from America.'

I stopped, suddenly calm. I picked up the receiver while Roche made mutinous noises in the background.

'Chuckie?'

'Jake. Hi.'

'Do you know what fucking time it is?'

Chuckie knew what time it was. Chuckie didn't care. If he'd been in Eureka Street, I might have driven round to beat the shit out of him but he knew it wasn't worth an international flight.

Chuckie had called me for two reasons. First, he wanted me to give up my job and start working for him. He told me he was worried about Luke Findlater. He was a nice guy and good at his job but Chuckie wanted someone he could trust on the inside there. Besides, Luke kept saying things like *soigné* and *egregious*. It was getting on Chuckie's nerves.

I told him wearily that I didn't know anything about business or money. He refuted my objections. I was so tired and pissed off that I said I'd work for Chuckie for a grand a week. I was astonished when he said yes. It wasn't that he'd agreed, it was that he'd barely noticed.

'What was the other thing?' I asked fuzzily.

'What?'

'You said you'd called me for two reasons.'

'Oh, yeah.' He paused.

The line burred and chirped. It wasn't very atmospheric but I wondered what Chuckie was working up to.

'I'm going to be a dad.'

'What?'

'Max is pregnant. We're gonna get married.'

'I took a deep breath. 'That's great. Congratulations, Chuckie.'

'Yeah. Listen, don't tell my mum. I'll tell her when I get back. How's she doing?'

'Ah, fine,' I said vaguely.

'Good. I'm really grateful for what you've been doing with her, Jake.'

'What do you mean by that?' I snapped nervously.

'Looking after her. It means a lot to me.'

'Oh, yeah, right. Don't mention it.'

'I gotta go,' said Chuckie.

I felt a surge of affection for him. I was even beginning to wake up. 'Hey, Chuckie. I'm openly jealous.'

'Of what?'

'Fatherhood, Chuckie. Fix that short-term recall. It's fine news.'

'Thanks.' There was a slight tremble of emotion in Chuckie's voice. He hung up.

I found my eyes had grown misty. Chuckie a father. I wasn't sure what I felt.

'Did he give you the grand a week?' asked Roche.

'Yeah.'

'Fuck. Put it there,' said the awestruck boy.

Roche held out a grimy paw. I groaned and headed for the kitchen. I made some coffee, lit some cigarettes and fed the cat. It was 6.15 a.m. I don't think I'd ever woken up this early. I was surprised to find it quite so beautiful. The light was exquisite, somehow energizing. Even Roche didn't look so bad. I made the kid some breakfast, we sat at the table and I apologized for chasing him round the flat.

'I don't suppose you'd consider the possibility of going to school today?'

Roche munched his toast implacably. 'What do you think?'

'Thought so.'

'What, are you like my dad now or something?'

The cat vaulted onto my lap. He'd finished his breakfast. I seemed calm so he started purring. I felt like some kind of respectable patriarch there, cat and kid at six in the morning. I quite liked it.

'What's the deal with your old man? Does he knock you about?'

The boy lodged a large slice of toast in his mouth. He stood up and lifted his shirt over his head, toast and all. He swivelled slowly.

'Fuck me,' I said.

His chest and back were sown with rich bruises of varying ages. Over his back, the patches of unbruised flesh were in the minority. He pulled the shirt down, almost dislodging his toast in the process, and looked at me imperturbably. I had been planning to end breakfast with the advice that he couldn't stay with me for long. Perhaps he'd guessed that before he'd flashed his tits. I lit another cigarette.

'Hey,' I said, 'you've got margarine all over your shirt.'

My first executive decision as an employee of Chuckie was to take the day off. I rolled down to the hotel to quit my job and say goodbye to Rajinder. I had to bid a variety of fond farewells to the others as well. I had planned to discuss the tragedy of his initials with Ronnie Clay, but in the end I didn't have the heart. For a sectarian racist moron, Ronnie wasn't so bad.

Since I'd just increased my annual income more than five-fold, I spent the rest of the morning shopping. I bought myself another suit and even, pathetically, got some stuff for Roche. In the act of buying socks and underwear for a twelve-year-old boy, I knew the world would frown upon such a situation. I would have to do something about the kid before I got arrested. I decided to visit Slat.

I called into his offices. It was a swish Golden Mile interior but the waiting room was full of people who looked as though they'd never even met anyone who had enough money. The place smelled of desperation and poverty. I hassled the receptionists. A variety of prim but attractive young women tried to frown me away but I persisted and after a few minutes Slat himself wandered out. I told him I needed to talk to him straight away. He told me to meet him in the Wigwam in half an hour.

I hadn't been in the Wigwam during the day. It somehow felt like a crucially different experience. The waitress who liked me slid up to my table. '*Slan leat*,' she said, mystifyingly.

'You work days too? You must be really shagged,' I replied.

She said something else in Irish and pressed a special smile on her features. I looked blank.

'I'm afraid I only speak one language,' I mentioned.

Her manner grew cold immediately. 'Can I get you anything?' she snapped.

In my embarrassment I smiled more widely than I should have. 'Coffee, please. Listen, I'm sorry – I didn't mean to . . .'

Her face softened again and she sat opposite me. 'Your name's Jake, isn't it?'

'Yeah.'

'I'm Orla.'

I felt myself flush to the skull. 'Hello, Orla. I'm glad to meet you.'

'Likewise.'

It was hard to get a cup of coffee, these days. She smiled expectantly at me. It didn't matter how humble I was, there was no mistaking this.

'What age are you, Orla?'

'Nearly eighteen.'

'Jesus.'

'What's wrong with that.'

'I'm nearly old enough to be your father's much, much younger brother.'

'So?'

I gave up on the coffee. I lit a cigarette. 'OK. Well, in that case, you know all that *Chuckie ar la* stuff you come out with?'

'Yeah.'

'Well, sister, that stuff really gives me the shits.'

She just walked away. I really seemed to have a knack with the women in my life. They kept on just walking away.

Slat arrived. He sat down. 'What's cooking?'

Orla came back with my coffee. She bent over the table and poured half of it into my lap. I sat in silence as she placed the near-empty cup on the table. She apologized insincerely and smiled triumphantly as she asked Slat what he wanted. He replied, in some trepidation, that he would like a cup of coffee but that he would fetch it himself if she liked. She simply smiled and stalked off.

Things between men and women were very modern these days. That was nice. Girls chatted you up now. But it looked like you still weren't allowed to turn them down.

'What was all that about?' Slat asked.

'Revolutionary politics.'

He looked nonplussed and uninterested. 'Speaking of which,' he said, 'have you heard?'

'Heard what?'

He laughed. 'Yeah, I forgot. You always switch the radio off when the news comes on.'

'Have I heard what?'

'There's been a ceasefire.'

'What?'

'The IRA have declared a ceasefire.'

My initial deep surprise faded. 'They've had plenty of ceasefires before.'

'This is different,' Slat insisted. 'They're saying themselves that this is the end of their war.'

'Fuck.'

'Big news, huh.'

'What about the Prods?'

'People think the UVF and all their chums will call their own ceasefire in a few days.'

I sipped what was left of my coffee and tried to wipe my trousers with a napkin. 'So, it could really be the end?'

'Looks like it might be.'

We had a silent, sombre reflection there, Slat and I. We were sensitive and intellectual that way. Then I told him why I'd wanted to see him.

'He's sleeping at your place?' asked a shocked Slat, when I'd finished.

'Yeah.'

'Jesus.'

'I couldn't let him sleep on the street. He's only twelve.'

'If anybody finds out, they'll think you're having sex with him.'

I frowned. 'What can I do?'

Slat smiled sadly. 'There's nothing you can do.'

'What about social workers or something?'

'Social workers can't take a child-care referral from some guy on a building site, Jake. It's got to be the cops or a GP or something.'

'Brilliant. Somebody has to do something. When I was a kid, I got Matt and Mamie. There's got to be something like that for Roche.'

'Things are different now, Jake. Social services are an arm of the state. They don't mediate between state and individual any more. It's the new Britain or the new Northern Ireland or whatever you want to call it. What do you think I do all day? It's why I do the work I do.'

'Should I let him move in, then?'

'No!' Slat almost shouted. Some diners looked round at us and my revolutionary waitress sneered.

'No,' he repeated. 'Tell him he has to go back home. He should tell his teachers about his troubles. They can put the wheels in motion.'

'His teachers? Jesus, Slat, this kid probably can't remember what street his school's on.'

'That's the way it is.'

And that was fair enough. That *was* the way it was.

I tried to spend the rest of the day shopping but found that I quickly ran out of things I wanted to buy. This depressed me somehow. After lunchtime, something Protestant in me made me go down to Chuckie's office and start some form of work. Luke Findlater was there and he did his best to explain the main areas in which he and Chuckie were doing business. He was rational and clear, but after twenty minutes I still had to lie down and breathe deeply.

Chuckie's ventures were almost all wildly improbable. It was as though all his corrosive yob fantasies had been given grotesque flesh. To my horror, I discovered the rejected proposal for the chain of ready-to-wear balaclava shops. I was told how much money they had made from the leprechaun walking-stick scam. I saw how much money the various government investment agencies had granted Chuckie for no reason I could readily identify.

Additionally, Chuckie's rapid accruing of wealth had not been without its amorally democratic grandeur. He had ripped off and duped Protestants and Catholics with egalitarian zeal. He was a pan-cultural exploiter. I discovered that he had bought a controlling share in a regalia company that supplied the Orange lodges and Loyalist bands that marched so Protestantly on the Twelfth of July. He had just negotiated a contract for this company to supply the Vatican with various regalia and uniforms. If anyone heard about this, Chuckie would be hung upside down from some street-lamp in East Belfast.

After an hour or so, I'd got a pretty fair picture of the state of his business machine. Soon, I grew bored. I didn't know what I was supposed to do. Luke, thankfully, was kind.

'I'll get a desk brought in and get you a phone and stuff.'

The telephone rang. He answered. He listened, then cupped his hand over the receiver. 'You speak French?'

'Sure,' I bluffed.

'Here,' he passed the phone to me, 'we've opened a chain of Irish restaurants in Paris. You can deal with this. Tell them you're the executive director or something like that.'

It took fifteen minutes – my French was but a halting thing – but I worked out that Jean-Paul or whoever was complaining that he had been told to put Irish lasagne on his menu and he didn't know how to make such a thing. They were opening the next day and could I please tell him the recipe.

It was a dreadful predicament. I racked my brains but I had run short on French nouns in general and French nouns describing foodstuffs in particular. The only one I could remember was *pommes de terre*. At least it was vaguely Irish – amazingly Irish, in fact. I gave it to Jean-Paul or whatever his name was.

He was mystified. 'Pasta *aussi*?' he enquired.

'No. Fuck it, *pas de* pasta.'

'*Merde! Vraiment. Pommes de terre?*'

'*Absolument.*'

'OK.'

I hung up. It wasn't my problem. It wasn't my idea.

I spent the rest of the day there. I didn't do any real work. I just told young Luke all about how bad my life was. It took hours. Then we talked about the ceasefire. He seemed to think that there was big money to be made if it panned out. I almost dreaded the thought.

He went home early. I hung around the office for another couple of hours. As I sat there, looking at the house that Chuckie had built, I felt real envy. He was getting everything I'd ever wanted. The great woman, the great business and now a baby.

It was my big secret. I was hilariously broody. I desperately wanted to procreate. It was a need in me that made me sweat in the middle of the night. For months I had been assailed by dreams of ready-made sons and daughters arriving on my doorstep (importantly motherless), five years old and already reading Pushkin. Roche would never constitute an adequate substitute for the beribboned marvels of my fantasies.

It was one of the reasons that I was pissed at Sarah. I couldn't live with the thought of her killing the kid.

I had one other big secret of the day. It was why I was lurking pointlessly in Chuckie's empty offices. It was why I didn't want to go home. I couldn't face telling Roche that he had to leave.

Septic called me there. He chatted tensely about nothing for a while and then tried to persuade me to go to Aoirghe's big Amnesty thing. He said if I helped him out he stood a chance. I told him I wasn't going to grease any wheels for him. I didn't lose the bap. I was actually pleased. It sounded like Septic had been invited round to Aoirghe's for the unsexy task of leaning on me. It nearly cheered me up. Septic was still my friend but it had been some years since I'd liked him.

When I could bear Chuckie's office no longer, I drove around the city for forty minutes. When I got bored with that I called in at Eureka Street and said a brief and prim hello to Chuckie's mother. Caroline Causton was there and although Peggy blushed at my arrival, the heat seemed to have gone out of our exchanges. As I sat there for half an hour, I sensed that something was going on. When I left, I had the crazy sensation that they might be sleeping together. I even shook my head to rid myself of that impossible thought. I drove around the town at slightly illegal speeds for another twenty minutes. Then I called in at Mary's bar. She wasn't there and a friend of hers who didn't like me bought me a beer. I left. I drove around some more. I went home.

Roche was watching the television that Chuckie had given me. To my surprise, he was avidly absorbed in a news special about the IRA ceasefire. We watched Mickey Moses, the Just Us spokesman, thank the brave volunteers for their efforts in the long struggle. Mickey had the kind of twitch in one of his eyes that made me feel that he was missing the sniper's scope already.

'You like to keep up with current affairs, then?'

'There's money to be made out of this,' said Roche.

'You'll go far.'

I went into the kitchen to make some coffee and feed the cat, whose dish was already piled high. Roche had cleaned up my kitchen. Many months of my household habits had dulled its sheen somewhat but now it glittered as it had when Sarah had lived there. It must have taken him ages. I felt like weeping.

'I cleaned up a bit.'

I turned round. The boy was standing near the door. There was something crucially different about him.

'Fuck,' I said. 'You're all clean.'

'You're big with the personal comments, aren't you?'

'Sorry.'

Horribly, Roche seemed amazed that I had apologized. I could have sworn that his eyes watered. His voice quivered uncharacteristically. 'Aye, well, don't do it again.'

I threw a plastic bag towards him. 'Here, I got you some stuff. I wasn't sure about your size and they didn't seem to stock *runt* so it might be touch and go.'

He snickered, happier with the abuse than the apology. 'You got some calls. Some woman with a funny name and an old dear called Mamie. I had a big chat with her. She said you had no folks. And there was another one I can't remember.'

I was just about to complain that he hadn't written it down when I remembered Roche's textual sensitivities. I called Mamie.

Mamie had, indeed, had a long chat with Roche. She quizzed me about what was going on. I tried to minimize my own piety but she couldn't disguise the delight in her voice. I could even hear it in the pauses when she didn't speak. She thought I'd joined their club. She thought I was repeating their benevolent pattern. For the first time since I'd met her, she told me she was proud of me.

I tried telling her that it wasn't that simple. I wanted to tell her that my largesse was temporary, that I was about to tell the kid he had to leave but I couldn't muster the courage. So I just listened to ten minutes' worth of what a lovely man I'd become. Then she told me that this thing they wanted to give me was a letter from Sarah. She'd given it to them before she left. She'd told them to give it to me when they thought I was ready. Apparently, that auspicious time had arrived.

I got her off the phone quickly after that. I found, to my annoyance, that my heart was racing and I felt nauseous. A letter from Sarah. I was furious. I didn't want any explanations from her. For the first time, I felt something other than supine longing for the woman who had left me.

This new preoccupation somehow made me feel better about telling Roche he had to go. My anger would be useful in being butch with the kid. This was a form of emotional diversion with which my cat was familiar. It was time I tried it on the higher species.

It was made more difficult by Roche suddenly walking into the kitchen, modelling his new clothes for me. In this neatly pressed, brand new costume, he looked almost ridiculous. He looked like any other kid. Only the filthy, ripped trainers on his feet gave any hint of the true urchin.

'Very nice,' I said.

He smiled almost boyishly. 'Are you sure they don't make me look spazzy?'

'Spazzy?'

'You know . . . geeky.'

I lit my last-ever cigarette. 'Listen, kid. I spoke to a friend of mine today about you.'

Roche's smile shut itself down as tracelessly as a Belfast shipyard. 'You want me to leave,' he stated.

'It's not like that,' I pleaded.

'Forget it. I was leaving anyway.' He stalked off to his bedroom.

I tried to follow him. 'Listen, you don't have to go straight away. Stay a few days.'

He shut the door behind him. He did not reply. I knocked for a few minutes but he wouldn't talk to me or open the door. I decided to have a shower and give him time to cool down.

As I stood under the imperfectly warm water, I heard the unmistakable bang of my front door. I had known perfectly well that Roche would leg it while I was in the shower. That was why I had had the shower in the first place. No cowardly ruse was beneath me. Guiltily, I soaped my testicles.

The rest of that evening was grim. Roche had left behind all the stuff I'd bought for him. He had, naturally, stolen my new ex-Eureka Street television and VCR but he had rejected my gifts. I was not surprised. It was his style. I knew he'd nick them. I hoped it might make me feel a little better. It did.

Nevertheless, I felt so bad about the kid I even forgot to think about Sarah's letter, my new prosperity or how much I disliked Aoirghe, a subject upon which I had dwelt of late. My cat wisely avoided me. I listened to the radio for hours. Roche had pinched the major electricals, after all. It was all news on the radio that night, what with the ceasefire and all. I didn't bother switching it off. In the previous twenty-four hours, there had been five fatal shootings and seventeen kneecappings. The IRA had cleared its backlog of murders and punishment shootings while it still could. How charming of them. How confidence-inspiring.

After four or five hours of this, I grew so depressed that I went outside to clear my head and breathe some air. It was another warm night and I sat there on my step for an hour, trying not to think about ceasefires or twelve-year-old boys with domestic problems. Sometimes, Belfast looked like the past, remote or recent, the confident Protestant past. I couldn't see how any of its fires would cease.

How did I feel about the big-deal ceasefire? It was news. It was event. What did it mean to me and the tiny group of mine?

Sitting on my step that night I felt three things.

First of all, I felt as though Belfast had finally given up smoking. A twenty-five-year-old hundred-a-day habit had just stopped. I dreaded the withdrawal. What were we supposed to do with our afternoons now? How were we going to look cool?

Then I felt fury. Nothing had changed. The boys in the ski-masks had called it a victory but their situation was exactly the same as it had been a quarter of a century before. Three thousand people had died, countless thousands had had bits blown or beaten or shot off, and all of the rest of us had been scared shitless for a significant proportion of the time. What had this been for? What had been achieved?

Additionally, I couldn't help thinking that if I was husband, wife, father, mother, daughter or son to any of the twenty-seven who'd died in the last eight days I'd have been highly fucking miffed at the timing of this old armistice.

Actually, I felt four things. I also felt like they'd start it all again any time they fancied – any time they got pissed off or menstrual.

As I began to think of going back inside I saw a girl walking alone on the road at the junction of my street. A trio of skinheads was walking towards her. The girl noticed them and quailed. Her step veered to the edge of the pavement. Her head drooped and she tried to make herself small. I shared her fear but there was nothing I could do. She was almost jogging by the time the rough boys drew level.

As I had dreaded, one of the youths put out an arm and grabbed her. She stopped, terrified, her arms thrown up to ward off a blow. One of the velvet-heads bent down to pick something up. He handed her the thing I hadn't seen her drop and the three boys walked on.

It wasn't much, I knew. It was only a small event but suddenly Belfast seemed again a place to be.

Because, sometimes, they glittered, my people here. Sometimes, they shone.

Sixteen

In the high-capacity car park outside the shopping mall, Chuckie Lurgan sat behind the wheel of a rented Subaru watching the lugubrious women sitting silently in their cars. It was 9.30 a.m. and, although it was summer, the air was cold. Chuckie was beginning to find American mornings beautiful. On his only morning in New York City the light had been early but already tired, the sun on the buildings smoky and dry, like it didn't have enough gas to get through the day. But the Kansas version of 9 a.m. was enchanting. The ground frost breathed up its wisps like a landful of cigarettes.

Chuckie wound down his window and looked up at the sky. He knew that it was getting thinner. The ozonosphere was degrading at a rate that negated replenishment. The earth was being dug up and scattered with corrosive filth. The seas were being fished out and the people were growing everywhere. Every day a hundred species became extinct. (Chuckie had been watching an environmental TV programme the night before and found himself newly concerned. What had previously seemed the worst kind of style-free tree-hugging now seemed crucial to father-to-be Lurgan.)

Chuckie felt that his skin was crackling and warping under

the toxic light of the unfiltered sun. In ten years he felt that he would be bald and shrivelled with radiation. The planet, too, would lose its hair and juice. His own city would warp and buckle. Desert Belfast, dry and dead. He found his eyes begin to water.

He was waiting for Max. She was in the mall deli trying to buy chocolate croissants. At breakfast, that morning, she had mildly desired these croissants. Though he thought it absurdly early in her pregnancy for cravings, Chuckie had strenuously insisted that they drive the twenty miles to the nearest deli. She had grumbled but had complied.

After the old lady had told him about Max's pregnancy, Chuckie had spent a couple of days in his hotel room. For thirty hours he had contemplated fatherhood amongst the cloistered plastics and nylons of the little roadside motel. Then he slept for ten hours, rented a car and drove out to see Max.

When he drove up she was sitting on a rocking chair on her porch. The gentle motion of her chair did not falter as he got out and approached her. His heart failed and surged a hundred times in that thirty-second walk, but Max, Max looked serene. Max looked like she had expected him.

He mounted the porch and stopped a few steps from her chair. She looked blankly at him, rocking gently back and forth. There was no welcome in her eyes but there was no refusal either. The Ulsterman took the initiative.

'Marry me,' said Chuckie Lurgan.

It grew dark and chilly out on the porch while they talked. Max told him about the secret thing that had happened to her when she had run away after her father's death. At the end of those two missing years, she had found herself pregnant and too stoned to know by whom. She promised herself that she would have an abortion but, somehow, she never seemed to get around to it. It was a drag to organize, the telephones, the doctors and the clinics. She didn't have the money. She didn't have the time. There were occasions, late at night, just as she was falling asleep when she knew well that she was leaving it late. But the bed was always warm and it was always nice just to dream the bloody thing away so that she would wake up slim-bellied, unfertilized.

But she left it late past the legal termination date. She was six months gone when she finally decided to give it a go.

But that night she and a retired boxer from Tulsa had a party with some cheap crack. Her arm rested on the bump of her belly as she slotted the needle there. She knew exactly what she was doing but she did it anyway.

The people in the hospital had said bad things to her. She remembered one doctor. A young man, unshaven and weary. His voice had been gentle and he had smiled but she had been startled at the thing that she had seen in his eyes. She saw the shame he felt for her.

She had hit him and scratched his face with her ragged nails. A big nurse had rescued him, thumping her back onto the bed. She called Max a dirty whore, pronouncing it broad in the Southern fashion, making it a much uglier word . . . *hoor.*

And there was much time after that. There was a broken time in big rooms where the walls were cold as floors and no one spoke to her. It was like headaches she had had when she was a girl. She knew that there was a thing to endure and only by thinking of its end would she see it out.

She was only truly frightened when they told her that the child had lived. She wept and chided them. That night she dreamt of monstrous births and repulsive babies. The thing had seemed like a virus in her. She had expelled it. That was enough. They could expect no more of her.

For a week or more, she refused to see the child. The nice doctor, his face still scarred from her nails, made a list of all that she had taken when pregnant. As his hand had written down the second page, she understood what she had done. The child would be a monster, made of chemicals and nightmare. One nurse let it slip that the baby had been born addicted and her fears were confirmed. She saw the loathsome little thing with its lizard eyes glittering with greed and narcotic hunger.

When they brought it to her, she wept as if to die. Her heart was glass and broken. That wizened thing was all that she was. She had made it so.

And it seemed that when her baby died only she was surprised.

This was why she ran back to America when she discovered that she was carrying Chuckie's child. When she finished talking, Chuckie simply asked her, gently, caringly, what that had to do with anything. That was then and this was now. He had found it a simple task to persuade her that leaving him was not an option. He found it a simple task to tell her he loved her. He found it a simple task to look at her flawless belly and hope that the child would not, eventually, come to look like him.

The old lady neighbour came round for a while, keen to stay as long as Chuckie. She fought it out for an hour or two but when she looked at the acquiescence in Max's face, she decided it wasn't worth getting tired for. Chuckie spent the next hour and a half gauging the weight of Max's now placid breasts and asking her again to marry him.

He spent a short week there, pitilessly uxorious. He followed Max around the house and yard. He practically helped her to sit and stand. The old lady openly tittered at his excessive attentions. Sometimes Max grew vexed at his solicitude. One night, after the old lady had gone home, she snapped at Chuckie that he should stop clucking. But it was impossible to be long angry with him and within ten minutes she was rolling on top of his comprehensive belly, urgently whispering, *Cluck me, cluck me*, in his ear.

It was a joyous, absurd, consequential week. They spent those days more happily than Chuckie could have thought possible. He was drawn deep into all manner of metaphysical speculation. He found himself considering his own mortality for the first time.

By the time the week had passed Chuckie had grown abashed by such thoughts. He knew himself to be a pragmatic man (actually, he knew himself to be a fat, lazy bastard but he was now too rich to merit that summation). Mystical profundities ill-suited him.

There was something appropriate in his new situation. Something that he felt was more his speed. He was about to have a child – the Ulster Protestant in him guaranteed it would be a son. It was time to provide for his international family. It was time to make some more money.

Chuckie saw Max walking across the parking lot towards him. He felt his customary surge of pleasure to think that this spring-heeled, healthy American woman was his. Her genetic contribution to the child would dilute much of the unwelcome Lurgan inheritance.

Max opened the Subaru's passenger door. 'No chocolate croissants,' she said morosely.

'OK, we'll drive out to Shaneton. You said there was a mall there.'

'Chuck, that's forty miles from here.'

'So what?'

Max glared at him. 'I bought some croissants and I bought some chocolate.'

Chuckie looked question marks.

'We can put them together, Chuck. Or you can have a bite of one and then a bite of the other in quick succession. Mix them in your mouth and it's the same thing.'

'Don't get humpy. This was your craving.'

'It wasn't a craving. I just fancied some.'

'Fair enough.'

'Chuck, stop that. Not in the parking lot.'

Chuckie moved back into his own seat.

'Jesus, Chuck, for a fat guy you're always surprisingly horny.'

He smiled. 'For a horny guy, I'm always surprisingly fat.'

He stared at her. She failed to fall off her seat at his comedy.

Max and her mother were the only Americans who did not find him hilarious. 'You love me,' said Chuckie.

'Don't I know it?' replied Max.

That night they talked about the future. They talked about where they would live. Chuckie knew that a return to Belfast was not assured. He would go anywhere that Max took him.

'Here or there. That's the big question, I suppose,' she said, trying to remove his lips from her nipple and bring him back to the point.

He looked up at her vaguely. 'Here, there, makes no difference to me.' He smiled. 'I can turn a buck anywhere. The world's my can of Tennant's.' He moved back to her breast. Max sighed at the thought that she would marry this man. She rubbed her hand on the back of his sparse, almost sandy head. She wondered if this was how it had been for Peggy Lurgan.

'Yeah,' she said, suddenly mindful. 'You should call your mother.'

That night Chuckie called Eureka Street. Caroline Causton answered. She told him that Peggy was out shopping. Chuckie felt a momentary thrill that his mother felt so much better. This brief pleasure was quickly replaced by bewilderment that Caroline should be answering his telephone.

'You think it's better that you still hang around for a while longer?' he hazarded, as vaguely as he could.

'What do you mean?' Her tone was exacting.

Chuckie grew tense. 'Relax, Caroline. I was just asking a question.'

'Am I not welcome or something, Chuckie?'

'Don't be stupid. I'm just trying to work out how my mother is.'

There was a brief silence.

'She's much better but she wants me to be with her. Is that all right with you?'

There was something in her tone that Chuckie didn't like. There was something in her tone that he hated.

'OK, take it easy.'

'I will if you will.'

'Tell her I called, will you? I haven't spoken to her since I left.'

'I'll tell her. She's fine. Don't worry.'

There was another silence. Chuckie had wanted to tell his mother. Now he wished he could wait but he found that the news was too big inside him.

'Caroline, I'm going to be a father.'

'I know.'

'What?'

'Peggy told me.'

'Who told her?'

'That American girl of yours. The night before she left.'

'That's nice.'

'You getting married, then?'

'Aye.'

'Congratulations, son. I've got to go now. You take it easy. 'Bye.'

She hung up. Chuckie felt deflated. His big news had depreciated in value on its first telling. And, although Caroline's tone had been warmer towards the end, there had still been something in it that Chuckie had not liked.

He called the office immediately. He told Luke instead. He hadn't known Luke very long and wasn't yet sure how entirely he liked him but at least the man was graciously animated at Chuckie's momentous news.

'John Evans has been calling again,' Luke told him.

'Who?'

'The billionaire you met on the plane. Jesus, Chuckie, what did you tell him?'

'Why?'

'You must have given him the best snowjob in history. He wants a part of everything we're doing. He calls every day. He's even threatening to fly over. He wants to know what our action is, or something transatlantic like that.'

'What have you told him?'

'Nothing. I was too embarrassed to tell him. This man is a very big cheese. I'd heard of him. He's famous. I wasn't going to tell this Rockefeller about our twig-dipping franchises. I still have a reputation.'

'Don't get poncey.'

'It drove him nuts. Absolutely crazy. I don't think he's used to secrets being kept from him. I think his money usually gets him what he wants.'

'Gimme his number,' said Chuckie grimly.

'Are you sure you're in the right mood for this?'

'Gimme the fucking number.'

Chuckie called Evans but he called Slat first. He called Septic and Deasely, he called his cousin, he even called Stoney Wilson. He called old schoolfriends, old enemies. He called people he had once passed on the street. He told them all that he was going to be a father. Despite the reservations of some about the continuance of the Lurgan genetic strain they were all pleased for him. He felt better. Then he called John Evans. He told him the truth about all the bullshit businesses and the ridiculous ways in which he had raised capital. As he had expected, Evans offered him five million dollars on the spot.

'I'll get back to you,' said Chuckie casually.

Then he went off to make some money.

One week later Chuckie found himself in a swanky high-rise in Denver.

'Mr Lurgan, we get a lot of advice about places we could capitalize,' said a man in a New York suit.

'I don't give advice,' said Chuckie.

'We're worried about the war there,' said another man in a New York suit.

'There's a ceasefire,' retorted Chuckie.

'It could all start again,' suggested yet another besuited man.

'We're worried about what your guys are doing in Israel,' said the last of the three-pieces.

Chuckie smiled blankly.

'We do a lot of Jewish business in New York. We don't want to irritate anybody there,' the man explained, only partially.

'Well,' Chuckie began, 'I know what you mean.'

He stopped. He had no idea what the man meant. He stared at that trim, tanned foursome. It struck him that they might actually believe that the IRA were some kind of Arab terrorist group. He changed tack quickly. 'If you think that's a problem, then the best option for you is to invest in this region and thus get some leverage with these . . . *Muslim* guys.'

The man with the Arab theory nodded, as though admitting the justice of this point.

'Also, Belfast is a crucial Western port in a vital geographical area.' The men murmured uneasy assent. It took some minutes but Chuckie finally deduced that several had supposed Ireland to be just off the west coast of Africa. He thought hard before he corrected their misapprehension.

An hour later, he had made another eight hundred and seventy thousand dollars. He had persuaded them to give him the money to help buy a factory unit, which Luke had told him they already owned. He would use their money to set up the Stateside utilities companies about which he'd so long dreamt. Irish-American Electricity, the American-Irish Water Company, US Hibernian Gas.

In a week he had bamboozled, bluffed, duped and outwitted a selection of America's finest and hardest-headed businessmen. It had barely troubled him. They knew nothing about his country and sometimes believed wildly inaccurate stories. One man, perhaps thinking of Iceland, thought there were no trees; another firmly believed the island of Ireland to be situated in the Pacific. Chuckie found that their ignorance was not the product of stupidity. These men simply didn't want to know much about the rest of the world. News that was not American was not news. Such had always been the case but now that there had been a couple of ceasefires, Northern Ireland was much televised. It was by no means a lead story but it was on television all the same. Americans found themselves forced to have an opinion. There was a gap, a void between what they actually knew and the opinions they felt they must now hold. Chuckie Lurgan aspired to fill that void.

He was not alone. Jimmy Eve and a coterie of Just Us celebs had flown to Washington immediately after the announcement of the first ceasefire. Despite having less than 12 per cent of the Northern Irish vote, they ambled into the White House and hung out with the President. Chuckie briefly considered telephoning the leader of the low-polling British Liberal Democrats and charging him ten grand for the idea that if he wore a C&A suit and shot a few policemen he'd get an audience with world leaders.

The Americans loved Eve. Several matronly Irish-American women insisted on describing him as hunky, despite his patent lack of physical beauty. The *New York Times* compared him with Clint Eastwood. He had a patchy beard which grew up to his eyes and a mouth like a guppy. There was no way around it, the man looked like a weasel. Chuckie was mystified.

Eve did television shows coast-to-coast. His hairy, carnivorous smile was everywhere. He talked the language of American civil rights to interviewers too ill-educated in their own country's history to notice. He talked about South Africa. He talked about equal rights and democracy. He talked about Eastern Europe. He talked about inclusiveness and parity of esteem. One anchorman asked him when he thought Irish Catholics would be given the vote. Eve fought hard with his temptation to say something like, Never too soon, or, I hope I see it in my lifetime. But he also resisted the temptation to correct the anchorman's profitable error. He just ignored the question and started talking about what a bunch of fuckers the British were.

However, the finest moment came when he was interviewed

simultaneously with a stray Ulster Unionist and Michael Makepeace, the leader of the Ulster Fraternity Party, a collection of vegetarian middle-class doctors who did much lamenting and quite a lot of unsatirical body repairing. For twenty minutes, it was the usual back and forward. Chuckie, watching TV in a Minneapolis hotel room, had seen this hundreds of times but America obviously loved the way these guys just bad-mouthed each other so happily. It was like the trailers for a boxing match or like the fake badinage of professional wrestlers. It was fun.

But then something extraordinary happened. The Ulster Unionist had persisted in claiming that the ceasefire was no ceasefire until the IRA gave up their weapons. The man obviously considered it his best, if not only, point. Finally, the anchorman put that very question to Eve. He asked him if there was any chance of IRA arms being handed in. Eve did his usual waffle about democracy and military occupation and Chuckie was about to change the channel when the anchorman turned to the Fraternity leader with his bright but sincere American smile. 'And what about you, Mr Makepeace, will you, too, give up your weapons?'

Chuckie lay back on his bed and howled like a hound. His delight was complete. By the time he regained an upright position, Makepeace's mouth was still moving but sounds still failed to issue. Chuckie heard an off-mike titter, probably from Eve, and he believed – he would always believe – that the leader of the lentil-munching, fête-giving Fraternity Party looked almost pleased that anyone would think he looked butch enough to have a few Kalashnikovs stashed.

As the days passed and Eve received the vital presidential imprimatur, his progress took on some of the glamour and resonance of a rock tour. Chuckie saw him stand outside a Boston public building with the poet Shague Ghinthoss by his side. Both men were shaking hands, their faces turned towards the bank of cameras, their smiles wide. Journalists shouted questions but Eve and Ghinthoss ignored them until one man shouted that he was from Swedish television. At those enchanted words, both men abruptly assumed a tender, sensitive expression, their four eyes pleading and mild. Then they glanced at each other, each man calculating the unlikelihood of the other being the first to a Nobel.

In New York, one dissenting protester, who carried a placard reading *Stop the Punishment Beatings*, was arrested and punitively beaten up by a trio of zealous New York cops. Several of the Just Us entourage could be seen casting admiring glances at the NYPD technique. Just Us were triumphant. America didn't know Protestants even existed. Many thought that Great Britain had actually invaded in 1969. A passing English historian was interviewed and mentioned that the Army had been drafted in to protect Catholics.

'Well, you would say that,' the interviewer replied, an indomitable, investigative smile on his brave and trustworthy American face.

It wasn't so much that real history was rewritten. Real history was deleted. Its place was taken by wild and improbable fictions. Ireland was the land of story and Just Us campaigners had always been the best storytellers. They told the world a simple story. They edited or failed to mention all the complicated, pluralistic, true details. It had always been thus and the world had always loved it.

Theirs was a narrative in which the innocent, godly CATHOLIC Irish were subdued and oppressed by the vicious English and their Protestant plantation spawn. Italian socialists, French Maoists, German Communists and the entire population of Islington swallowed it all whole, but every now and then inconvenient voices were raised. Why do you guys shoot young boys for stealing cars? How socialist is that? And that business of blowing up shops, bars, cafés, it doesn't feel enormously left wing, does it? How come you have to kill so many Irish to liberate the Irish? Although these were infrequent objections, they still nonplussed the boys and girls from Just Us who had no logical riposte.

This simply didn't happen in America. The United States presented a trusting, sentimental face for Jimmy Eve. He puckered up whenever possible. True, in America he diplomatically downplayed Just Us's supposedly socialist credentials. But he hardly had to. The Americans were not going to draw any parallels between Just Us and the spick Commie rebels in South and Central America. Just Us was full of white guys. That was enough.

All this had a superbity that Chuckie could not match but he incorporated Eve's Broadway-hit status into his own spiel. He began to develop two separate *personae* for dealing with these businessmen. If required, he could be the ultimate croppy boy within seconds, lamenting the filthy English invasion of his land. He became the ultimate Catholic, he grew misty-eyed when talking of the Kennedy clan and blessed himself, inaccurately, before signing any documents. He even began to affect a spurious command of spoken Irish until one sharp-eared *Star Trek* fan pointed out that the noises coming from his mouth sounded suspiciously like the Klingon for 'Phasers locked and ready, Captain'.

Alternatively, he sometimes found it useful to assume an entirely English manner. East Coast WASPs responded to this particularly well. They had a vague belief in some vestigial Northern Irish aristocracy. Chuckie knew he sounded more like Perry Mason than James Mason but they seemed to go for it.

There had been one frightening occasion upon which Chuckie had made an initial miscalculation. He had sailed into an important meeting in Boston doing his full Mick routine. 'Top o' the mornin' to yous all, now. What say we get all our aul jawin' done and then we get down to Maloney's for a few o' the fine stuff?'

He was just about to start complaining about the health of

his pigs when he noticed the frowns on the faces of the four men around the table. Then he noticed their striped ties and highly polished brown brogues, the pictures of old college rowing eights on the walls. It looked like there were fancy old WASPs in Boston too. His transition was immediate and effortless. He smiled thinly at the only man he'd met previously.

'I do apologize, old boy. I've just been listening to some unspeakable bog-wog called Eve on the motor car wireless. They're always banging on about something or other these days. Drives me barmy, I must confess.'

He sounded dreadful. His phoney David Niven accent was mangled by his customary broad Ulster tones. He thought the men might punch him for taking the piss but, as always, it worked a treat. They gave him some more money.

He saw many parallels between the bullshit that Eve was selling and his own success. Indeed, he began to watch each television appearance that the Irish ideologue made, and as Eve's lies and fantasies became more abhorrent and fantastic – and ever more successful – Chuckie stepped up the wildness of his own approaches. Chuckie Lurgan and Jimmy Eve sold Ireland long and short, begetting their monstrous perjuries in tandem, united in an hallucinatory jubilee of simulated Irishness. Chuckie even began to feel something like a grudging affection for his hirsute counterpart.

This uneasy twinship came to a riotous head near the end of Chuckie's second week away from Max. In Washington to tell some lies about a textile company he wanted to start in Dungiven, Chuckie had become so famous that he gave a newspaper interview. In this piece, he had mentioned that he was a Protestant. Jimmy Eve was in town for a few nights, giving head to any Irish-American congressmen who came his way. Spookily, it was the first time that he and Chuckie had coincided geographically. Eve was scheduled for another multitude of television appearances. The producer of one network show happened to see the little piece about Chuckie and decided, uncharacteristically, that it might be a good idea if, just for once, Eve was confronted by an alternative view. He called Chuckie's hotel and booked him to appear the next night.

Chuckie had been missing Max for near a fortnight. He felt himself growing rather grumpy. He called her every couple of hours but it didn't begin to be anything like enough. He grew mutinous and peevish.

Additionally, on the night before his first television appearance, Chuckie failed to sleep. He was remarkably agitated. All his life, this fame business had been magical to him and now he was about to achieve some small renown on his own part. And, whatever he believed about Jimmy Eve, he could not deny that the man was becoming increasingly famous. Chuckie, veteran Protestant Pope-chum, was familiar with this sensation of reluctant awe.

By the time Chuckie arrived at the television studios the next evening, he was so nervous he had practically stopped breathing. While in Make-up, the producers came to see him and were concerned about his evident anxiety. He could see that they were considering cutting him from the show. He was ashamed. He excused himself and sat unhappily in a cubicle in a nearby restroom.

After a few lonely minutes, he heard footsteps. A cubicle door was opened close by. Chuckie waited, scarcely breathing. The business of defecation had always embarrassed him and he decided to wait until this invisible man had finished his task before he himself could leave.

He grew conscious of strange noises: scrapings and small impacts. Suddenly uneasy, he looked up and saw a man staring down at him, obviously perched on the cistern of the next-door cubicle.

'How ya doing?' the man asked, airily.

'Fine. Thanks.'

'You on the show tonight?'

Chuckie nodded.

'Got the jitters?'

Chuckie nodded again.

'Hold up.'

The man disappeared from his position. There were more scuffles and then Chuckie heard a polite knock on his cubicle door. Bewildered, he opened it. The man pushed into the cubicle beside him, locking the door behind him. He took a mirror and some small papers from his pocket. He set them on top of the cistern behind Chuckie's head.

'Outa the way, man. I got just the thing for confidence problems.'

Happily, he proceeded to cut four fat lines of cocaine on the little mirror. He pushed it in Chuckie's direction. 'Go for it, big guy. If you get this in you, you'll be a star. You'll get a fucking Oscar.'

He put a thinly rolled-up dollar in Chuckie's hand. Chuckie stared at the little mirror and its four tracks of powder. Now Chuckie was not altogether a drugs virgin. He'd done a little speed, he'd smoked dope – but rejected it as a thin person's vice. He was, in essence, a conservative man. But he was also an anxious conservative man.

He stuck the tube of money in his nose and inhaled one of the lines of powder. His eyes pricked and his face appeared suddenly delicious. He felt as though he would like to eat his own lips. He put the dollar in his other nostril and hoovered up another track. This time, his very gonads grew elated. He had an ecstatic sense of simplicity. He cursed himself for never having previously investigated the Wonderful World of Cocaine.

The man protested only mildly when he snorted up the last two chunky portions of the substance. Chuckie felt as needy and blameless as a greedy superpig and the man felt a certain evangelical satisfaction at introducing such a keen newcomer (and Chuckie pressed a fistful of money into his hand, which also helped console him).

Chuckie straightened up and strode out of that pisser like

another man, like several other men. He felt absolutely fucking tremendous as he was quick to inform the waiting TV people in the make-up room. Surprised at this new super-bullishness, the producers decided that he was ready for broadcast and the make-up artists went to work, dabbing at his sweat patches, smudging his spots, failing to damp the lunatic glitter in his eyes. When they finished their work, Chuckie leapt to his feet and strode unaccompanied into the studio, godlike, austere, filled with glorious chemical rectitude.

Thirty-five minutes later, the interview was coming to an end. On the periphery of his vision, Chuckie could see the floor manager signalling that a countdown was imminent. He was broken-hearted. He tried to look pleadingly at the interviewer but the man paled visibly under his demented gaze. He ignored the crumpled figure of Jimmy Eve and tried to finish what he was saying before they were counted out.

'And the other thing is that it always comes down in the end to cold, hard cash. That phrase is no accident. Those are its attributes. America, fabulous America, understands this. All you wonderful Americans out there don't need to listen to our moronic politicians. You don't listen to your own, why should ours be any different? What America understands is what I understand – making a dollar, cutting a deal. There are no nationalities, only rich and poor. Who gives a shit about nationhood if there's no jobs and no money? Bread before flags, that's what I say. I'm here in America to do a bit of business. It's the real peace. Don't listen to assholes like this.' Chuckie gestured towards the silent Jimmy Eve. 'This man wouldn't know an economic policy if it came up and bit him on the bollocks. Interested Americans should invest in my country. They should give their money to men like me.' Chuckie smiled a ghastly smile.

The tirade continued for another minute or so. Chuckie saw the floor manager counting down the seconds and he helpfully reached some notional full stop. There was a moment's dreadful silence, until the presenter managed to gasp a flabbergasted good night.

The red lights on the cameras went dead and the men and women behind them started to bustle importantly. Chuckie removed his own chest mike, shook hands with the presenter, chucked the Just Us leader under the chin, waved a cheery farewell to all and sundry and went off looking for the man he had met in the toilets.

Jimmy Eve had said nothing during those seventeen and a half minutes of national television. He had made several attempts to speak but Chuckie had charged him down with coked-up exuberance. The politician had sat silently, pale and sweating, while the lunatic Protestant had ranted, only sporadically interrupted by the flailing presenter.

Afterwards, Eve's entourage had been mystified. As they bundled him into a waiting limousine, they quizzed him as to what had gone wrong, why he had not performed. Eve said nothing. He looked close to tears and his forehead was cold and damp. When they reached their hotel, they called a doctor. The doctor could find nothing wrong with Eve although he manifested some of the symptoms of shock.

This was not surprising. Something shocking had occurred. Ever since he had arrived in America, Eve had made a big event out of who would shake his hand and who would not. He had tried to discomfit British government officials and opposing Irish politicians by offering his hand whenever there were cameras around. He knew that these people could not possibly shake his hand and he knew that that looked so unreasonable on American television. There he was, making the ultimate gesture of peace and amity, and those unreasonable reactionaries continued to reject him.

Thus when Chuckie Lurgan had surged into the television studio, Eve had offered his hand in his usual demonstrative and significant manner. He had never heard of this Lurgan guy but he knew he was a Protestant and that he was there to put forward the Unionist position. Thus, he was enormously surprised when this excited fat man took his hand firmly and shook it vigorously. His surprise increased when the man moved close to him and hugged him one-armed in the American fashion, putting his face close to Eve's own.

The two men remained in that position for what seemed like a long time. The smile on Lurgan's face was so joyous and the way he murmured so intimately in Eve's ear led the producers to think that they had been set up and that these men were related. They did not notice Eve's abrupt pallor and immediate sweat. They did not remark the tremble of his hands as he regained his seat.

When Chuckie was seventeen he had suffered a brief fad for rugby football. He began to play for the third fifteen of a club situated in the nearest bourgeois area to Eureka Street. He had not lasted long. Chuckie had not fitted in. His own team-mates disdained him and opposition players treated him with open contempt. Chuckie was neither good enough nor butch enough to reply with any on-the-pitch heroics, but he found a way to unburden himself of some of his resentments.

He began to place himself in the front row of scrums. When both front rows locked shoulders, his face would be inches from that of another player. Chuckie would proceed to hiss nauseating and vile abuse of a nature that sometimes shocked himself. He told these nice middle-class boys that he had had sex with their mothers and sisters, sometimes their fathers and brothers as well. Sometimes he threatened to have sex with the boys themselves, sometimes he threatened them with arcane amputations and extractions: penises lopped off, bottoms burnt, testicles torn apart. Occasionally, to vary the monotony, he did this to one of his own team-mates.

It always worked. It produced in the victim a state of something approaching catatonia. The dazed individual, a rabbit in headlights, would then be haplessly mashed in some hospitalizing tackle. The obscenity or level of threat was not the effective ingredient. What worked so brilliantly was the sheer surprise. These young men were astonished to have their bourgeois pastime invaded so abruptly by this back-street coarseness.

And this was what had produced the uncustomary silence in Jimmy Eve. Fired by a million years' worth of resentment against this duplicitous Nazi (Chuckie had never felt so Protestant before, he had never felt Protestant at all), Chuckie's rage had been massive. He had whispered things so appalling in Eve's ear that he would always prefer to forget exactly what he'd said. It was bound to be his finest performance. The four fat lines of cocaine had helped.

Two days later, Chuckie and Max boarded a 747 bound for London. They had settled the here-or-there question in the way both had known they would. After a difficult parting from the old house in Kansas, during which Max tried to be stoic but blubbed like a baby, they flew to New York and spent a night there. With Max beside him, that city was a different and much more appealing experience.

Once they had boarded the British Airways plane and Chuckie heard the – relatively familiar – accents of the cabin crew, he breathed a sigh of European relief. He had liked America enormously but his last two days had been mayhem. His television appearance had made him briefly famous. Excerpts were shown on other networks; the entire event was even repeated. Other stations called him and asked him to be interviewed in tandem with American politicians, one even offered him a job as their political correspondent. The CLAD.(Campaign to Legalize *All* Drugs) called him. Max had to deal with much of this telephone traffic. Her mulishness protected him. He was referred to as the MFG in Irish politics, the Mad Fat Guy. There were even rumours of T-shirts being printed. Jimmy Eve skulked home a week early.

This sudden fame upset Chuckie. It shattered the love for celebrity that had never left him. If someone as unevolved as Chuckie himself could be celebrated, however briefly, then notoriety was not worth the having. It was oddly appropriate to his experience of America. That country ran on the fuel of celebrity. It was the true spiritual currency of the nation. In America, actors and actresses were gods, the populace hung on their every word. Chat-shows were the discourses in which these beings diagnosed for the people.

When first in New York, Chuckie had felt that movie-unease was a feeling restricted to him. Every step he took on those famous pavements was self-conscious. That, he felt, was a visitor's sensation. By the time he got to New York second time around, he had established that this sensation was the common experience of the inhabitants as well. Everyone behaved like the movies they'd seen, like the movies in which they'd want to star. The streets were full of men and women acting out images of what they wanted to be. The cops acted like movie cops. The young bloods acted like movie young bloods. The men in suits were motion-picture men in suits. Chuckie even saw a street-sweeper who wielded his brush with a discernibly cinematic air.

In New York, there was a glitch in reality, a hair in the gate, a speck on the lens. There were gross parodies of machismo and arcane street competence everywhere he looked.

The fact that Chuckie now knew that everyone on the planet was an infant who watched too many movies meant that he would never be able to stop making money.

But as the aircraft flew away from America and Max rested her head on the plump shelf of his belly, Chuckie knew that making money had, perhaps temporarily, lost its mystique. He needed to look for something else to give substance to his life. As he looked at her slumbering face, he knew he didn't need to search.

When they reached Aldergrove airport, Chuckie felt his spirits lift. Through the Atlantic air his mood had been subdued, but as soon as that Ulster drizzle smacked his fat chops, he knew he felt better. Max bought some flowers and laid them on the spot where her father had been shot. Her face was red and Chuckie said nothing.

Even the taxi-driver's predictable churlishness moved him. As they drove at speed down the motorway, he found himself becoming grotesquely sentimental. Moving south on the motorway towards Belfast, the mountains hit him like a friend. It was near dusk. The city was laid out beneath him, flat, shyly illuminated. The sky looked like litmus paper and Chuckie knew that there was no excitement in the world like the excitement of this dour provincial cityscape.

They drove to Max's flat first. Aoirghe helped them unload Max's baggage. She embraced Max, but merely scowled her habitual scowl at Protestant Chuckie. He wondered if she had found out about his run-in with Eve. It didn't seem likely. He parted from Max after ten minutes of nuzzling embraces on the pavement while the grouchy driver looked on.

Max went inside and Chuckie told the driver to take him to Eureka Street.

'Are you sure you don't want to do any more fucking snogging there, mate?'

Chuckie, New York veteran, fascist-slayer, MFG, spent the rest of the journey telling the driver what the trouble with him was.

A few hours later, he sat in the jumbled living room of little No. 42, oppressed by a burgeoning sense of unease. His welcome had been all that he could have hoped. His mother was much better, Caroline Causton had attempted courtesy and the house had been cleared of the majority of his recent madcap catalogue purchases. But there was something about the two women that began to perplex him. As the evening went on, he kept waiting for Caroline Causton to stand up and announce that she was going across the street to her own house. This persisted in not happening.

Chuckie tried to ignore the unspoken restraint under which both women mysteriously laboured. He gently questioned his mother about how she was feeling. He told them about his trip to America. Caroline stayed still. He told them some more about his trip to America.

'. . . and all these big Yank tycoons, they were all scared shitless of China. They thought it was the coming place and they didn't want those slit-eyed bastards taking all their money so, of course, the dumb fucks went and sent all their money to China and invested there . . .'

His voice trailed away. He felt like he'd been talking for hours (he had). He noticed that both women had now stood up. Peggy Lurgan bent over him and kissed his face. 'Welcome home, son.' She straightened up. 'We're going to bed now,' she said casually.

Chuckie stared his question marks all around the little room as the two women headed for the stairs.

His mother paused in the doorway. Both women looked at him. 'Yeah,' Peggy said lightly, 'Caroline's moved in with us. 'Night, Chuckie.'

She started to climb the stairs and Caroline favoured him with the merest ghost of a wink before following her.

Chuckie sat in his favourite armchair, mouth open, breathing slow. His flesh grew cold and he began to think he was in shock. After a while, however, he calmed down. He even began to smile. What he had been thinking was, of course, absurd. His mother and Caroline were simply too middle-aged and unsophisticated to have mastered the meaning that might have been imputed to their words. They probably didn't even know what lesbians were. His mother had forgotten to tell him that he would have to sleep on the sofa because Caroline would be sleeping in his bed. He nipped upstairs to check.

His heart raced faster when he saw his room empty. But the fact that his bedroom was unoccupied proved nothing. They had been friends since they were little girls. They probably felt it natural to share a bed, especially since Caroline had been looking after Peggy so recently. He would maybe drop a gentle hint to his mother the next day, demonstrating that such an arrangement might be unseemly.

Chuckie was confident that he was right and could not explain the sweat on his palms and the sensation of bloodlessness in his face. He stepped across Eureka Street and knocked on the Causton house front door. There was no answer. He knocked again.

The door of an adjacent house opened. Old Barney came out in his slippers. Chuckie had known this man all his life. He had always seemed old. Chiefly notable for his extraordinary smoker's cough and the velocity of his spitting, he had a habit of opening his front door to spit onto the street. He never looked first and most of the Eureka Street residents had been inadvertently spat on at some time or other. He didn't do that so much any more – no one liked to think of where he now spat – but many would still cross the street instead of passing his house.

'Ach, what about you, Chuckie? Back from the United States of America, then?' He coughed, rumbled and hawked.

Chuckie ducked. He heard the phlegm splash on the street behind him and straightened up. 'Are the Caustons not in?'

Barney looked vaguely shifty. 'Aye, well, they've gone away for a few days. I think there's been a bit of a dispute in the family.'

Chuckie experienced a surge of relief. His mother had merely taken her friend in because her husband was maltreating her. 'Yeah,' he said, 'Caroline's staying with us.'

Barney coughed again. Chuckie ducked and waited for the splash. It did not come. He looked up at the old man. He realized that, for the first time in his life, Barney had just executed a nervous cough.

'I know,' the old man said quietly. He looked up at one of the upstairs windows of No. 42. Chuckie followed his gaze just in time to see a light extinguished. The old man's face quivered in panic. 'Gotta go, Chuckie,' he muttered. He started to call his old dog.

Chuckie was bemused by his urgency. 'What's going on, Barney?'

The old man continued to call his dog with increasing urgency. Chuckie noticed that another neighbour had opened her door and was trying unobtrusively to recall her own pet. Both kept glancing at the upstairs of the Lurgan house with petrified expressions.

'Barney?'

But Barney had collared his old pooch, swiftly skipped inside his front door and banged it shut behind him. Chuckie walked towards his other neighbour but she, too, grabbed her dog and went indoors hurriedly.

Chuckie Lurgan stood stock still in the middle of Eureka Street. It was quiet. He felt like laughing. It had been like some bad western when all the townsfolk rushed indoors before the bad guys rode into town. He stood bemused in the pleasant silence, his sparse hair sticking to his skull because of the rain. From America to this. But, as he stood there, he could not help but feel fond. Wind-whipped drizzle darted around the street-lamps. In the haze of the sodium lights he could see serried ranks of heavier drizzle swoop in time to the wind's gusts. His mind cleared.

It filled again as he began to hear the noise that had obviously cleared his street. It was a low, spectral wail. The sound chilled his blood. The noise died away and then commenced anew, louder and deeper. It was eldritch, ghastly.

It took Chuckie some time to comprehend that the sound was issuing from his own house, it took him some more time to understand that it was being made unmistakably by his mother, and a final brief period to guess what might be provoking her to howl so.

Chuckie sank to his knees in the middle of wet Eureka Street. His hands went out before his face and his world went black.

Seventeen

'You can't be serious,' I said.

'I swear to God,' said Deasely. 'Apparently he fainted on the street. The milkman found him in the morning.'

'That's got to be a spoof.'

'Straight up.'

Luke Findlater looked daggers at me. He'd been trying to get me off the phone for the last ten minutes.

'Have you seen him?' I asked.

'No,' said Deasely. 'Have you?'

'I've tried. He was in bed and wouldn't open the door. Peggy says he hasn't been out of the house for a fortnight. He won't speak to her and he doesn't come to the phone when I call.'

Another phone rang and Luke picked it up. I ignored him.

'Do you think he'll come to the Wigwam tonight?' asked Deasely.

'Max said she'd told him she'd leave him if he didn't come out. She seems to think he'll be there.'

'Should we avoid referring to it?'

'I think that would be best, don't you?'

'Maybe.'

Luke cupped his hand over his telephone and whistled to

interrupt. 'It's John Evans,' he hissed, *sotto voce*.

'Who?' I asked.

'The Yank billionaire. He wants to speak to you.'

'You talk to him.'

'He doesn't want to talk to me because I'm English. He thinks I'm some kind of office boy. He thinks you Micks are the big operators. He's desperate to know where Chuckie is.'

'Tell him I'm on a call.'

'This man is giving us millions of dollars. I can't do that.'

'He loves it when we treat him rough. It sets his pulse racing.'

I turned back to Deasely and finished my gossip.

It took a long time. There was such a lot of gossip around. Events had been moving apace. For instance, Peggy Lurgan was now a lesbian living with Caroline Causton. This was spectacular news. People had called press conferences. Peggy and Caroline were the most Protestant and the most working-class women I had ever met. Such women did not normally end up munching blissfully at each other, or so everyone had believed.

The news had had a seismic effect in Eureka Street and Sandy Row. Indeed, much of working-class Protestant Belfast was in uproar. Uncomplicated men watched their wives with new attention and fear. Several gave their wives preventive beatings just in case they might have considered stepping out of line in this most unProtestant fashion.

The effect on Chuckie was less seismic than coma-inducing. He had gone into deep hiding. No one but Peggy and Max had seen him since the night he had come back from the States and Peggy had only seen him in his rare trips out of his room to eat or evacuate his bladder and bowels. He was obviously traumatized. Chuckie's liberalism had often surprised me. For a Prod prole, his politics were uniquely unimpeachable; his almost exclusively Catholic acquaintance was proof of that.

But he drew the permissive line at his mother putting out nightly for another woman. My concern was that, since Chuckie did not leave the house and Eureka Street houses were famously small and thin-walled, he would be presented with the most detailed auditory impressions every night. In that house, he would be able to hear the rustle of their pubes.

For me the news of Peggy's conversion came as a relief. It meant that I definitely didn't have to think about her sporting provocative underwear any more. I could put all that behind me.

In some ways, the impact upon Donal Deasely had been the most surprising. Encouraged by Peggy's unexpected Sapphic courage, Deasely came out. He told us he was gay. It was something of a shock for those of his friends who had known him for ten years and more. No one had noticed. Which showed how sensitive and perceptive we all were. We'd noticed that he had had very few girlfriends but they had definitely been girls.

When he told me, I felt like a liberal parent presented with a homosexual child. I was delighted to be able to demonstrate my permissiveness. I was, frankly, a little jealous. Deasely was leading a life completely free of PMS. What was I thinking? It had been so long since I'd got laid there hadn't been too many menstrual storms for me either. Apparently, Deasely was going to bring his current boyfriend to the Wigwam that night. He was called Pablo, it seemed. I could barely wait.

Other news. Roche had disappeared more effectively than Chuckie. No one had seen him since the night I'd so unceremoniously kicked him out of my flat. Faithfully, I kept my eye out for him at the office and checked around Eureka Street. I even called at his house. His big-vest daddy didn't answer and the broken woman who spoke to me had no idea where he was nor any real interest.

Oh, yeah, there was the ceasefire as well. We were a fortnight in and there had been several more ceasefires. The UVF and all the Protestant paramilitaries had laid down their arms. To my amazement, they had even apologized. The INLA, the IPLO had declared ceasefires. The IJKL, the MNOP and the QRST (both members of the latter turning up to the press conference in a mini-cab) had all followed suit. A fortnight in and only five people had been shot murkily dead and thirty-eight people beaten half to death with baseball bats.

In Chuckie's second absence, Luke and I had managed to bring his grotesque financial empire into some kind of trim. With the aid of constant and unsolicited cash injections from the patently barmy John Evans, we had managed to pay for several of the businesses that Chuckie had already bought and set up a few new ones of our own, though thoroughly in the Lurgan style. We had started to export High Quality Irish Garden Soil to American gardeners – in reality, it was the cheesy side layer from the big municipal landfill by the motorway.

Business was easy. A few years ago, I'd met a man who owned a garage in West Fermanagh. Any time business was slow, he would go out with a pickaxe in the middle of the night and chip out a sizeable hole in the road half a mile away from his joint. For weeks afterwards, his casual trade would soar, ripped tyres, bent wheel rims, fucked axles. He had the gift.

Of course, Chuckie's gift was something infinitely grander but the principle was largely the same. On the day I was gossiping with Donal, Luke and I were doing our sums and making an attempt to calculate what Chuckie Inc.'s current assets might be. We worked hard and tirelessly. By three o'clock that afternoon we came up with a figure that scared the piss out of us both. We gulped. We looked at each other silently. We stood up. We put on our coats. We said we'd meet at the Wigwam. We took the rest of the day off. I drove out to see Matt and Mamie, trying not to think about how scarily plutocratic the invisible Chuckie had become.

Still warm in the belief that Roche was shacked up round my place, Matt and Mamie were flushed with pleasure to see me. They stood, arm in arm, beholding the philanthropic marvel I had become. They wittered on for ten minutes about how proud they were.

'The kid's gone,' I muttered.

'What?'

'He's left. He left a fortnight ago. He only stayed one night.'

'Where is he now?' asked Mamie sharply.

'I don't know.'

'Have you looked?' said Matt.

'Yes, I've looked.' My voice had grown edgy.

Mamie turned on her heel and walked into the kitchen.

'She'll get us some coffee,' Matt mumbled feebly.

I followed Mamie. I tried to explain to her the advice that even Slat had given me. Neither of these generous old folk could properly understand why I might come under sexual suspicion when harbouring a homeless twelve-year-old boy. That idea revolted them but I persuaded them that that was the way it was. I failed to mention that Roche had walked off with all my new electrical goods.

It took some time to persuade Matt and Mamie to talk about something else.

'You could have sent him to us,' Mamie suggested.

'I thought you said you'd been forcibly retired from the kindness business.'

'We have. We could have looked after him unofficially for a while.'

'I'm sorry, Mamie. I should have thought of that.'

'Yes. You should have.' She turned to Matt. 'You better get him his letter, then.'

Matt sloped off like an uneasy pooch.

In the meantime, Mamie told me some secrets. She'd been sick. I knew this. Matt had already told me he'd been worried for a while but that the doctors had finally said she was OK. Mamie told me that, at the height of their anxiety, they had discussed the possibility of her dying. Matt had freaked out, apparently. He had raged and broken furniture (that, I wished I'd seen). He had told her that he couldn't live without her, and if he thought she was going to die, he would kill himself first.

Even I could see that this was not very supportive.

Mamie had always been the strong partner but she told me that there was no way she was going to let him die first. The thought of a future without Matt bled her of all her courage and stubbornness. She would make sure she would be the first to go. It might be cowardly, she admitted, but it was the way it was going to be.

Matt came back. I'd never envied anyone as much as I envied Matt and Mamie.

'Here you go.' Matt handed me the red envelope while looking suspiciously at Mamie. It was Sarah's style. She'd always used fancy stationery. I decided, as my hand first touched it, that I didn't necessarily have to read it straight away. I was sure it was just another recipe for what the trouble with me was. So many people had told me recently that I didn't need any textual confirmation.

'I'm sorry we didn't give it to you before,' Matt said. 'Sarah asked us to wait.'

'I understand,' I lied.

I spent an hour in the city centre buying things I didn't need. What with Belfast being such a small town, I bumped into about forty people I knew. I chatted long each time. I encountered Rajinder with his new girlfriend, Rachel. It was good to see him but after a few minutes I was uneasy. I drew him aside and whispered, 'Is she Jewish?'

'Yeah,' he said.

'Aren't you a Muslim?'

'Yeah, but I'm Sunni.'

I smiled kindly. 'Yeah, Rajinder your disposition is very pleasant but you're still a Muslim.'

'No, no. I mean I'm a Sunni Muslim. We're more moderate.'

'I knew that,' I muttered quickly.

There'd been a couple of ceasefires and suddenly Belfast was the city of love. Muslim and Jew at it like rabbits. By all accounts Rachel's and Rajinder's parents had yet to call their own ceasefire but Rachel and Rajinder didn't care.

I met a dozen more folk I knew. Some I liked nearly as much as young Rajinder. I'd never been so glad of casual street encounters. I'd always responded well to kindness but that evening I'd have licked your hand for a gentle word.

I still felt like shit, though. So it was with joy that, on my way back to my car, I saw someone who was doing worse than me.

Surrounded by what looked like a foreign film crew at the rails beside the City Hall, I could see the unmistakable figure of Ripley Bogle, tramp, waster, tosspot, holding forth to some journalists. I hiked across the road to see what was going on. I sidled up close and could hear Bogle spouting on in French to the interviewer. The cameraman moved in tight and I saw my indigent ex-schoolmate pull an urbane expression and deliver his final *bon mot.*

The director made a signal and the camera crew dispersed. Bogle shook hands with the producer and the interviewer, and pocketed an envelope obviously stuffed with cash. I waited until the French guys had moved off a little and then I approached old Bogle there. He spotted me and smiled in surprise. 'Jake Jackson?'

'*Ça va?*'

He laughed and shook my hand. 'I can hardly believe it,' he said.

He looked dreadful. In the midst of the ample evening sunshine and all the summer greenery of the trees around us, he looked wintry and decayed. He'd always been the good-looking type, but he was as faded and grimy as an old photograph, white face and bloodless lips. I felt a sudden shock of grief, as though someone had died.

'Jesus, man, you look like shit,' I said, tactfully.

'Thank you.'

'Sorry.'

He stuffed the envelope into his pocket and made to move on.

I changed the subject. 'What was that with the telly people?'

'Peace dividend. Lots of foreign TV crews and I'm the only polyglot *clochard* in town. I turn an honest and superbly educated dollar. I've gotta meet a German crew in a few minutes. Gotta go.'

He tried to walk off. I put my hand on his chest, arresting his progress. 'Look, I said I was sorry for what I said.'

'Yeah, forget it.'

I offered him a cigarette. He accepted. We ignited manfully, leant our backs against the rails and watched a series of heart-breaking women dawdle past.

'You like the way you live?' I asked him.

'What do you think?'

'How long has it been like this?'

'Decades.'

'Why do you live this way if you don't like it?'

'I have a problem.'

'What's that?'

'I don't have enough money.'

'Jesus, you went to Cambridge, you'd get a job with your eyes closed.'

He smiled. 'Look at me,' he said. 'Would you give me a job?'

'Wouldn't take much to clean you up.'

'It would take more than I've got.'

I tore a piece off my cigarette packet and scribbled a telephone number on it. I handed it to him.

'What's this?' muttered Bogle, perplexed.

'You know the thing about depending on the kindness of strangers?'

'If you say so.'

I tapped the piece of paper I'd given him. 'Call these people. He's called Matt. She's called Mamie. You've got something they need.'

He looked at me strangely. 'I remember. Your foster-folks, right?'

'Your long-term recall's still firing, then.' I tried to move off.

Bogle put his hand on my chest. His face was animated, somehow younger. I had a sudden memory of what he used to be. 'Why are you doing this?'

I laughed. 'You're frightening, Bogle. You're very expensively educated. It's spooky to see all that going down the plug. You're a symptom of the grand malaise in our society.' I removed his hand from my chest. 'You scare the piss out of me,' I added.

He laughed appreciatively. His teeth were still good and he looked momentarily healthy and almost winsome. 'Are you sure it's not just because you're a soppy old fucker? You were always a soppy old fucker at school.'

I patted his hand away. 'I'm hard,' I replied. 'I'm a very tough individual.'

I walked on, reasonlessly elated. I had no idea whether he would get in touch with Matt and Mamie. I thought it was more unlikely than likely. I didn't imagine I'd done anything to patch up that spectacularly damaged life. But the trees were bright in the sun and the women were pretty and half dressed and I was stubbornly jubilant.

As I waited at the pedestrian lights to cross into Bedford Street, a youngish mother walked past me wheeling a three-year-old boy in a pram. The mother ignored my casual glance but the little boy looked straight at me.

'Keep it country,' he said ringingly.

'OK,' I replied.

Amongst the gossip that I hadn't related to Deasley was a piece of news I couldn't share. The people I knew had taken to confiding in me recently. Perhaps their confidences were provoked or encouraged by the aura of failure and celibacy I was giving off. It was worrying when too many people liked you. Mass likeability wasn't always a good sign.

Luke Findlater told me his big secret. He had been bothering me – and everyone else – ever since I'd met him. It felt

disturbed him most, he simply walked the streets and inspected the men's white socks, moustaches and windcheaters again. He could only concede that he was different. That there might be something to like.

He went to Belfast and quickly rented an apartment there. He had barely worked for three weeks but he cared little. He called a couple of people in London and New York. He told them that Ireland was the coming place and that he had decided he needed to be on hand. He could still work contracts elsewhere. The place had airports. A fortnight later, he was working again.

It was a place that suited him. It was a life for which he had been made. He was besotted with Irish girls because they were so easily besotted with him. Elegantly, handsomely, he had dated twenty-four working-class Irish girls in his first four months on the island. He loved them for their vigour, their vulgarity – he loved the whole sublime atmosphere of post-colonial eroticism. Most of them were gobsmacked by his looks, his eloquence, his sophistication and his unarguable *poshness*. The others just thought he was gorgeous, great in the sack and they tolerated the rest.

He knew that it was wrong. The crucial element was condescension. They had to be both surprised and honoured by his attention. In surrendering his birthright amongst these women, he was crucially rewarded for being his graceful, accomplished self. There was also a gentle pleasure in playing out an extra life-size version of himself in their back-street world of tiny interiors, where he glittered like some exotic beast amongst their colourful (sometimes criminal) parents and gum-chewing siblings.

After five or six months, he began to feel guilty. He felt then that he had used up the thrill of dating yob Irish girls. If he was becoming scrupulous, then the reason had gone. He thought briefly about going to South Africa to scour the townships and see how he fared amongst the surprised and grateful black girls.

But he fought his way through the intermittent prickings of his conscience and started all over again. Belfast, Derry, Lurgan, Antrim, Ballymena, Enniskillen, Portadown. They gave their daughters to him. He felt that he exploited no one and no one exploited him. If he gave them a small part of the joy and gratitude that they made him feel then it was no robbery.

They were funny, these Deirdres, these Siobhans. They were fun, these Aoifes, these Sineads. They gave him so much – pleasure, happiness. There was much of beauty in the exchange and more tenderness than might be supposed. But the best thing they gave him was their version of him. For them, he was something special, something unique. He knew that, to them, it must have seemed really great to be him.

When they were around, these Orlas, these Mauras, these Medbhs, they were right – it was really great to be him.

Slat Sloane had only recently confessed a tandem peccadillo to me. Slat was the only socialist I knew. Slat was the only socialist any of us knew. But Slat told me that because of an erotic incident during the last election with a Democratic Unionist Party canvasser called Margaret, he could now only sleep with right-wing women. It was the only thing that worked for him. The more overtly Nazi the better. DUP women were wonderful, naturally, but he coveted Free Presbyterian females.

In the last couple of years, Slat's sex life had become a hunt for right-wing women of a certain age. He started going to DUP and Official Unionist meetings, and even Conservative ones, in the hope of scoring with the treasurer in the toilets. (Sometimes it worked.) On a week's holiday in Houston, he stayed in a hotel where a Republican convention was being held and got criminally boffed by the wife of a rabidly xenophobic Ohio senator – although she ruined the experience by disagreeing with some of her husband's more excessive notions.

Slat told me that he slept with these women for several reasons. It was naughty because they were so entirely right-wing, because they were so entirely middle-aged. But mostly he slept with them because they hated him. That was a sensation difficult to replicate with non-political girls.

The upshot of this was that Slat was forced to inform me that he had got engaged a week before to someone ominously called Wincey. That sounded right-wing, Protestant and middle-aged all at once. She would be in the Wigwam tonight. I could hardly wait.

I had often worried that my friends and I seldom talked about politics. There we were, living in Northern Ireland, the country of calorific nationalisms, Christolatry and a splittable and splitting populace. We never really mentioned it. It was good to see that local conditions weren't entirely passing us by. I was glad that my friends' sex lives were incorporating the sectarian and post-colonial experience. It meant I didn't have to think about them myself.

Eight fifteen p.m. Usual table in the Wigwam. Everyone was there. Slat was there, Donal was there, Luke was there. Even Chuckie was there. He was completely silent, true, and Max seemed to be holding him down in his seat, but he was there. It had been a month since any of us had seen him. Septic had started a rumour that he was hiding out because he'd had a hundred grand's worth of plastic surgery in California. He and Max had arrived late and even the sceptical amongst us had been half expecting to see a new slim, epicene Lurgan. When the same old fat, balding Chuckie walked in – pushed by Max – we were much relieved.

When we'd said hello, he had grunted reluctantly. With her usual skill, Max had smoothed it over and made us comfortable. Pregnancy suited her. She was more beautiful and serene than before. As she talked and joked to fill Chuckie's silence, she made the rest of us feel that we lacked something.

Donal was there with his new boyfriend. Pablo seemed a nice enough young man, if pointlessly good-looking and well-muscled. I caught Septic staring distastefully at the inordinate bulge in Pablo's trousers. It was easy to see precisely what Donal was getting these days.

Slat had brought Wincey, who looked like she was the mother of everybody else at the table. She must have been fifty. Brown-haired, well made-up, plump but trim, she was the kind of woman that Chuckie's mother might now go for. Slender, intelligent, sensitive, Slat looked like her youngest son. But Slat was obviously besotted. They persisted in whispering close together like amorous teenagers. I heard her ask how many of us were Catholics. I heard the distinct erotic and colonialist quality of her gasp when Slat told her that we were almost all Catholics.

Septic, too, was accompanied. His escort was, to my infinite surprise, young Aoirghe. I was trying not to think about the irritation this was causing me. They weren't exactly swapping sweet nothings and Septic's hands only seldom fluttered near her airspace but they were together and that pissed me off.

It wasn't the usual Wigwam scene. Bar Luke and me, the boys had all paired off. It was Couple City. It was like the last scene of a Shakespearian comedy: everybody was getting married off apart from us minor comic characters. I'd always hated Shakespearian comedies.

At first, the chat was general. Current weather conditions. Sharon Stone. Garden furniture. Jimi Hendrix. There was more unease, more discomfort than we'd ever experienced on one of these evenings. Some of that was to be expected. We no longer had a quorum. Our numbers had doubled. We'd been forced to spread out and grow up. But there was much strangeness: even Chuckie's silence was not particularly remarkable amongst all the newness. None of us boys seemed to have spoken so far.

'Was he that black boy who killed himself years ago?' asked Wincey.

'That's right,' replied Pablo. 'A beautiful man.'

'Didn't he take lots of drugs?'

'Whenever possible.'

'That's terrible.'

'Probably.'

I saw both Donal and Slat shiver with pleasure and affection. The exchange was obviously characteristic of each of their paramours and this they found infinitely sweet, it seemed.

'Jimi Hendrix was a victim,' declared Aoirghe. Septic flinched. We all flinched as she went on, 'He was a black man in a white man's world. It had to end the way it did.'

I laughed. 'He was a stoned man in a white man's world. That had more to do with his death than the accident of his skin,' I suggested.

'He made beautiful music,' sighed Pablo.

'It was the music of the oppressed,' Aoirghe hissed at me.

I laughed and Slat rapidly began talking about Chelsea football club. He supported Arsenal so it was an eccentric choice.

'If they don't buy a central defender early in the season, they'll be relegated.' He fizzled away into silence and everyone but Wincey and I glared at him.

'Oh, I am sorry,' Aoirghe said with a theatrical air. 'I wouldn't want to annoy Jake by being too committed.'

How could she open the door for me like that?

'I'd have no problem with you being committed, sweetheart.'

Slat and Donal gave me their cheap-shot looks and Septic practically clapped his hand over Aoirghe's mouth to prevent her reply. The moment passed without violence.

'Did you hear the OTG guy has been arrested?' piped up Donal, over-brightly.

'What?' I asked, suddenly interested.

'I heard on the radio.'

'Nah,' said Slat. 'The cops waded in after a student party. A whole lot of the kids had taken a bucketload of speed and fucked off round the Holy Land with spray cans. Not the real McCoy.'

'Mass action. That's so sixties,' squeaked Wincey.

We all stared at her in silence. I tried to smile at her.

'Absolutely.' I grinned. I liked Wincey. I nearly began to wonder what she'd look like in some high-thigh Lycra . . .

'So the real guy hasn't been found?' asked Max.

'How do you know it's only one guy or even a guy at all? It could be several people.'

'Roche saw him,' I told them.

'When?'

'A couple of times. It was definitely the right guy.'

'Nobody knows what it means yet?' asked Max.

'No,' said Septic.

'Feeble pacifist bullshit,' murmured Aoirghe.

I laughed into my beer.

'I have an idea what it means,' said Donal quietly.

'What do you think it means?' asked Slat.

'Nothing,' replied Donal.

Everyone pulled their disappointed faces.

'I'm serious,' said Donal. 'I think it's entirely random. It could be any three letters of the alphabet. It doesn't really matter what they are. This is the city of the three-letter initial written on walls. I think someone's satirizing us.'

'Well, it's worked,' said Pablo.

'It has to be someone very persistent,' grumbled Septic.

'He must just have wanted to see what happened. To see if other people copied him – which they did. It must have been touch and go whether it was going to start a terrorist gang, a religious cult or a political party.'

'So, it's ultimately pointless?' I suggested.

'Not at all, satire is never pointless. It makes us look stupid and besides it's just a pretty good wheeze.'

I felt suddenly depressed. The same conviction had been growing in me. I didn't like to have it verified in this manner. I wouldn't say I'd been placing any hopes, spiritual or political, on this OTG thing but I'd been glad to have it around. I liked the way it had pissed everybody off.

The conversation stuttered on uncertainly.

'It's pointless now that it's all over anyway,' said Septic.

'What precisely is all over?' I asked him.

'You know, the Troubles,' he glanced at Aoirghe, 'the war.'

'Five dead and thirty seriously assaulted,' I mentioned. 'Doesn't sound very over for them.'

'Cut it out, Jake,' said Max kindly. Even Chuckie looked up when she spoke.

'Yeah, it's over, right enough,' said Donal diplomatically. He raised his beer. 'Here's to all of us making it through unscathed.'

We raised our beers and toasted that notion. It was no surprise to me that we'd all made it through. We were all so middle class now. We'd never been in any danger.

Post-toast, the conversation lightened rather. I didn't look anywhere near Aoirghe and smiled only grimly at Septic Ted. We rumbled on, talking, eating, drinking. Even Chuckie began looking up from his plate. There was a difficult interlude when my revolutionary waitress, obviously just finishing her shift, leant over our table and murmured at me, 'I worked it out, shithead. It wasn't my politics that bothered you. You just didn't like me because I'm working class.'

She stomped off and everyone started chatting in a charitable attempt to conceal my humiliation. I noticed that Luke Findlater followed her to the door and stopped her there. Even at that distance, I could hear the excitement in his voice as he said: 'So, you're working class, then? Would you like to tell me about that?'

They left together, hand and glove, foot and shoe.

So, now everyone had scored. Everyone had got some love in their life. Earlier that evening, I'd even seen my girl from the supermarket walking down the street arm in arm with her spotty colleague with the hearing-aid. I wished them well but I was a little miffed that she had recovered so quickly from her pash for me.

I ate some strings of lettuce and watched mournfully as my friends talked around the table. Apart from Aoirghe and Septic, they were all guilty of sundry hand-brushings, thigh-meetings and face-touchings. Their limbs twined like some amorous undergrowth. I felt like a monk or a referee. Nobody was twining anything with me.

Yeah, Belfast felt like a city of love that night. A city of sex. It felt strange. It felt uncharacteristic. It felt slightly illegal and it felt like I hadn't been invited. I drank some beers.

A couple of nights before, I had found myself listening to a Muddy Waters record four times in a row. I'd been hearing the blues non-stop for a month or more. I'd always loved it when depressed old black men sat on bad wooden chairs in the middle of New Orleans and sang about some woman, yeah, who'd left them, yeah, 'cos they loved some other man, yeah, and it was all right, yeah. Except that it wasn't all right, yeah. It was awful, yeah. I was settling myself into this solitary, unloved predicament. I was beginning to enjoy it.

I blamed Chuckie. I had to blame someone. I looked up at my fat, silent friend.

'Hey, Chuckie,' I said aggressively. 'Hey, Lurgan.'

There was silence. Chuckie wasn't looking at me: he was staring over my shoulder at the door with a mute and horrorstricken expression. I turned round and looked in the same direction.

'Shit,' I whispered, to no one in particular.

Peggy Lurgan and Caroline Causton had walked into the café uncertainly enough. It was new to them and they were surrounded by people twenty years younger, but when they saw our table, they approached with a confident step.

'Hello, everybody,' smiled Peggy. 'This is Caroline.'

I kept Chuckie in sight right down Shaftesbury Square and Great Victoria Street. He pulled a sharp left down Glengall Street and I cursed myself for not having jumped in the car in the first place. I simply had no idea that Chuckie could run so fast. Sitting around like a fat cabbage, it was hard to imagine him getting much over six miles an hour. But here he was, a hundred yards in front of me, really travelling. My own lungs were bursting and I felt inches away from a heart-attack. I smoked too many cigarettes for this kind of lark. Nevertheless, I skidded round the corner on my metal-tipped heels and pelted up Glengall Street after the fat fuck.

He'd simply burst out of the café when his mother arrived with Caroline. Plates, bottles and waitresses were sent spinning in his chubby wake. I had told the others to stay where they were and had sprinted after him. What were friends for? Something else, probably.

By the time we were half-way past the traffic-only, double-lane Westlink, Chuckie's pace had slowed to a vivid jog. I could see bits of him wobble under the exertion. Unfortunately, I was so fucked by this point that it was all I could do to match his pace. Motorists braked and swerved wildly. Horns blared and drivers shouted. Chuckie ran on and I had to follow, guts churning, arteries bursting.

But when he turned up the foot of the Falls, I stopped and lay down. After a couple of minutes while my lungs started working and my heart-beats became distinguishable again, I lifted my head from the pavement to look for my friend. A bottle crashed and splintered on the spot where it had been.

I looked about me. The street was full of people running, shouting and throwing things at each other. An armoured police Land-Rover had pulled up close by and the bottle that had just missed me had been destined for them.

'Fuck ye.'

'Bastards.'

'Up the Ra.'

Oh, good, I thought. A riot. Just what I needed.

At each end of the dark lamp-lit street, masses of people had started charging towards me. On one side, I had the helmeted and shielded Royal Ulster Constabulary, and on the other, the forces and supporters of national liberation. I sat like a prick in the middle, pebbles and bottles failing to bounce all round me.

The first few baton rounds of plastic bullets woke me up. I'd seen these things in action before. They might have been made of rubber but they really messed you up. I stood up and charged into the midst of the rioters – at least they wouldn't arrest me.

Sure enough, the wave of people parted and I made my way to the rear of the charging throng. I could see that various types of desultory rioting were taking place all along the length of the Lower Falls. Bunches of kids were throwing stones and breaking windows with no apparent end in mind. I looked around for Chuckie.

My search was interrupted when the charging rioters, having clashed with the police, retreated again and charged back the way they had come, straight towards me. I ducked into Divis to avoid them. I watched as the rioters and police tore up the slight hill and then moved on. I had a peek round the foot of the flats to see if Chuckie was there. I didn't hang around too long. I could hear shouts and impacts from high up. I hadn't seen a riot in a few years but I was still too much of an old hand to get banged on the bap by a tower-block trash-can dropped from the fifteenth floor. Some people would do something like that just to see what it felt like.

I moved up the Falls, ducking the trouble, keeping close to the buildings, running in the shadows between street-lamps. The Army were out now and I didn't want to go making anyone anxious. The soldiers ran after the rioters and the rioters ran after the soldiers. Bottles were thrown and heads were kicked. A few cars were burning, up by the swimming baths, and some kids with scarves round their faces had stopped a bus and were hauling the passengers off. The riot was a halting thing (it had been a while, after all) but rioting was a bit like riding a bicycle: no matter how long it had been, you never really forgot how to do it.

There were only a couple of TV news crews so far, but wherever they went, the riot would surely follow. Gangs of kids chucked bricks to order. If they'd been asked for retakes, they'd have gladly obliged. The sinister figures of older men could be seen amongst these kids, obviously directing them where to go and what to do. I'd seen lots of that kind of stuff. I'd seen riots on this road where these guys had openly passed out cash to the stone-throwing youngsters. I'd seen riots where five kids chucked a few bricks surrounded by twenty or thirty photographers who had broadcast pictures of mayhem to the world. It was boring, frankly.

I saw some kids with milk-bottle petrol bombs. They stood on the side of the street and chucked their bombs at cop Land-Rovers as they whizzed up the road. After all the cops had passed, the kids had one petrol bomb left. They looked at each other in confusion until the kid with the bomb just threw it at one of his mates. I suppose he had to do something with it. They all laughed but at least they helped pull the burning jacket off the bombed boy.

I watched two chunky policemen hold a young rioter down by the hair while they both kicked him repeatedly in the face. The cops kept losing their balance but always leapt up quickly and resumed their work. The sound was distinct amongst all the clamour, a horrible wet repetitive sound. I headed over there through the crowd, but by the time I crossed the road, cops and rioter had disappeared.

I saw two masked men with guns rob their local off-licence, completely unnoticed amidst the chaos. I saw an old lady being mugged by a plump young skinhead. He punched her to the ground and ripped her handbag from her hands. I saw a big heavy, who looked like one of the Just Us stewards, jump on the skinhead and beat him to the ground in his turn. The guy then took the handbag and sloped off.

I saw the cutting edge of Northern Irish self-determination.

I was attacked a couple of times myself. I put both my guys down without too much trouble. Rioters were never much cop at actual fighting and I was, by now, in a very bad mood. I didn't go mad or anything. I just put them down. They were very neutral events, more like callisthenics than combat. I found a tooth lodged in the elbow of my jacket later but that was hardly my fault.

What was this riot about? There had to be a reason. This was Catholic Land. The war was over. These guys were supposed to have won. Why, then, were they so pissed off?

I learnt later that the riot had been caused by the early release of a British soldier, who had shot a couple of joy-riders dead a few years before. The squaddie had been convicted of murder, untypically, but had only done about ten minutes for it. It had been a tactless move but the reaction surprised me. The IRA themselves routinely shot young folk who stole cars and were always campaigning vigorously that all their imprisoned members who had murdered and maimed people should be released. Everyone seemed to have a very shaky grasp on jurisprudence these days. I wondered what the old lady who'd had her head bashed and her bag stolen would have said.

I wandered around hopelessly as the riot faded away. I was wrong about rioting, it wasn't really like riding a bicycle. It had been a pretty crap riot. Everyone had looked a little embarrassed, slightly existential. Several motorists had been badly beaten up by people who wanted to disguise their uncertainty and confusion.

I wandered but Chuckie was nowhere to be found. On the wasteground by Leeson Street, some people had gathered round a couple of burning cars, making something almost festive out of the night's events. I asked a few if they'd seen any fat, balding Protestants. *Only in uniform*, they replied good-naturedly. The heat seemed to have gone out of these people. They were now normal citizens again, far from atavistic.

I heard some of them gossiping about a kid who'd been given a baseball-bat beating by the boys down at the bottom of Leeson Street. He'd broken into a senior IRA man's car at the beginning of the riot. He hadn't driven it away, he had simply urinated on the driver's seat.

I knew it had to be Roche. That was his style. I skipped down Leeson Street as fast as I could. By the time I arrived, two paramedics were already shunting the victim into the back of the ambulance. I stopped them and had a peep. One eye was beaten closed and much of the upper part of the face and head was matted with old blood but it was definitely ugly and stunted enough to be Roche.

I was impressively calm for quite a long while. In the ambulance I was calm. All the way to the hospital, as Roche lapsed in and out of consciousness, I was calm. In Accident and Emergency, I was placid as Roche waited his turn for treatment. The riot had produced one or two serious injuries, including a lorry driver who had had bleach poured down his throat while his truck was hijacked (what were they doing with bleach?). I was even-tempered when one of the nurses told me that Roche had a broken leg, a broken arm, cracked ribs and a fractured skull. I was composed as I waited to be allowed in to see him. All in all, I was serene, collected, tranquil.

But when I saw the TV crews arrive. When I saw the Amnesty International man arrive. When I saw Aoirghe arrive. When I heard they'd all come to see a senior Just Us councillor who'd been arrested after the incident with the bleach and endured a four-stitch head wound. When I heard that this man's car had been vandalized and urinated on by the police. When I heard the Amnesty guy start prosing on about human-rights violations to the TV cameras.

Well, what do you expect? It was me. I flipped. I lost it.

Laudably, I didn't hit anyone, but one of the nurses told me that the things I screamed at these people didn't include any recognizable forms of human speech. I bellowed. I frothed and champed. Several people looked like they wanted to go home.

I grabbed the Amnesty guy by the lapels and gave him some nuclear lip about why he should be monitoring the right of twelve-year-old boys not to have the crap beaten out of them.

It was pointless, however. He couldn't understand a word I said. I couldn't understand a word I said.

By the time I'd finished, my voice had dried to a scraped-out croak. Sweat dripped off my face onto my shirt. I grabbed the back of a nearby chair to steady myself. Everyone stared at me in aghast silence. Then they moved off muttering and went to visit their wounded political hero. Only Aoirghe remained. She looked me full in the face. Her expression was different – something I couldn't associate with her. She came closer to me and put her hand on my arm. I flinched.

'What are you doing here?' she asked.

I had no excuse. I'd never done the like before but I grabbed her by the front of her shirt and dragged her to the booth where Roche lay tubed and bandaged. The kid looked awful, his face was mutant and swollen. To Aoirghe he must have looked as though he were dying.

I didn't scream this time. I did unleash a torrent of extraordinary abuse in Aoirghe's direction but I tried to keep the volume down. I said dreadful, unforgivable things to her. I had had a lot of experience with people telling me what the trouble with me was. I gave it a go from the other end.

When I paused for breath and cardiac massage, I saw that she was crying. It was an amazing sight. She crumpled up – her shirt had been ripped by my wrathful hand. Some people can look pretty when they cry. Most people just look like wet snails. Aoirghe was one of those who didn't look their best. Her nose ran, her eyes were red and her face was creased like a clam. She looked pitiable. My heart might then have misgiven me and I might have stopped shouting at her.

What did I do? I did what all the unjustly angry do – I really fucking went for her. I piled on in.

After a few minutes, she ran out into the corridor, sobbing. I followed her all the way to the exit, abusing her viciously. She fled the building. As the swing doors banged shut behind her, I stopped shouting and tried to be calm. I knew I should have felt much better but I didn't. I shook my head like a dog. It didn't help.

I waited for hours there. The cops had gone to fetch Roche's parents but Roche's stepfather (or whoever he was) had told them to fuck off, that the kid didn't interest them. A social worker was coming in the morning to try to sort out a foster home or something for him. Meanwhile I waited.

I called Peggy and she told me that Chuckie had arrived home about an hour before. He was talking now, apparently. It seemed that the silent routine was over. I wanted to give him a piece of my mind for leading me into the riot so I asked Peggy to put him on the blower. She thought it was better if I waited until he calmed down a little. She said he was manic. She asked me to call the next day. I could have sworn she blew me a kiss as she hung up.

I waited on for Roche. I watched as the Just Us guy was discharged with a small plaster on his forehead. Two cops led him gently out as he struggled and screamed cinematically for the news crews. I watched the Amnesty guy give another brief statement about police brutality and the rule of law. I thought about making him wait with me to see Roche but I decided, accurately, that he didn't want to know.

I felt so bad about what I'd said to Aoirghe that I didn't even have the heart to fall in love with any of the nurses and doctors. I just drank Casualty coffee and nipped outside every fifteen minutes for a smoke.

I was finally allowed to talk to Roche at about four o'clock that morning. When I went in to see him, I was more upset than I needed to be. Amongst the bruises, bandages and cuts, I could easily discern the wide-boy presence of Roche's conscious self.

'How are you feeling?' I asked lumpily.

'Fabulous,' said the kid.

'You don't look so bad now,' I said.

He glared at the quiver of my lips and the bulge of my firmly uncrying eyes. 'Don't you start bawling,' he warned. 'All them good-looking nurses will think you're my boyfriend or something.'

I smiled. 'There's a social worker coming to see you tomorrow. Did they tell you that?'

'Aye.' He laughed indulgently.

'What's funny?' I asked.

'They take photographs of you to show foster parents. I was just thinking of the groovy foster mum I'd get if they take the photographs tomorrow.' He gestured at the wreckage of his tiny body. 'The way I look I'd arouse the maternal instincts of any late-twenties piece of ass you'd care to mention.'

'You're disgusting.'

'Hey, Jake.'

'What?'

'You coming to see me tomorrow?'

I got all emotional again. 'Yeah, sure thing.'

'Well, get the doctors to give me more of these drugs – I'm flying, boy.'

I laughed again. 'I think I hate you,' I said fondly.

A nurse came in and asked me to leave. I said goodbye to Roche. I patted the only undamaged portion of him that I could find and he yelped in pain anyway.

'That was some routine with the girl there,' he said, as I was walking away.

'What?'

'Your big screaming match with your woman with the funny name.'

'Aoirghe?'

'Aye.'

'I thought you were asleep,' I said guiltily.

'Nah, I was keeping an eye on you. You really gave it to her.'

'I was very uptight.'

'She seemed sorry,' said Roche.

I looked closely at him. Roche could not have made his eyes twinkle if he'd tried.

'I don't think so,' I replied. 'She's not the sorry type.'

Roche settled down into his bed. 'Yeah, maybe not. Nice tits, though.'

I left.

I had to walk back to the south of the city. I had left the Wreck parked near the Wigwam. I was tired and lugubrious after my big night. I walked slowly. My right hand hurt from when I had hit someone during the riot. I had run out of cigarettes a couple of hours before and I had no cash. I started humming blues riffs to myself. It sounded bad but appropriate.

I cut across the motorway and the industrial estate, heading in a straight line for the railway track near Poetry Street. I bummed a fag off a drunk lying near the Park Centre. I saved it and walked on.

There was a dampness in the air and a dampness in my spirits. The riot had depressed me and Roche had an infinite capacity for making me feel bad, but that did not explain the droop in my mood.

I'd overstepped the mark with Aoirghe Jenkins back there. She deserved a little and I'd given her more than a lot. Her politics were poisonous but she hadn't beaten up any twelve-year-olds. My heart sank as I remembered what I had said to her.

It was after five by the time I crossed the railway tracks at Adelaide Halt. I stopped on the footbridge. I was only a few hundred yards from Poetry Street but I sat down on the steps of the bridge facing the mountain. I fished in the pockets of my ruined suit for my borrowed cigarette. I found the fag and I found Sarah's letter as well. I smiled and decided to read it. It was getting pretty light and it seemed like the right time. I lit the cigarette and opened the letter.

I read Sarah's one-word letter and sat thinking and smoking for quite a long time. I looked up at the hill. It looked down at me. The fields from the mountains rolled out towards the city like a proffered tailor's cloth, checked and regular. Clouds of liquid grey issued and gathered over the city like witchbrew.

The one word in Sarah's letter was *Forgive*.

It was minutes before dawn. The birds were anxious. They suffered last-minute, curtain-up nerves. A yellow spider of crane metal picked itself out in the gloom, its noselight winking bright against the faded mountain. The slopes were a gradual beginning on which buildings dotted themselves with increasing density. Houses, farms, quarries, stations and schools. They tumbled into ensemble and merged urban and flat at the foot of the hill.

I thought about forgiving.

Yet the sky didn't lighten. The atmosphere thickened like gravy and all seemed stained. A man crossed the footbridge, a white plastic bag drooping from his motiveless hand. He shuffled onto the footpath parallel to the rails. His bobbing back faded into flatness until he seemed like a tiny shimmer on a painting: cuckold, worker, citizen.

I thought about Chuckie and Max. I thought about Peggy and Caroline. I thought about Donal and Pablo. I thought about Slat and Wincey. I thought about Luke Findlater and the Maoist waitress. I even thought about the boy and the girl from the supermarket.

Now the mountains were beginning to clear, show themselves, gaining form and colour. On each side of their broad sweep they were fringed with tassels, trees on one side and the regular cadence of a sloping quarryworks on the other. They looked like a cheap sofa. They looked like something Chuckie would buy. They were beautiful.

I thought about Aoirghe.

I went looking for my car. I had stuff to do.

Eighteen

When she had been a young woman, Chuckie's mother had been obsessed by the beauty of her breasts. She had loved their firmness, their fullness, their marvellous unlikelihood. Her breasts had been magical to her. For much of the time between sixteen and twenty, she had longed to show them to the world. To walk the streets of Belfast with her dress around her waist. She had longed to astonish and gratify one of the dull boys who dated her by opening her blouse without a word and letting him fill his mouth with their taut abundance.

Needless to say, Peggy Lurgan had astonished and gratified no one. Her breasts had languished in glorious privacy seen only by herself and occasionally by her friend, Caroline. By the time Chuckie's father had finally penetrated to the mysteries beneath her clothes, the magic had somehow gone.

But Peggy had always remembered the bliss of her bosom. Indeed, as she grew older, her remembrance of the early to mid-sixties was indissolubly linked to the memory of her chestly beauty. The Kennedy Assassination. The vague beginnings of American and Northern Irish civil unrest. Such recollections were hazy adjuncts to the historical fact of her private prize.

Recently, the obsession had returned. It had been so long since she had taken her sleeping pills and tranquillizers that many such unbidden memories flooded her unfogged brain now but her breast-vanity was the chief revenant. She was glad that she had felt that way and was glad that she was beginning to feel that way again. They were still pretty good. For a fifty-year-old woman, they were spectacular.

Then there had been that thing with Jake Jackson, Chuckie's friend. She had noticed that he had noticed. The fact of making an attractive young man obviously uncomfortable in that manner intoxicated Peggy. She felt that she was beginning anew.

The memories that came to her made her spine tingle with joy. One night she conjured the image of a woman washing her hair in the scullery tub of a poor house near the markets while her husband, sturdy but idle, scraped his scraped limbs in the hottest tub in Templemore Avenue baths. These were memories of her father and mother.

Her childhood surged back. She remembered how everyone on her street had avoided the Friday tickman, on his bike, motorbike or old tin car. Pay up and shut up. No palms were laid before his feet. She remembered sneaking down to the covered market when the Antrim women came to the iron-bound stalls to show what they would sell, throwing dappled light on the ground from the red shawls they used as awnings. She remembered their shrill shouts:

Tupporth here!

Aggie, where's the calico?

My man's going.

See youse in the tram shed.

She remembered childhood sweets and secrets. She remembered the smell of her father's cigarettes and shoe polish. She remembered fifties Belfast, buttoned-up, Presbyterian. She remembered winter mornings, her fingers growing cold in the scullery, losing the stored heat of sleep as her mother lit the fire.

Most of all she remembered Caroline. Her friend seemed to be a constant presence in almost all her recollections. They lived on the same street. They were in the same class at primary school. Their mothers were friends. They even played together on the same rope swing on the lamp-post at the bottom of their street. For forty-five years or more Peggy and Caroline had been together.

In Peggy's nitrazepam-free mind, their early years together were most vivid. The years that followed their girlhood and adolescence were smudged and murky in comparison with the glitter of those early times.

She could not have said that the friends loved each other dearly. It was more that their pasts and futures would have been unthinkable without the other. As they grew into women, this unspoken indivisibility increased. A few days after the bomb at Fountain Street, Peggy had spent a morning looking through all her old papers for a photograph of the two friends. She wept throughout the morning as she found photographs of her parents, obituary notices, letters from cousins she had forgotten, cheap old jewellery.

After a couple of hours, she had found the photograph, which was both more and less than she had remembered. Written on the back in faint pencil was the legend: Peggy and Caroline, May 1962. She started to cry again. She stared at it ruefully for an hour.

The picture, milky rather than faded with age, showed the girls sitting on the railings beside the City Hall. They wore patterned dresses with exuberant skirts. They smiled wide black-and-white smiles in a bright black-and-white world. They were eighteen. They were both beautiful. Their youthful hair and skin, the sheen in their eyes and the brightness of their smiles gave Peggy a desperate sensation in her stomach.

She remembered the day vaguely. A hapless bright Saturday, they had wandered the town, window-shopping with two boys from the Newtownards Road. One of the boys, Andy, the one who had taken the photograph, had been pursuing Caroline for weeks. Caroline had been joyously uninterested. In a few weeks' time, Andy, exasperated by their solidarity, would give Peggy a pair of old work trousers, telling her she might as well be Caroline's boyfriend since they did everything else together.

The photograph made Peggy feel indescribable things. It made her deeply sad and filled her with joy simultaneously. The photograph represented a junction in their lives. A time before Peggy had met Hughie and Caroline had met Johnny. Their black-and-white 1960s selves were frozen in the photo. A time when everything was different. When Belfast itself was different. She inspected the soft grey out-of-focus metropolis in the background. Buildings had disappeared and new ones had sprouted; violence and husbands had come, their effects equally devastating.

But the picture showed two pretty eighteen-year-olds for whom all possible futures were possible futures. It showed the point where the road had forked. It demonstrated where it had all gone wrong. And, yes, her breasts had looked amazing in that dress.

For days, the suddenly untranquillized Peggy had stayed quietly in her bedroom, thinking. She kept the photograph by her bed and constantly referred to it as if for cues or clues. She thought about the man who had come soon after the photograph had been taken. She remembered Hughie's drunken, inexpert fumbling amongst her clothing. She remembered how old he had seemed. She couldn't remember having said yes. She couldn't remember having been asked.

Peggy became pregnant and Caroline had perhaps married Johnny out of pique. Hughie failed to marry Peggy and Peggy had moved into Eureka Street and produced her fat, bald baby. Few now could remember the kind of courage which that then took. Hughie didn't even live with her. He stayed sometimes but, as he told Peggy, he had other commitments.

She vaguely remembered marrying him just before her

parents had died. She recalled that it did not dull the shame for them. She could not remember Hughie leaving. His latest absence just stretched out and became permanent. She remembered being left alone with her only son. After a couple of years, Caroline and her family had moved into the house across the street. Her life took on the gloomy pattern that would not alter for nearly three decades.

Thirty years of loneliness. Twenty years of growing old. Ten years of various tranquillizers, sleeping pills and anti-depressants.

Then Chuckie got rich.

Then she stood on Fountain Street and watched everybody die.

That view had changed Peggy for ever. The two women, thrown so violently together again, probably realized at the same time. What had seemed like ever-presence had been love.

It happened on the night that Chuckie had called from America to say he was flying back in three days' time. He was getting married and having a baby, she didn't have to worry about him any more.

They had both been ashamed, they had both been scared. But in the end it was pretty easy. They took off their clothes and smiled. Both women had thought in their private hearts that this event would lead to disgust as they beheld again each other's bloated old flesh, but that did not happen. Each could only find beauty in what they saw.

Caroline was surprised that she was not surprised. Peggy was surprised by this thing between her legs that she had ignored for so long. Peggy had had little sex: Chuckie's mother had slept with only one man – Chuckie's father. They had copulated only thirty or forty times. This double score of erotic incidents came to represent the world of sex for Peggy. It was a small and slightly vicious world. Despite the infrequency of their love-making, she came to know Hughie's habits well. She extrapolated at first, using her experience with Hughie to represent the activities of all men. She concluded that all men wiped their dripping foreskins on their women's thighs after sex, that they all got that brutal look in their eyes when they came. Then she stopped extrapolating, considering that it was unfair to attribute Hughie's foibles to the entire gender. In the end, from what Caroline told her, she changed her mind again and extrapolated like mad, suspecting that, after all, knowing one was knowing them all.

The next morning, the two women had chatted like girls over breakfast. Sunlight flooded the kitchen and the little house was transfigured. A bridge had been built between them as they were now and as they had been in the photograph. For the first time in her adult life Peggy had decided that this was what she wanted.

It was difficult, of course. Sandy Row was scandalized. Caroline's husband went unviolently berserk and left Eureka Street with the eighteen-year-old youngest son. Peggy and Caroline were visited by vicars and missionaries and no one on Eureka Street spoke to them. They nearly got into the newspapers. It looked like Protestant Belfast would never deal with their consensual but idiosyncratic behaviour.

Then Chuckie had returned home and spent a fortnight in the front bedroom, speaking to neither woman. At first, Peggy had been upset by her son's reaction. He had passed out on the street on his first night home. Caroline had intolerantly suggested jet-lag. Chuckie's subsequent gloom and silence made his message clear. It wasn't so much that he didn't like what she was doing. He hated every micro-second of what she was doing. She didn't want to change anything for Chuckie. She would give up this new joy for no one, although she tried to modify it a little. But the walls were so very thin and her delight was ungovernable.

After a comatose fortnight from Chuckie, Peggy and Caroline grew restive. They enlisted Max's help – the American girl had been sympathetic from the beginning – and she persuaded Chuckie to go to the Wigwam and meet his friends again.

That night Peggy and Caroline breathed free. It was blissful to be rid of Chuckie's morose, disapproving presence. The two women played Eddie Cochrane records and told each other that this was love. But after a couple of hours, Peggy was unnerved. She missed Chuckie. It was her big secret. It was what had filled her last thirty years. It was what had brought the little light to her tranquillized decade. Chuckie had been a miracle child, a presence she could never have expected. Peggy loved her son like she would never be able to love anything else. For thirty years Chuckie had ruled her thoughts like a government of love. She decided that it was time she told him.

She put on her coat and asked Caroline to come with her. Caroline had been slightly rebellious but they went to the Wigwam looking for Chuckie.

Peggy failed to see why he ran away when they got there.

The morning after the riot on the Falls Road, Chuckie woke late. His curtains were open and his head ached from having slept several hours in direct sunlight and from the nitrazepam he'd nicked from his mother's neglected bottle. He shook his groggy head, lurched out of bed and stumbled into the bathroom.

He fumbled with his pyjama trousers, dozily trying to find his member.

'Ah, Chuckie.'

He leapt softly into the air and spun round to confront the two hitherto unnoticed naked women sloshing around in the bath. Caroline and Peggy both smiled mutely at him.

'Fuck it,' said Chuckie.

He went downstairs and urinated in the kitchen sink.

Afterwards, he switched the kettle on. Uncertainly, he walked to the foot of the little staircase. His voice quivered slightly as he said, 'Hey, I'm making some tea. Do you two want some?'

There was a hesitation. Then he heard some splashing and what he could only describe as whoops of delight rendered tinny and echoey by the tiny Eureka Street bathroom. A door opened and Peggy stood at the top of the staircase, wrapped in a flimsy towel. Caroline, obviously still naked, slipped her head around the banister and stared at him. His mother looked happy. The silence was over. It was how Chuckie had intended his mother to look. Son and mother stared at each other, silent and almost loving.

'Some time this week, Chuckie,' said Caroline. 'Milk and two sugars.'

Later that day Chuckie decided that this base-level, low-income-group resolution over a cup of tea was typical and commendable in equal measure. No rapprochements, no negotiations or accords could be made in deep Eureka Street in any other way. He decided that this was one of the nice things about being working class.

Chuckie sat in the swanky office of the enormously expensive architect whom he had just hired to build him a new house and decided that he didn't care what his mother did with her private parts. He didn't approve but it was not in his remit. His mind was full and he didn't have space to think about Peggy and Caroline munching at each other every night.

'What about that?' asked the expensive, well-dressed, suntanned architect. He held a sketch in front of Lurgan's unseeing eyes. 'What about that?' he repeated.

'That's fine,' murmured Chuckie absently. 'That's just grand.'

Somehow, he had understood how much his mother loved him. He had never comprehended this before. It had come as something of a shock.

'And the price?' asked the architect.

Chuckie was silent.

The architect touched his Corbusier spectacles nervously and scribbled a figure at the bottom of the sketch. 'That's the absolute minimum,' he suggested.

Chuckie dragged his weary gaze to the paper in front of him.

'Sure thing,' he said. 'No problem.'

The architect gulped in surprise. He was disappointed that he had not scribbled a rather higher figure if this fat yob had found his original estimate so unexceptionable. He started scribbling again.

Chuckie had first known the tempestuous extent of his own mother love when Peggy had been exposed to all the ordnance down at Fountain Street. That was when he learnt that the frail and the harmable had to be loved. But it had only been when he'd parked his fat gut in the midst of last night's riot that he had guessed she might feel the same uncontrollable thing for him.

'Of course,' the architect elaborated, 'there might by contingency and add-on costs of all kinds. It might come to something like . . .' He pushed the paper with his revised total at Chuckie.

'Uh-huh,' mumbled the fat man.

He had realized that he and his mother were both so small, so breakable, that each merited more love than they knew. He didn't want to spend too much time thinking about it, but he knew that Peggy and Caroline could do whatever they liked to each other and there was simply no room for him to mind.

'And if there are any planning problems then it will be likely to come to something close to . . .'

The architect thrust another scribbled number in front of Chuckie's face. Chuckie woke up. He grabbed the pad from the man. He scored out all the numbers, wrote a figure almost half of the man's first estimate and spoke clearly for the first time. 'If you can't do it for this, I'll get some other yuppie fucker to do it instead.'

Then Chuckie Lurgan walked out of the building, thoughtfully.

That night in Max's flat, he watched television absently, one hand gripping a can of beer, the other rhythmically stroking Max's astonishingly occupied belly. Aoirghe had gone home to Fermanagh after some big fight with Jake Jackson and they had the flat to themselves. They had been watching news programmes for hours. The ceasefires were still playing to big houses on Northern Irish television. The situation had developed in eccentric fashion. The IRA had said they had given up violence but were going to keep their guns (just in case?), the UVF had said they were sorry for killing all those people, the US State Department had said that the ceasefire was all its own work (a claim disputed by several messianic Irish politicians), the Irish and British governments were having Exploratory Talks about the possibility of having some other Exploratory Talks, and around two hundred teenagers had been beaten with baseball bats and car tools by a selection of extremely unofficial policemen in balaclavas and leather jackets.

Some prisoners had been released early. Chuckie had been worried about this. These were men who had killed people, sometimes quite a lot of people. It was how they expressed their aspirations. Two or three hundred assassins were being released back into the melting pot of his Belfast. These were men who did not easily deal with the frustrations of normal life. And with the confessed inadequacies of his driving skills, Chuckie didn't want to go cutting up any of these guys in traffic.

Shague Ghinthoss, the poet, had been awarded a knighthood and the Just Us party's very first Hero of the Revolution Award. This unfortunate conjunction had caused him some unease until a fresh-faced young hack had asked him whether he was going to accept both awards as some kind of pan-ecumenical gesture, an attempt to build bridges between the divided traditions. Ghinthoss's eyes had gleamed suddenly. 'Yes,' he had said. 'Funny you should mention it.'

A television special had been broadcast showing Ghinthoss, looking disturbingly like Santa Claus, receiving both awards. Picking up his knighthood, he had spoken of the cloudiness of nationality, the New Europe and the breaking up of borders. He had smiled twinklingly when someone asked him about the suddenly vacant poet laureate job. At the Hero of the Revolution Dinner and Disco, the very next day, he had told the rapturous crowd how he had always been an Irishman and how he would always be one. No one noticed any contradiction. A Shague Ghinthoss cookery book and a new collection of his *Rejected Poems (1965–1995)* was already in the pipeline. Chuckie damned himself for not having thought of that first.

As Chuckie watched television, something simmered in his non-stick mind. When he had been in America he had grown sentimental about his home town. America had seemed so vivid, so jumbled and chaotic. He had pondered affectionately on how Belfast had stayed gloriously the same throughout the thirties, forties, fifties and sixties. It had been unfortunately Protestant but thrillingly provincial. Political violence had somewhat disrupted the sleepy obscurity of the place but Chuckie felt that there was something in the heart of his birthplace that was profoundly everyday.

And now, as he watched television beside his wife-to-be (and son-to-be), Chuckie listened to a variety of people tell him that the Troubles were at an end. Peace had come at last. The war was over.

Then Chuckie lit on what he had been clumsily attempting to think:

What war? No one he knew had been fighting.

Initially, it seemed ludicrous to him. It was such an obvious thought. It was too simple to have any real significance. But, as the belly-rubbing minutes passed, the enormity of this notion impacted upon him. He babbled confusedly to Max about what was on his mind. She ignored him mostly. (Max had always believed Northern Irish violence to be distinctly overrated. The Irish were a bit precious about their trauma. They should have tried Manhattan on any Saturday night.)

That day, Chuckie had gone back into the office for the first time in a fortnight. Luke Findlater was glad, if disturbed, to see him. They had made a lot of money in those two weeks, and ever since Chuckie's American success, Northern Irish television companies had been looking for him desperately. His debate with Jimmy Eve had not gone unnoticed. Several cisatlantic broadcasters were queuing up to stage a local rematch.

Chuckie had ignored these blandishments and had told Luke that he was not interested. But, as he listened to Max's television telling him things he didn't believe, Chuckie changed his mind. He called Luke and told him to say yes to all the interviews he had declined. Luke was grumpy and mystified but, as always, Chuckie prevailed.

'Hey, Chuck,' said Max, 'what are you up to?'

Chuckie kissed his way down her stomach.

'Mnrth thaghth orfthf njr thruhhth,' he replied.

Chuckie spent most of the next day borrowing money. With all his new skills and massive reputation, he found this an easier task even than hitherto. John Evans alone promised him fifteen million dollars. He ended the day with pledges of more than twenty-five million pounds from various people and organizations. Chuckie was happy.

He and Luke grabbed a pizza and dined in the office, talking tactics. Well, Chuckie dined and talked. Luke was so bewildered by the fund-raising he had witnessed that day that he was barely capable of speech and unable to eat solid food. Chuckie explained that he intended to use his television appearance that very night to launch a new industrial initiative. Jimmy Eve was scheduled to appear with him, but after his last experience Chuckie was confident of settling his revolutionary hash within the first few minutes. He could then devote the rest of the programme to announcing his new project. Massive reinvestment in the city of his birth, nothing less than the industrial rebuilding of Belfast. He told Luke that the riot had proved to him that

Belfast people had amounts of energy they didn't know what to do with. Chuckie knew what to do with their energy.

It had struck Chuckie that the political conflict that had occurred during his entire adult life had been a lie. It was a war between an army that said it didn't want to fight and a group of revolutionaries who claimed that they didn't want to fight either. It had nothing to do with imperialism, self-determination or revolutionary socialism. And these armies didn't often kill each other. Usually they just killed whoever of the citizenry happened to be handy.

Chuckie was too stupid to think he understood a great deal of anything but he deeply understood the majority politics of Northern Ireland. The majority politics in Northern Ireland were not political. The citizens were too shy to give the grand name of principle to any of the things that they believed, but there were still things that they believed. And that peaceful majority spent its life keeping down jobs or failing to keep down jobs, buying washing-machines and houses and vacuum-cleaners and holidays and carry-cots. The way they were doing these things had changed the face of the city in the last ten years. Protestant areas were Protestant no longer. Working-class areas had become bourgeois. The city was moving outwards like a spreading stain. That was what cities did and that was what Chuckie, correctly or incorrectly, understood as politics.

He was confident that his pragmatic announcement of massive job-creation projects would silence Jimmy Eve's feeble ideological spoutings. Ideology was a thick enough blanket but it wasn't as warm or sustaining as employment. Eve could arrange for the odd bomb here and there but he, Chuckie Lurgan, would bring back work to the city single-handed. He would be a hero.

He called his mother before he went to the television studio. She asked him what he would wear. His blue suit and his new Doc Martens, he told her. She told him that the outfit would look nice. Chuckie was faintly disturbed. Only a month before, she would have disapproved strongly of the DMs. Chuckie wondered if sexual deviance liberated everyone's sartorial tastes.

'I met a woman in the supermarket who wanted your autograph,' said Peggy. 'She's the first woman from Sandy Row who's spoken to me in a fortnight. You're very famous, son.'

The faint Lurganish awe in his mother's voice pleased him.

'Caroline sends her love and says good luck,' Peggy continued.

Chuckie swallowed nervously. 'Ah, thank her for me.'

'OK.'

'I have to go now,' he said. 'I don't want to be late.'

'Hey, Chuckie,' said his mother.

'What?'

'You love me,' said Peggy, confidently.

'Sure thing,' said Chuckie. 'No problem.'

The interview had been going for about fifteen minutes before Chuckie sensed that it wasn't going the way he had intended. When he arrived at the studio, he had been bundled into a separate waiting room, obviously at the request of Jimmy Eve and the Just Us crew. He was to be the third guest and, as he watched the show on the monitor in his dressing room, Chuckie was delighted to see that there was a small group of Americans in the audience wearing MFG (Mad Fat Guy) T-shirts. They had flown all the way from the States on the off-chance of meeting him.

The first guest was an academic who had been wheeled on to give his views on the current ceasefire and to explain his theory that the mysterious underground OTG movement was the missing dynamic in Irish politics. It was this man's profound belief that OTG were the initials of the Omagh Trotskyist Group.

Eve was the second guest. Chuckie was pleased to see that he was nervous and trembling unmistakably.

Jimmy Eve had been trembling constantly for nearly three

weeks now. Ever since his televised meeting with Chuckie Lurgan, it had all been going wrong for the Ardoyne ideologue. At Just Us meetings, his unease was evident and remarked upon. It was particularly bad, however, when he had to make public appearances. It made him angry and unappeasable. He had even seen his doctor about it. The situation had not been improved by his six-year-old daughter who, having asked him what a unitedireland was, had walked away only half-way through his explanation. The ostensible flush on his face was bad enough but it had brought a return of his old complaint, the inward tremble, the private shame.

Jimmy Eve had known for some years that almost everything he said was untrue. Mostly, that had not mattered. After a decade of Margaret Thatcher, he had learnt to believe his own lies in some careless, auto-pilot way. The consciousness of deceit was one he found easy to repress, to tuck away somewhere dark in his unthinking mind. But the sensation of being a liar was ever present again. It was disturbing his equilibrium and ruining his peace. He had even begun to wonder guiltily whether other prominent members of Just Us were conscious of what liars they were. His own lies were talismanic, mathematical. When he said that he only wanted dialogue he meant that he only wanted total victory. When he told reporters that he respected the rights of the Protestant community he meant that soon they wouldn't have any. When he called publicly for international monitoring of human rights in Northern Ireland, he certainly didn't intend them to poke their noses into any of the naughtinesses of his chums in the IRA.

The only lie he could still believe was the most important one, thank goodness. Whenever he said that everything was all the fault of the British Government, he still deeply believed that. That lie still held good.

Enough of Eve's uncertainty was visible to make Chuckie confident as he watched his dressing-room monitor. But fifteen minutes into his appearance it had all gone wrong. Chuckie had stepped onto the set to applause and cheers from his MFG fans, and as he had approached Jimmy Eve to shake hands, the man had stepped back as though to ward off a blow. Chuckie had shaken hands with the man with the Omagh Trotskyist theory and had launched happily into the announcement of his investment plans.

But it had been a damp squib, an irrelevance. The audience had applauded politely but Eve had wiped the floor with him. He had criticized the right-wing private enterprise and exploitation of plutocrats like Chuckie. He had accused Protestant businessmen of not building cross-border links towards an all-Ireland business community. He had interrupted Chuckie several times, confidently telling him that he didn't know what he was talking about, derisively doubting the totals that Chuckie said he had already raised. After ten minutes the man's tremor was stilled and Chuckie felt himself falling apart. He could see his T-shirted American fans whispering anxiously amongst themselves. He could not understand why he was not performing as well as he had on his last TV appearance.

Then he remembered. Cocaine. As Eve talked on, dominating the broadcast, Chuckie racked his brains. Then he held his breath.

Chuckie watched Max sleep. It was barely past midnight but she slumbered deeply. He envied that. She twitched and whimpered. He smiled. Strangely, she had told him that she still only dreamt of America. Same here, thought Chuckie.

He had been listening to the radio for the last twenty minutes, waiting for news about himself, but between the records, the people on the radio had only talked of percentages – 30 per cent off all curtain fabrics, 10 per cent unemployment, 12 per cent fall in sterling. Chuckie had turned to tell Max that she had 100 per cent of his love but she was already asleep. He would tell her when she woke. He hoped she would be happy with it. He was.

Both Max and Peggy had given him some grief for his television performance. They had disapproved of his final efforts but Chuckie didn't care. He had had no choice.

He had held his breath for almost three and a half minutes. He noticed by the end of the second minute that some audience members were tittering openly and that Jimmy Eve was staring at him aghast. He could feel his face grow taut and purple. Thankfully, the political academic talked on blithely for another minute and a half. In the third minute, Chuckie's world had gone aqueous and black, he had temporarily lost the power of sight and was just losing consciousness when the interviewer turned and nervously asked him a question he could not hear.

Chuckie breathed in.

Blood flooded places he didn't know he had. The noise was dreadful and he felt sure that his face had changed colour in some grotesque way but he launched happily into his answer. His head was less than light, it thumped with pain, his neck bulged and his heart banged like the Ligoniel Young Defenders' massed pipe and drum band. It wasn't quite cocaine but his blood was definitely moving.

He sailed into a wild diatribe against Eve. Eve himself, who was probably close enough to spot the thin trickle of blood from Chuckie's ear, immediately quailed. Chuckie bellowed abuse. He said Eve reminded him of Joseph Goebbels, who had said that if you were going to tell a lie you had better make it a big one (Chuckie almost pissed himself with pride at remembering any kind of historical fact). He ran through a semi-conscious version of his thought of yesterday: What war? No one he knew had been fighting. He barked and whinnied a variety of sound man-of-the-people platitudes at the palely sneering Eve. The crowd warmed to him, he could see – cloudily – his American fans squirming with pleasure.

But Eve had been able to interrupt him – Chuckie had had to take a fairly extensive second breath. He mocked such idle demagoguery and said that it was easy for non-contributors like Chuckie to make fun of the work of real politicians who had to work on proper solutions to the political difficulties of Northern Ireland. He wanted to know if Chuckie was going to do something constructive about his many complaints.

Now, as Chuckie watched Max sleep, he wished that his second breath had taken even longer and that he had been unable to answer Eve's taunt. But, starved of oxygen, pulse hammering, the goaded fat man had announced his plans to set up a new political party, an effective and non-sectarian third force in Ulster politics. It had certainly shut Eve up but, unfortunately, it had rather shut up Chuckie himself. He had absolutely no idea what he was talking about. The audience had gone quiet for a few moments and then applauded strongly. The interviewer had questioned Chuckie about his new party and Chuckie had waffled grandly. A press conference would be held at the end of the week. He was confident of success. In tandem with his business enterprise, he felt he could bring prosperity and other stoned bullshit. He had even included a white-guy version of Martin Luther King's *I-have-a-dream* speech.

Jimmy Eve had interrupted one last time. With all the contempt he could muster, he asked Chuckie what this new party would be called. On the verge of actually passing out, Chuckie had gasped that his new party would probably be called the OTG, he had been having talks with that group and they would announce all the details at the press conference.

The audience went crazy. Young women threw their underwear at him, and as the floor manager counted down the last five seconds Chuckie gracefully lost consciousness.

It had been madness, but after the programme he saw that Eve and his Just Us advisers were terrified. Chuckie couldn't understand it. As he fought off the autograph-hunting volunteers, he failed to see that the Just Us people considered him the charismatic Protestant of ancient republican demonology and that he was the kind of imponderable in Ulster politics that they wanted to avoid.

But what chiefly amazed him was that everyone seemed happy to believe that he had been having secret meetings with the mysterious OTG organization. Now Chuckie knew that he moved in a credulous universe, credulity was the only thing that could have set him in motion, but even he was impressed by this new gullibility.

Peggy had called an hour ago. She said that the Eureka Street phone had been going crazy with journalists calling to find out about the new party and the press launch. Chuckie knew that he had gone too far and that, once again, his private fantasies were taking on a form and colour that he had not intended.

He walked to Max's bedroom window and looked out. The moon hung high like a bare bulb in a cheap room. The mountain was a rim of glow, a flat, wide thing. Chuckie had never been too impressed by the horizon. To him it had always been just a distance. Nevertheless, he conceded that it looked fine that night, it looked dandy.

In his panic, he had gone round to Poetry Street to see if he could find Jake. He sat on his friend's doorstep, practically sobbing. Jake was not in. He didn't know what he could do. He would never be able to make up a meaning for the letters OTG on his own. He needed his friend.

Jake's cat appeared from underneath a hedge and screamed happily at the disconsolate Chuckie for a few minutes. The cat looked hungry and neglected but Chuckie knew he tried to look like that all the time and decided to take him for a walk anyway. It was the only one of the animal's idiosyncrasies that he could bear.

So, cat and fat man set off up Poetry Street, both anxious and confused in their different ways.

Then Chuckie saw the OTG man. He was half-way up a ladder, which leant against the wall of the Irish Institute. It took Chuckie a few moments to determine that he wasn't a workman. It was only as he saw him paint the word The, the letters

OTG and the rest of the sentence that he knew who it was.

He was just as Jake had described Roche describing him. Jake's age and height, dressed in shabby, priestly black. Chuckie saw him carefully paint out the words around the OTG itself and then the fat man went charging up the street after him.

The man saw Chuckie coming and panicked. He slid down the ladder like a fireman and ran for it, paint and brush in hand. Chuckie zoomed on after him.

He was very quick and by the time Chuckie got to the Lisburn Road, the OTG man had gained some yards. But Chuckie saw him turn down one of the little terrace streets on the other side of that road. The fat man increased his speed and followed. His quarry ducked down a little alleyway. Seconds later, Chuckie skidded in behind him.

Imagine Chuckie's surprise when he saw the words LEAVE ME ALONE painted on the alley wall. The paint was wet but the typography was composed. Jesus, he thought, how had he managed that? Chuckie ran on, shouting at him now.

The man came out of the alleyway on to another terrace street. Chuckie was gaining on him. Quickly, the man dived into the alleyway opposite and turned a sharp corner. When Chuckie turned the corner there was more fresh writing in that steady, unmistakable hand. FUCK, YOU'RE QUICKER THAN YOU LOOK, it said. Chuckie began to lose his mind but he didn't check his pace.

By the time the OTG man made it on to the next street, Chuckie was almost within diving distance of the spooky bastard. As he sped into the last alleyway available, Chuckie thought he had him. The man vaulted a wheelie-bin and turned again. Fat Lurgan's heart was bursting as he turned the corner, banged into the wall and collapsed on the ground. He looked up through the sweat in his eyes and saw the words THIS ISN'T FUNNY ANY MORE perfectly written on the wall above him. He raised himself on his elbows and stared down the alleyway. The OTG man had stopped and was staring at Chuckie with something close to a smile. Chuckie could have sworn a wink trembled in one of his eyes.

'Fuck it,' said Chuckie.

The OTG man smiled again and jogged off towards the railway tracks, towards the mountains, towards fuck knew where.

When Chuckie regained his breath, he beat a painful path back to Poetry Street. Jake's cat was sitting near the foot of the ladder. There was some more paint there and the cat had got some on his paws. Chuckie approached him smiling, in the hope he could get close enough for just one kick, but the cat was too cute. He ambled off, leaving white-paint paw marks on the pavement behind him.

Chuckie stood on the ladder looking up at the wall. In his panic, the guy had inadvertently dragged his brush over the OTG. It was a meaningless blur of wet paint.

Chuckie stared at it blankly.

Then he picked up the paint. He climbed up the ladder.

OTG, Chuckie wrote, OTG.

Chuckie turned away from the window. Seeing the OTG man had been fortunate but it had solved none of his problems. He still had to think of something believable that might be represented by the initials OTG. If only he could think of something Catholic that began with O and something Protestant that began with T, he would be laughing. As he pondered, he began to believe that the Omagh Trotskyist Group wasn't such a bad idea.

He wished Jake had been in when he had called. He needed his Catholic friend's guidance. He thought with pride of their friendship. Protestant and Catholic, their casual brotherliness was the ultimate example of what he meant when he said that no one he knew had been fighting. He and Jake had a friendship that the world supposed could not exist. Chuckie thought with horror that it was exactly this kind of platitude that was bound to get him elected. Political office was probably only months away. His fantasies of wealth had been much more unlikely and he had achieved those while barely noticing. Things seemed to come easy to him now. Perhaps he was becoming a force of nature.

He looked over at the sleeping Max. It was all her fault. Because of her, he had wandered the streets of his city bewildered by the mathematics of people. And now he couldn't think of a time when he might have walked a street without thought of her as company and motor. Because this wasn't love, this was punishment.

She had made a music of his heart. Now, the beautiful things smacked him in the mouth like a bar-room fly-weight: motorways, cheap cafés, cigarette smoke in a still room, dull days with dirt in the air, car parks.

There are things so beautiful that they let you not mind that you will grow old and die. There are things so beautiful that growing old and dying seem like pretty good ideas, rounded and generous. For Chuckie, Max was one of those.

Chuckie's chest swelled with unfashionable grandeur and he headed for the fridge to drink something calming, something cold. Max's fridge was full of bottled yuppie water, open bowls of spices and a solitary tub of margarine. On the lid of the margarine, printed in large yellow letters was the advice:

KEEP COOL

Yeah, thought Chuckie, that's a good idea. Yeah, I'll try.

Nineteen

Today the sky was an amazing thing. The clouds were city clouds, thick with dirt and matter. The light was the colour of tea, badly stewed. At midday, I walked out to buy cigarettes. It surprised me that the people could walk, drive and stand on those streets with me.

I'm in that kind of mood. Tonight, the sweet, sweet world makes me wanna lie down and take my clothes off. In another room the radio's on and a man reads a letter from a woman who says her heart is cold and broken. Then he plays a song that means much to her. And that banality makes me faint with tenderness.

Yesterday, she only smiled, she only wiped a strand of hair from her face, she only kissed me.

And tonight the world is a big world, grand and marvellous as the story you never knew when you were a child. And tonight the sky is an amazing thing.

I'll never forget that morning. She had gone home to her parents' house in Fermanagh. It took me two days to find a firm address. Next morning, I drove the ninety miles to her town in a mood like an opening chapter. The radio was on but I needed no music. Her little town was beautiful. It rose on both sides of a thin river. Dozy houses, too many churches, it looked like an impossible place, a child's drawing. It looked fine to me. Across the bridge in the little townland, I was stopped at a checkpoint. The young policeman leaned on my open window.

'Going far?' he asked.

'I hope so,' I said, 'I certainly hope so.'

It took me five hours to work up the courage to knock on their door. I wandered around the little town, hoping that I would bump into her. As the day matured, I worked up the guts and strode on up there.

I met her brown-haired mother. I met her wheelchaired father. They watched uncomfortably as I apologized to their daughter for something they didn't understand. Restrained in their presence, she could only listen, she could only accept my regret.

The parents invited me to stay for dinner while their daughter glowered mutinously. The mother suggested that in the meantime her daughter show me round their land. Silently she stood up and beckoned me to follow. The mother smiled approvingly at me as we left.

We walked out into all the green and the shit and the spiders. It was the first time we'd been alone since I'd arrived. My face was hot and my lips did not move. She, too, was silent, her face not turning my way. It looked like this would be an unproductive walk.

We walked in virtual silence for nearly twenty minutes. The sun got low and the hedges and trees went all red. Sheep baaed, cows mooed, birds chirped and all the beasts did their thing. We stopped at a five-bar gate at the edge of their land. Aoirghe turned to me for the first time.

'Jake,' she said.

I drove back to Belfast that night. Aoirghe was going to follow in a couple of days. I called Chuckie to see if he was OK. Chuckie seemed to be OK. I told him I wasn't coming in to work for a couple of days. He continued telling me how OK he was. I hung up after twenty minutes or so.

I checked up on Roche, too. He was still in hospital but only had a few days to go. He greeted me with a volley of complaints so obscene that one of the nurses turned green. He'd met his foster-folks. They'd met him. Despite this, they had agreed to take him on when he got out of hospital. He told me they lived in a big house near Dunmurry. He was disappointed that the wife was a little out of his age-range (the woman was in her late thirties) but apparently they had a whole shitload of seventeen-year-old nieces. The little creep tried to rub his hands with glee but his arms were still too fucked.

He asked me about Aoirghe. I told him. He laughed like a drain.

The new foster-folks came in. They seemed like a nice couple, good-natured and amiable. They had talked to the doctors. Roche would be allowed out in a couple of days but would have to miss at least a month of school. Roche looked confused as though he couldn't understand what difference this would make to his life. They hadn't been informed of his truancy rates. They were nice, these people, but they had a lot to learn.

I said goodbye.

'Hey, Jake,' said Roche. 'Thanks.'

'What for?'

'I don't know. Just thanks.'

I waited expectantly. There was silence. They all looked at me.

'What?' I asked. 'No snappy line? No obscenities?'

Roche settled back comfortably amongst his pillows. 'Nah,' he said. 'I'm too fucking sick.'

Later that day, after much sweating and swallowing, I called Sarah. I had never used the number she had left. It was near a year now. My heart hammered as I tapped out the number.

'Hello,' said a man's voice. My chest went hot with jealousy and fear.

'Could I speak to Sarah, please?'

'She's not here, I'm afraid. Are you Jake?'

'How did you know?'

'The accent.'

'Right.'

There was a pause.

'Could you tell her I got her letter and I was just calling to see how she was,' I said.

Somehow the next pause felt more comfortable, more generous.

'She's fine and my name's Peter,' said Peter. 'You don't sound like such a wild man to me.'

'You should see how I look.'

And, well, we had a long old chat there, Peter and I. Soon I was feeling disconcerting amounts of warmth for Peter. It was tricky at first. We weren't talking about the size of our penises or anything like that but it was a little tense, a little territorial. Then he asked me whether I had anyone in my life. I told him that I had. He warmed noticeably after that. It was endearing. Soon enough we were burbling like old ladies in a hairdresser's.

He sounded OK, Peter. He sounded like the kind of boy I'd have wanted my daughters to date. Level-headed, funny, gentle. A part of me wondered why I was so glad. But only a part of me.

'Make sure and tell her I called,' I said finally.

'I won't forget,' said Peter.

I did a lot of other stuff. I checked out my friends. I checked out everybody I'd ever met. I even called in at the Europa and said hi to Ronnie Clay and Rajinder. I seemed to have reserves of goodwill that were suddenly enormous. I wandered around the city greeting the citizens.

Then she came back to Belfast. She came round to Poetry Street that night with an uncertain expression and eyes like a forties film star.

'Hello,' I said.

Now, she's sleeping four feet behind me and my room is magical with her presence. A solitary cat yowls its own melancholy klaxon. I'm forced to admit that it sounds like my cat. I ignore it.

My curtains are open and I'm looking out tonight. I've had two good hours to myself. I've never felt less lonely. It has rained and the raindrops on the outside of the window panes glitter like cheap beads. We're talking about spilt beer, we're talking about the end of the world.

I light a cigarette. I'll give up some time soon. The window starts to shed light, a dubious rumour of dawn. I look out as the thing speeds up. It's getting glossy out there. Buildings and roads begin to look pale and flat, hung over in the ebbing strength of the street-lamp shine.

She stirs in the bed. The dark smudge of her face settles against my pillows. I'm tired but I think I'll watch her sleep some more. I think I'll wait for her to wake.

Chuckie called me a while ago and ranted about all kinds of stuff. He told me he'd seen the OTG man and that he was setting up a political party. I'm worried, frankly. Chuckie will probably succeed. When Chuckie's around, comedy isn't funny. Comedy is serious.

And that was what the OTG man didn't even know he was for. You want to know what OTG means?

Almost everything.

That was the point. All the other letters written on our walls were dark minority stuff. The world's grand, lazy majority will never be arsed writing anything anywhere and, anyway, they wouldn't know what to write. They would change their permissive, clement, heterogeneous minds half-way through.

That's why OTG was written for them. It could mean anything they wanted. It *did* mean anything they wanted. Order The Gammon. Octogenarians Tote Guns. Openly Titular Gesture. One True God.

I make coffee. The percolator gurgles and clicks. Dazed, my head is filled with the lush music of euphoria. I don't know. Maybe she won't make me feel like this in a year. Maybe six months. Maybe some day I won't even remember the velocity in my veins tonight. Maybe some day some other woman, some other sleeping presence will make me feel like this again and I'll think I've never felt it before. I don't know and I don't care. Maybe we'll all be dead six months hence. It's a big world and there's room for all kinds of endings and any number of commencements.

I don't care because this is enough.

I pour some coffee and put the cups on a tray. The birds gossip loudly outside my kitchen window. I look out into that murk and see my cat swipe inexpertly at a swooping sparrow. He misses and then starts licking his fur, pretending he wasn't really trying. I knock on the window and he looks up. I just wanted him to know that I saw. I think I'll get a new cat.

I go back into the bedroom and leave the tray on the bedside table. Gently, I brush her hair from her brow and she stirs slightly. She'll be awake in a minute. I have only a few moments left on my own.

The mountain looks flat and grand. In the greyness, it is stupidly green. It looks like all cities this morning, Belfast. It's a tender frail thing, composite of houses, roads and car parks. Where are the people? They are waking or failing to wake. Tender is a small word for what I feel for this town. I think of my city's conglomerate of bodies. A Belfastful of spines, kidneys, hearts, livers and lungs. Sometimes, this frail cityful of organs makes me seethe and boil with tenderness. They seem so unmurderable and, because I think of them, they belong to me.

Belfast – only a jumble of streets and a few big bumps in the ground, only a whisper of God.

Oh, world, I think, aren't you pretty?

Aren't you big?

I hear a noise and I turn towards the bed. She has woken. She stirs slowly. She sits up and runs her hand through her disordered hair. She turns in my direction.

She smiles and she looks at me with clear eyes.